W9-DGA-075

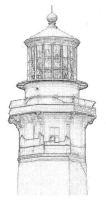

Grays Harbor Publishing

Published by Grays Harbor Publishing.
graysharborpublishing.com

Cover design by Clayton Swim.

Westport (Grays Harbor Series: Book 1) First Edition

ISBN 978-1948714013

This book is dedicated to my Mom and Dad,

and to everyone else who encouraged me.

I should also thank certain other members of my

very strange and sometimes twisted family,

for providing me with inspiration — but I won't.

PROLOGUE
WESTPORT

In her relatively short twelve years of life, Amanda has seen her share of disaster preparations, virtually everyone living on the coast has — but the scene outside of her window today is something altogether different. There's no storm or shipwreck causing the chaos on the streets, or even a world war, this is something far more frightening and mysterious, something that has even the most hardened members of the community panicked with fear.

Even under ordinary circumstances, you might expect that life in Westport is filled with stress and anxiety, given that its location is wedged between two massive bodies of water, Grays Harbor and the Pacific Ocean — but the truth is, life here is predictable and oftentimes uneventful in the eyes of its longtime residents. In fact, most people in the area never seem to be fazed by much of anything at all. Even the massive windstorms that are a regular occurrence in the winter months are met with a stoic resolve, and not the hysteria and mayhem that one would expect from less experienced souls. The harsh environment and violent weather are simply considered a way of life here.

Fear had actually started to creep in several weeks before now, when news of a deadly virus first began making headlines in the newspapers and on television. Panic, however, didn't set in until yesterday, when communications were suddenly cut off from the world around them. Within a fraction of a second they went from being concerned about an illness making its way through their town, to finding themselves with no electricity, no phones, no Internet, no

1

radio, and no way of knowing if the outage was limited to only their area. Even worse was their limited access to medical needs here on the peninsula — the nearest hospital is in Aberdeen over twenty miles away. For most, this latest setback proved to be too much, and packing up and leaving the small fishing community seemed the only sensible option left.

Amanda's own household wasn't immune to the panic either. Both her father and stepmother were busy behind her, throwing essentials haphazardly into boxes, bags or any other containers lying around the house. Her seventeen-year-old brother, Aaron, has been making trips back and forth between the house and the family car, loading what they hope will be enough supplies to get them someplace safe.

Throughout all of this, Amanda hasn't shown the least bit of concern, something that her stepmother, Diane, feels grateful for. She's raised Amanda from infancy, and the last thing in the world that she wants is for her to feel the stress and agony that the rest of them are experiencing.

As Diane hands Aaron another handful of bags to take to the car, she turns to Amanda and watches her for a moment — noticing a slight smile on her face.

"Sweety, what are you looking at?" she asks Amanda.

"The neighbors. Mrs Morgan is out on their lawn throwing up."

Diane stands beside her step-daughter and looks out at the scene across the street. Kate Morgan, a good friend of Diane's, is on the ground on her hands and knees, vomiting what appears to be mostly blood. Her husband is standing about ten feet behind her, holding their three young children back at a safe distance, while cars passing by on the street speed up as they drive by.

Diane feels horrible for her friend, and guilty for not running to her aid, but she knows it's too late — Kate will likely be dead in only a day or two, if not sooner. They've all seen it happen before.

2

Her real concern is Amanda's reaction to it — the smile.

"Amanda, what were you smiling about?"

The girl looks up at her, straight faced and serious. "I wasn't smiling Mother..."

Amanda's gaze returns to the neighbor's house, and Diane watches her face to see if the smile returns — and while her mouth doesn't move, the excited glint has once again taken over her eyes. An uneasy feeling creeps into Diane's mind, watching her child enjoy someone else's misery.

"Come on, help me sort through these clothes in the bedroom. We can't take all of them."

She pulls her away from the window and leads her into the master bedroom, where Amanda's father, Paul, is on the far side of the room beside the bed, staring out of the window toward the harbor in the east.

"The whole town is gonna be empty by nightfall," he says, still looking outside.

"Do you think maybe we should stay another night? I can't imagine how packed the road is going to be..." she answers back, handing Amanda a pile of clothes to sort through.

"No, the longer people stay, the more desperate they'll become. We'll find someplace safe down the road." He motions for Diane to come closer, then points outside in the direction of the marina. "Looks like the rest of the boats are leaving..."

Diane stands next to him, wrapping her arm around his waist and squeezing. She can see that most of the marina is already empty, and the few dozen boats that are left are beginning to leave. Other than the people boarding them, the area around the marina is completely deserted.

"I wonder where they're headed," Diane says.

"The same place we are — anywhere but here."

3

Diane leans in close to Paul, then whispers... "Kate is sick."

He turns to face her. "You can't go over there, you know that..." he replies, his voice filled with sympathy.

"I know, I just feel horrible about her kids."

Paul leans over and kisses his wife's forehead, then grabs a large suitcase off of the bed and starts to walk out of the room — pausing for only a moment to speak. "We should leave soon, we might be able to beat at least some of the traffic."

Diane nods in agreement, then looks back out the window. A man walking on the next street over catches her attention. He's wearing a pair of filthy pajama bottoms and a t-shirt, moving so slowly that for a second she's not certain if he's standing still or not.

"Paul..." Diane calls out, curious if he saw the man or not. She leans over the bed to see if her husband is still in the living room, but she doesn't see anyone. She focuses her attention back to the man outside, who's still making his way down the sidewalk cautiously, as if he's in excruciating pain.

"I think you're right, I don't think we should leave either," Amanda blurts out, startling Diane.

"No, your dad is right, things are just going to get worse around here."

"What if it's worse everywhere else?"

Diane had to admit, she raises an excellent point. She can't let on that she feels that way though, somehow it seems important that she and Paul appear to agree on everything, at least in front of the kids anyway.

"That's not something you should be worrying about. Your dad and I will find someplace, you'll see."

"How will our mom find us?"

Diane's heart sinks when she hears the question. The two kids haven't seen their biological mother for almost three years, and that

4

was only under court supervision. As far as Diane knew, she'd been in and out of jail or rehab ever since — making absolutely no effort to see her children. Her last known residence was a halfway house in Aberdeen, but that was over a year ago.

"Once the phones are working again I'm sure things will be fine," Diane answers, trying to hide her emotions.

Amanda finishes separating the pile of clothes in front of her into two heaps, not bothering to actually sort them. As she tosses one of them into an empty bag, she notices something shiny in a box at the foot of the bed. Making sure that Diane is still facing the window, she moves closer to inspect it.

"What are you looking at?" Amanda asks, hoping her step-mother doesn't turn around.

"Nothing. Just a guy."

As Diane remains glued to the scene outside the window, Amanda reaches into the box and pulls out a large kitchen knife, the weight of it so heavy that it shakes in her hand. She quickly wraps it into a small towel, and then holds it to her side while she slides into a sitting position beside Diane — placing her head on her step-mother's shoulder as they both look out of the window.

"Where is the guy?" she asks Diane.

"Over there, next to the yellow house..." she answers, pointing in the man's direction. He's just standing there, with his mouth hanging wide open, staring up at the sky, his face gray and sunken.

"What's the matter with him?"

"He's delirious."

"What does that mean?"

"It means he's sick, and he doesn't know what he's doing."

"Is that what happens to everybody who gets sick?"

"No, most people just die." She looks down at Amanda, ignoring the man for a moment, and notices that the sweet and innocent look

5

has returned once again to her eyes. "Don't worry about it, we'll figure everything out."

"Mom, what if we get stuck on the road?"

"I told you, your father and I will figure it out."

"But wouldn't it be safer to stay here, once everyone else is gone?"

"We'll be back home before you know it, just as soon as all of this is over," she answers, kissing Amanda on the forehead.

When Diane looks out the window again and sees that the man is no longer there, she stands up and faces the bed, figuring that she's wasted enough time as it is. As she opens her mouth to tell Amanda to continue packing, she lets out a loud moan instead, and nearly collapses to the floor in pain.

Afraid to move with any sudden motions, she slowly reaches behind her back for the source of the pain, and feels something warm and wet just below her ribcage. As her legs begin to go numb and become unsteady, she looks at her hand and discovers that it's completely covered in blood. She looks over at Amanda and tries to speak, but for some reason she's unable to say anything. Amanda's face is entirely expressionless, with no hint of worry or surprise. It takes Diane a moment to notice the knife in her step-daughter's small hands, both fists wrapped tightly around the handle. The blade is bright red.

"Amanda..." she manages to whisper.

The girl smiles warmly, then plunges the blade deep into Diane's chest, pulling it out quickly before she falls to the floor. Careful not to come into contact with any of the blood, Amanda sits beside Diane on the carpet, wiping the knife off on the towel before wrapping it up once again.

Despite her stepmother's desperate gasps for air, and the panicked look on her face, Amanda patiently sits and waits for her to stop breathing — her eyes never looking away from Diane's. Finally, after

6

hearing the front door open in the next room, she decides that she can't wait any longer, and begins to push her stepmother under the bed and out of sight — leaving the towel-wrapped knife lying next to the body. When she's finished, she stands up and pulls a pile of clothes off of the bed and onto the floor, covering the large bloodstain on the carpet. Just as she returns to sorting through clothes once again, her father enters the room behind her.

"How is everything coming along?" he asks, surveying the progress on the bed.

"Fine, almost everything is packed."

"Good. Where's your mom?"

"She left."

"Where'd she go?" he asks, confused.

"I don't know, she went outside and said she'd be back in a bit."

"She went outside? What for?"

"She didn't say..."

Paul walks back into the living room, with Amanda following closely behind him. Just as they enter the room, Aaron comes in through the front door and sits down on the couch, exhausted.

"Did you see your mom outside?" Paul asks Aaron.

"No, I thought she was in here..."

Paul turns around and faces Amanda. "Are you sure she went outside?"

Amanda nods.

"And you're sure she didn't say where she was going...?

"I'm sure."

Paul walks to the window and looks out at the town beyond. The sun is beginning to fall west toward the ocean, and the street in front of their house is filled with cars, trucks and even hikers — all of them heading south and away from Westport. The Morgan family is still sitting on their front lawn, overcome with grief, but Diane isn't with

7

them. Part of him is worried about Diane, and what might happen to her out there — but another part of him is furious with her for leaving without telling him.

"Should I go out and look for her?" asks Aaron.

"No, it's too dangerous. Besides, we have no idea where she went."

Paul waves at Aaron to move over, then takes a seat next to him on the couch, then motions for Amanda to join them.

"Dad..." says Amanda, as she takes a seat on his lap.

"What is it, sweety?"

"Does this mean we're not leaving?"

"No, we're still leaving. We just have to wait until your mom gets back."

It's nearly dark outside, and the only objects illuminating the Williams household are two small candles burning on the kitchen counter, and an old propane lantern that sits precariously on the edge of a coffee table in front of Paul and his two kids. It's been nearly three hours since Diane disappeared, and Paul is growing increasingly worried about her safe return.

Aaron stands up and walks to the door, staring out at the street. "Maybe I should go look for her, just around the house..."

"Do you see anybody on the street?" asks Paul.

"No, it's still empty. I think everyone is gone."

Paul gets up and stands next to his son, both of them looking at the dark, empty streets of a seemingly abandoned town outside. "Why don't you and Amanda check inside the house, and I'll look around outside."

"What are we checking for?"

Paul gives him a stern look, a look that tells Aaron not to ask anymore questions.

"Don't let your sister out of your sight..."

As his two kids disappear down the hallway toward the bedrooms, Paul quietly opens the front door and steps outside into the damp air of Westport. Somehow it feels different tonight — the air is warm and fresh, almost like summer.

As he makes his way out onto the street, looking in all directions for any sign of his wife, or of anyone else for that matter — he suddenly realizes just how isolated and alone his family has become. He can hear the ocean striking the jetty off in the distance, and he can see the light of the first stars overhead as they appear and disappear through the clouds. What he doesn't hear, or see for that matter, are signs of life in the town itself. Even his neighbor, John Morgan, who lives across the street, left with his three kids less than an hour ago. Paul can only assume that his wife is still inside the house, no doubt on the verge of death from the looks of things earlier in the day.

He can't imagine what must have gone through John's mind as he drove away, sacrificing the love of his life to protect the only three things in the world that meant more to him. He doesn't know if he has that kind of strength inside of himself, and he's afraid to find out.

As he makes his way around the house, his flashlight beam leading the way, he calls out to Diane, hoping that in these breezy conditions his voice reaches far enough for her to hear. When he comes back to the patio and faces the harbor in the east, he can see the faint lights coming from some of the boats still anchored in the harbor. What he doesn't see are the lights coming from Hoquiam and Aberdeen on the other side. Normally there's a bright glow in that direction, but late last night everything changed, and the skies turned dark in that part of the horizon.

When he approaches the front door again and begins to reach for the handle, he notices that the door is already partway open. Knowing

9

for certain that he'd locked it when he came out, he peeks in through the antique glass window at the living room beyond, but doesn't see his kids anywhere — only the lantern still burning on the table where he left it.

He gives the door a slight push, slowly opening it enough to fit through, then takes a single step inside — his heart pounding in his chest.

"Aaron... Amanda..."

No response.

"Are you guys in here...?"

He starts to take another step inside, then sees a bright flash coming from the hallway, and the sound of gunfire echoing throughout the room. Feeling a dull pain in his stomach, he looks down and discovers a gaping wound in the middle of his abdomen. He looks up, hoping to catch sight of his attacker, but the hallway is pitch black once again. As he carefully backs up, holding his right hand firmly on the wound, another shot rings out, this time striking him in the chest and sending him to the ground.

When he comes to, the world feels like it's slowly spinning, and his eyesight is slightly out of focus. Eventually things begin to clear up, and he realizes that he's facing the sky. Then something else comes into view, a person. At first he doesn't recognize her, and then he notices the dress, its white fabric now tinged in red. Amanda kneels down beside him, stroking his hair and smiling. He tries to open his mouth, but he's too weak.

"Shh, don't try to speak. It'll be over soon," Amanda whispers in his ear. Sitting up, she unfolds the kitchen knife, then holds it against his throat. "Don't worry Papa, I'll be fine."

10

CHAPTER 1
ASTORIA

Even in darkness, passing over the Astoria bridge is an impressive sight. With the tidal waters of the Pacific Ocean moving underneath, it spans some four miles over the mouth of the massive Columbia River, anchored by the town of Astoria on the Oregon side, and the ghostly remains of a once prosperous fishing community on the Washington side, where today only the wooden pilings of the canneries and docks can be seen.

Tonight the air is exceptionally clear, and the lights spread over the hills of Astoria to the south cast a golden shimmer on the water below, broken only by the unusually long line of ships heading west for the Pacific.

As beautiful as it is, Curtis Lockwood notices none of it. His thoughts are focused on the strange events that are currently unfolding around him, and whether his life would ever again return to normal. He was leaving Oregon, and although he doesn't realize it yet, this would be the last time he would ever see his home state.

His wife, Sarah, is sitting beside him in the passenger seat. In the light of the midnight moon overhead he can't tell if she's awake or asleep, they'd barely spoken since they left Portland over two hours ago. In the backseat of the pickup are their two sons, Matt and Ben, aged twelve and ten — both sound asleep as well. Annie, their daughter, is in California attending college. For two days they'd tried desperately to bring her home for the trip, but air travel had been suspended, and all traffic in and out of Oregon would be shut down in only a matter of hours. Despite the pleas from his wife, Curtis had

11

made the decision to take the family to the Washington coast without Annie — a decision that would ultimately haunt him for the remainder of his life.

This trip wasn't a vacation. It was a desperate move by a desperate man trying to protect what was left of his family — and he wasn't alone. In the past few weeks the population of Portland had declined by more than two-thirds. Cars were lined up for miles in every direction out of town, most heading for the wooded hills both east and west of the metropolis. Most had simply left with no warning or reason. Truth be told, no explanation was necessary — they were all running from the same thing. They were running from a virus.

This particular virus wasn't a normal flu or cold, although it acted just like one during the first few days of infection. Soon after, it began to show it's differences. Death came quickly for most, but for others the illness lingered on, torturing its victims with the hope of recovery — a recovery that would never come. Curtis knew little else about it, few people probably did. Their world had been turned upside down in only a matter of weeks. Stores were closed, gas stations were running out of fuel, it was even rumored that hospitals were turning away patients that showed signs of the sickness. It was a world unrecognizable from the one they knew only a month before — a world where a simple conversation or greeting could send someone to an early grave. It was a world Curtis no longer wanted to be part of.

Sarah's argument for staying was actually a legitimate one. Not only did she want to stay someplace their daughter could find them, but their neighbors had already left, making them the only residents within a four block radius. Staying made sense, he couldn't deny that — but it also made him feel uneasy. He'd become afraid of other people. Afraid that others might be infected, and afraid they might be looters or rapists looking to take advantage of his family's unquestionable vulnerability. He knew he had to take his family

12

someplace safe, a place where the passage of time and the unrelenting pressures of society didn't exist. In only a few short hours they would be there, safe and hidden, and miles away from the rest of civilization. They would simply disappear for a while, deep in the woods of the coastal mountains of Washington.

At least that was the plan.

Things have a strange way of working out — sometimes for good, and sometimes not.

After thirty minutes of driving their truck and small utility trailer up and down the same roads, Curtis is glad to see that his family is still sound asleep and unable to witness just how lost he'd become. Even though he'd been here dozens of times as a kid, and several times as an adult, he'd never driven here at night before — and certainly never like this. On his third trip down a road he was certain was wrong, he finally finds it. It's a small, narrow driveway that used to be topped with gravel and lined with rhododendrons — but today it's overgrown with ten years worth of blackberries and salal, the first of which is already showing signs of autumn drawing near, even if it is only the middle of September. Now that it's directly in front of him, illuminated by the headlights of his truck, he's almost sorry he's come. It's a cabin, of sorts. Most would call it a shack. Nestled into the woods less than a mile from the Pacific Ocean, it was once a treasured possession in his family for three generations — and he's hoping it could be again.

He glances over at his wife, who still seems to be asleep — and at his kids in the backseat, who have been out since they left the outskirts of Portland. His first instinct is to get out and check the place over, and maybe dredge up some old childhood memories of the place, but he's afraid that opening the truck door would probably just wake everybody up. Instead, he closes his eyes and tries to relax, hoping for a few hours of rest before morning comes. Who knows,

13

the place might look better in the light.

"Shh, you're going to wake up your Dad..."

Curtis had woken up to that same sentence more times than he cared to remember. Looking out the windshield, he sees Sarah and the two boys sitting on a half-rotten picnic table in front of the cabin — a cabin that looks even worse in the daylight as it turns out. As he stumbles his way to the table, still fighting the sleep from his eyes, he hears something that brings a sudden clarity to his mind — the sound of crashing waves echoing through the trees. If not for a stand of ancient Douglas Fir, he could probably see the surf from here. It wasn't just the sound though, it was also the smell. The salty, rich organic smell of saltwater, mixed with the sweet aroma of rotting fir needles and wet moss from under the canopy of trees. It was a smell only encountered in the coastal forests of the Pacific Northwest.

As the crow flies they actually weren't that far from the ocean, but walking the twisting roads and pathways through the forest and sand dunes was a different story. For just a moment, he was transported back in time, to a childhood that didn't seem so distant now that he was here.

"I was starting to wonder if you'd get up..." says Sarah, with a smile on her face.

"What time is it?" he asks.

"Almost noon."

"How long have you been up?"

"Since about seven. I thought you could use the rest"

He sits down across from her, facing the cabin he was hoping would be their home for the time being.

"Have you been inside?" he asks, pointing to the cabin.

14

"Yeah. I'm not sleeping in there, neither are the boys."

"That bad, huh?"

"Go see for yourself."

She doesn't want to be difficult, but she also doesn't know quite how to respond. None of this was her idea. Not the sudden midnight trip to Cohasset, not crossing a bridge that was scheduled to close right behind them, and certainly not the cabin.

Curtis stands up without saying a word and strolls toward the cabin. Ben quickly follows behind him, a bright smile in his eyes.

Sarah grabs his arm as he passes by. "Ben, not so fast."

"He's fine," says Curtis.

She looks at Curtis, not convinced, then back at Ben. "Don't touch anything."

"I won't Mom."

As they approach the front door, Curtis starts a mental checklist of repairs and maintenance that need to be done if they're going to stay here. It doesn't take him very long to realize that writing it down might be a good idea.

To call the cabin rustic would be a severe understatement. It was pieced together from scraps of wood that Curtis' grandfather had found around town. Some of it he'd actually found on the beach, the last remnants of a shipwreck according to his father. Now it looks as though the ship had wrecked on the clearing in front of them.

As he opens the rough and splintered front door, its hinges shrieking loudly in protest, he realizes that he can't really blame Sarah for being upset with the situation. He'd practically forced the three of them to move to a falling-down shack when they had a perfectly nice house in the suburbs of Portland. There's no possible way they could have stayed though, not after what happened.

"Did you used to live here?" asks Ben.

Curtis smiles. "No, we just stayed here on vacations."

15

"Did it look like this?"

"No, it didn't. It looked nothing like this..."

It had been a decade since he'd laid eyes on it, and nearly another decade since he'd spent the night inside. When he was fifteen his father had died in a car accident, hit head-on by a drunk driver on his way home from work. His death devastated Curtis' mother, who overdosed on prescription drugs only a few months later, a mixture of sleeping pills and painkillers. Whether it was an accidental overdose or not nobody knows for sure, but the details made little difference to Curtis. His parents were both gone, and with their passing his childhood abruptly ended within the span of a single season. With the death of his father, the cabin became the property of his Uncle Brian, his dad's older brother — and so too did the custody of Curtis. The trips to Cohasset were few and far between after that. Uncle Brian never really cared much for the place, and Curtis was only reminded of better days when his family was still together. For reasons he's never fully understood, the absence of his parents seemed stronger than their presence when they were alive. A lesson he learned only after they were gone.

"What is this?"

Curtis snaps out of his daydream to find Ben holding a small oil lamp covered in dust. "That's a lamp, and you're not supposed to touch anything, remember?"

"Where does it plug in?"

"It doesn't, there's no electricity here."

"Not even TV?"

Curtis smiles. "I guess you'll have to figure out something else to do."

"So are we going to sleep in here?"

"That's the plan. It needs some work though."

Ben looks around at the room they're standing in, but this time

16

through the eyes of someone who might actually live here. Seeing past the dust, cobwebs and animal waste was proving hard for him — despite his normally endless enthusiasm.

"What do you say, do you think we can we make this a home?" asks Curtis.

"Nope."

"That's the spirit. You sound like your mom."

Seasons change slowly at the beaches of the Pacific Northwest — in truth almost everything does. The cold maritime flow is a constant presence in the air, producing a climate that never gets especially warm — yet never becomes bitterly cold either. It carries with it a dampness that permeates everything it comes into contact with. The people who call the area home find the feeling both comforting and uncomfortable at the same time, a strange mixture that even they can't explain. It's the same feeling you experience on a rainy afternoon, relaxing in front of a fireplace or wood stove, enjoying life despite the retched weather outside. It's nostalgic somehow. At the beach that happens nearly every day, regardless of the season.

For Sarah and her two sons, living on the coast was becoming unbearable — and they'd only been here a day and a half. They'd slept through the first night without a problem, but the truck was still relatively warm by the time they woke up. The second night wasn't passing as smoothly. The boys were sleeping in the front seats with the backs reclined as far as they would go, while Curtis and Sarah decided to try an air mattress in the pickup bed under the canopy. They left the window between the cab and the bed open, unsure of whether it might hurt or help the temperatures in either

17

compartment.

"Can't we start the truck for a few minutes?" whispers Sarah.

"We'll run out of gas."

"We're going to freeze if we don't."

A dim blue light suddenly appears, the glow coming from Curtis' watch next to his pillow. "It's only fifty-two in here, it just feels colder."

It wasn't just the temperature that bothered Sarah, it was the noise — or lack thereof. She was used to camping — she'd spent half of her childhood camping, but this wasn't anything like that. There were no crickets, no owls, no crackling of the campfire, no sudden gusts of wind to break the silence. Instead, the wind blew at an almost constant speed, which somehow made it disappear from your senses. She was left with a silence so complete that she could hear her own heartbeats, something that was growing more distracting by the minute. The only solace she felt was when the fog horn in Westport sounded. It was startling, but it was at least something.

She whispers into his ear again, this time so quietly that he has a hard time understanding. "We need to talk about what's going on."

"Can it wait until morning?"

"No."

An awkward silence suddenly fills the space. Curtis didn't really want to talk about it, he didn't even want to think about it. One of the advantages of staying in a place as remote as this was not facing the problem head-on. Apparently she felt differently.

"What did you want to talk about?"

"How long did you plan on us staying here?"

"I guess until things settle down."

"And how will we know when that happens?"

"We'll listen to the radio."

"They've been repeating the same news for a couple of days. I'm not sure we'll learn much."

18

"That's a pretty good sign that there's still a problem."

A gentle rain begins falling on the canopy above them, cutting through the deafening silence in an almost hypnotic way. Outside the tinted windows Sarah can see the leaves and branches of the maple trees swaying in the wind, and the tops of the evergreens rocking back and forth in a rhythmic motion, all of it illuminated by the moonlight that's somehow found its way through the clouds. It was beautiful, but dreary at the same time. Maybe if she were seeing it under different circumstances she wouldn't feel this way. She was tired, but not sleepy — drained of all energy by stress and fear.

"What did Annie say earlier?" Curtis whispers.

"She's sleeping at a friend's house. Becky I think her name was."

"She's staying inside?"

"That's what she said."

Annie was staying at a friend's house, that much was true. What she didn't tell Curtis was that Annie was also complaining that the school was shut-down and its classes canceled. She suspected that their daughter wasn't being as careful as she should be. She didn't want to worry Curtis though, he had enough on his mind without stressing over things he had no control over. That's what this trip was really about, feeling in control of something. She'd watched him glued to the TV for days on end without eating or sleeping. He watched intently as cars passed by in front of their house — some of them slowing down according to him, although she never noticed it herself.

"So I take it we're not going into town for supplies?" she asks.

"The trailer has enough food for several weeks if we're careful."

She knew trying to convince him to go home was a waste of time. For one thing, they couldn't go back now even if they wanted to — the bridge closed soon after they crossed it. Now that they were here, she'd have to learn to make the most of it.

19

"What are your plans for the cabin?" she asks, trying to sound hopeful and upbeat.

"Honestly, it's in worse shape than I thought. It might be best just to burn most of what's in there — anything that can't be cleaned anyway."

"It might be quicker to burn the entire thing down."

"It's just been neglected. You'll be surprised what it looks like when it's fixed up."

They lie in silence again, staring into almost complete darkness — both of them with minds too active to go to sleep, like kids during a sleepover after their parents have turned off the lights.

"Isn't it strange that there's this killer virus that we're all afraid of, and we don't even know anyone that's had it?" asks Sarah.

"Rob and Marie got it."

"Rob from work?"

"Yeah."

Curtis had worked with Rob for years. Over time they'd become friends too, although Sarah had probably only had two or three meaningful conversations with him during that time. His wife, Marie, was a different story. She considered her a close friend, and an ally with her against the power-hungry supermoms on the school activities board. They had a boy and girl only a few months younger than Matt and Ben.

"Are they alright?" asks Sarah.

He doesn't say anything, and wonders if telling her was the right thing to do.

"Curtis...?"

"They died a few days ago."

"They what?"

She sits up in bed and turns on a flashlight she had lying beside her, flooding the area with light. Curtis grabs it from her and turns it

20

off. "You're gonna wake up the kids. Lie back down."

Instead of lying back down, she reaches for the handle on the canopy and opens it, then climbs out into the fog that's now rolling through the trees from the ocean below them. Still holding onto the flashlight, Curtis follows her, closing the latch behind him.

"What about their kids?" she asks with a slight tone of anger in her voice.

"The kids died first."

She suddenly feels as though she's in a dream, like all of this is a figment of her imagination. Her head spins, her legs feel wobbly, and for a moment she isn't sure if she's going to pass out or throw up — or both.

"Why didn't you tell me any of this before?"

"I just found out a couple days ago."

"And that somehow makes it better?"

He pauses for a moment, trying to remember exactly how he'd planned on explaining everything to her. "We had to get out of there, we had to leave the city. Would you have left if I'd told you?"

"Why wouldn't I?"

"Annie."

He can tell by the look on her face that she finally gets it, finally understands the determination behind the trip. This wasn't a simple family vacation that their grown daughter was missing out on. They were leaving her behind. As the world fell into chaos around them, Annie was falling with it.

She stares at Curtis, not really sure what to say. She doesn't know whether to be angry with him for deceiving her, or thankful for protecting her and the two boys. Without saying a word, she turns around and walks back to the pickup, unable to feel the cold dampness for the first time tonight. She grabs the handle on the canopy, then stops and turns toward Curtis again. She speaks, but this

21

time without emotion or volume, still feeling sick to her stomach. "Who else?"

"I don't think everyone in the neighborhood simply moved away."

CHAPTER 2
HOODSPORT

Hoodsport is like most towns on the Olympic Peninsula — overflowing with tourists during the warm summer months, and then quickly turning into something that resembles a ghost town as soon as the first leaves fall. It's a small, picturesque community in Washington State that rests along the shore of Hood Canal, a sixty-five mile long natural waterway that runs north-south, paralleling the Puget Sound. Glacial runoff from the eastern portion of the peninsula flows into the basin through countless mountain streams that wind their way past towering old-growth rainforests just to the west of town.

At one time it was a thriving logging community, taking advantage of some of the world's largest trees that conveniently grew along one of the world's deepest ports. As the trees were cleared, they farmed the same land, adding another source of revenue to an area that was wild only a few years before.

Tall trees still surround the area — but are rarely ever harvested. The fields and pastures that once fed the families in and around Hoodsport are still here too, but they mostly sit empty now, waiting for the forest to encroach and take them over once again. The town now survives on one industry alone — tourism. Secretly, or not so secretly in some cases, the locals find the vacationers a necessary annoyance. They fill up the RV parks, hotels and summer cottages, trading their money for tolerance — and for a few short months each year the residents do just that, tolerate them. Most of the tourists leave just before school starts, which was ordinarily still a week away, and the rest clear out when the cold winds make their way down from

23

the mountains a few weeks later.

Tonight the canal is quiet. One by one people have been leaving, most of them not even bothering to checkout of their hotel or park. Not a single car has been spotted on the highway in nearly three days, and despite their growing curiosity, none of the locals have attempted to leave either — not until tonight that is.

Marinas are scattered along the shore from one edge of town to the other. Some are home to several dozen boats, and some are private docks with barely enough room for one. The shabbiest of all of these belongs to a man named Larry Gossman. The boat tied to it happens to be the only one in the area with light flickering through its windows.

Standing in the shadows of the building, shivering from the cold air moving in from across the water, are Jake and Beth Wilson. They're both watching the highway intently, but the only thing even faintly visible is the movement of the windsocks in front of the general store down the street. Aside from a couple of streetlights and a few houses up on the hill, the entire town is dark.

"Are you sure he's coming?" asks Beth.

"For the tenth time, yes. He'll be here," replies Jake.

"What time is it?"

"Ten to eleven. Are you sure you don't want to wait on the boat with Larry? I'm sure he could use some help getting ready..."

"He'll be fine."

She knows he's trying to get rid of her. They've only been married a year, but they've known each other since they were toddlers. Sometimes she wonders if they were better off friends rather than husband and wife, but deep down she knows better. They're both in their late twenties and married to their best friend. That doesn't happen very often, at least in her experience anyway. Larry is Beth's older brother, and is the only person they know that has access to a

24

boat — even if it isn't entirely his. The man they're waiting for is Sean, Jake's friend and coworker. Beth has only met him briefly a couple of times, but had already seen enough to dislike him. She wasn't even sure what it was that she didn't like. He was polite enough, he was a guard at a local prison the same as her husband — but it felt like he watched her when she wasn't looking. It was an uncomfortable feeling she just couldn't shake. And now here they were, about to board a boat with him, bound for who knows where.

"You're still sure you want to do this?" he asks.

"Do what?"

"Take the boat."

"Of course. As long as Larry is fine with it."

"And you're positive he's okay with Sean coming along?"

"He's fine with whatever, you know him. Why all the questions?"

"I just want to know you're comfortable with everything."

She rolls her eyes, unsure of whether he could see it. In all honesty she didn't care if he did — he'd been getting on her nerves for days and she was getting tired of it.

They wait in silence for a few minutes, listening for the sound of a car, or the crunching of gravel under footsteps — but all they hear are the sound of the waves lapping at the rocky beach behind them, and the distant screech of an owl from the forest on the other side of town.

"It's strange isn't it, how quiet everything is?" asks Jake. "If everything is going to hell you'd think there would be some activity to stop it."

"Maybe there is. We certainly wouldn't see it here in Hoodsport."

"Yeah, maybe so. It feels like we're hunkered down though, waiting for a storm or something."

Beth points toward the road, where a pair of headlights can be seen turning off the highway and down the driveway in front of them.

25

"That must be him," she says.

"I guess we'll have to make a decision about where we're going," says Jake.

She turns toward him with a cold look in her eyes. "Listen, he's along for the ride, but he's not one of us, and he certainly doesn't get a vote." She turns around and walks back to the boat, leaving her husband to greet Sean alone.

As Beth climbs onto the deck of the boat, which has the name 'Larry's Obsession' plastered onto the side, she sees Larry himself digging through a box in the pilothouse. As rough as the boat looks on the outside, it's surprisingly clean and well-kept on the inside. It was originally a 45' fishing boat that served most of its years operating out of Sitka, Alaska. Today it's in a constant state of repair and upgrades, all of which are time consuming, and most of which aren't necessary. Larry is a lot of things, but organized and ambitious are not among them. He talked his friend into loaning him the money, went to Alaska to pick it up, and then quickly lost interest in it altogether. His 'obsession' lasted nearly three weeks. Now he spends part of the day fixing imaginary problems on the boat, and the rest of it drinking beer at the local tavern — a habit his business partner isn't aware of. As much as she loved her brother, and as much as she wanted to be with him right now, Beth worried about pinning the survival of herself and her husband on him — especially in his current state of mind.

The idea of this expedition wasn't sudden. It started soon after the outbreak began, when Larry's neighbor developed a nagging cough — something that would have been dismissed as allergies not so long ago. Larry and his wife, Jennifer, decided they would take the boat the

26

following day to her parent's house in Poulsbo — returning only after the virus ran its course. The trip, however, was delayed when Jennifer came down with the same cough later that same night.

She was dead five days later.

That was nearly two weeks ago — an agonizing two weeks that's been filled with the fear, or hope, that he would suffer the same fate.

Climbing up the ladder that reaches the bridge, Beth can hear Larry before she catches sight of him. He's overweight, breathes heavily, and seems to be incapable of buying pants that completely cover his ass — a look he's become famous for locally.

"How's it coming?" asks Beth.

"It's coming. Did your friend ever show up?"

"He just got here, and he's not my friend. He's Jake's friend."

Larry glances up at her, noticing the hint of hostility in her voice. "Anything I should be concerned about?"

"No, he's just not my favorite person."

He stares at her for just a few seconds, then goes back to digging through the box.

"What are you looking for in there?" she asks him.

"Charts, although it might help if I knew where we were going."

"I figured we'd get away from town first, then decide."

"Whatever works, as long as we're out of here tonight."

Looking around from this high up, she's amazed at how empty and lonely the town looks. Granted, at this hour it usually doesn't look all that different — but there's a feeling that wasn't there before. It was either fear or sadness, she couldn't tell which. Maybe it was both. The fog is just beginning its slow roll in from the north, an event seen year-round in this area, but this time she can see the faint glow of headlights through it, and for a moment she finds herself nervous at the site of activity in town.

"Do you have your gun with you?" she asks Larry.

27

"Yeah, it's around here somewhere."

"Maybe you should find it, just in case." Hearing Jake and Sean walking onto the bottom deck, she leans toward Larry and whispers... "Don't let anyone know you have it."

He looks back at her with a look of concern, but it's clear she doesn't see it. She's too busy watching her husband and his friend loading suitcases and duffel bags on-board.

Without saying a word, Larry reaches into a side compartment next to the wheel and pulls out a .38 revolver and places it into his jacket pocket. Then he leans over the railing of the flying bridge, finally seeing Sean for himself. Usually he's conflicted about the people his sister finds offensive, or the people she finds attractive for that matter — they've always been incompatible when it comes to friends or enemies. If this were any other day he'd probably greet Sean with open arms, but this isn't just any other day. All things considered, he's not completely comfortable having someone on his boat that he's never met, and he's not sure why someone would volunteer to board a boat with no set destination either. Even he's uncomfortable with that.

"If you guys are ready, go ahead and untie us," he tells Jake.

Behaving as calmly and rationally as a teenager about to drive for the first time, Jake manages to fumble his way out of the knot, nearly leaving the rope lying on the dock. "We're good to go!"

As the sleeping town of Hoodsport grows smaller with every passing mile, the group slowly makes their way through the thickening fog and rough waters, eventually losing sight of the shoreline completely. Ahead of them to the north is the Strait of Juan De Fuca, and to the west of that lies the Pacific Ocean. Once the lights

28

of the town disappear altogether, Larry shuts down the engine and joins his passengers on the outside stern deck. They're all seated on a wooden bench that surrounds the entire deck. It looks out of place considering how nicely made it is — one of Larry's proudest accomplishments.

"All right, where are we going?" he asks.

An awkward silence falls over the boat, which is further accentuated by the rhythmic lapping of water against the hull. They've had this discussion before, on several occasions in fact — but they could never agree on where to go. Beth wanted to go to Vancouver Island, in British Columbia — to take advantage of its vast natural resources. Jake had his mind set on the San Juan Islands in the northern Puget Sound, an area only accessible by boat or plane. Larry wanted to go to California for reasons he couldn't, or wouldn't, explain.

"Are you sure you want to do this?" Larry asks after no answer.

"Obviously we're doing this. We can't stay here, not after what happened," answers Beth, sounding more assertive than she meant to.

Jake sits down next to her and places his arm around her waist. "I guess the question is, do we go someplace familiar where we know people, or do we hide out?" He looks at Sean, who has been quiet ever since his tour of the boat. "What about you, Sean? Any thoughts?"

Beth gives Larry an annoyed glance. Of course Jake would ask him that.

"I'm just along for the ride, whatever you guys decide is fine with me." says Sean.

"Your family are from out of state aren't they?"

"Yeah, Colorado."

"Have you heard anything from them?"

"My Dad lives in Denver. I talked him a couple days ago."

"And...?" asks Beth.

29

"He was sick."

In that instant Beth felt sorry for Sean. Not sorry enough for her instincts to change, but rather something resembling sympathy. "Can I ask you a question, Sean?"

"Sure."

"Why are you coming with us when we don't even know where we're going?"

"Where else would I go? Shelton is practically a war zone at this point." He looks directly at Beth, his voice just the right balance between grateful and confident. "I think I'd rather take my chances with you guys."

"Do you remember Aunt Jessie's house in Astoria?" Larry asks Beth.

"Yeah, what about it."

"What about going there?"

"Astoria? In Oregon?" Jake asks Larry.

"What's wrong with Oregon?"

Jake is baffled by the suggestion. "How long would that take? How much fuel would we burn through getting there?"

"We should have plenty of fuel."

"And if we don't...? The fueling stations are gonna be closed."

"Even better, we won't have to pay."

Jake turns to Beth, waiting for her to call Larry an idiot, or worse. Instead she shrugs.

"He's right, the place is kind of perfect. It's right on the water, it has a dock of its own, and it's kind of isolated from the rest of the neighborhood," she says.

"What makes Astoria any better than Hoodsport?" asks Jake.

Beth glares at her husband, who of all people should know better than to ask a question like that. He knew how desperate Larry had been for the last couple of weeks. He was there the night Larry had called for an ambulance — the night Jennifer died. He watched him

30

endure fifteen minutes of busy signals and dropped calls until he finally reached somebody, an actual person, only to be told they wouldn't be sending anyone to a home that had already been infected. People were terrified, and rightfully so — this was an epidemic like nothing the world had ever seen. Even now, some eleven days after her death, her body is still lying on the bed where she fell asleep for the last time. Whether it was by himself, or surrounded by family, Larry was leaving town — and he had no intention of ever coming back.

Larry notices the glare — and part of him even appreciates it — but as much as he hates to admit it, Jake has a point. "Astoria probably isn't any different, you're right... but maybe it is," he says. "All we know for sure is that Hoodsport is disappearing, one person at a time, and we're next if we stay here."

For a moment nobody says anything. Jake is embarrassed about what he said, Beth feels embarrassed for him, and Sean hasn't had much to say since he boarded the boat.

"So, Astoria?" Beth asks everyone, including Sean.

"Sounds good," says Jake.

Sean just nods in approval.

Larry stands up and walks to the ladder leading up to the bridge, already out of breath and red in the face for his efforts. "Okay, at least that's settled. Jake, why don't you and Sean go down below and organize everything. Make sure nothing can roll around or fall over if the water gets rough."

"What about me?" asks Beth.

"I want you up top with me."

The boat, which was made sometime in the 1960s, has three levels

31

to it. There's the pilothouse where the controls and navigational equipment are located, the main cabin directly below it, and finally the engine compartment below that. Although perfectly seaworthy, it looks like an absolute mess. Part of the outside has already been stripped and sanded in preparation for its next paint job, and the decking outside still hasn't been finished since it was prepped almost three months ago. Inside the main cabin, however, most of the surfaces are already done. There's new paint, new hardwood flooring, mostly new appliances in the primitive kitchen, and a retrofitted bathroom complete with a marble counter-top. Larry was sure to spare none of his friend's money in making sure the boat was ready for his own personal comfort.

Once he makes his way up the ladder, he wastes no time in starting the engine and getting underway. In only a few minutes they're pushing their way through the fog and light mist and into the deep waters of the central canal.

"I take it you can see where you're going...?" asks Beth.

"More or less. I seriously doubt anyone's out here anyway, not on a night like tonight."

"How long do you think it will take us to get down there?"

"A few days maybe, if everything goes okay." He motions for her to come closer, then says quietly... "Does Sean know about Jenn?"

"I don't think so. Did you want him to?"

He begins running his hand through his hair, a nervous habit he's had since childhood.

"Maybe he has a right to know. I can't be certain I wasn't infected."

"None of us are certain. That's one of the reasons I'm not comfortable with a stranger on-board with us."

"But this is..."

"What, different? Listen, we were all around Jenn while she was sick, and none of us have come down with any symptoms. She got sick after what, half a day?"

He nods. "Something like that."

"There's no reason to tell him about it, he'll start freaking out the first time one of us coughs."

Larry taps her on the shoulder, then points to their right, toward the eastern shore. At first she can't see anything through the fog, and then it becomes obvious what they're looking at. It's another boat, and although it's still some distance away, it seems to be heading in their direction.

"What do we do?" she asks.

Larry kills the engine, then turns to Beth. "Turn off the lights."

Beth reaches to the light switches on the wall behind her and flips them both off. "What about down below?"

"All of them, and no sound."

She hurries down the ladder and runs through the small doorway that leads to the main cabin. Inside she sees Jake and Sean, both of them busy re-stacking the totes and bags that they've thrown haphazardly around the living area. They're both laughing about something when they look up and see the sober look on Beth's face. Their smiles instantly disappear.

"What's wrong?" asks Jake.

"Turn the lights off, and keep quiet," she whispers back.

"What's going on?"

"There's a boat coming toward us. We have to disappear — now."

Without hesitating, Jake quickly turns off all the lights in the cabin, while Beth turns off the lights to the stern deck. Every trace of the moon overhead has been obscured by the fog that's settled over the water, and as a result the cabin is suddenly swallowed up into complete darkness. Still standing in the doorway, hearing only the water lapping against the side of the boat, Beth realizes that her heart is pounding so hard that it's almost uncomfortable.

33

"Does anyone have a flashlight, just in case?" she whispers.

"I have my phone if we need it, there's a flashlight app on it," answers Sean.

With her heart still racing, she slowly feels her way into the room and finds a seat near the starboard window. At first she can't see anything, then her eyes slowly begin to adjust to the darkness. Off in the distance, and still dim through the fog, she can see the lights of the other boat again.

"It's out there, on the right side."

She can hear the other two as they make their away across the cabin, finally settling onto the same bench she's sitting on.

"See it?"

They both answer. "Yeah."

"Jake, do you have your gun on you?" she asks.

"No, I left it in the bedroom."

"I have mine," answers Sean.

"Good, keep it handy. Just don't shoot one of us."

"I'll try my best." he says jokingly. He can't see it, but Beth isn't amused. She knew all along that he was probably armed, and she wasn't exactly happy about it — except for this one instance.

"It's getting closer," Jake says, a hint of concern in his voice for the first time since they left the dock.

He was right, it was getting closer — a lot closer. Beth couldn't tell if it was heading straight for them or not. What she *could* tell was that their engines were at or near full throttle by the sound now making its way into the cabin. Only moments later she can hear them slow down, but not stop. Even though the boat is relatively close now, only a few hundred feet, she still can't make out any details on it — not even the size of it. All she can see are the blurred yellow lights filtered through a thickening wall of mist.

"They have to see us," whispers Jake.

34

"I don't think so. That light has to be reflecting off the fog quite a bit," Sean replies. "It's not headed directly for us either."

Beth watches as the boat moves behind them, then slows down again — this time to a crawl. With the cabin door still open, a subdued light is now leaking into the area around them, illuminating the hallway just enough for Beth to see Sean with his pistol pointed toward the door.

The boat is moving at a painstakingly slow speed around to their port side, shortening its distance as it does. As much as they want to, none of them make a move to the other side for fear they might be seen or heard. Instead, they sit and wait for what seems like forever, occasionally having to remind themselves to breathe. Then everything goes quiet, deathly quiet, and the lights of the other boat go out. For a moment Beth wonders if it was actually real, or just some ghost ship they all hallucinated — a figment of their collective minds. The silence doesn't last long though. They can all hear a voice, loud and clear, coming from the boat that's sitting less than fifty feet off their port side.

"Is everybody okay over there?" a man's voice asks in a concerned tone. Then more quietly... "Hit the light."

Just a few seconds after hearing those words the cabin is filled with a bright white light. All three, who were still sitting on the bench, drop to the floor and hide behind the bench on the opposite side. Sean immediately starts coughing the moment his body hits the carpet. A deep, painful cough that he tries to muffle inside the crook of his arm. Beth knows that if they didn't see them, they could certainly hear Sean's coughing.

"Shh... They're going to hear you," she whispers to him.

Red in the eyes, and still struggling not to cough, Sean finally manages to stay quiet. "No shit."

"Are you okay?" Jake asks him.

35

"Yeah, just breathed in some dust. I'm fine."

"Do you guys think we might be overreacting?" asks Beth.

"No," answers Sean. "These guys aren't just out searching for somebody to help. If they were, they wouldn't have shut off their lights when they spotted us."

Before she has an opportunity to respond, the man speaks again, his voice sounding calm and reassuring. "Listen, we know you're in there, and we don't want any trouble — but there's a quarantine in place that prohibits any travel across county or state lines."

Beth feels a tap on her shoulder, and when she turns around she sees Sean pointing against the starboard wall opposite them. Two red laser marks are darting around.

"Where are you heading?" the man asks.

They can hear a voice above them, in a tone more commanding than Beth had ever heard from Larry. She'd almost forgot about him up in the pilothouse.

"Friday Harbor, we were just down here for the weekend."

Beth knows instantly what Larry is doing. Friday Harbor is a town in the San Juan Islands, in the opposite direction of where they're headed.

"I'm afraid you'll have to turn back around and head into Hoodsport, at least until the quarantine is over."

"That's not going to work. We're going to Friday Harbor, one way or the other."

"Is that a threat?"

"We don't want any trouble either, but if that's how it ends up, so be it. I can guarantee we have the firepower."

Sean looks thrilled, giving Beth and Jake an enthusiastic thumbs up. They clearly don't feel the same way. They know Larry, they know how out of the ordinary this is, and they hope he's not finally cracking under the pressure. They can hear talking from across the water, but

36

the voices are too low to make anything out. After a minute or two the light goes out, leaving them in the dark once again, followed by the roar of an engine as the boat moves to the south.

"Are you guys okay down there?" yells Larry.

"Yes, we're fine!" answers Beth, not bothering to whisper anymore.

The lights on the stern deck come on, and they can hear Larry making his way down the ladder, his gun still in his hand. When he reaches the cabin he flips on the lights, his face and clothes drenched in sweat.

"We'll wait a few minutes before taking off again, but we're gonna have to run with minimal lights from here on out."

"What the hell was all of that?" Beth asks. "We're threatening cops now?"

"Those weren't cops."

"How do you know that?"

"Because they were in Sam Keller's boat, and Sam left for Alaska two days ago — along with his wife and kids."

"They also didn't identify themselves," adds Sean.

Larry walks to a cabinet at the front of the cabin and pulls out a gun and a box with several small flashlights in it. He drops the box onto the bench in front of the other three, then hands the gun to Beth.

"From now on, everyone carries a gun and a flashlight — day or night. No exceptions."

CHAPTER 3
COHASSETT BEACH

Sometimes after having a bad day, a good nights sleep can make all the difference in the world. You wake up and realize that what seemed catastrophic the night before wasn't actually so bad in the light of the next day. It really makes no difference how or why it happens, sometimes the weight of the world somehow seems to disappear the moment your head hits the pillow.

Sometimes.

For Sarah Lockwood, that didn't happen.

Her night was filled with endless thoughts about what was happening around them, and what might happen if even one member of her family became sick. When she did manage to fall asleep it was only for a few short minutes, and even those were occupied by strange dreams about stressful situations, most of them concerning her husband. She still didn't know quite what to think of Curtis' motives, but she began to notice things about him that she didn't see the day before — a coping mechanism that whether by design or by accident, seemed to work. He was throwing every ounce of effort into making a new life here, as if their life in Portland never existed. Watching him now she hopes his enthusiasm rubs off on her, and on their kids. More than that, she hopes this madness will end soon, and that the life they once knew will return to them again. Right now it was beginning to feel like a distant memory.

Curtis started the day out by promising that their next night would be spent inside the cabin — a bold move considering the shape that it was in. Nonetheless, Sarah was determined not to be negative from

38

here on in, or at least until nightfall. He said their first priority would be to burn anything flammable that was of no use to them, inside or out. For Sarah and Ben that meant using some of the tools in the cabin to tackle the monstrous tangle of blackberry vines that now surrounded it. Curtis said he would clean out the inside of the building itself, and Matt quickly volunteered to listen to the handheld radio for the day, as though it were a job they all despised. Ignoring Sarah's disapproving looks, Curtis agreed to let him.

By late-afternoon, their hard efforts managed to turn a small clump of branches and firewood into a slash pile that rivaled the cabin in size.

"Isn't this getting a little large, considering it's so close to the cabin?" Sarah asks Curtis.

"Everything is so wet I doubt it'll burn at all. We can start another pile on the other side if it makes you feel better."

"What's in the box?"

Curtis looks down at the open cardboard box he's carrying. "Stuff from the cabin."

"Like what?"

He smiles a little. "You don't want to know. They used to be alive."

"You're right, I don't want to know. How is it looking in there?"

"It's not fancy, but another hour or two and I think it'll be livable."

She looks at the picnic table where Matt is sitting, the radio firmly in his hands. "Maybe you should talk to him, try to get his mind off the radio, and everything else."

"Yeah, I've been thinking the same thing. We haven't really talked to them about all of this."

"Maybe the three of you can check out the beach while I make dinner. We can finish this up afterward."

As Curtis approaches the picnic table, he can hear the same robotic voice he's been listening to for days, likely giving the same worthless advice too.

"Any news?" he asks.

"They keep repeating the same stuff, even the music."

"Music?"

"Yeah, some of the stations are playing music, but they're just playing them over and over again."

"Have they said anything about the hospitals?"

"Just to stay away, the same as before."

The lack of news doesn't really surprise Curtis. Either the news reports are being controlled by the government, or the reporters themselves have disappeared. One is just as likely as the other. Curtis reaches out and takes the radio from Matt and switches it off.

"Go get your brother, we're gonna check out the beach."

"What about the radio? What if we miss something?"

"The rest of the world will wait for us, I promise. Now go get your brother before we run out of daylight."

Although the cabin is only a short distance from the ocean, walking there is anything but easy, especially for a slightly out-of-shape guy that's spent most of the last several years sitting behind a desk. There isn't one straight stretch on the trail leading from the cabin to the highway, which gives you the feeling that you're following in the footsteps of a drunk. The part after the highway — which is most of the distance — winds its way through a maze of sand dunes, each one higher and less stable than the last.

"Do you hear that?" asks Matt.

"Hear what?" replies Curtis.

"It sounds like a woman."

Curtis stops, then motions for the boys to do the same.

40

"Do you hear it?" Curtis asks Ben.

Ben listens, then nods in the affirmative. Curtis tries to tell himself that he's distracted by the other sounds of the beach — like seagulls, wind and the crashing of the surf. Deep down though, he realizes that his ears aren't so young anymore, and that age has selectively tuned out the parts of life it no longer finds interesting. Then suddenly, he hears it too — and it's definitely a woman. What Matt didn't pick up on, and apparently still doesn't judging from his lack of response, are the blood-curdling screams coming from her — like every part of her soul is in agony.

"Follow me, and don't talk," he whispers.

He leads them back toward the highway about twenty feet or so, and into a crescent-shaped pocket that the wind has carved into the dunes. Like most of the dunes along the coast, this one only has grass growing on it, providing little to no protection from being seen.

"It sounds like she's screaming," whispers Ben, in a voice so low Curtis could barely make it out.

"Shh. I know she's screaming."

The screams were coming from the beach, and they didn't seem to be getting any closer as far he could tell. There were only one or two dunes between them and a clear shot of the beach, and he wanted more than anything to see for himself what was going on — but he also couldn't leave his sons behind, not as scared as they were.

"I'm going to peek over the dune and take a look, but I need you two to stay here."

"But..." starts Matt.

"I'll be right over there, in plain sight of you. Can I trust you?"

They both nod, more out of fear than anything else. As he makes his way up the dune, crawling on his stomach the entire way, he realizes that Sarah might be able to hear the screaming too. After a quick glance back toward the highway, which still looks empty, he

41

decides the sound of the yelling probably wouldn't carry as far as the sound of the surf does — at least he hopes that's the case. The last thing they needed right now was for her to come running down the trail.

When he finally reaches the top, it doesn't take him long to spot the woman. She's standing at the edge of the water, facing the ocean, stark naked, with both arms raised straight in the air. Very slowly, she lowers them down to her waist, then stops the maniacal screaming. After standing there silently for a moment, watching the waves crash against her bare feet, she bends down and picks something up. He can't see what it is, but she's clutching it to her chest like it means the world to her. Looking straight ahead again, she turns around and faces the dunes. Curtis immediately ducks, afraid she might be able to see him somehow. When he looks up again, he's horrified at what he sees. The woman looks awful. Her hair is dirty and tangled, her face and chest are covered in what looks like vomit, and her eyes look cold and vacant, like someone in a trance. It's hard to guess how old she is. She could be twenty-eight or eighty-eight — neither age would surprise him. She takes what he can now clearly see is a knife, and begins to violently slash at her own throat, making absolutely no sounds while she does it — she doesn't even look upset. After several hard thrusts he can see blood running down her arm and into the water at her feet — a sight that makes his stomach turn — but it doesn't seem to faze her. He looks back at his boys, hoping his face doesn't give away the gruesome images now seared into his mind, then he looks back at the woman. At first he doesn't see her, and then he notices a crumpled mass stretched out across the sand — motionless and pale.

His first instinct is to walk down to the water, out of curiosity if nothing else. If this were any other time he probably would have— but as bizarre as the scene was, he knows with absolute certainty what caused it, and that the same thing would undoubtedly happen to him if he were to go anywhere near her body. He'd heard rumors about what happened to some of the sick, rumors that until today he disregarded as wild stories and outright lies. He felt sorry for the woman, sorry that she was driven to such madness, and scared that even in the most remote corners of his world, the sickness had still found them.

He slides back down the dune and walks back to where his sons are still hiding, motioning for them to get up.

"Let's go back home, it'll be dark soon."

"What happened to the woman?" asks Matt.

"Nothing happened to her."

"Why was she screaming?"

"I don't know, maybe she thought she was alone. We all do strange things when we're alone sometimes."

"Is she going to be alright?"

He stops them, then looks both of them in their eyes. "Listen to me. The only thing in the world that's important to us now is our family, that's just how it is right now. Just the four of us."

"And Annie..." says Ben.

Curtis hangs his head down, feeling horrible about forgetting his oldest child so easily. The guilt has been intolerable in the week leading up to this move, but up until this moment he hadn't realized how far the thought of her had slipped from his mind.

"Of course, and Annie."

Looking up at the sky, Curtis knows they won't be sleeping in the cabin tonight. A thick, dark band of clouds was pouring in from the west, obscuring nearly all of the light from the already diminishing sun.

Their trip to the beach had been filled with nearly constant chatter between the two brothers, both of them excited about the prospect of

43

finding treasures washed up from the bottom of the ocean. The trip back, however, was silent. Neither of them had actually witnessed anything, but they both knew something significant had happened.

As they walk into the clearing that surrounds the cabin, Curtis sees Sarah waiting for them by the front door. With the radio in one hand and two raincoats in the other, Sarah holds out the coats to Matt and Ben. "Why don't you two gather up your stuff and put it in the truck. It looks like it's going to rain again tonight."

"We're not sleeping inside tonight?"

"One more night in the truck, I promise," she replies.

Curtis waits for them to leave, then turns to Sarah. "I have to tell you something..."

"Me first, but let's go inside."

Maybe it's the fact that it's so dark inside, or maybe he's just getting used to it, but the cabin is actually looking halfway decent. It's certainly roomier than the bed of their F150 pickup. A good washing tomorrow and they should be able to move in — that is if the well out back is still operable.

"It looks great," he says.

"That's not what I wanted to talk about."

He notices that she's almost shaking. "Okay, what is it?"

"I tried to call Annie, but my phone went dead. There's no signal at all."

"Yeah, I can't say I'm surprised. It probably happens all the time during these storms."

"That's not all. The radio went out too, every station."

"Did you try the truck radio?"

"It's out too, and so is the satellite radio."

He holds out his hand. "Let me see it for a minute."

He starts flipping from one station to the next, hearing the same monotone static on each one. Switching from AM to FM doesn't yield

44

any results either, or the weather band. He switches it again, and then slowly changes the frequency, listening closely to every dial setting.

"What are you listening to now?" Sarah asks.

"Shortwave. You can pick up signals from all over."

Hearing raindrops on the roof overhead, she glances outside to make sure her kids aren't getting soaked before they climb into the truck. To her surprise, they're already inside. It's usually a battle.

Curtis switches the radio off, then sits down on a wooden chair covered in a decade of dust and cobwebs.

"Nothing. All the channels are dead."

"What does that mean?"

"I don't know, but it's not good."

CHAPTER 4
HOOD CANAL

Since their encounter the night before, Larry was all the more determined to leave Hood Canal for good, but the fact that he felt that way was heart-wrenching. This was where he was born — it was where he grew up, got married, and one day hoped to raise a family of his own. Today those hopes and dreams are gone, leaving behind only an emotional scar as a reminder of what his life almost was.

In a strange twist of fate, it felt as though the world only consisted of Beth and himself, just as it had during most of their childhood. Their father had left when Larry was six, and Beth was only an infant. That resulted in a string of stepfathers and boyfriends in and out of their lives — some of them horrible, and some of them wonderful. It was the latter that hurt so much. With them came the promises of a normal life, of summer vacations and Christmas parties — all of them eventually ending in disappointment when he suddenly realized they wouldn't be coming back. To make matters worse, their mother didn't seem to notice his heartache and disappointment, or care if she did notice. That cycle of broken promises ended the day he met Jennifer — or at least he thought it did. He was beginning to wonder if this was all part of that same cycle, a small section of an endless loop he's only now beginning to recognize.

Afraid of being seen in the canal during the day, the group have spent the last sixteen hours hiding in the winding channel of a small, but deep creek — tucked out of sight from the rest of humanity. Now that they were once again in the cover of darkness, Larry was determined to make up for lost time.

46

"Mind some company?"

Larry turns around and sees Sean halfway up the ladder to the pilothouse.

"Not at all, come on up."

Sean sits down in the chair next to Larry, taking in what little view there is. There's no fog tonight, and the moon hasn't yet risen overhead to illuminate the shore on either side of them, or the water in front of them.

"It's dark tonight isn't it?" asks Sean.

"Yeah, but I don't really want to run the main lights. Might arouse too much suspicion."

They sit in an uncomfortable silence for a moment, each one feeling obligated to say something, and both wondering if smalltalk was appropriate in a time like this. Finally, Larry breaks the ice.

"So you're from Colorado?"

"No, that's just where my dad ended up. I grew up in Oregon, just outside of Salem."

"And you work at the prison with Jake?"

"I used to. I doubt I have a job anymore — considering what happened and all."

"What did happen exactly? I've only heard bits and pieces from Beth."

Sean nervously shifts around in his seat, folding and unfolding his arms — like he's had too many cups of coffee.

"It's all a bit of a blur to tell you the truth... I guess it started a couple of weeks ago, the regular supply shipments stopped coming in. Just the laundry service at first, then soap, toilet paper — that kind of stuff. That didn't go over so well with the inmates, as you can imagine, but about a week ago the food shipments stopped too. Things got a little interesting."

"What, like riots and stuff?"

47

He gives Larry a small, awkward grin — which Larry considers inappropriate considering the seriousness of the subject.

"I guess it started that way, yeah. I can't really blame them really, they knew what was going on outside the walls, at least as much as we did. If you're hungry you're capable of some serious shit."

Sean begins coughing, a slight, shallow cough — then controls himself again. Larry notices it, he's even alarmed by it, but he tries to hide his suspicions from Sean.

"So what did they do?" asks Larry, trying to speak as nonchalantly as possible.

"It's not so much what *they* did, it's what *we* did. The second day of rationing we had a small group of prisoners escape, maybe six or seven at the most. They headed straight for town — stealing cars, stealing food, killing people that got in their way, just going nuts. The next day the boss brings all of us in for a meeting, telling us that we're the only chance the town has, that if any of these people get out they'll destroy the town."

"So what did you do?"

"We went in and killed what was left of the prisoners, or at least we tried to."

"Jesus."

"Yeah, that's what I said."

"You said some of them weren't killed?"

"A bunch of them got out. As far as I know they're tearing the hell out of the town as we speak — the warden got that part right."

Larry doesn't know what to say. He's trying his best not to judge the man sitting next to him — after all, he might have done the same thing if the roles were reversed.

"So what do you think is really going on?" Sean asks him.

"With the virus?"

"Or whatever it is."

48

"I don't know, I guess it's like the flu or something, only a lot worse."

"I've heard entire cities back east are gone, wiped out overnight," says Sean.

"I think we've all heard those stories."

"Yeah, it's probably a bunch of bullshit."

Larry points to the starboard side, toward the east. "You notice anything strange over there?"

Sean looks, but can't see anything, just the blackness of night. "No, I can't see a damn thing."

"Exactly. You don't find that odd?"

"Why should I?"

"About fifteen miles in that direction, as the crow flies, is downtown Seattle. And about five miles in the same direction is Bremerton. That sky should be lit up like a baseball field."

"Fuck..."

"Oh, that's not the eerie part. Just ahead of us, about a thousand yards away, is Bangor, the naval ballistic sub base. It's a little quiet, don't you think?"

Sean peers into the night ahead of them, trying to spot some glimpse of light from the shore, but there is none. The only light around is coming from their boat, and the stars overhead, which seem unnaturally bright.

"Those stories you've been hearing, the ones about cities dying and the end of civilization... Yeah, I think they're bullshit stories, created by people like you and I that don't know what the hell is going on — but they might be right."

Sean begins coughing again, this time more forcefully than before. His eyes quickly turn bloodshot.

"Everything okay over there?" asks Larry.

"Yeah, it's just allergies. I've had them all my life. It's this fucking

49

damp air."

"Still, it might be a good idea to wear a mask, just in case."

The expression on Sean's face suddenly turns hostile, and even in relative darkness it's noticeable to Larry.

"I'm not sick. It's just allergies," Sean says sharply.

"I'm not making accusations. I'm just simply..."

"I haven't even seen a sick person. I certainly haven't had a wife die of it."

In that instant, Larry knows Beth was right, it was best not to let anyone else know about Jennifer — it's just too bad she never passed that wisdom onto her husband. He looks Sean directly in the eyes, but the look coming back is filled with venom.

"How long is your shift?" Sean asks.

Larry tries to stay as calm as possible on the outside, but inside he'd like to throw Sean overboard for what he said. "There are no shifts. We're going to Port Townsend. We'll spend the day there, maybe top the tanks off if the station is open."

"Why don't you let me take over when you're done, we can push straight through to Astoria that way."

"I appreciate the offer, but we're spending the day in Port Townsend."

"Uh huh..."

Larry can feel him staring, and for the first time tonight he's painfully aware of the gun Sean has strapped to his side. Sean stands up, still staring at him, then turns around and walks to the ladder. "I'm off to bed, just holler if you need me."

"You can count on it."

When Jake walks out of the only bedroom on the boat, and into

50

the main cabin, the first thing he sees is Sean dressed in full uniform — complete with a sidearm and pepper spray. Beth and Larry are outside on the deck behind him, with a look of concern on their faces.

"What's going on?" Jake asks Sean, still trying to wake up.

"Look who decided to finally get up! Get your shit on, we're going to shore."

"Where are we?"

"Port Townsend. The captain wants to see if we can buy fuel."

"What time is it anyway?"

"Quarter after six. You brought your gear, right?"

"Yeah, I brought it."

Beth walks into the cabin, giving a courteous smile to Sean as she walks by him. "Can I talk to you, in private?" she asks Jake, walking past him and into the bedroom.

"Sure..." He turns around, winking at Sean.

After they leave, Sean yells... "Don't you two make too much noise, this boat has thin walls!"

Beth waits for Jake to enter, then closes and locks the door behind him.

"Wow, you really are in the mood..."

"Shut up and listen," she whispers. "You have to get rid of Sean, today."

"Whoa, where did this come from?"

"Larry had a talk with him last night, and he all but threatened his life."

"Wait, this is Larry we're talking about. You know how Larry can be..."

"This is different, he even brought up Jen. Thanks for telling him that by the way."

He sits down on the bed, completely overwhelmed. "Do you have any idea what you're asking? You're talking about tossing him out like

51

he's a stray dog or something. This is my best friend."

"He's sick."

"I've known him for years, he's fine."

"No, I mean he's really sick. He's got this flu or whatever."

"He has allergies."

"Are you willing to risk your life on that? Are you willing to risk mine? He's too much of a liability."

He gets up and paces what little floorspace there is, a million thoughts running through his mind.

"Alright, any thoughts as to how this might happen? If you hadn't noticed, he's armed for war out there — and I doubt we'll be able to talk him into staying, especially if he's gone all psycho on us."

"Go to the store with him, acting completely natural, and we'll leave his bags on the dock."

"And then what?"

"Make up an excuse, say you forgot something on the boat. By the time he figures it out we'll be gone."

"Fuck, this can't end well. He's gonna be pissed."

"You'll be fine, just get dressed." She gets up and walks to the door, then turns around again. "Do whatever it takes, just don't let him come back."

Port Townsend isn't like most towns along the Washington coast. The other towns have either modernized or fallen apart from years of neglect, but Port Townsend looks almost exactly as it had over a century ago. Thanks to strict building codes and city ordinances, every house and business in the historic district uses the same architecture and paint colors as they did during the Victorian age, giving you the impression that you've traveled back in time — aside from the occasional hybrid car or smart phone that is.

Walking down the dock toward downtown, Jake is trying to keep his cool, and trying to tell from Sean's face if it's working. While his physical expressions aren't giving anything away, Sean's mood has been cheerful all morning, indicating that he's probably oblivious as to what's about to happen.

"You see anybody?" asks Sean.

Jake looks at the streets in front of them, a perfect view of the hill that makes up downtown. "No, it looks empty. Might be too early."

"It's Wednesday morning, it should be busier than hell."

"That was before. Things are different now."

"Ain't that the truth. That must be the store up there on the left."

"Did Larry tell you what to do if they're closed?"

"Yep, find the key to the pumps."

If Jake's mind weren't filled with anxiety he'd probably find the situation humorous. Here they were, two prison guards, planning to steal diesel from a dock, and their getaway vehicle maxes out at ten knots.

"It says open on the window," Sean points out.

"It looks dark inside though — in fact the whole city looks like it's out of power."

Sean tries the handle, but it's locked. He looks in through the window, but can't see anybody inside, just half-empty shelves. As he knocks on the door and window, Jake walks to the intersection behind the store.

He'd never liked living in town, he always preferred the peace and quiet of living in the country, where the only constant noise was the wind. As much as he disliked the bustle of the city though, standing in the middle of one with no sound or activity at all was decidedly worse. It was like looking at a still photograph, where everything looks like it should, but it's somehow lifeless and without character. He notices the

53

cars still parked along the streets, and a cat sitting on the front porch of a house washing itself. He sees everything but people.

"There's nobody inside. I'm just gonna break the window," Sean hollers.

Jake walks back toward the store. "Whatever you do, make it quick. This place gives me the creeps."

Sean takes his nightstick out and puts it through the window beside the door, then reaches in and unlocks the deadbolt.

"I always wondered what that felt like..."

Jake follows him inside, an uneasy feeling building in his gut. The store is mostly empty, with no sign of food anywhere. It looks as though they weren't the only ones looking to replenish their supplies. As Sean heads behind the counter, looking for any sign of the keys, Jake sees it as a perfect opportunity for a getaway.

"Shit, I forgot the list that Beth gave me."

"From the looks of the shelves I doubt we're gonna find any of it anyway."

"You never know. Besides, she'll be pissed if I didn't try."

"Just hold on a minute and I'll head back with you."

Jake can feel the beads of sweat forming on his forehead, and the pain shooting through his jaw as it clenches. This isn't going to plan.

"I'll be back in just a second, then we'll both look."

He starts to head out, and then just as he makes it through the door he hears Sean.

"You leaving me behind?"

"Yeah, right," Jake says, hoping to pass the remark off as a joke.

"I think it's best if we both stay — you know, for security and all. It might be in both our interests." His tone is serious, even somewhat threatening.

Jake is still standing just outside the door, with a slight smile still plastered on his face. "Did I do something?"

54

"No, but your brother-in-law said plenty last night. I'm just looking out for myself. You understand, right?"

"Yeah, I guess so. We're in this together though, all of us."

"Right, so lets find the key and get the hell out of here."

Jake slowly walks back inside and joins Sean behind the counter. "Are we okay? I'm not really sure what's happening."

"We're fine, we just have work to do."

All Jake can think of are Sean's bags waiting on the dock beside the boat, and what his reaction would be if he saw them. He hates the position he's been put in, and he's pissed at Larry and Beth for placing the burden on him.

"We're still friends, right?" Jake asks, extending his right hand for Sean to shake.

"Always."

As Sean extends his hand, Jake grabs his stun gun with his other hand and pulls the trigger, sending the electrodes directly into Sean's neck. He hits the ground instantly, his body shaking from the electricity coursing through his nervous system. Jake watches him for a moment, in disbelief at what he just did — then he sees Sean's hand reach down to his side in an uncoordinated effort to unsnap his revolver. Jake bends down and jerks his arm away, then unsnaps the gun himself and takes it.

"I'm sorry man, I really am. I'll leave this on the dock in front of the boat. I hope everything works out for you, I honestly do."

"Fuck... You..."

The words sound painful, and bitter.

Jake reaches down and takes out Sean's stun gun, then unzips his armored vest, exposing his v-neck shirt underneath.

"Again, I'm sorry about this, but it has to happen this way, and you know why."

He stands up, aims the stun gun, and fires another round at his

55

bare skin. This time he doesn't wait around — instead he bolts for the door and runs toward the dock, hoping to find Beth and Larry waiting for him. As he gets to the halfway point he realizes that the dock is empty, and he sees the two of them standing on the deck, staring in his direction. As soon as they spot him Larry climbs up to the pilothouse, and Beth starts throwing bags out of the cabin and onto the stern deck.

"Why didn't you already do that?" Jake screams as he jumps onto the boat.

"I didn't know if you were going to go through with it!" Beth replies, her voice frantic. "He's still alive?"

"Of course he's still alive, but he's gonna be pissed when he wakes up."

As Larry starts the engine, Jake joins Beth in tossing the bags onto the dock. He pulls Sean's gun out of his pocket, then throws in onto the dock with everything else.

"Why did you do that?" she asks.

"I'm not leaving him here unarmed."

Beth picks up the last piece — a hard, black case that looks like a over-sized briefcase, then throws it overboard with the rest — just as the boat starts to slowly move away from the dock.

"Not that one!" yells Jake.

"Why?"

"That's his rifle."

"So? You just gave him a gun..."

"I gave him a pistol, not a rifle." He looks up to the pilothouse. "Larry, is there any chance you could go back?"

Instead of answering, Larry points in the direction of the store, where Jake sees Sean staggering out of the doorway and onto the wooden planks of the dock, his feet almost dragging across the decking.

56

"Fuck!" Jake climbs partway up the ladder, making eye contact with Larry. "Is there any way you can get us out of here any faster?"

"I'm at full-throttle already."

He climbs back down, trying to clear his head enough to think this through rationally. Sean is about fifty feet from the bags they left behind, and his pace is getting quicker with every step. Their pace is picking up too, but it still feels agonizingly slow.

"Why can't you just shoot him?" asks Beth, her voice filled with fear.

"I'm not going to shoot him."

She grabs the .38 from out of her pocket, the one that Larry gave her, then points it at the docks. When Jake sees it he grabs it out of her hands.

"He's going to kill us if he gets to those guns!" she screams.

Jake's voice turns calm and reassuring. "No he won't, we're out of range now."

"What about the rifle?"

"It's in pieces, he'd have to put it together."

They watch as Sean finally reaches the bags. He picks up his pistol first, placing it back in its holster, then looks around the dock. He jumps onto a boat sitting nearby and breaks the cabin door down, then disappears inside. After thirty seconds or so, he reemerges and steps back onto the dock. Then just as they start to lose sight of him behind a waterfront hotel, they see him throwing the bags onto the boat, one by one, slowly and calmly.

"He's coming after us, isn't he?" Beth asks.

"Yeah," responds Jake, his voice grim. "I think he is."

57

CHAPTER 5
PORT TOWNSEND

There are three large bodies of water that make up the Salish Sea — the Puget Sound, the Strait of Georgia, and the Strait of Juan de Fuca. These, along with the Columbia river to the south, the Olympic mountains to the west, and the Cascade mountains to the east, create some of the world's most complicated weather patterns. They can also cause severe, and often unpredictable currents in the ocean. In the heart of the Salish Sea is Port Townsend, where all of the major components come together as one. Directly to the west, through the rough waters of the Strait of Juan de Fuca, lies the Pacific Ocean.

From the strait just northwest of town you can see the city of Victoria on Vancouver Island — and also Whidbey Island, the San Juan Islands, and the jagged peaks from two mountain ranges, some of which soar over fourteen-thousand feet. Despite the breathtaking view surrounding them, Beth and Jake Wilson are focused on only one thing — a small glimmer of reflected light that seems to be following them. Even with the assistance of binoculars, they still can't tell what it is, or who.

"That has to be him. Can he shoot us from that range?" Beth asks.

"No, he's still too far away."

He puts the binoculars down and sits on the bench, noticing for the first time the sights that surround them. The sun is just beginning to descend into the horizon in front of them, creating a glare on the water that shimmers in the tidal flow.

"God, it's beautiful here isn't it?"

"Yeah..." she answers back, not taking her sight off of the object.

58

He turns his view toward Victoria to the north, a city that sits in one of the most picturesque locations in the world, and yet still suffers an identity crisis in its quest to be more like another city halfway around the world, London. He picks up his binoculars and looks toward the city, but the normally busy streets look as empty as the ones in Port Townsend. He faces his wife again, feeling exhausted, like an escaped convict watching every movement, or lack thereof.

"Did you notice how empty the town looked?" he asks.

"I didn't really pay any attention. I had a few other things on my mind."

"It was eerie, like everyone just disappeared without a trace. You couldn't even hear anything."

She turns away from the object and looks down at him, recognizing the fear in his voice, then she sits down.

"Maybe they were hiding," she says.

"You'd think there'd be looters though, right? The shelves in the store were mostly empty, but there was still some stuff left, and the door was still locked when we got there."

Beth picks up her binoculars and looks at Port Townsend, its streets still visible, but only barely.

"There aren't any boats out here either, except for the one following us," says Jake. He stands up and looks toward the object again. "That's definitely a boat, you can see it better now."

Beth joins him, and can tell even with her naked eyes that he's right, they're being followed by a boat. "If we can see him better that must mean he's gaining on us."

"I should have killed the son of a bitch when I had the chance."

"At this rate you might get that chance again." Leaving Jake on the main deck, she climbs the ladder to the pilothouse, where Larry is sitting behind the wheel. "Did you hear all of that?" she asks Larry.

"Yeah, sounds like we're gonna have company."

59

"Is there anything you can do to speed us up?"

"The best I can do is try to make it to Port Angeles by nightfall."

"How will that help exactly?"

"We'll hide in the marina, and hope he keeps moving."

"He'll still find us. He knows where we're going."

"My guess is he'll end up on the sandbar just outside the jetties, if he even finds his way down there."

"I'm sure that boat has GPS."

"That doesn't seem to be working very well for some reason." he says, pointing at his own GPS screen.

"Maybe it's just yours."

"I have another one, and they're both giving the same location. They have us approximately two miles the other side of Highway 101."

She looks more closely at the screen, and sure enough, it shows them moving across dry land, several miles off-course.

"Is that going to be a problem navigating?"

"Not for me, I never liked the damn thing anyway. As long as the compass and sonar keep working, we'll be fine."

They finally lose sight of the boat following them as they move past the town of Sequim, a town with a large population of retirees, and referred to as 'God's waiting room' by many in the area. Although the boat is drawing closer with every passing minute, the slow veil of nightfall is making its way across the water from the east, and they're now only a few miles from Port Angeles. Larry has ordered both Jake and Beth to turn off every light on the boat, and to cover as best they can the most reflective surfaces on-board. Whether or not it will help remains to be seen, but if they have any shot at slipping away during the night they have to remove as much visibility as possible.

60

As they pass each small town and community along the waterway, Jake watches them closely, hoping to see another living person or moving car somewhere, if for no other reason than to know they aren't the only ones left alive. So far all he's seen are what looks like the after-effects of a war. A scattering of houses and trees burned to the ground, cars with no lights lined up on the highway, dogs and cats running free through otherwise empty neighborhoods, and at least one person he knows for certain was dead. There were several other things that could have been people, alive or otherwise, but at this distance he couldn't be sure one way or the other. Now with darkness obscuring his view, even the unrecognizable objects are disappearing.

He climbs up into the pilothouse, where his wife and Larry are already seated.

"How long until we get to the marina?" he asks.

"Another twenty minutes maybe. It'll be nice and dark by the time we get there," answers Larry.

"Are there usually a lot of boats there?"

"A couple hundred under normal circumstances. I'm hoping he doesn't even see us go in."

"What do we do after he passes us? He might spot us if we just follow behind him," Beth says.

"I thought maybe we'd hang out in town for a while, let him think he's chasing us down the coast," replies Larry.

As the boat turns south toward town, the waves hit the boat against the starboard side, causing it to rock side to side. With only two chairs in the room, Jake sits down on the floor before he loses his footing. Between the wind and waves crashing against them, and the sound of the engine as it forces its way through the current, the only way they can hear one another is to yell.

"Maybe we should double-back instead," says Jake.

"What do you mean?" asks Beth.

61

"I mean go back to Sequim for a while. He won't expect that, not after he's chased us this far."

"For how long?"

"I don't know, maybe a week or two. We'll just stay low for a while."

"At some point he'll catch on, he might come back..."

"If he keeps moving it'll be morning before he realizes he's not following us." The boat lurches to the side violently, nearly throwing Jake down onto the deck below. "Where would he be by then?" he asks Larry.

"It's hard to say, he could be clear to Astoria if he ran all night. I'll bet he stops in Neah Bay before hitting the ocean though."

"Why is that?"

"It's at the end of the strait, right at the opening to the ocean. When he tries to go around the cape he's gonna feel like he's been kicked in the gut. This is mild compared to out there."

Beth looks out the window at the city of Port Angeles, which is quickly disappearing as the sunset vanishes from the sky. Soon the only illumination they'll have left will be from the moon overhead. The city itself is dark, and the buildings look like shadows against the snow-covered mountains in the distance.

As they reach the outskirts of the marina, Jake watches behind them carefully for any sign of their pursuer. The docks are only about half-full, but Larry weaves his way through them anyway, trying to pick out the perfect spot. After about ten minutes of searching he finally finds one. As he straightens the boat out with the space, he cuts the engine, gliding into place with only a slight jolt as they collide with the dock. Looking over the marina they can see a ripple effect on the other boats as they sway from side to side. There's a reason Larry chose this spot — not only does it sit back in the middle of the other boats, it also has a perfect view of the entrance from the strait. If anyone comes in they'll be able to see them, and that might give them

62

a crucial advantage.

"So, I guess we wait," says Beth.

"Yep," replies Larry.

Jake lowers himself down to the stern deck and looks around at the other boats, and at the city. At first everything is quiet, almost too quiet, and then he hears a noise coming from down the dock — a low thumping, like the muffled sound of footsteps from inside a building.

"I'll be back in a minute," he whispers to the others.

"Where are you going?" Beth asks.

"I hear something, I'm gonna go to check it out. Stay here and keep an eye out for Sean."

Clearly not happy, she spins her chair around, shaking her head as she faces Larry. As Jake sneaks down the dock, trying to discern where the noise is coming from, he notices a boat that's rocking more than the others. He ducks his head down low and carefully creeps closer, until he comes close enough to reach out and touch it. The boat is moored only four spaces down from them, and aside from the sounds, looks to be completely lifeless. With his gun firmly in his grasp, he leans in closer and listens. Somebody, or something, is inside, thrashing around and throwing things. Back and forth they walk, pacing from one end of the boat to the other. He looks at the windows, trying to get a peek inside, but the curtains are pulled shut, and there aren't any lights on inside anyway. As he starts to make his way back, a hand suddenly appears from behind the curtain on the side window — their palm pressed firmly against the pane. Slowly they begin scratching the window, a high-pitched steady screech coming from the glass as their nails glide down the surface. When it reaches the bottom it disappears, then slams into the glass, the hand still stretched out flat. Again and again it hits the window, and each time it does, Jake expects it to break — and then it stops. He stands there for a minute, waiting for something to happen, waiting for

63

someone to come outside — but nobody does. The night is suddenly silent again, and the only noise aside from the dock itself is coming from the direction of the city. It sounds like the rattling of chain link fencing.

He walks quietly and quickly down the dock to their boat, then jumps on-board and climbs up to the pilothouse.

"What was it?" asks Beth in a normal tone.

"Shh... I think we should get ready to leave, now," he whispers back.

"Why?" she replies, her voice now soft, but concerned.

"We're not the only ones here..."

"Did you see somebody?" asks Larry.

"Sort of, and I don't think they were well."

Beth excitedly taps both of them on the shoulders. "Look!" she whispers.

Just beyond the jetty, at the entrance to the marina, is another boat easing its way into the calm waters that surround the docks. Its lights are out, but they can hear the sound of its engine. As it makes its way down the first aisle, three down from where they're at, they see a spotlight appear. They all drop their heads to the dash, but they keep watching. The light is moving from boat to boat, taking only a few seconds to examine each one.

"He must have seen us..." Beth says.

"He couldn't have, it was too dark," answers Jake. "Besides, it'll take him half an hour to search this place at that rate. He won't waste that much time."

"He'll find us in half that..." replies Larry.

As they watch the boat ahead of them, all three suddenly become aware at the exact same time that someone is behind them, staggering down the dock. They turn around and sit on the floor, hiding in darkness, and wishing they had a door on the pilothouse to provide at least some cover. Jake pulls out his gun, then holds up his hand at

64

Beth and Larry, motioning for them to keep their guns concealed. The last thing he wants is for one of them to get scared and pull their trigger, alerting the entire marina of their location. With only a small portion of the dock in his sights, he waits, listening to the uncoordinated steps grow louder. Then he finally sees someone, fully illuminated by the moon overhead, walking from the direction of the city toward the end of the dock.

The man is dressed in what looks like a hospital gown, his bare feet dirty and bloodied, and his face wearing no expression at all — like he was in some sort of a trance. He looks either drunk or drugged by the way he's moving, stumbling and stubbing his toes with almost every step. Jake spreads himself out on the floor and stretches forward as the man walks past them, never leaving him out of his gun sights. Beth slowly creeps up beside him, her body shaking with fear. With their heads sticking out from the pilothouse doorway, they watch as the man casually walks off of the edge of the dock and into the water, hitting the back of his head against the wooden deck on his way down.

After a quick look up and down the rest of the dock, Jake and Beth pull themselves back into the pilothouse.

"What the hell was that?" Beth asks Jake.

"Fuck if I know, he looked like he was half-dead."

Larry pops up to his feet, looking the marina over to see where the boat ended up — but he sees nothing.

"Where is he?" asks Jake, now back on his feet beside him.

"I don't know, I don't see the light anymore."

"Fuck! He could be sitting out there, just waiting for us."

"We'll wait until midnight, then we'll go."

"What if he *is* out there? He's faster than us..." says Beth.

"It's three against one. The odds are in our favor in a shootout," replies Larry.

"Yeah, but he has the rifle, and he's trained to use it." says Jake. "I

65

think you're right though, we have to move. If he's still here he'll find us eventually anyway."

They wait, watching the area for any sign of Sean, or anyone else. At ten after midnight Larry starts the engine, keeping it at low throttle. He inches out of the space, then moves down the aisle toward the entrance and into the strait. With no sign of another boat, Beth glances back at the streets behind them. What she sees doesn't register at first, it's the last thing she expected to see as they left Port Angeles — in fact it's the last thing she expected to see anywhere.

She sees people.

"Jake, look!" she says, pointing to the street behind the marina.

At first he sees just a few of them, shadows on the other side of the fence from the docks — then as his eyes adjust, the rest of them appear. There must be dozens, maybe more, wandering the area just beyond the barrier — crowding the closed gate only fifty yards from where they were moored.

66

CHAPTER 6
COHASSETT BEACH

Sarah Lockwood had kept an open mind since the outbreak first began. Too many times over the years she'd listened to one expert after another give dire warnings about the latest epidemic, only to find out that their predictions were nothing more than hysteria. It seemed every news outlet in the country had one — a doctor with a kind personality and warm smile, and a talent for convincingly crying wolf with uncanny regularity.

On July 22nd, doctors from around the world sounded the alarms once more, this time concerning a flu that was spreading rapidly throughout Europe. Few people on the continent listened, and those that did were too late to do anything about it. For her own part, Sarah didn't listen to anything in those early days either — and neither did the rest of the United States. As the days passed, however, bizarre stories started to make their way into the news cycles — and with them came fear and confusion throughout the nation. There was talk of missing towns throughout the mainland of Europe, of planes landing at empty airports, even reporters for news agencies that were disappearing overnight. Then on the morning of the 26th, there was nothing.

For the first time in an age, the entire continent was silent.

Rioting and overall mayhem was spreading throughout every major city here in the states, fueled mostly by misinformation on social media, and by a deepening distrust in officials that were trying their best to control an already uncontrollable problem. At this point nobody in the country had actually fallen ill, but the mere fact that

67

the virus existed had been sufficient to bring the system to its knees. Adding to the problem was the fact that information about the infection itself was scarce.

By the time the virus did arrive on our shores, the news media and Internet had been virtually shut-down, and replaced with continuous loops of generally worthless advice on what not to do. People were being told not to leave their homes, not to drink water from public supplies, not to visit crowded shopping centers, and not to go to the hospital for any flu-like symptoms. It was the last one that broke Curtis, that made him aware of just how much danger they were in. Looking back on it, Sarah knows that it should have affected her too, but she chose not to see it, chose not to believe that the world around her was changing. Ultimately it was the sound of radio static that opened her eyes, that made her recognize that her children would never grow up in the same world that she and her husband had. Those days were now gone.

It was now shortly after midnight, and the Lockwood family has huddled up around a small campfire that sits beside the cabin they now call home. They'd spent the previous day cutting wood for the wood stove and getting the cabin ready for habitation. They had beds to prepare, cupboards to stock with food, and a seemingly endless amount of disinfecting. When they were finally done, they decided to start a campfire and spend some time outside, telling themselves and each other that they shouldn't waste such a beautiful evening. The real purpose, however, was avoidance. They wanted distance, from both the cabin and what it represented.

The two boys, Matt and Ben, are lying on the ground, gazing at the few bright stars that are visible through the trees. The radio hisses quietly in the background, creating a sound that seems more lonely and empty than when its off, but they listen anyway. Earlier in the evening, both Curtis and Sarah waited impatiently for the glow of lights that normally come from the nearby towns of Westport and Grayland, but the lights never appeared. Also gone was the fog horn from the state park, and the sound of traffic from the highway in front of their place. All that was left was the roar of the ocean, the wind in the trees, the birds overhead, and a radio searching for something that no longer existed.

"How long are we going to stay here?" asks Matt, looking quite comfortable.

Sarah looks at Curtis, who looks back and shrugs, unsure of what to say. "We could be here a while." she answers back. "Don't you like it here?"

"Its kinda cool. Can we go back to the beach tomorrow?"

"We'll see. There's still work to do around here," says Curtis. "How much do you guys know about what's going on?"

"What do you mean?" asks Matt.

"I mean this whole virus thing, and why we left..."

Matt and Ben both shrug.

"I don't know." Matt answers dismissively.

"You know its killing people, right?"

"Yeah..."

"And you know that's why we left...?"

"Yeah, I guess..."

Sarah places her hand on Curtis' knee, then shakes her head. They hadn't really discussed when to talk to their sons, and this seemed like the perfect opportunity to him, but it obviously didn't seem that way to his wife.

"We'll talk about it some more another day," he says. "It's getting late, we should probably head inside and get some sleep, we've got

69

another busy day ahead of us."

As Curtis shuts the cabin door behind them, closing out the world from their senses, he misses something unusual — something that would never be seen again. To the north, just barely visible from the steps of the cabin's porch, is a line of hundreds of lights, stretching for miles down the highway. None of them are moving, and none will be seen by the time the sun comes up. Throughout the night, one by one, they slowly fade away.

CHAPTER 7
COHASSETT BEACH

Nearly two months have passed since they first arrived at the cabin, and although it looks completely different on the inside, the outside looks virtually unchanged. How it stays watertight Curtis will never know, but the pathetic excuse for a home has been just that, a home. It's a two-room, single story, unpainted mess of half rotten wood and rusty nails, and yet it's kept them warm and dry through the most difficult time of their lives.

He can't imagine what his grandfather would think if he could see them now. As a boy, Curtis and his family would spend summer vacations here, and even the occasional weekend in the winter months to dig for razor clams on the beach below. He remembers those days fondly, and it bothers him deeply that his own sons' memories of this place will be full of sleepless nights listening to the radio as their world disintegrates around them.

A storm had moved through only a couple of days ago — not exactly a rare event for late October, but being the first real wind storm of the season, it left the air feeling fresh and brisk, and the deciduous trees around them leafless. It was the first time his family had witnessed an event like that, a windstorm so powerful that it moves the earth beneath your feet. Explaining to them that it was actually tree roots moving the ground didn't seem to help matters, or the fact that he couldn't wipe the enjoyment off of his own face. He loved the storms at the beach, he always had — even when he was a kid. He remembered his Dad staying up with him, sitting in front of the wood stove, watching the flames dance every time a gust would

71

come down the chimney. They could watch it in silence for hours, words being unnecessary in a moment like that.

Walking up the driveway, he can smell the woodsmoke from the same tiny cast-iron stove. He wonders if it was smart to leave his wife and kids alone with such an obvious sign of life visible for miles around. Today was different though, today he walked down the beach to the edge of town for the first time since arriving here. He was determined to take the family into Westport tomorrow, but before they did, Sarah insisted that he check everything out first.

Standing in front of the cabin window, he sees his wife folding clothes on the bed, an old-fashioned wifely duty that she would've expected him to share only a few months prior. She'd become just like her mother, and although she'll never admit it, especially to Curtis, the role somehow made sense in their current situation.

Sarah didn't look her age, she never had. When she was in high school she looked like one of the teachers, and now that she's over forty she really doesn't look any different. These last couple of months have been tough though. While her face looks exactly the same as it did last year, her eyes have lost their sparkle, and her skin tone has changed to a color bordering on gray. She tells herself that it's the almost complete lack of sunshine on the coast that's done it, but she knows the real cause runs much deeper. Although she's grateful that she has her husband and sons with her, she hasn't yet come to terms with the fact that her daughter is hundreds of miles away, if she's even still alive. From the day they arrived at the beach they've been living day to day, hoping for a sign that things will return to normal. Tomorrow could be their chance to find out, and she's afraid of what the answer might be.

As Curtis walks around the back of the cabin, he sees his sons playing some sort of game that apparently involves throwing sticks and yelling, as most games do when you're their age. Last summer it would've taken a small miracle to get the kids outside, and today they're playing the same types of games he and his friends used to play when they were young. Moving to the middle of nowhere seems a drastic way to get his kids to play something besides video games, but he has to admit, it is rather effective. The oldest, Matt, is exactly like Curtis was when he was twelve — quiet and reserved, and secretly the wild one of the two. Ben is different. He's talkative, energetic, playful, and without a trace of deception. Curtis feels close to both of his sons, but he's worried what this new world might be like for Ben. His cheerful attitude would either save him from the darkness yet to come, or he would find himself lost and incompatible in a society that no longer has any use for such behavior.

Lost in his own thoughts, Curtis hadn't noticed his wife standing next to him, holding out a glass of water.

"Thanks." he says, swallowing the mineral-rich contents in a single swig.

"What did you see in town?"

"Not much. I went down to the boardwalk in front of the park, then walked to the grocery store."

"Did you get anything?"

"There wasn't much to get, the shelves were already empty."

"Did you see any... you know..."

"Dead bodies?" he asks.

"Yeah."

"A few. It's mostly bones though, scattered around in the streets like litter."

Curtis sits down on a wooden swing next to the cabin and motions for Sarah to do the same. He notices a slight tremble in her hands, but says nothing about it. Although he knows this new information has probably startled her, the visible manifestations of stress and anxiety are something they stopped talking about weeks ago. Some things can

73

be mentioned only so many times before the meaning wears off. In truth, neither of them cared to talk about it anymore. Instead, he simply takes her hand into his and holds it.

"We can't take the kids into a place like that, can we?" she says.

"To be honest, I think the town is safer if everyone *is* dead. At least then we don't have to worry about catching anything."

Sarah says nothing. A small part of her wants to be angry, to yell at him for making such an outrageous comment — but she doesn't have the energy to be judgmental or righteous anymore, and a growing part of her agrees with him. Her moral and ethical boundaries are in constant shift these days, leaving her feeling empty and numb.

"You didn't answer my question," she says.

"If there was rioting in the streets I would agree with you, I wouldn't want to go either — but there's nobody there." He takes out his cell phone, then opens up a photo. "I hope and pray that this is the worst thing they ever see in their lives..."

The photograph he's showing her is of a sidewalk covered in leaves, with several bones sticking out from underneath them. She takes the phone from him and starts flipping through the other photos. When she reaches one that shows a street view she stops.

"Where are the cars?"

He looks at the picture closely, and not a single car is parked anywhere in the shot.

"I don't know, I didn't really notice that."

"So your view is that everyone is dead, and Matt and Ben have to see it eventually... Right?" she asks, her voice calm.

"Right."

"And if they aren't dead, then what?"

"Then we keep our distance."

She keeps the volume of her voice low, so the kids can't hear, but her tone becomes more indignant. "For what purpose? Why do we

74

need to go?"

"We're running out of supplies."

"That's not an answer, you could go get the supplies without us."

"And what if I didn't come back? Would you come search for me, or just figure that I dropped dead someplace?" He waits for a response, but gets none. "We have to stay together in this, no matter what."

She looks at the boys again, watching them run around like fools in the woods surrounding the cabin, a glimmer of innocence still bright in their eyes. From her own childhood she knows how easily that innocence can be damaged, even destroyed.

"Okay," she says softly.

"Okay what?"

"We'll stay together. No matter what."

After dinner they decide to walk to the beach and relax before heading off to bed, hoping the fresh air and the sound of the waves might take their minds off of the hike tomorrow. The sun is beginning to make its slow decent into the ocean when they finally cross the sand dunes and catch their first glimpse of the water. A sun setting red in the sky is seen as a bad omen in many parts of the world, but somehow over the ocean it seems tranquil and calming — even hopeful. As the boys divide their time between digging in the sand and chasing seagulls, Curtis and Sarah sit on a flattened piece of driftwood that a storm had conveniently left on the beach. They'd been to this spot before, but this time the wind seems cold and penetrating, a sign of the changing seasons. Although she's wearing two layers of clothing, Sarah can feel the icy breeze clear to her bones. Curtis doesn't feel anything. He has something else on his mind.

He'd seen things in town, things he couldn't share with Sarah. Horrible things.

CHAPTER 8
SEQUIM

Although he'd spent nearly two weeks obsessing over the trip, Larry Gossman hadn't actually thought a lot of it through. One could argue that it could have been grief over the death of his wife that caused it, or the overwhelming stress of a worldwide epidemic taking place all around him — but neither of these is actually true. The real reason Larry never followed through with the planning was simple — he never planned on living long enough to leave.

Shortly after his wife died, Larry developed a cough. It was exactly like Jennifer's in every way — except in his case , he lived. To this day he's never told another soul about it, not even Beth. There isn't a day that goes by that he doesn't wonder why he lived and his wife died, or whether he was actually sick from the same virus that killed her. In his mind it seems far-fetched to believe they contracted two different illnesses within only days of each other. The odds would have to be astronomical.

He also feels an incredible amount of guilt — not concerning his wife, but for possibly exposing Beth. He'd managed to keep her away during the entire sickness, even threatening to disown her if she stepped foot inside their house — but after Jennifer's death he became weak, both emotionally and physically. When he called her that night to tell her the news, there was no hesitation on her part, and within minutes she was standing beside him as they stood over his wife's body. Part of him knew that he was likely condemning his sister's life with that phone call, and the fact that she likely knew it too meant the world to him.

His lackluster planning had nothing to do with supplies. They'd brought hundreds of dehydrated meals, dozens of cases of filtered water, medications and first aid supplies, extra clothes, fuel, and even a sewing kit for reasons still unknown to Beth and Jake. What he didn't count on was sitting for very long. As long as it was moving, the 'Obsession' ran perfectly, except for one small problem — a leak.

Larry had known about it for months, but it never seemed a great concern as long as the bilge pumps were working. Out on the water they ran off the boat's own electricity, and in the marina they ran off of power at the dock. Sitting in the middle of Sequim, however, was a different story. They'd been here for over a month with no electricity, forcing Larry to waste precious fuel by running the engine every other day just to keep the boat from sinking into the strait.

None of them wanted to be in Sequim, it was in the opposite direction from where they needed to be. They'd much rather be heading west toward the Pacific Ocean, and from there south to the Oregon coast — but they all agreed that backtracking to the east a few miles might help to throw Sean off of their trail. So far it seems to have worked, since they haven't seen a single sign of him all month.

They hadn't actually planned on staying this long. After reaching the marina they all agreed that a week should be sufficient, but a series of storms blowing in from the Pacific changed their itinerary, and now they have no choice but to pray that the weather holds out for just a couple of more days as they make their way to Astoria.

It's late-evening, and Jake is standing on the stern deck watching downtown Sequim in the distance. Beth climbs down the ladder from the pilothouse and stands beside him.

"Larry says as long as the skies look clear in the morning, we're headed out," she tells him.

"Sounds good."

"Did you know that Sequim gets less rainfall than Phoenix?"

77

"Everyone knows that." he responds, his voice more blunt then he intended, a consequence of being forced to live in such tight quarters for this long. They stand in silence for a moment, his gaze focused on the city, and hers at the decking between her feet. "Why the smalltalk?" he asks.

"Because I'd rather talk about anything else, anything other than that..." She nods in the direction of town, the direction that Jake is staring. From one end of town to the other, hundreds of shadows are making their way out into the streets, just barely visible enough to be recognized as the citizens of Sequim. They've been watching them for weeks now, coming out at dusk, and completely disappearing just before daybreak. During the last several weeks they've come up with a million ideas of what the people are doing, or who they are, but after studying them for countless hours now, they really have no clue. They seem lost, wandering with no purpose or direction, mindlessly walking with no routine whatsoever. They've watched some of them go in and out of buildings, apparently at random, always staying in motion — and yet others simply stand in one location for hours on end.

"I hate it when they do that," says Beth.

"Do what?" asks Jake.

"Scream like that."

They've been listening to them every night for so long now that apparently he's grown used to it. For some, it's a high-pitched, blood-curdling scream, and for others it sounds more like a primal howl — almost full of pride. Some of them do it all night long.

"Do you think Astoria is the same way?" she asks.

"Probably." He sits down, still keeping an eye on the commotion across the water. "It's like the entire fucking world has gone mad, and we're the only ones unlucky enough to witness it."

"I wonder what they eat...? They must be running out of food by

78

now."

The thought hadn't really occurred to him, but she's right. Somehow, miraculously, a portion of the town has survived the infection, and apparently the only cost to them has been their humanity and intelligence. They've yet to see any sign of foraging or gathering of supplies from the crowds of people on the street, even if something useful is literally at their feet in front of them.

He points out some people holding onto the fence that surrounds the marina. It looks to be a woman and two men. "Why don't they ever try to climb that fence? That woman has been there almost every night for the last week, and she's never tried to climb over."

"I'm just glad she doesn't." Beth takes her eyes off of the crowd for a moment, and instead watches her husband, his face a mixture of emotions as he looks from one diseased soul to the next.

Some of the shadows are walking in stiff, uncoordinated steps, as though it causes them great physical pain to move — but most are moving almost normally, with only a slight carefulness in their gait. More than anything, they seem to be confused.

"I'm sorry about Sean. I know I pressured you to bring him..." he says, finally taking his eyes off of the people.

This was the first time he'd actually apologized to her. In fact it was the first time she could ever recall him expressing remorse at all. Normally they would ignore disagreements and awkward moments, letting them slip away outside of their consciousness, and into a place where they could fester and grow. It wasn't ideal, she knew that, but it had always worked for them — even when they were kids.

"I know. He was your friend, I understand that."

"I thought he was perfect for something like this. He stays cool under pressure, he knows his way around weapons — he's even saved my life a couple of times. I thought I owed him something."

"Don't feel guilty about what you did to him... You *had* to do it."

79

"I'm gonna have to kill him — that's the only way to stop him."

"If Larry is right, you might not get the opportunity. The ocean he's headed into is deadly this time of the year."

He looks back at the city, where the crowds of people are slowly disappearing in the looming darkness. "You should get some sleep, I'll take the first watch."

"Yeah, I'm getting a bit tired. Wake me up for the next shift, Larry needs all the rest he can get. It's gonna be a long trip tomorrow."

CHAPTER 9
COHASSETT BEACH

Just south of Westport is the extinct town of Cohasset. It was once a bustling and prosperous community during the great depression, one of the few that were, but the town slowly disappeared following World War II, and today remains only a suburb of its larger neighbor to the north. The houses along Forrest Street were mostly built in those early days, and most of them look it. The level of upkeep these last two months has been relatively the same as it had been during the past century — virtually nonexistent.

Sarah knew the houses were empty, but walking past them she was struck at how lonely they felt, a glaring reminder of just how isolated they'd been living. They were walking through what used to be a close-knit community, a neighborhood that had grown accustomed to banding together when times were tough. Today the street looked defeated.

Having already found nothing on the beach, Curtis decided that a walk down the highway might shed at least some light on whatever happened to everyone — but after traveling less than a mile, the mystery was starting to solve itself, and it wasn't good. A line of cars, stretching as far as they can see, are parked in the middle of the road in front of them — most of them with their doors open and keys in the ignitions. A thieves paradise, except there were no thieves in sight. It didn't take a genius to figure out what happened. All it took was a dozen or so cars clustered together in the roadway, blocking both lanes of traffic. Every car behind them was essentially trapped, caught between the soft and unstable sand dunes on the west side, and a

81

flooded cranberry bog on the other.

"Why didn't we hear this?" asks Sarah, stopping to take in the scene.

"It's hard telling when it happened. It could have been weeks ago," replies Curtis.

"What happened?" asks Ben.

"It looks like a traffic jam that never got cleared up," answers Curtis.

"Where did the people go?"

"I don't know, but that's a good question."

The cars surrounding them look abandoned and forgotten, like tombstones in an old graveyard. After spending several minutes examining them, the family decides to move on, hoping that things look better as they get closer to town.

It's an unseasonably warm and sunny morning for this time of year, a rare autumn event that sometimes happens in the aftermath of a storm. It was a perfect day for their seven-mile hike into Westport. Sarah had hardly been off the property since they first came to the cabin, and she was both excited and nervous about going. Curtis had warned her that she would see things today that she wouldn't soon forget, and so would their sons. She wanted more than anything for their youth to be preserved, to feel like kids without the weight of the world being placed on their shoulders — but their youth has ended prematurely, and the cold reality of adulthood has taken its place. Early this morning, as they prepared for their hike, Curtis and Sarah sat both of their sons down and tried their best to explain what they would see today. They'd spent much of the night discussing how to do it, but in the end they decided there really wasn't a right or wrong way, just an honest way.

As they make their way through the endless maze of cars and fallen tree limbs, she was trying hard not to think about Annie, but she couldn't help it. Though it caused her an incredible amount of emotional agony and guilt, her mind wouldn't let even a trace of time

82

go by without thinking of her. Looking back, Annie's innocence had disappeared without her even noticing. It was less than a year ago when she walked into Annie's bedroom while she was packing for college, realizing for the first time that her child was no longer a child, and wondering what had happened to the girl she once knew. It was a bittersweet moment that all parents must come to terms with, despite the heartache they feel. As hard as it was, that feeling was natural though, you're supposed to feel those emotions when your child grows up. For Matt and Ben it wasn't happening like that. She noticed it, she recognized every heart-wrenching step into maturity — despite her best efforts to keep them grounded in a childhood that no longer existed.

She had taken walks in the woods around the cabin nearly everyday, but only a couple of miles into their journey she was already feeling the effects of her backpack. They were all wearing what seemed like a ridiculous amount of cargo — but Curtis had insisted on preparing for anything, and she wasn't in the mood for an argument. They had extra clothes, food, essential medical supplies, and of course the revolver that seemed to never leave Curtis' side these days. Sarah wasn't a fan of guns, in fact she despised them — but considering the circumstances she felt better that he had it with him today.

Looking around, she realizes that the family is now walking through a stretch of extremely well-kept homes, a sight not often seen in the Grays Harbor area these days.

"Do you know any of the people that live in these houses?" she asks Curtis.

"A few of them."

"What about this one?" she asks, pointing to a particular house.

He stops and looks at the house in front of them. It's an unusually nice house, even for this neighborhood, with an immaculate yard out

83

front — aside from the knee high grass. The house itself is an older two story Victorian with over-elaborate moldings and even a widow's walk that looks as though it once had a view of the ocean. Today, several majestic maple trees stand in the way of the view, trees that were no doubt younger than the home.

"That's Ms Wilson's house. She died a couple of years ago, a stroke I think."

"You knew her?"

"Sort of, I used to follow her around in her garden when I was young. I think her son owns the place now."

As soon as the words leave his mouth he feels awkward. Her son was probably dead, which didn't really bother Curtis. He was an asshole as a kid, and from what he'd heard from people around town he'd likely died an asshole.

Looking back down the road he sees Matt looking into one of the cars with a strange look on his face. "Matt, what are you looking at?"

"There's somebody inside," he says, pointing at the driver's seat.

Sarah holds Ben back as Curtis approaches the car. Sitting in the driver's seat, slumped over the steering wheel, was a body. Whether it was a man or a woman he couldn't tell, but they were definitely dead, and had been for some time.

"Don't look at it," Curtis tells him, gently pulling his shoulder. Matt couldn't take his eyes off of it though, and finally Curtis pushes him away. "Nobody look in the cars," he says, looking at all three of them. Then looking directly at Matt, and in a stern voice... "I mean it."

They walk in silence for the next twenty minutes, an image of horror still freshly imprinted on Matt's brain. As they walk, Sarah's thoughts wander into places she never knew existed until today. Her son had just witnessed something horrible. It wasn't just the idea of seeing death for the first time, everyone at some point will experience that — some younger than others. This meant more than that. At

84

almost any time in the last two-hundred-thousand years, people have awakened to a world with more souls in it than the day before. Progress was seen as something that required hard work, but it was also inevitable. This world, however, was entirely different from the one she grew up in. Thousands of years of progress has been reduced to ashes in only a few months, and adjusting to that reality was proving to be overwhelming.

It was all so surreal — walking into a town, hoping they weren't the only people left alive, and praying that whoever was left was still uninfected. What made these ideas even more unreal is what surrounded them. They were walking through a picture of serenity. Towering fir and spruce trees were hanging over the road, giving shelter to birds who chose to winter over on the mild-weathered coast rather than fly south. The air was filled with the thick, salty and nostalgic fragrance of the ocean. The sun had even managed to find its way through the clouds and the ever-moving trees, giving the road in front of them a golden shimmer.

This all contrasted sharply with the image of chaos left along the roadway. Whether the scene around her was getting worse, or whether she'd only now allowed herself to pay attention to her surroundings, she didn't know, but Sarah began to notice details about the cars left stranded. Most of them were simply left behind, as though they'd been left in a parking lot for the past several weeks. Others were more difficult to look at. Some held the remains of family pets, or even family members. Heavier pieces of garbage still littered the asphalt, the lighter scraps having been removed long ago by the constant wind. There were places where the road had been jammed completely, an obvious sign that people had tried to drive around the gridlock, and failed. These were the areas that displayed the worst side of humanity.

Sometimes you have to do whatever it takes to get by, leaving compassion and the wellbeing of others behind. Even the most well-intentioned person is capable of cruelty, if that's what it takes to survive — but none of these people did.

Even in the advanced stages of decomposition, it was obvious that a large number of the people around the gridlocks were murdered, with some of their skeletons still tangled in a struggle. In one spot alone, Sarah counts at least fifteen bodies strewn across the roadway and ditches, some of them quite young judging from the size of the bones.

Curtis looks up to see a sign alongside the road, saying simply 'Welcome to Westport!' It seems ironic in a way, being welcomed to a town without any residents.

"This is it, Westport," Curtis says.

Sarah looks around, seeing the same sparsely populated houses as she'd seen for the last hour.

"How far until we get to the actual town?" she asks.

"You act like you've never been here before," Curtis says, a smile on his face.

"I've never walked into town before."

"Fair enough. It's just a little farther, probably half a mile." He looks behind them at the two boys following. "Are you kids getting hungry?"

"No," says Ben.

"What about you Matt?"

Matt shrugs his shoulders. "Not really."

"We'll get something to eat once we get there. When I was here yesterday I saw soup, crackers, potato chips, all kinds of stuff."

As they get closer to town, Sarah notices the houses growing closer together, along with empty side streets that look like something out of a horror film. She felt like she was dreaming. It wasn't only the emptiness, it was also the silence. The woods had always seemed quiet, but here the constant noise of civilization was expected, and its absence seems to suppress the silence even further. She could hear the crashing of waves and the annoying screeches of the seagulls coming from the beach to her left, but beyond that the only sound came from their shoes kicking the fallen maple leaves across the asphalt as they walked along the road.

"I thought you said the stores were empty...?" Sarah asks.

"They are."

"So where did you see the food?"

"Take a guess."

"We're going into people's homes?"

"Don't worry, they aren't home." A quick glance toward Sarah shows that she's not amused. "They're dead, we're alive, it's as simple as that. We'll find whatever we can, and if we find enough we'll come back with the truck and load everything up."

"Ah yes, the truck we couldn't bring today, because gas is in short supply..."

"We'll just siphon some out of the cars."

Sarah notices that Ben is starting to lag behind, dragging his feet with every step. "Are you getting tired, buddy?"

"Yeah, are we ever gonna get there?" he replies.

She turns to Curtis. "What time is it?"

"About four-thirty. We should have gotten an earlier start, we haven't made very good time."

"Maybe we should spend the night here, then go into town at first light," she replies.

"There *is* a hotel in town, the Regency. It's pretty nice."

"I'm not spending the night in town. I'd rather stay out here where it doesn't feel so strange."

Curtis stops walking, prompting the others to do the same. He looks around at the few houses nearby. "I guess it's one of these then. Which one is it?"

87

"I don't suppose we can sleep outside...?" she asks.

"If you want to freeze to death you can."

Matt points at a house on the ocean side of the highway, a single-story faded yellow rambler that's the least impressive of the bunch. "What about that one?"

Curtis looks confused. "Why that one? The porch is falling off, and the roof looks like it's about to cave in."

"It has a chimney."

Sure enough, it does have a chimney, which is something the other two houses don't have.

"I'll be damn, so it does. Good eye, son."

With a broad smile plastered on his face, Matt leads the way across the overgrown lawn, walking right past an old apple tree with fruit hanging from its branches.

Sarah stops underneath it and begins picking the apples up off the ground. "You and Matt go check it out, I'm gonna stay out here with Ben," she tells Curtis.

"I wanna check it out too!" says Ben, his voice frantic with desperation.

"You can stay here and help me pick some apples. We'll make them into something for after dinner."

The first thing Curtis does when he approaches the front door is to lift his hand up to knock, and he's still not sure if it's the appropriate thing to do or not. For all he knows, the place still belongs to someone who is very much still alive — in fact they might still live here. With his son standing beside him, he decides that using proper manners would be best, to set an example if nothing else. After knocking a couple of times, waiting for the sound of footsteps after each one, he grabs the doorknob and opens the door — surprised to find it unlocked.

"It smells," says Matt, covering his face in the crook of his arm.

88

"It's been shut up for a while, It's just musty." He takes a couple of steps inside. "Hello? Is anyone home?"

"They're probably dead, Dad."

"Yes, I know that. A little common courtesy doesn't hurt though." He strolls farther in, followed by his son. "That doesn't bother you, knowing that all of these people died?"

"I guess. We didn't know them though."

Curtis sighs and shakes his head. He can't really argue the point.

"What's that spot on the ceiling?" asks Matt.

Curtis looks up to see a sagging dark spot on the living room ceiling. "That's the roof leak I mentioned. Lets check out the bedrooms."

It takes all of about two minutes to thoroughly search the house for any residents still left, and when they're done they find absolutely no sign of anybody living there. The house would be considered old in many neighborhoods, but not in this one. Curtis figures it was probably built sometime in the late-50s or early-60s. It has no electricity, no running water, a nagging smell of mold and decay, and a roof that's seen three or four winters too many — and yet he's quite certain that it's an improvement over the conditions they've been living in.

The kitchen looks like someone had simply walked away in the middle of cooking dinner, with moldy food still sitting inside the pots on the stove-top, and three empty dishes arranged around the small table in the middle of the room.

"Don't open the fridge," says Curtis.

"Why"

"It's probably full of rotten food. We'd never be able to get rid of the smell."

He touches the silverware, still aligned neatly on either side of the plates, then remembers the unlocked front door. For reasons they

89

may never know, these people left in a hurry. A quick check of the cupboards only confirms that suspicion — they left all of the food behind.

"Go get your mom and brother, tell them it's all clear."

With a fire roaring in the wood stove, and all the windows propped open to get rid of the stagnant air, the Lockwood family sits comfortably in front of the flames, waiting for their dinner of canned meat and vegetables to finish cooking. Sitting beside the pot of stew on top of the stove is also a mixture of apples, sugar and cinnamon — a rare dessert that they all have high hopes for.

"I'll be the first to say it, this is a lot more comfortable than the cabin," says Curtis.

Sarah smiles. "The cabin was only a slight improvement over the pickup — it doesn't take much."

"Are we gonna move here?" asks Matt.

"No, it lacks some essentials," answers his father.

"Like what?"

"Like water. The cabin has a hand-dug well, I'm sure this one doesn't."

"Don't some of the older houses?" asks Sarah.

"Yeah, they could, if they haven't filled them in already."

"Why would they fill them in?"

"Some of them collapsed on their own in the sand, and the rest were filled when they brought in city water."

Sarah stands up and lifts the lid on the pot, stirring the contents inside — then she looks around the room, noticing for the first time some photos hanging on the wall. "It feels odd."

"What does?" asks Curtis.

"This place was somebody's home just a couple of months ago. They were probably sitting here watching TV without a care in the world, having no idea that in just a few weeks they'd be dead, and that we'd be sitting in their living room eating their food."

The mood in the room turns sullen as the others consider the thought. Then Curtis speaks, his voice somber... "Well, tomorrow we'll be robbing them blind, imagine how they'd feel about that..."

CHAPTER 10
DUNGENESS BAY

After waking up before daybreak, Larry spends most of the early morning hours arguing with Jake over whether or not to steal another boat — and in the end they compromise and decide to only take the fuel from a few of the boats docked alongside of them. Despite its current condition, Larry doesn't want any other boat besides his own. He's grown accustomed to every quirk and trick that's proved necessary to keep it running. More importantly, he has experience with it on the ocean — although some might not call the inside passage from Alaska the ocean. Still, the waters off the Washington coast really weren't all that different, at least not until they got to the mouth of the Columbia River.

The four-hundred mile long stretch of water from Tillamook Bay, Oregon to the northern tip of Vancouver Island has been known as 'The Graveyard of the Pacific' since the early days of exploration along the western coast of North America — and for good reason. Through the years, thousands of ships and nearly as many lives have been lost to the sea in this region, most of them at the Columbia Bar, a sand spit that provides only a small window into the river beyond. The sand there shifts continuously and unpredictably beneath the water, manipulated by both the tidal forces of the ocean, and the seasonal flows of the river.

This wouldn't be Larry's first time crossing the bar, he's done it several times in the past. It will be his first time doing it with untrained crew members though. Even though he's spent much of the last few weeks preparing them for what they're about to take on, you never know how a person will react when faced with a life or death situation until it happens.

While Beth prepares everything below for the journey ahead of them, Jake and Larry untie the boat from the dock, then take a final look at the city — its streets now empty in the bright sunlight overhead.

"It's strange how they disappear in the daylight, isn't it?" asks Larry.

"Beth is half convinced they're vampires or something."

"I'm pretty sure vampires could figure out how to climb a fence."

Jake smiles at the thought, then points to an overturned school bus sitting right outside the marina fence. "Do you see that bus over there...?"

"Yeah."

"A week ago, Beth and I saw twenty-two of those things crawl out of it right after sunset. Every night since then, the exact same group comes out, minus one person."

"How many came out last night?"

"Fourteen."

"How can you tell they're the same people?"

"It's not hard, they never change their clothes. A couple of them aren't even wearing clothes."

Larry gives the dock a kick, pushing the boat away from the wooden deck and into the lane of the marina. He's overheard Jake and Beth talking about the people on the other side of the fence in the past, both of them coming up with theories about what's going on, each one more fantastic than the last.

He watched the crowds himself the first few nights they were here, desperate for what few answers existed — but as the days turned into weeks, his search for the truth became muddled with a need for blissful ignorance. Eventually he stopped paying attention all together.

93

"Well, I'm sure there will be others to watch down the road." he tells Jake, coiling the rope up and securing it on the deck.

Jake glances toward the cabin, where he can see Beth organizing things in the front berth — then he leans down, speaking in a low voice that he hopes Beth can't hear. "I've been meaning to talk to you about something..."

"Yeah, what is it?" Larry replies in full voice.

"I was wondering if we could make a stop in Dungeness Bay."

"Why?"

"There's a police station there, I know the layout pretty well."

Larry stands up, looking at Jake suspiciously. "So?"

"You guys gave Sean most of our ammunition back in Port Townsend. I'd feel a lot better if we could stock up again."

This time Larry is the one whispering. " That doesn't sound the least bit crazy to you?"

"I know it sounds..."

"Yeah, it does... What if those things are inside?"

"We could watch it for a while... make sure nobody is there..."

"It's not gonna happen. There's no marina at Dungeness, just a shallow boat launch."

"So you're saying there's no possible way to get there?"

"No, I'm saying there's no good reason to risk it."

"Thirty-four."

"Thirty-four what?

"That's how many bullets we have left. Is that enough of a reason?"

The small town of Dungeness is only a few miles north of Sequim, protected from the rough waters of the Straight by one of the longest natural sand spits in the world. In some respects it seems like an ideal

94

place to lie low for a while. Calm waters, small businesses and houses nearby to scavenge, an open view of the Straight to the north — and of course, a police station that at one time was the training center for all of the officers on the peninsula. It was perfect, except for one small detail... it has no seaport, not even a dock.

Larry is keeping a close eye on his depth finder as he guides his boat through the narrow inlet and into Dungeness Bay. Silt and sand cover much of the shallow bottom, forcing him to stick to man-made channels that are slowly filling in with every change of the tide.

"That's the station over there," says Jake, who's standing next to Larry, and pointing to a large, white concrete building near the bay.

Larry nods his head, then turns the boat toward a paved launch that's only a short distance from the station. The building sits by itself near the beginning of the sand spit, surrounded by nothing but tall grass and sand — and a couple of police cars in the parking lot. The rest of the town is a few blocks to the east. Everything seems quiet and deserted, with no sign of human activity in sight.

"How close can you get us?" asks Jake.

"Not very, you'll have to swim part of the way. Are you sure you wanna do this?"

"We need the ammo, and whatever else they might have."

"What if those people are in there? There isn't much for cover around here."

Larry was right, the only trees visible were far off in the distance, leaving both the station and the town exposed for everyone to see. The only plant life in the area is tall grass and short shrubs.

"If they are, I'll deal with them."

Larry pulls the throttle back, letting the boat slowly come to a stop about a hundred feet from the launch. He turns around just as Jake starts making his way down the ladder to the deck below.

"When you say 'deal with them', you mean kill them, right?" asks

95

Larry.

"Is that a problem?"

"There doesn't appear to be a lot of people around anymore, I'd just hate to see anything happen to the few that are still with us."

"Yeah, well, I'll do my best not to kill anyone."

After watching Jake and his sister swim toward the boat launch near the police station, Larry sits down in the pilothouse and watches both the station and the town through binoculars for any signs of life. They all agreed that if he saw anything at either location, they would call off the mission and move on ahead to Neah Bay. Besides a couple of small fires burning on the outskirts of town though, everything else seems to be quiet. For reasons they've yet to figure out, fires seem to be a common occurrence in the communities they've come across so far — even when the area is seemingly abandoned.

As the soft, sandy bottom of the bay changes to concrete under their feet, Jake knows that he and his wife have finally reached the boat launch. Just up ahead is their destination, a large, spread out single-story block building with over-sized windows along the entire wall facing the Straight — many of which are cracked or shattered. Jake is already beginning to wonder whether or not this was a good idea.

As soon as they step out of the water and onto the gravel roadway that leads away from the launch, they both stop in their tracks when they smell something foul in the air.

"Jake..." Beth whispers, pointing to the marshy edge of the bay just to their right. Sticking out of the water, only a few feet off shore, are at least a dozen human bodies — none of them recently deceased.

Jake stops for a moment to take in the scene, then continues on

96

without saying anything until the gravel under his feet turns dry, then he unzips a duffel bag he's been carrying and examines the contents. There's only four items inside — a bottle of water, a box of gallon-sized sealable kitchen bags, and two .40 caliber semi-auto pistols that have been sealed in two of the bags. He grabs both guns, closes the duffel bag again, then hands one of the guns to Beth.

"Be careful, there's only a few rounds in each one."

"You still want to do this?"

"Why wouldn't I?"

"Someone dumped these bodies here... Whoever did it could still be around."

"I doubt it. Look at 'em, they look like they've been here for weeks."

Looking closely, Beth can see that he's right. Most of the bodies have little to no flesh left, and those that do are so deteriorated that it's impossible to tell if they're even a man or a woman.

"Still, we can't assume anything..."

"We also can't assume that these people didn't have it coming," he says, pointing to the bodies. "Besides, they could have washed up from anywhere."

Jake picks the bag up and begins walking up the road, his eyes fixed on the station just ahead of them. Beth's attention, however, is on the small community of Dungeness to their right. The houses, shops and farms that occupy the area are fairly spread out, separated by rolling pastures and gardens that still look somewhat managed. She can see a few cows grazing on top of a hill in the distance, and a horse standing in the front yard of a large house only a few blocks away. The only things missing are people, which at the moment is a huge relief to both Beth and her husband.

"Is it me, or is Larry acting a bit odd lately?" Beth asks Jake, as both of them climb the road away from the launch.

"Larry always acts odd."

97

"No, I mean more so than usual... He never wants to talk about what's going on."

"We're in the apocalypse, I think we've all earned the right to act a little strange."

"This is different, it's not healthy."

"Let's just focus on the task at hand. We can figure out your brother after we're done."

She shakes her head, wondering why she expected to have a decent conversation with her husband. As much as she loves him, he's always had an annoying habit of ignoring uncomfortable conversations — an attribute that doesn't seem all that useful given their current situation.

They finally reach the top of the rise where the gravel surface flattens out and turns to pavement. As exhausted as they are, the view from this spot stops both of them in their tracks. In front of them are lush green meadows and golden wheat fields spreading for miles around, interspersed with mostly older Victorian-era homes surrounded by small orchards and gardens. In the background, only a few miles away, the sun is shining brightly on the snow-capped Olympic mountains that rise up seemingly out of nowhere.

After taking in the view for a minute, neither of them saying a word about their surroundings, Beth notices a nearby farmhouse that sits across the road from the police station. Its front door and windows on the ground floor are boarded up.

"That house over there is all closed in. I wonder if there's still people around here...?"

Jake starts walking again, his eyes focused on the farmhouse. "They're pretty isolated, maybe it hasn't reached them yet."

"Wanna check it out?"

"No, I doubt they're in the mood for company."

She looks over at the empty streets of Dungeness. There's something surreal and eerie about the town, about the way it looks.

98

The other areas they've come across have looked abandoned, or worse. Some, like Sequim, look war-torn and defeated, with homes and buildings burned to the ground or severely damaged by the large crowds of people roaming the streets at night. Dungeness is different though, its streets are more or less clean, and its buildings all look to be in one piece. Even the lawns and flowerbeds in front of the houses look well cared for. Normalcy though, or even the appearance of it, is something to be suspicious of these days.

"Do you ever wonder what things will be like from now on?" asks Jake.

"You mean after this is all over?"

"I don't think it's ever going to be *over*. I think this is it."

She stops, looking at him as if she feels sorry for him. "You don't really believe that, do you? That everything is gone?"

"The fact that the GPS wasn't working on the boat isn't exactly a good sign — or the lack of any radio signals for that matter."

They continue once again, glancing back and forth between the farmhouse and the station — and occasionally back at the bay where Larry's boat is still waiting for them to return. As they turn off the road and start down the driveway to the station, Beth turns her head and takes a look back at the house again, this time seeing movement in one of the second story windows.

"I just saw something move in that house..."

"What did you see?"

"The second story window, all the way to the right, the curtains just moved."

He watches for a minute, but sees nothing. "It was probably just the wind, maybe the window is open."

"No, it looked like someone shut it."

They watch for a few minutes longer, but neither of them see any other movement. The house looks dark and empty, but he notices an

99

extension ladder resting on the porch roof, accessible only from the second floor. Whoever is in the house has apparently been coming and going.

"Come on, lets check out the station."

Beth follows Jake to the entrance of the station, but continues to keep an eye on the house behind them. She can't shake the feeling that someone is watching them.

When they reach the double glass doors at the front of the police station, Jake pauses once he realizes the doors are unlocked. *'Could the station still be open?'.* As he looks through the partially shaded glass at the front desk and waiting area beyond, however, he can clearly see that the place has been ransacked. File cabinets, tables, chairs and virtually everything else has been tossed around the room in front of him. Almost the entire floor has been covered with scattered papers and garbage.

"Looks like someone beat us to it," whispers Jake.

"Should we head back?"

"No, they might have missed something. We might as well check it out while we're here."

With his gun held firmly in one hand and his flashlight in the other, he slowly pushes the door open and steps inside, his wife following right behind him. They make their way to the left past the waiting area and into a large room filled with desks and cubicles, all of which are in the same disarray. The main aisle runs along the edge of the room and leads to a hallway in the back. Rows of desks, a dozen in all, are off to the left, with a wall of windows beyond them looking out at the rolling meadows in the background. Nearly all of the windows are broken, just like the wall looking out at the water on the other side of the building. The only sound they can hear is from the wind whistling through the broken panes of glass.

As they walk down the aisle, both of them looking closely at the

100

cluttered desks beside them for anything useful, Beth looks up and notices something written on the wall just before the hallway. The message is scrawled in huge red letters, reading... "THEYR COMING".

"Jake..." she whispers, pointing at the writing. "Is that blood?"

He walks closer to the message, shining his light on one of the letters. "No, it looks like it's just paint."

"Who do you think they're talking about? Who's coming?"

"It was probably just some kids or something, trying to scare people."

"Well, it worked."

Jake shines his light down the hallway in front of them, then sniffs the air. "Do you smell that?"

"It's horrible."

"Yeah, it smells like something dead."

Jake starts down the long hallway at the end of the room, the smell becoming stronger with every step, and he wonders to himself what they might find if they venture farther into the building. Beth follows closely behind, but keeps her gun down at her side, with her finger off of the trigger. About halfway down the hall, Jake stops at a heavy steel door with a single small window in it. Beside the door is a sign that reads 'Armory'. As he reaches for the handle, Beth grabs his arm.

"Did you hear that?"

"No, I didn't hear anything."

"It sounded like crying."

"Like a baby?"

"No, someone older."

He takes his hand away from the door and they both listen closely, and then it happens again, this time sounding more like a low-pitched moaning coming from farther down the hallway.

"Did you hear it?" she asks.

"Yeah, I heard it."

101

"Are we gonna check it out?"

Jake shines the flashlight through the small window in the door, revealing once again, a completely ransacked room. The only things still left inside are a couple of cardboard boxes — most likely case evidence with no real value to them.

"Shit, the armory is cleaned out — someone beat us to it."

"Hon, what about the sound?" She can tell by the look on his face that he has no intention of finding the source of it. Part of her can't blame him, they could be walking directly into a trap — but another part of her is disappointed in him for being so uncaring. "If someone is in trouble, we can't just leave them..."

Jake, obviously not thrilled about checking on the noise, starts walking down the hallway toward the sound — which is getting more intense by the minute. "Stay behind me, and don't say anything unless it's absolutely necessary."

The farther down the corridor they walk, the louder the voice becomes. As far they can tell, it's coming from only one person, although it's impossible to tell whether it's a man or a woman. Sometimes it sounds desperate, like they're pleading for help. Other times, however, the sounds turn more sinister, like the devil himself has been confined somewhere in the building.

Jake stops and turns toward a door beside him, then motions for Beth to stand back while he listens to whatever is happening on the other side. Beth backs up about ten feet, then watches down both directions of the hall while Jake shines his flashlight through the small window of the door. She sees a sign next to it that reads... "Holding cells".

After watching through the window for a couple of minutes, Jake turns around and faces Beth, his face pale white, like every ounce of blood has been washed away.

"What's wrong?" she asks him.

closing in front of them, followed by footsteps walking through loose papers and trash.

"I know you guys are in here!" shouts the voice of a man. "You might as well come out and show your faces." The footsteps stop, leaving the building quiet once again.

Jake places his index finger to his lips, motioning for Beth to keep quiet.

"I saw your boat in the bay. That's an awfully nice looking boat..."

Jake leans over and whispers quietly into Beth's ear... "Wait here for just a minute."

Before she has a chance to respond, he heads down the hallway, carefully stepping around anything on the floor that might make a sound. About twenty feet forward he catches a glimpse of something, the silhouette of a rifle barrel against the bright white color of papers scattered on the floor. Another step and he can clearly see the man holding it. Even better, it's obvious from the man's face that he doesn't see Jake standing in the shadows — at least not yet anyway.

Looking almost directly at Jake for a moment, the man sits down on a large wooden desk and begins looking over the framed photographs on top of it. He looks to be in his early to mid thirties, dressed in blue jeans and a bright orange hunting vest. Not exactly what Jake expected to see. "I just wanna talk, that's all..." says the man, who once again is looking around the room, his voice loud enough for the whole station to hear.

As the man looks back at the entrance, Jake aims his gun right at the man's chest and fires a round. Instantly the man crumples to the floor and lets the rifle fall from his grip. Jake can hear Beth crying behind him, but instead of looking back, he keeps his eye on his target as he slowly makes his way toward him. When he reaches him, he bends down and grabs the rifle, then he turns the man over and searches his clothing for any other weapons. All he finds, however, is a pocket knife and two boxes of .22 ammo.

"You... shot... me," the man says with some struggle.

"Are there any others with you?" Jake asks, his voice steady and calm.

"No..."

"Do you live in that house across the road?"

The man nods.

"Do you have any other weapons in there? Maybe some of the stuff from the armory?"

He shakes his head and coughs slightly, a small trickle of blood running from the corner of his mouth. "The police... they ran off with it weeks ago..."

Jake turns around and sees Beth standing behind him, her eyes still filled with tears. "What did you want with our boat?" he asks the man.

"Nothing... I swear... I was just making conversation..."

Jake stands up and turns to Beth. "Lets get back to the boat, there's nothing here."

"What about him?"

"I think I punctured his lung."

She looks down at the man, whose breathing is becoming labored and noisy.

"Go on ahead, I'll be right be right behind you," Jake tells her.

"What are you gonna do?"

"I can't leave him like this, it's not right." He places his pistol in his pocket, along with the man's knife, then cocks the rifle.

Beth is in shock at her husband's behavior. Not in a million years did she think he was capable of something so callous. "Jake, this isn't right..."

"What was I supposed to do? Hand over the boat?"

"You can't just kill him though..."

Jake looks at the man again. He looks terrified, and it's obvious that

105

he's in an incredible amount of pain. Part of him is still worried that the moment they leave the room, this guy will find some sort of weapon to use against them, or at the very least send a distress call to someone close by. Deep down he knows that Beth is right though, as much as the line between good and evil seems to be blurred lately, something about this does seem wrong. He reaches into his pocket and pulls out the knife he took from the man, then opens it and lays it down on the man's lap.

Still holding onto the rifle, he leaves the man and walks out of the building and into the bright sunlight, Beth following closely behind with their nearly empty duffel bag. The peaceful scenery outside contrasts sharply with the horror inside the police station — that is until he looks at the farm house across the road. Standing on the porch roof, struggling to pull the ladder back up, is a young woman and a boy that can't be any older than about ten. Behind them is a girl, a few years younger than the boy. Jake can only assume that they're the family of the man he just shot. He knows what Beth must be thinking of him, although he knows she won't say anything. Part of him feels horrible for the pain that he might have caused, and for the mental anguish that he's instilled in his wife. Another part of him though, the part that enjoyed pulling the trigger, really doesn't give a shit.

CHAPTER 11
STRAIGHT OF JUAN DE FUCA

With their fuel tanks near the three-quarters mark, and the town of Dungeness fading behind them, Larry steers the boat toward the Pacific, riding the outgoing tide into the west. They couldn't ask for better weather — the sun is bright in the sky, with only a few clouds lingering to the north — and the wind has stopped blowing down the strait from the Pacific, giving the water an unusually smooth appearance. Visibility is also high, which they have mixed feelings about. On one hand, it should make it easier to spot Sean while there's still some distance between them — but it also leaves them in the open, unprotected from anyone else, Sean or otherwise.

Halfway to Neah Bay, hopefully their last stop on their journey before they reach Astoria, Beth joins Larry in the pilothouse, keeping her eyes toward the southern shore for any sign of life.

"What time do you think we'll get there?" she asks.

"Around four or five hopefully, it all depends on whether this current holds up."

"Is there a fence around the marina in Neah Bay?"

"Not that I remember."

"Maybe we should spend the night away from town, just to be safe..."

"I wouldn't mind some more fuel before we head south. Neah Bay has a decent fueling station."

"I'd be willing to bet they also have no power."

"Those places always have a generator ready, we'll get it somehow."

As much as she disagrees with docking for the night, Beth knows that she has no choice but to trust him. She used to hate arguing with her brother when they were younger — his opinion always seemed to differ from hers on a fairly regular basis, to the point where it was oftentimes suspicious. Today though, when so much is on the line, she feels incredibly appreciative that she can lean on him for support.

"So what exactly is the plan for the next few days?" she asks, hoping to put her mind at ease with some clarity.

"We'll spend tonight in the bay, then we'll make our way to Astoria tomorrow."

"How long should that take?"

"All day. We'll probably have to spend the night anchored just outside the bar, then tackle it in the daylight just before high tide."

"Why just before?"

"Our best chance of getting through is when the tide can carry us, and when the water is at its highest level. Otherwise we'd sit there all day trying to run against the flow of the river. Trust me, that's not a lot of fun."

The eastern shores of the Strait of Juan de Fuca are dotted with cities and towns both big and small, but as you move west toward the ocean, the towns begin to disappear, and large checkered patches of forest take their place. The timber companies log the land in sections, giving the landscape a look reminiscent of a quilt. Some of these sections are newly cut areas almost completely void of anything but stumps and fireweed, while others are full of towering trees ready to be harvested when the price of lumber is right. It's a sight that often goes unnoticed by the longtime residents of the area. Their eyes have grown used to it over the years, accepting it as a way of life in the northwest.

108

The very northwestern tip of the Olympic Peninsula is named Cape Flattery, a point of land that's been disastrous to ships over the years. On the ocean side of the cape is Tatoosh Island, which sits less than a mile offshore in the Pacific Ocean, and is little more than a rock with a lighthouse in the middle of it. On the inland side of the cape is Neah Bay, a small Native American fishing village sheltered by the relatively calm waters of the strait. This is the first time Beth has ever been to the town, and as they approach its marina, she's beginning to regret never seeing it in its original state.

In better times the place may have looked perfectly fine, but today a portion of it lies in ruin, burned by a fire that apparently spread throughout most of the town. Many of the damaged buildings are covered in black char, and small wisps of smoke are still rolling from the timbers that are left standing. Fewer than fifty structures are still there, most of them near the water.

The sun is still visible in the sky as Larry guides the boat into a space at the fueling dock in the marina, giving them an opportunity to carefully examine the streets before shutting down the engine for the night.

"Would you recognize Sean's boat?" Beth asks Larry, who in turn looks over the three or four dozen boats moored around them.

"Yeah, I don't see it here. Hopefully he moved on weeks ago."

Beth zips up her coat, freezing despite the thick sweater she has on underneath her parka. She can already feel the wind coming off the ice-cold waters of the sea beyond.

"I'm gonna check out the store before we start searching for the generator. You never know, they might actually be open," says Larry, already climbing onto the pier after tying the boat to the dock.

Beth jumps overboard right behind him. "I'm coming with you." Still walking away, she turns to Jake. "Keep an eye out for Sean."

"Wait a minute, we have no idea what the hell happened here. If

109

anyone goes it should be me..." Jake protests.

Beth stops and faces him. "I need to get off this boat." She holds up her revolver. "I'll be careful."

Jake frowns, disgusted at the idea of them walking into the unknown without him. After what happened in Dungeness, he has serious doubts about his wife's trust in him — and he can't really blame her. In the previous world, what he did would've been considered murder. The fact that he's shown no remorse, or felt any for that matter, he realizes is a cause for concern.

When Larry and Beth finally finish climbing the hill into town and reach the store, they find that its door is already open, saving them the trouble of breaking in. Even though there doesn't appear to be any damage inside, the place reeks of smoke and burned plastics. There's another smell too, something that's oddly familiar to Beth, but she can't quite place it.

They start walking the aisles, looking for anything they might be able to use on their journey to Oregon.

"Do you see any food?" asks Larry.

"No, there's not much of anything left." Then she stops and begins to load something into her pockets.

"What did you find?"

"Deodorant."

"We're supposed to be looking for necessities..."

"Trust me, this is. We've been on the water for too long."

As he begins to shake his head in disbelief, they hear something outside. A crashing sound. Both of them take their guns out of their pockets and creep toward the front window.

"Maybe it's Jake," Beth whispers.

Larry pulls out a radio from his other pocket, then speaks quietly into it. "Jake, are you still on the boat?"

He waits a few seconds, then... *"Yeah, I'm still here. Why?"*

"We heard something outside the store. I'm gonna check it out."

"*I'm headed that way.*"

"Stay where you're at, I've got this. I need you to watch my boat."

After a few seconds of silence, Jake answers back in a voice that doesn't sound thrilled. "*Be careful, and keep your radio handy.*"

"Affirmative." He puts the radio back in his pocket, then peeks through the window to the street out front. It looks empty. With his gun in his hand, he turns the doorknob and slowly opens the door, taking a final look around before stepping out onto the sidewalk. Then he hears it again.

"It's coming from the next building," says Beth, startling him. He had no idea she'd followed him outside.

"Fuck, don't sneak up like that! I thought you were staying inside," he silently screams.

She shrugs in a somewhat apologetic way, following Larry as they make their way to the building next door — which looks to be a house with only an alley separating the two. As they walk past it, Beth notices a window in the house facing the alley.

"We might be able to get a look inside through that window." she tells him, already walking toward it.

"It's over my head, how are we supposed to see anything?" he whispers.

"Give me a boost."

"Why don't we just look through the front windows?"

"Because it's dark in this alley. They won't be able to see us."

"Alright, but be quiet."

He bends down on one knee, then lifts her up on his shoulders, putting her at a perfect height in front of the window.

"It's the kitchen." she whispers down to him. "There's someone sitting under the table... It looks like a boy, maybe sixteen or seventeen."

111

"What is he doing?"

"He's just sitting there, staring at the cabinets. He looks like he's in a trance or something."

The teenager suddenly goes wild, pulling at his hair and clothes, and biting at the back of his hand. When he finally lets go of his hand, blood starts streaming down his arm and onto the floor. He reaches up and lifts the table, then lets it come crashing down under its own weight. Beth ducks her head below the window as he thrashes around the room, throwing objects and screaming at the top of his lungs.

"What the hell is going on up there?" Larry asks.

"Shh... He just went crazy all of the sudden."

She glances to her right at the next street over toward the middle of town, and sees Sean walking by, in perfect view of her.

"Let me down, now!" she whispers.

"What is it?" he asks, lowering her to the ground.

"Sean just walked by. He's right behind the store."

"Shit, did he see you?"

"I think it's too dark."

Larry grabs the radio again... "Jake, are you there?"

"*I'm here.*"

"I'm gonna make this quick... Sean is on the next street over from us. We're gonna try to make our way back, but you have to get out of sight. Do you copy?"

"*Got it.*"

"I can hear him in the store," says Beth. "Maybe we should take him out, while we have the advantage..."

"It's too risky, he'd be able to see us. We need to get back to the boat and get the hell out of here."

"We're gonna have to wait until dark to do that. There's nothing to hide behind between us and the docks."

Larry looks around, then spots an old half-rotten pallet leaned up

112

against the side of the store. "We can hide behind that."

After informing Jake of their plan to wait until dark, and watching Sean stroll out of the store and in the direction of the marina, Beth and Larry are still hiding in the alley between the store and the house.

"It's getting pretty dark. Do you think we should leave?" asks Beth.

"Let's wait a few minutes longer, I can still see the houses on the other side of the street."

As Beth glances over to the next block to see for herself, she notices something moving by the corner of the house. Without looking away, she hits Larry on his side to get his attention.

"See it?" she asks, her voice barely even a whisper.

"Yeah, but I can't tell what it is."

"It's that kid from the house."

They both watch as a man stumbles in front of the alley, walking as though he were stoned or drunk — then he stops and faces the side wall of the store. He just stands there, slightly slumped over, his feet occasionally scuffing the pavement, seemingly in an effort to find his balance. Then he starts to walk again, reaching out to grab the wall of the store as he passes by. Moving out of sight, they can still hear the dragging of his shoes as he makes his way down the road.

"We'd better go now, before he comes back," says Larry.

Walking as quietly as possible, they exit the alley and move out into the open ground in front of the store. The moon is just beginning to rise in the sky, making long shadows over the road between them and the waterfront. Somewhere down the street they can hear wind chimes moving in the breeze, creating a noise that hasn't stopped the entire time they've been in town. Annoying as it seemed only an hour ago, it's proving to be quite useful now, masking

113

their footsteps as they walk on the gravel driveway. As they move down onto the pier they pay close attention to the boats in the marina, trying to spot signs of activity from any of them — but they all look the same, dark and quiet. Finally, they reach their own vessel and enter the main cabin carefully and quietly. The room inside is pitch black.

"Jake?" Beth whispers.

"I'm here, on the starboard bench." he replies in an almost normal volume.

"Have you seen Sean?" asks Larry.

"Yeah, he's down on the other side of the marina, at the last dock."

"What kind of boat does he have?"

"It's about the same size as ours, maybe a little bigger than the one he had before."

"Did you see a name on the side, or a make?"

"It said 'Harbor Cruiser' on the side."

"That's a make, and not a particularly good one for where we're going."

"Can it survive on the ocean?" Beth asks Larry.

"A dinghy can survive on the ocean when the conditions are right. We're just gonna have to hope things get worse."

"Is he faster than us?" asks Jake.

"I'm not sure, I've never run one."

Jake can barely see the outline of his wife and brother-in-law as they sit in the chairs opposite of him. "If you look closely you can see a light in his cabin, really faint."

"I can't see anything," says Beth.

"Here, take the binoculars."

She reaches out in front of her and finds them, then searches the area to their left, where she can barely make out a glow coming from the boat, just as Jake said. She also sees something moving in front of

114

it, like a silhouette. "It looks like a candle. I can see it flickering." She hands them over to Larry, then switches seats with him so he can get a better view.

"So what's our plan? Do we make a run for it?" asks Jake.

"He'd hear us, and as small as this place is he'd definitely get a shot off," replies Larry, still looking.

"What if we wait a while, then sneak down and tie a second line to his boat?"

"He'd still shoot us. This thing isn't designed for covert operations, everyone in town is gonna hear us start up. I don't know how in the hell he missed us when we came in."

"What about a diversion?"

"Like what?"

"I don't know, maybe we could do something in town, like fire a gun."

"You're forgetting about the people in town... I don't know about you, but after seeing one of them up close, I'd rather take my chances with your buddy here."

"Well, that was my last idea. Feel free to share some of your own."

"Hey, knock it off," Beth responds. "We're not going to solve anything by insulting one another. Larry, do you have any ideas?".

"No, I don't."

"We have to do something, we can't just sit here. You know he's gonna see us when the sun comes up..." she replies.

"What if we create a diversion on the pier?" asks Jake.

Only in an attempt to please Beth, this time Larry sounds interested. "What did you have in mind exactly?"

"We're gonna need something flammable."

After waiting for more than an hour, they finally see the light in Sean's new boat go out shortly after nine-o-clock. At eleven, the nervous group decides that now is as good a time as any to carry out their plan.

Shortly before leaving Hoodsport, Larry set a thirty gallon tank full of gasoline into the main fish hold, which sits under the stern deck. He's spent the last twenty minutes drawing fuel from it and placing it inside of a pair of smaller cans. Jake, dressed in his full armored uniform, has gone over his mental checklist seven times, and is about to go over it again when Beth taps him on the shoulder.

"What can I do? I feel like I'm a spectator or something," she tells him.

"Larry will keep an eye on Sean, but I need you to watch the town behind us."

"For people?"

"Yeah, just let me know on the radio if they're coming down the dock. I'll take care of the rest." He walks out onto the stern deck, where Larry is tightening the cap on the last fuel can. "Are we ready?"

"Ready when you are. You realize this is about a third of our gas, right?" asks Larry.

"I guess it's a good thing the boat runs on diesel."

"Is that gonna be enough?" Beth asks Larry.

"It's ten gallons, it'd better be enough."

"It'll be fine," says Jake.

With the fuel cans in his hands, Jake slowly walks down the wharf toward the last pier, while Larry takes his spot in the pilothouse — readying himself for a quick getaway. Beth watches her husband as he disappears into the darkness of night, then remembers that she has a role in this as well. She sits on the deck and watches the town above, letting her eyes adjust to lack of light once more. Within a minute or so her eyes do adjust, and reveal a pair of obscure figures moving

116

around on the street that leads to the marina — but they don't seem to be getting any closer.

Jake knows this plan is risky, and not just because he's planning to burn half the marina down. The layout of the marina makes it almost impossible to reach Sean without making at least some noise. It consists of a raised wharf, and from that the individual piers run perpendicular into the deep waters of the strait. While the wharf itself is secured firmly in place to pilings that are embedded into the rocky ground below, the piers float on the water, making room for the tidal action that can change the water level by as much as ten feet in a normal cycle. Both the wood decking and the polystyrene foam beneath it shift with every step, creating a squeaky groan no matter how carefully you move.

Sean moored his boat at the end of the very far pier, a move that was no doubt strategic. It places him closest to the strait, and the farthest from the town — not to mention the fact that the dock itself was now acting as an early detection system. Sean is a lot of things, but stupid isn't one of them.

As Jake steps down onto the last floating pier, he unscrews the cap off of one of the cans, then begins pouring its contents onto the decking as he continues walking forward. Although the deck is groaning slightly under his feet, most of the noise is coming from the water below, slapping against both the pilings and the polystyrene blocks that hold the pier into place. He trickles the gas out, making the first can last almost to the end of the platform. After opening the last can, he covers the area in front of the boat heavily, saving the last couple of gallons for the boat itself. Beads of sweat run down his face and back as he pours the liquid over the windows and decking of the cuddy cabin, listening carefully for any indication that he's been detected.

With the last drop gone, he inches his way back in the direction of

117

the wharf, being especially careful not to slip in the oily surface that now covers the entire dock. Only a few feet from the boat, he hears something behind him, a series of muffled thumps. He turns around and sees a light shining through the curtains of Sean's boat, and movement in front of it. For a moment he's unsure of what to do — should he make a run for it, or stick with the original plan? At this point neither seems a particularly good idea. Instead, he decides to compromise between the two by walking down the pier at a normal pace, all the while keeping an eye behind him for any sign of trouble.

He only makes it about twenty feet when he hears the slamming of a door. When he turns around, he sees Sean closeup for the first time since their encounter in Poulsbo — a mixture of both anger and madness in his eyes. Sean is holding a gun, but it's not his rifle — it's a semi-auto pistol that's still hanging at his side. From his physical demeanor he doesn't seem like much of a threat, but the expression on his face tells another story, and Jake knows that it's only a matter of time before he makes a move.

Sean is armed with an expensive European-made pistol, capable of finishing someone's life with a single shot.

Jake is armed with a wooden striking match.

Making sure his feet aren't in the fuel, he tightens his grip on the match, knowing he only has one shot at this. In one fluid motion he reaches into his pocket and pulls out a box, then strikes the match on the side of it, throwing the burning stick as close to the boat as possible. Without looking back, he runs down the pier, feeling an intense heat following him, and noticing that the entire marina is now lit up in a bright orange glow. Almost to the halfway point he slips, landing face-first in the stream of gas that he'd left on the wooden planks. As he struggles to get up, he knows he only has a few seconds before the entire length of the pier in engulfed. Instead of standing, he rolls off the side and into the icy water below, a dampened sound of gunshots vaguely noticeable after he enters.

Even underwater, the fire is burning bright enough to almost hurt your eyes, but Jake knows that the inferno will be short-lived. In just a couple of minutes the gas will have burned off, lifting the temporary veil he's risked his life to create. With some effort, he climbs onto the next pier, then runs to the wharf that leads to their boat. When he finally reaches the boat, which is already beginning to pull away, the first thing that catches his eye is the look on Beth's face. She doesn't look relieved to see him, or grateful that they're actually on their way to safety — her horrified gaze is aimed at the buildings of Neah Bay. He pulls her inside the cabin, fearful that Sean might still be alive to take a shot, and then he sees for himself what she's been staring at. The young man that Beth and Larry had seen, who seemed to be walking around in a trance-like state only a few hours prior, was now standing just inside the light of the fire, holding what appears to be two human heads in his hands. Although it's hard to tell from this distance, it looks as though he's covered in blood.

As the shock wears off, Beth begins to breakdown, crying and shaking uncontrollably.

"Listen to me, we're going to be fine, we did it," Jake tells her, trying to make eye contact. "Our plan worked, Sean is gone."

"Jake, could you come up here for a minute?" hollers Larry from the pilothouse above.

"I'll be up in a minute!"

"Now would be better!"

Jake sits his wife down in a chair, stroking her hair and kissing her on the forehead. "I'll be back in a minute, okay?" There's no answer from her, no acknowledgment that he's even there. Wrapping a blanket around her shoulders, he steps out onto the stern deck, seeing for himself the aftermath of his plan. The pier is still burning, along with part of the wharf, but the flames have diminished greatly,

119

leaving behind scattered flares of light up and down the floating boardwalk. It's too dark to see any of the boats though.

He climbs the ladder, then sits down beside Larry. "Beth is freaking out."

"We can deal with that later, we've got a bigger problem," says Larry, pointing at a blinking light on the dash.

"What is that?"

"That's the water sensor in the bilge. It means we're taking on water — a lot of water."

"What do we do?"

"I need you to go down into the bilge and see what you can find."

Jake practically jumps down the ladder, then rushes into the cabin where Beth is still sitting in the same place. He walks by her, brushing his hand against her shoulder as he passes by, then kneels down on the floor at the bilge hatch. Immediately after opening it he can hear the sound of running water, and two bilge pumps working to clear it out. He leans inside, shining a flashlight around on the walls. He can't see much below the waterline, which is about two feet deep by the looks of it, but what he can see are three holes in the side. The holes are at different levels, but otherwise they're identical — each one sharing the same size and shape, strikingly similar to a bullet.

He pulls himself up, then uses his radio. "Larry, it looks like at least three bullet holes. There's quite a bit of water coming in."

"*Find a permanent marker and draw a line an inch or so above the waterline. That way we can keep an eye on it,*" answers Larry.

"I'm on it. Any sign of Sean?"

"*Look to the stern.*"

Jake puts the radio in his pocket, then walks across the cabin to the doorway. Several hundred yards behind them is a boat, and not just any boat. This particular boat still has flames licking across the top of the canopy.

120

"He's still alive?" comes a voice to his side.

Jake looks over to see Beth standing there, a look of clarity and focus back in her eyes.

"For now he is."

CHAPTER 12
WESTPORT

None of the Lockwood family wanted to get up. Even though they were unwelcome guests sleeping in a strange home, it was still a home with real mattresses, not the inflatable kind they were unfortunately getting used to. Before going to sleep the night before, Curtis and Sarah talked again about the prospect of living here — if not in this house, then perhaps another one nearby. In the end, they decided that the isolation and security of the cabin was unparalleled compared to what they'd seen closer to town — and considering the circumstances, the safety of their children meant far more than simple comfort. As rested as Sarah felt this morning, however, she was considering the idea of staying here again on the way back, only this time she'd sleep in.

As torturous as it is climbing out of the comfort of an actual bed, they all manage to drag themselves out onto the street at daybreak, just as they'd planned — but each one of them could feel the effects of their walk yesterday. Their feet are sore, their legs are heavy and weak, and feelings that range from tingling to sharp pains are running down their spines from the weight of their backpacks.

Only twenty minutes into their walk, they reach Westport, and it quickly becomes obvious that the town has seen better days. The storm that had swept through only a few days before has decimated the trees in the area, and the damage is far worse here in town. The seemingly never-ending line of cars they'd walked past the day before had finally disappeared, leaving the town almost completely devoid of them. The roads are so littered with trash that in places they have a

122

hard time spotting the pavement beneath. Here and there they can see bones scattered in the debris. Some of them are obviously human, some of them obviously aren't — and most of them you can't tell. Power lines are lying everywhere, forcing the family to walk around them carefully — all of them feeling somewhat foolish fearing a technology from the past. Beyond a few missing shingles on the roofs, the only damage done to the buildings themselves are the broken windows and glass-paned doors, giving the ground beneath their feet a slight crunching sound as they walk past. How much of the damage had been done during the evacuation and how much was caused by the constant barrage of weather they might never know, but seeing it in this shape was heartbreaking for Curtis. Relatively few of his childhood memories were made here, but almost all of the cherished ones were.

The Westport he knew, the one he remembered as both a child and an adult, was that of a picturesque fishing village separating the blue waters of the Pacific, from the dark waters of Grays Harbor. The small peninsula it's built on was used as a fishing source for generations of native tribes in the area, and unlike many of the towns along the west coast, fishing has remained its primary industry even in recent times.

Curtis has fond memories of walking down the sidewalk in the marina district with his parents, an ice cream cone in his hand from a nearby shop, and watching as the commercial boats came in over the bar with their daily catch. Fishing wasn't merely a sideshow or roadside attraction in Westport, it was the lifeblood of the town, a way of life that the locals held onto with pride.

Looking at it today, however, Curtis saw something entirely different. Westport was now filled with darkened windows and empty streets — and despite the rare sunny skies and gentle breeze, the sight of it still managed to dampen his family's already unsteady spirits.

The highway they were walking on leads through the middle of town, with the ocean to the west, and the harbor to the east. Most of the tourist shops are on the harbor side, along the marina — while the ocean side is mostly made up of older houses and newer condominiums, the last of which is a sore subject for many of the permanent residents. Also visible from most of the west side is the Regency, a grand hotel not without its own controversies.

"Did it look like this when you were here the other day?" Sarah asks Curtis.

"Pretty much."

Waking up this morning, she assumed her first instinct would be to ignore the town — focusing instead on gathering supplies. Now that she was here though, she was surprised to find herself soaking it all in.

"It looks so unreal," she says.

"I was thinking last night about the stories my grandfather used to tell me. He said in world war two it was illegal to have any lights on after dark, inside or out. Even the headlights on your car had to be turned off."

"Why was that?"

"They were afraid the Japanese were waiting offshore, and that the lights would give away the location of the town. It must have felt something like this back then — at night anyway."

"It definitely looks like a war-zone now." She turns her head, noticing that Ben is drifting farther behind once again. "Ben! Keep up, don't fall so far behind." Her attention turns back to Curtis, whose mind seems to be elsewhere. "So where do we start?"

"I've only been in a couple of houses, so I guess any of them," says Curtis, snapping out of his daydream. He stops and points at an incredibly small house sitting on the edge of the dunes. "How about this one?"

"It's tiny."

124

"It also has a car in the driveway. They never left."

"So...?"

"If they didn't leave, they never took any of their food."

"It also means they didn't leave... They could still be in there."

He turns and makes his way toward the front door anyway, soon followed by his wife and two sons. As he reaches for the door handle Sarah grabs his arm.

"How do we know these places aren't still contagious?" she asks.

"We don't. That's why we don't touch anything we don't have to."

"Maybe the boys should stay out here." She looks back, and both of them are looking back at her, terrified.

"I don't want to stay out here!" cries Ben, tears welling up in his eyes.

Matt is too proud to speak up, but his expressions are betraying him. With Ben now wrapping his arms around her, Sarah kneels down to his eye level.

"We'll keep the door open, and we'll only be a few feet away. You can talk to me the whole time."

The reassurance doesn't seem to put his mind at ease, but it does release his grip from her waist. Curtis reaches into his pocket and pulls out a pair of latex gloves, then hands them to her. "Just in case..."

Not surprisingly, the door is locked, but after a swift kick it rips into several pieces, providing a clear path to walk through.

"It might be a good idea not to destroy *all* of the doors... Now anything could get inside," Sarah says.

"Yeah, you're probably right," says Curtis, feeling slightly embarrassed.

The air coming from the house is musty and damp from being closed-up for a long period of time, just like the house they slept in the night before. As they step inside it doesn't take her long to realize that the place had belonged to an elderly couple. Besides the decor,

125

there's also a walker and cane leaning beside the door — along with several coats and pairs of shoes, both men and women's. Curtis heads straight to the kitchen while Sarah stays in the living room in plain sight of her sons. Covering the walls and mantel are family pictures and keepsakes, a physical evidence of family memories that were now forever lost.

"These people must not have believed in canned food," says Curtis from the next room. "Everything is boxed or bagged."

"What's wrong with that? We can still boil it."

He steps into view with two big bags in his hand. "Boiled cereal?"

Sarah had to smile — despite feeling entirely uneasy in the house. She felt like they were thieves going house to house robbing people of their least valuable possessions.

Curtis walks back into the living room, empty-handed.

"There's not much in here. When we bring the truck we'll grab whatever we can use."

"We should get some mattresses too, I slept like a rock last night."

"That's a good idea."

"What about the rest of the house?"

"The only thing we really need right now is food. Whatever else is in here can wait."

After searching two of the neighboring homes with similar results, and no people, they head farther north to search the homes bordering the Westhaven State Park, an area mostly made up of sand dunes and pine trees that were planted by residents decades ago. On the south end is the lighthouse, a famous white beacon that had a much more useful purpose when it was first built. Back then it was used as a navigation point for vessels operating just off the coast — but in recent years it had stood merely as a relic of the past, a reminder of how unfortunate we were before modern technology saved us from our limited sense of direction. Today it serves no

126

purpose at all. It's a beacon without a signal, and nobody to notice if it had one.

They decide to continue their search toward the harbor. In this area of town the houses were few and far between, and businesses mostly catering to tourists or commercial fishing dominate the view. As they walk past a large, two-story building with a coffee shop in the bottom corner, Sarah catches a glimpse of movement from inside the glass.

"Did you see that?" she asks Curtis.

"See what?"

"I could have swore I saw something move in that shop."

Curtis watches for a few seconds, and after seeing nothing decides to get closer. Only inches from the glass window of the shop, he looks around at the empty tables and counter-top, spotting an impressive display of bagged coffee grounds and syrups.

"I don't see anything, but I wouldn't mind some of that coffee."

Sarah still feels apprehensive. She's almost positive she saw something. "We can get it later, along with everything else."

"Yeah, I guess so," says Curtis as he backs away.

"What about that store?" says Matt, looking across the street at a corner market.

"Might as well check it out," says Curtis.

As Curtis and the two boys make their way to the store across the street, Sarah takes another look at the shop. She has an eerie feeling that she can't shake, like she's being watched.

"Can we go inside this time?" asks Matt.

"Yes," says Sarah.

Curtis glances back at her, an inquisitive look on his face. "They can?"

"I don't want them out here alone," she tells Curtis. "Don't touch anything, do you understand?" she tells the two boys in a stern voice.

127

Both of them nod in agreement as Curtis walks to the door and breaks the glass beside it, then reaches through and unlocks it as if he'd been doing it all of his life. As they step inside, the first thing Curtis spots is a large stockpile of canned goods, but they aren't sitting on a shelf like one would expect to see in a grocery store. Instead, they're arranged neatly on top of a table behind the front counter. As he walks around the counter, he stops, then holds up his hand to stop his family.

"Wait a minute, don't come any closer."

"What is it?" asks Sarah.

"Go back outside for a minute."

"But... you said," cries Matt.

"I know what I said. Now go outside with your mom."

Sarah doesn't say anything as she escorts Matt and Ben outside, but when she looks back she sees Curtis staring at something on the floor. After a few minutes he comes to the door, then motions for her to come inside.

"Guys, just wait outside a minute," he says to his sons.

Once inside, he leads her back to the front counter. As she walks around the corner she sees a dark puddle of blood oozing across the floor, tracing back to a corpse slumped over onto his side.

"Oh my god..."

"Yeah, and it looks fresh..."

"How can you tell?"

"The blood is still wet, and his body hasn't deteriorated at all."

She starts to back up. "He could be infected..."

"He didn't die from the virus, he died from having his skull crushed in." He steps over the body, then points to the side of his head. "See, right there..."

She leans over, careful not to step in the blood. Most of the man's face has been bashed in, by numerous blows by the looks of it.

128

Whoever did this took their time.

"We should come back as soon as possible to get this stuff, before he starts to rot," says Curtis.

"I'm going back outside before I throw up..."

Curtis follows her back out, seeing two disappointed faces waiting on the sidewalk.

"Maybe the next one," he tells them.

"It's getting late, we should head back," says Sarah.

He points to the sky in the west, where a rolling band of black clouds dominate the horizon, blocking most of what's left of the sun.

"I think we're staying the night, it looks like there's another storm moving in."

CHAPTER 13
WESTPORT

The long band of black clouds stretching along the entire coastline and closing in on Westport is a perfect representation of how Sarah felt at the moment. The image of the man in the store and the thick smell of blood that refused to leave her senses seems to be permanently imprinted in her mind. The only good thing about the experience was that her sons weren't in the building to witness it.

Over the last two days, the four of them had come across dozens of corpses, most of them either along the highway or still lying in their beds covered with blankets or sheets, but none of them seemed as horrible as this. Maybe it's the fact that this one's death was more recent, or maybe it's knowing that he was killed at the hands of another person and not by some mysterious virus. Whatever the reason, the world viewed through her eyes was beginning to seem like a nightmare, and the heavily filtered light coming through the dark clouds overhead was completing the picture.

The part of town they're walking through used to be much closer to the ocean, but over the years the sand dunes have expanded, leaving the once-expensive homes and businesses with merely a distant view instead. One of those businesses is the Regency Hotel, which Sarah can now see sticking up over the pine trees in front of them.

"Do you hear that?" asks Matt.

They all stop and listen, but the only sound they hear is coming from the ocean on the other side of the dunes.

"What does it sound like?" asks Sarah.

"Like music."

"Honey, I'm sure it was just..." Before finishing the sentence though, she hears it herself. It's extremely faint, but it's definitely music of some sort — and it sounds like it's coming from the house across the street. She turns to Curtis and points toward the house. "I hear it too, I think it's coming from that house."

"Do you wanna check it out?" he asks.

She looks up at the house, a larger two-story home probably built shortly before the war. Despite the peeling paint and rotting trim boards on the outside, there's still a certain charm to it. There's no light coming from the inside, and no smoke coming from the chimney, which makes her question whether or not someone might actually be home. Part of her wants to find someone who survived, someone who might have answers as to what happened here during the past couple of months. Another part of her is scared, of both the disease and the people still left.

"I don't know, it's up to you."

Curtis takes another look at the clouds sitting off the coast, slowly making their way toward the town. "Let's be quick about it, we only have a few minutes before that storm gets here."

The four members of the Lockwood family cross the street, all of them looking both ways first, a habit not easily broken as it turns out. When they reach the porch, Curtis motions for his family to stay on the cement pathway while he knocks on the door. To his surprise, it's both unlocked and opened slightly, and as the door swings open even more, it reveals an immaculate front room filled with antiques and hardwood floors. Even stranger than the unlocked door is the fact that the air smells fresh inside — an indicator that someone might still be coming and going. As he steps inside, he reaches into his pocket and takes a firm grip on the revolver inside, then motions for his family to join him.

131

"Hello? Is anyone home?" he hollers, but there's no response. As he walks farther into the room he can plainly hear the music playing from a room upstairs. It's an old song from before his time, but one that he's unfamiliar with.

A stack of firewood is stacked up neatly beside the fireplace, a sight that surprises Sarah when she sees it. She'd assumed, perhaps wrongly, that nobody was left in town. The only dirt visible in the room is directly in front of the fireplace, which is odd considering the vast amount of fine sand that makes its way in from the beach every time the wind blows. She looks up the staircase at the far end of the room where the music is coming from, then at the ornate wooden railing that follows it to a second-floor landing. It's also completely free of any buildup of dust or sand.

"Somebody still lives here," she tells Curtis.

"It certainly seems that way, doesn't it?"

He steps past her and begins climbing the stairs slowly, trying not to make any noise — but the old wooden steps creak and crack under his feet regardless. "I'm gonna check out the upstairs, you guys stay down here."

"We're all going up," Sarah says firmly.

He stops for a second, trying to think of a good excuse why his family shouldn't follow him upstairs, but she's probably right, they need to stick together. After taking the revolver out of his pocket and holding it down at his side, he continues climbing the stairs to the top — where he can see an old-fashioned hand crank record player sitting in the closest room to the landing. The song being played is some sort of swing music from the 1930s or 40s. Ordinarily he wouldn't think much about it, but to hear it in an apparently empty house in a post-apocalyptic world, gives it a disturbing, almost frightening feel.

As the four of them enter what's clearly a bedroom and begin looking around, Curtis notices that all of the picture frames have

132

either been broken or turned face-down. He shuts off the record player, which turns the house eerily quiet, the only sound coming from a window shutter swinging in the wind outside.

"We need to get out of here," says Sarah, who's still standing just inside the door.

"I wonder how long these things can play before you have to crank them again...?" he responds, bending over to get a closer look at the record player.

Annoyed, Sarah gently pushes the two boys ahead of her and into the room, then stands next to Curtis. "We need to get out of here, *now*."

Curtis nods and stands up straight, then takes a single step toward the door before hearing something downstairs, a set of footsteps walking briskly across the hardwood floors. All four of them freeze, expecting at any moment for the footsteps to begin climbing the stairs — but they never do. Instead, they hear the opening and closing of the front door, and then nothing.

"What're we gonna do?" Sarah asks frantically, keeping her voice as quiet as possible.

Curtis looks out the bedroom window, hoping to find another way out of the house, but it's a straight drop onto the paved alley below. "I saw a back door out through the kitchen when we came in. I think that's our best bet."

Never taking his eyes off of the front door below, Curtis leads his family out of the bedroom and onto the staircase. His heart begins pounding with every creak and moan of the floorboards under his feet. When he reaches the bottom, he motions for Sarah and the two boys to head into the kitchen, keeping himself between them and the door he expects will open at any moment. As they all round the corner toward the back of the house, they hear a subtle knocking, too quiet to immediately know where it's coming from. Slowly, the

133

knocking grows louder, then faster, until finally it sounds like someone is trying to bust a door down.

"Where is that coming from?" whispers Curtis.

"Forget it, let's just keep moving," replies Sarah.

Curtis then realizes that a door near the staircase is shaking slightly, like someone is rattling it from the other side. "That's the basement — someone is locked up in there."

"That's their problem, we need to get out while we still can..."

Feeling a horrible guilt for leaving whoever it is behind, he leads the way through the small dining room and into the kitchen at the very back of the house. As they cross the room, they pass by mountains of canned foods and bottles of water. Nearly every square inch of the counter is covered in food and supplies. While Curtis slows down to look at the cache, Sarah moves around him and reaches the door leading to the backyard and begins to turn the doorknob. Before she has a chance to pull the door open, Curtis places his hand on her arm.

"What's wrong?"

"Nothing." he replies, as he looks out a window next to the door, scanning the yard for any signs of trouble. "I just want to make sure we're not walking into a trap."

"Do you see anything?"

"No... I don't. Go ahead and open it, but quietly."

She grabs onto the knob and slowly opens the door — and the instant that she does, the familiar sound of swing music fills the house once again, this time louder than before. Without hesitating, Sarah throws the door open and runs outside, looking back to make sure that her sons are still close behind. As all four of them run across the lawn and onto the street behind, Curtis looks back at the bedroom window, half expecting to see someone staring back at him — but the room is too dark to see much of anything at all.

134

"I'm not staying another night in this town!" Sarah says, her voice definitive.

"We have to, this storm could be dangerous."

She stops and turns around, just as the first drops of rain begin to fall from the dark clouds overhead. "There was somebody upstairs with us the whole time!"

"Yes, but..."

"That means they know we're here. They know we're in town..."

"I know..."

"And what about whoever they have locked in the basement...?"

"Hon, I'm not arguing that we should stay in that house — I'm saying we need to get out of this rain."

As the words leave his mouth, a massive flash of lightning illuminates the sky, followed by a crack of thunder that rumbles just over their heads.

Sarah knows that this entire trip was a huge mistake, that none of them had any business venturing into town this soon after the outbreak — not when they knew so little about what was happening. As much as she despises their new home in the woods, she'd give anything to see its warped floorboards and cracking paint right now. Curtis is right about one thing though, they're miles from the cabin with no possible way to get back before the full force of the storm reaches them. They need a place to hide, somewhere they can ride out the weather until daybreak.

"Where did you have in mind?" she asks.

"What about the Regency?"

"It's been closed for years."

"Good, it'll be empty then."

CHAPTER 14
WESTPORT

The history of the Regency Hotel is shrouded in secrecy and confusion, and is often told through far-fetched stories that do little to clarify the truth behind the place.

It was originally built in 1922 by a man named Joseph Embree. The hotel in those days was small, with only twelve rooms located on a cramped second floor — the first floor being entirely consumed by a grandiose entrance that looked completely out of place on the Washington coast. In 1942, shortly after the second world war broke out, the army took over the hotel and used it as a barracks, destroying most of the artwork and furniture in the process — and leaving Mr Embree broke for the first time in his otherwise productive life. Years after the war ended, and long after the Embree family disappeared from the area, the hotel was burned to the ground and rebuilt, this time on a much grander scale.

Size wasn't the only thing about the newly rebuilt hotel that surprised the residents of Westport — after all, it was still only a modest fifty rooms, with an extra floor added to take advantage of the ocean views. What set it apart was the style and elegance of the place, it was unlike anything the small coastal community had ever seen. The floor of the lobby was covered in white marble, giving the room a bright glow despite the often gloomy conditions outside. The ceiling over the entrance was nearly forty feet high, with windows that covered three sides of the building, and provided views of the ancient trees and sand dunes that surround the hotel. The most impressive element of all, however, just like the previous hotel, was the main staircase. Using the finest wood from the hills just outside of town, the carpenter spent almost nine months building what would ultimately become one of the greatest examples of Pacific Northwest architecture ever created. It swept across all three floors of the hotel, using a footprint so large that every guest and employee could actually stand on the bottom course of its maple inlay steps at the same time — something the staff went out of their way to prove every Fourth of July with a photograph. It was a tradition that would continue until 1957, when a horrible tragedy closed them down once again, only four years after the much-celebrated reopening.

That much about the hotel is widely considered to be true by historians and residents in the area. The numerous stories of hauntings, murders, the mysterious disappearance of the Embree family, and the true identity of the second owner, have been clouded in rumors and gossip throughout the years to the point where it's difficult to tell what actually happened there. Matters became even murkier a few years ago when yet another owner, this one veiled in secrecy as well, remodeled the building with the intention of matching its former glory.

The construction process was entangled with delays from the beginning, with men walking off the job, complaining of whispering and screams coming from the empty rooms on the second and third floors. People living adjacent to the hotel reported hearing strange noises as well, leading some to blame ghosts or specters for the disturbances, and others to postulate that the hotel might be sinking into the unstable sand dunes beneath its foundation.

In most cases, and in most towns, all of this would be quickly disregarded as foolishness by the locals, a pathetic attempt to draw attention to a business looking to attract curious guests. Westport, however, is no ordinary town. The waters along its shore are some of the most dangerous in the world, sending hundreds of fisherman to their death over the years, and causing its residents to firmly believe in the ever-changing laws of superstition.

Curtis grew up listening to his grandfather tell his own version of events concerning the hotel, leaving him both intrigued and terrified of the place. The stories would come like clockwork every time he visited the cabin with his parents, and despite his later suspicion that his grandfather was simply spinning tales to frighten an impressionable young mind, the stories never changed from one season to the next — which in his mind gave them legitimacy. Although he now considers his grandfather's stories nothing more than inspired fiction, Curtis had hoped to pass them onto his own children when they became old enough to hear them, and still young enough to listen.

Standing in front of the entrance to the hotel, with the wind already howling as it passes over the tortured trees behind him, it seems the perfect atmosphere for Curtis to recite the stories from his childhood — but as he walks up the chiseled stone steps, he turns around and sees the worn-out expressions of his wife and sons. It occurs to him that none of the stories he remembers are as terrifying or gruesome as the circumstances they now face, and little by little the magic of the grand hotel begins to wash away, until all that's left is an overly decorated building that's been built too close to the dunes.

"Did this place ever open again?" Sarah asks Curtis.

"I think it was supposed to open later this year."

Reaching for the doorknob, Curtis looks down and sees a set of keys still inserted into the keyhole. After figuring out that the door is locked, he turns the key and it swings open. At first he worries that someone might still be staying here, but after looking at the keys more closely he can tell they've been out in the weather for quite some time, and judging from the smell of mildew inside it seems clear that the building has been closed for a while.

138

As the four of them enter the lobby, their gazes all turn upward to the high ceiling above them, their slow footsteps echoing loudly throughout the immense space. Directly in front of them is the hourglass-shaped staircase, impressive even in subdued lighting. There's a landing in the middle of the stairs that provides access to the second floor, and another one at the top which serves the third floor. Hallways run both left and right from each landing. At the very top of the stairs, on the back wall that faces the ocean, sits a dirty and unkempt etched-glass window — barely clear enough to see the gathering storm outside. Two massive concierge desks sit on the ground-floor, one on each side of the staircase, both of them nearly swallowed up in the darkness that covers the far side of the room. The lobby itself has no rooms above it, the ceiling goes all the way to the roof, but the concierge desks are nestled under the second story, beneath the cover of shadow.

"Did you want to head straight to bed, or did you want to look around a bit?" Curtis asks his wife.

"I'm exhausted, let's just figure out where we're sleeping — then maybe you and the boys can come back down and explore."

Hearing a loud noise, Sarah wakes up, unsure of exactly what she'd heard. She listens closely for a moment, waiting for it to happen again, and trying to figure out just how long she's been asleep. Her body is unbelievably sore, especially her legs and feet. She knows if she feels this way in the morning she'll definitely want to stay another night in town just to heal up, and she hopes like hell that it isn't morning already. She knows it can't be though, the room is still pitch-black, and she's certain that she picked a room with an outside view.

Then she hears something again, a rhythmic thumping that at first

139

she mistakes for a branch blowing against the outside of the hotel. It stops for just a few seconds, and as it starts again she realizes what it is — footsteps from above her, on the third floor. Thinking that it could be Curtis and the boys, she reaches across the mattress to see if she's still alone, but instead finds her husband sleeping on the bed beside her.

"Curtis, wake up," she whispers into his ear, shaking him slightly.

"What?" he answers, still groggy.

"I can hear footsteps upstairs."

He turns on a flashlight and listens, but the sounds have stopped. After waiting a few more seconds, he kisses his wife's cheek, turns off the light, and pulls the blanket back over his shoulders. "It's probably just the kids. Go back to sleep."

"Why aren't the kids in here with us?" Sarah asks.

"I put them in the next room, they were going to build a fort."

"Hon, I don't feel comfortable with..."

She stops mid-sentence as a loud crash fills the room from directly above. Curtis turns the light back on and sits up in bed, then looks over at Sarah. "Did you hear that?"

"Of course I heard that." The footsteps start again, this time joined by the sound of something being dragged across the floor, like a piece of furniture. "That can't be the kids," she whispers. As soon as the words come out of her mouth, she hears a knock on the door from the adjoining room, startling both of them. Then the noises stop.

"Mom?" comes a voice on the other side of the door. She recognizes it as Matt.

"Come in."

Both Matt and Ben walk into the room, wearing pajamas and looking scared.

"Was that you two making that noise?" she asks them.

Matt shakes his head. "There's someone outside our window."

Curtis jumps out of bed and puts on his clothes, then grabs the revolver that he has waiting on the nightstand. He motions for the two boys to join their mother in bed, then closes and locks the door to the room. After shutting off his light, he waits by the window, watching for any sign of movement — but all he can see is darkness. Then just as his eyes begin to adjust to the lack of light, making the sand dunes visible through the filthy window, he hears something again, this time a faint rattling.

"What is that?" Sarah asks.

"It sounds like it's coming from downstairs. Maybe I should go down and check it out..."

"No! Are you crazy?" Sarah fires back, screaming under her whisper.

"We have no idea who they are. Hell, the hotel might be open for all we know..."

"Then we'll settle the bill in the morning. None of us should be leaving the room."

"Matt, did you get a look at the person you saw?" Curtis asks.

"Sort of, it was dark."

"Was it a man or a woman?"

"A man."

"Did he see you?"

"I don't think so."

Their eyes now fully adjusted, and with the moon momentarily shining through a small break in the clouds, they can now see each other clearly without the use of flashlights. Peering out the window again, he still can't see anything but the dunes between the hotel and the beach. He can see the blades of grass and the branches of the stunted pine trees whipping violently in the wind from the storm still raging outside, and the sheets of rain pelting the window in rhythmic bursts. Sarah almost screams as a flash of lightning fills the room, followed quickly by the loud crack of thunder overhead. Curtis looks at his watch, after suddenly realizing he has no idea what time it is.

"This is ridiculous, it's only a few minutes after nine... I'm not sitting here all night waiting for the sun to come up."

"What choice do we have?" asks Sarah.

"I'm gonna sneak down the hall and take a peek. Nobody will know I'm even there."

"We need to stay together."

"Nobody will see me, it'll be fine," he adds, walking toward the door.

Sarah throws her hands in the air, her face a mask of disbelief. She's too upset to even speak to him.

As he quietly unlocks the door, he tries once again to reassure her. "It's probably just a construction crew anyway."

"Yeah, for all the customers in town..."

Ignoring her remark, he opens the door and walks out into the hall, the door automatically locking behind him. The hallway is noticeably darker than the room, with very little visible except for the end of the corridor in front of him. As he begins walking, being careful not to step too heavily on the wooden planks that make up the floor, he can still hear something downstairs. Worse yet, he can also hear the creaking and groaning of the floorboards under his bare feet. When he reaches the staircase he waits and listens, but the noises have stopped once again.

The lobby below seems to glow in the dark, the bright white marble reflecting every speck of light that comes through the expansive windows surrounding the room. Crouching down, he watches the room closely, waiting for a flashlight or candle to appear, or maybe even the shadow of someone walking across the room. When nothing happens, he decides to walk down the stairs, his gun still firmly in his grasp.

Unlike the hallway, the steps leading down to the lobby make absolutely no noise at all, not even the slightest crack of dried-out wood. As he reaches the bottom, and steps out onto the cold stone floor, he catches a glimpse of something moving at the far end of the lobby to his right. His first thought is to run back upstairs to the safety of his room, but as the fear washes away he realizes how ridiculous that sounds — whoever else is in the room is probably as scared as he is. Still not comfortable being seen, he looks around for a spot that's hidden from the moonlight, and notices that a shadow extends a couple of feet out from the wall beyond the concierge desk. He places his back against the wall and begins moving slowly toward the other end of the lobby, his feet freezing against the hard tile.

About halfway down the wall he stops, his legs suddenly heavy with fear once again — someone is in the room, only twenty or thirty feet in front of him. He can hear them breathing, a deep rattling wheeze that causes a slight echo throughout the room. The moment he finally spots the man sitting at a table, the stranger stands up and coughs, nearly losing his balance in the process — then he walks slowly across the floor toward the main entrance, his steps awkward and unsteady. Curtis is still frozen with terror, realizing that he's been holding his breath since the moment he first saw the man. He eases a breath out, careful not to make any noise doing so, then watches as the figure's weak, trembling fists slam helplessly against the glass of the door.

Taking advantage of the man's distraction, Curtis glides down the wall and into the moonlight again — crouching over to make himself as small as possible as he steps onto the staircase. He turns around and faces the stairs in front of him, worried that someone else might be coming down at the same time — and out of habit he grabs the wooden railing beside him, releasing a loud creaking noise that rumbles across the room. The man in front of the door turns around and faces him, reaching his hands out in front of him, grabbing nothing but handfuls of air. He mumbles something completely unintelligible, ending with a low-pitched wail that stops Curtis in his tracks. He can barely see the man's face as he takes the first few steps in Curtis' direction. His steps are clumsy and jerky, and his breathing is audible even from this distance, but his face shows absolutely no sign of emotion. The features look sunken and withered, with glazed over eyes that look both dead and fixated at the same time. The sight of him sends a chill up Curtis' spine, and for a few seconds he does nothing but stand there and watch as the man creeps slowly toward him. Finally snapping out of it, he turns around and runs up the stairs, hearing once again the sounds of footsteps coming from the hallway on the third floor. As he reaches the second floor landing he turns and races down the hall, no longer caring whether he makes any sound or not. When he makes it to the door he grabs the knob and tries to open it, forgetting that it locked itself when he left.

"Sarah, open the door!" he whispers, still trying to turn the knob. After only a few seconds the door opens, with Sarah standing in the doorway, tears running down her face. After glancing back down the hallway to see if anyone is following him, Curtis rushes inside, closing and locking the door behind him. "Everybody stay quiet, and no lights."

"Who's out there?" Sarah whispers.

"Shh, they're coming..."

CHAPTER 15
WESTPORT

The room is nearly pitch-black, and the only sounds Sarah can hear are the frightened whimpers coming from behind her as her sons sit huddled on the bed. Her and Curtis are waiting nervously with their ears pressed up against the door, listening closely for any sign of activity in the hallway beyond — and although the hallway outside their room remains silent, in the distance they begin to make out the faint sounds of footsteps from seemingly all around them, and then the creaking of old wooden floors from the direction of the staircase at the end of the hall. Just as the footfalls pick up speed, a blood-curdling scream is heard, reverberating around the hotel and piercing through the walls as if it were in the next room. The screaming eventually becomes interspersed with shouting, coming from at least two people, each one as incoherent as the other. Curtis and Sarah both flinch each time one of the screams can be heard, their hearts beating so hard in their chest they have a difficult time concentrating on anything else. It's a noise unlike anything they've ever heard.

Then they hear a loud crash, like something, or someone, falling down the staircase — and then nothing. The noise disappears completely from the hotel, leaving only the sound of the storm outside.

Curtis listens to silence for a few minutes more, then whispers to Sarah... "I'm gonna block the door with something. Wait here and listen, okay?" Sarah nods, still staying silent.

Looking around the room, the only thing Curtis can see that might work is a cheaply-made wooden chair sitting by the window. On his way across the room, a hand reaches out and tugs on his shirt. His heart nearly jumps out of his chest until he recognizes the hand as his son's.

"Dad?" Matt whispers, still sitting on the bed with his brother.

"What is it, buddy?" replies Curtis, speaking in a voice as calm and relaxed as he can possibly muster.

"Can I turn on the flashlight?"

"Tell you what, why don't you get under the covers and turn the light on... That way nobody can see it."

"Okay. Who's out there?"

"I don't know, but I think they're really sick, and we need to keep away from them." Curtis lays his hand on Matt's shoulder, then looks back and forth between both boys. "Don't worry about it, your mom and I will figure it out."

He walks to the far wall and grabs hold of a chair, then on the way back glances out the window just as a flash of lightning illuminates the dunes in front of their room. Off in the distance, just barely in view from the hotel room, is an access road that leads to the beach. In the brief moment that everything was visible, Curtis could see what looked like dozens of people standing on the road, all of them staring in the same direction — toward the hotel. The sight catches him off-guard, and he nearly falls down as he backs away from the glass. After catching himself, he picks up the chair and carefully wedges it under the doorknob, his hands still shaking from the adrenaline.

"What did you see?" Sarah asks him.

"I saw people on the beach access road, dozens of them."

"What were they doing?"

"They're just standing around." He purposely leaves out the direction of their gaze, wishing that he didn't know about it either.

"Maybe they can help us. If we shine our flashlights out the

146

window..." Sarah says, her voice understandably desperate.

Curtis interrupts her mid-sentence. "Why would people stand around in the middle of the road during a storm?" He waits for an answer, but gets none. "This place is a ghost town. We've been wandering around it all day and we haven't seen a single person, not even a sign that anyone is still alive, and they're taking midnight strolls? It doesn't add up."

"Maybe I should watch out the window, just in case..."

"I don't think that's a good idea."

"One of us needs to watch the window in case somebody comes along that can help us, and someone needs to stay by the door — and I'm not guarding the door by myself..."

"Fine, just don't give us away unless you know for sure they can be trusted." He holds his hand out, drawing a confused look from her.

"What...?" she asks.

"Give me your flashlight."

"What's wrong with yours?"

"If we signal, it should be unanimous."

"When did that policy start? Was it before or after you went downstairs to look around?" Not waiting for a response, she turns around and walks to the window, careful not to stand directly in front of it. Beside her is the bed, with a faint glow coming from underneath the covers.

It doesn't take long for the next streak of lightning to hit, bringing Sarah's attention back to the world outside. Although it was only visible for a split-second, she could still see people on the access road, but not all of them are standing still — several are now walking in her direction along the sidewalk.

Little by little her eyes adjust to the darkness outside, slowly turning everything into a grayscale landscape of pine trees, sidewalks and people. As the veil begins to lift, she becomes aware that the

147

people on the road aren't the only ones out there. Standing on the sidewalk beside the hotel are two younger men that are soaked from head to toe, and looking directly at the room next to theirs, the room her kids were staying in just a short while ago. At first glance they look almost comatose, with mouths hanging wide-open and arms hanging to their sides like dead weights — but their eyes are different. There's a cold, heartless look to them, but also threatening and focused at the same time.

"Curtis..." she whispers, motioning for him to join her.

He moves up beside her, peering toward the road beyond. "What is it?" he asks.

"Look over there, at those men..."

She points toward the two people standing below them, just as their heads turn toward the street, almost in unison. Sarah and Curtis both look in the same direction and spot an older man about fifty feet away walking quickly down the sidewalk, making his way around others who are mostly just standing in place. He's wearing blue jeans and an unbuttoned work-shirt, exposing his bare chest to the wind and rain brought in by the storm. With a determined look on his face, and his mouth moving as if he were carrying on a conversation, he passes by an older woman who's slowly making her way down the sidewalk directly in front of the window. Just as he goes to pass her, she turns around and accidentally bumps into the man, stopping him in his tracks. He turns around with his back to the hotel, then swings what looks like a piece of driftwood at the woman's head. She falls to the ground immediately, but the man continues to smash the object onto her now-helpless body. As he straightens back up and turns around, Sarah spots a large pool of blood running down the sidewalk — coming from the old woman who now lies motionless on the ground in front of them.

Without thinking, Sarah lets out a loud gasp. She turns to Curtis, who's still staring at the scene with a look of horror on his face. Moving her gaze back out the window, she finds the two younger men below with their eyes fixed on hers. After sharing eye contact for a few seconds, she drops straight to the floor, trying not to scream or cry, and wishing she could simply wake up from the nightmare their lives have suddenly become. Just a couple of seconds later, Curtis joins her on the carpet.

"Those two men were looking right at me!" she says, her voice louder than she intended.

"Shh... The other guy looked up this way too. I think he saw me."

Her voice turns almost silent. "What are we gonna do? We have to get out of here!"

"I know..." He crawls over to the bed, pulling his upper body onto the mattress. "Matt, turn off the light for a minute."

"But..." comes the reply.

"Do it, right now." His voice is calm, but stern. After watching the light disappear, he rejoins Sarah.

"Do we have another gun?" she asks him.

"No, it's back at the cabin."

"Maybe we could move to another room. Maybe across the..." Her sentence is cut-off by the sound of footsteps coming from down the hall, moving slowly in their direction.

Curtis stands up and rushes back to the door, careful not to make too much noise. As the steps get closer, he places his free hand just above the doorknob, then braces his feet against the floor, wishing that he'd put his shoes on while he had the chance.

He can hear them breathing as they reach the door to the room, and then the footsteps suddenly stop, and the sound of a deep, raspy breath is all that can be heard. Curtis looks behind him and sees Sarah standing at the foot of the bed, and their kids right behind her with scared expressions on their faces. Then without warning, the person

149

in the hallway begins to pound on the door, screaming each time their fist makes contact.

Although frightening, the hits really aren't all that strong. They sound weakened, even desperate, and after only thirty seconds or so they stop altogether, along with the screaming. A moment later, the doorknob starts to jiggle, and Curtis almost reaches down to grab it out of instinct. He knows it's locked though, and holding onto it would only prove to whoever is out there that someone is in the room. He decides it's better to stay quiet and not make himself known for the time being.

After what seems like an eternity of heavy wheezing and throat clearing, the footsteps make their way farther down the hall and into a room that apparently wasn't locked.

Curtis turns around and lets out a sigh of relief, crumpling to the floor with his back to the door.

"We have to find a way out of here," says Sarah, sitting on the carpet beside him.

"From the looks of things, it doesn't look any safer outside..."

"So what are we supposed to do? The sun is gonna be up before we know it, and we can't hide in broad daylight." She stands up again and walks to the chair beside the bed, then opens her backpack and starts pulling out clothes. "We have to get back to the cabin before it's too late."

"Why are you unpacking?"

"I'm putting on the darkest clothes I have, you should do the same."

"What the hell is wrong with these people? It's like the entire world has gone insane..." says Curtis. He's still sitting on the floor, wringing his hands nervously. His eyes are growing vacant as he falls deeper into thought.

"Curtis!" snaps Sarah. He comes back to reality once again, looking fatigued and beaten. "Stand up and go through your clothes..."

Without saying a word, Curtis gets to his feet and starts unpacking his clothes. "What about the kids? Their clothes are still in the other room..."

Sarah looks at the two of them sitting on the bed, their bodies shivering. "Are you guys cold?"

"No," says Matt.

"A little," says Ben.

Sarah turns back to Curtis. "You're gonna have to go into their room and grab their things. They can't walk back home without shoes."

"That guy is right down the hall..."

"If he comes after you, shoot him. That's why you brought the gun isn't it?"

Finding out that the adjoining door had apparently locked itself when the boys came through it, Curtis steps out into the hallway and closes the door behind him, the first thing that catches his eyes are the blood-splattered markings on the outside of their door — all of them more or less the size of a fist. Looking down the hall toward the lobby he sees footprints of blood staggered across the floor, like they were left by a drunk. They continue past his room and disappear behind a door only a few rooms over. Judging from the amount of blood left behind, it appears that whoever is down the hall is badly injured — and barefoot.

Hearing the click of the lock behind him, Curtis keeps his flashlight as low as possible as he creeps down the hallway to the next room over. He watches the floorboards carefully, trying not to slip in the puddles of blood left on the floor, and feeling grateful that he's wearing his hiking boots once again.

151

When he reaches the door to their room he finds it wide-open, which he knows they didn't do. He walks in and closes the door partway, leaving only an inch or so still open, then spots the backpacks on the floor next to the bed. As he bends down to pick the packs up, he hears the sound of another door opening, right across the hallway from him. He quickly backs up and positions himself in a corner of the room behind the door, turning off his flashlight as he does.

He counts only five footsteps before hearing the hinges next to him squeak, and even in the darkness he can see the door moving as it swings into the room, followed closely by a shadowy figure that reeks of human filth and god only knows what else. It's a man, that much he can tell — but it's not the same man he saw downstairs. There's almost nothing to this guy. His frame is tall, but extremely thin, with long arms that are hanging loosely at his side. When he reaches the bed he nearly falls into it face-first, then catches himself and sits down on the edge of it — facing directly toward Curtis.

Squeezing the gun in his hand just a little bit tighter, as if he's reminding himself that it's still there, Curtis lifts it up and points it at the man's head, waiting for him to make a move — but the man doesn't budge. He simply sits and stares ahead, either not seeing Curtis, or not caring. His breathing has gotten worse, and every strenuous breath he draws in gurgles as his lungs fill up with fluid. It's not long before the gasps become desperate and hard to listen to, forcing the man back to his feet as he tries to draw air in. He stumbles around the room, stretching his neck out and moaning loudly, then finally drops backward onto the floor on the other side of the room.

Curtis flips the flashlight back on and shines it on the man, who he can now see is shirtless and sprawled out on the carpet only ten feet in front of him. Although his body is still twitching slightly, Curtis is almost certain he's dead. He quickly places the gun back into his jacket pocket, then grabs the backpacks and shoes and heads out of the room, trying his best to hold his breath as he passes through the infected air left behind.

As Matt and Ben get changed on the other side of the room, Curtis and Sarah stand by the window and look out at the dark sidewalk that surrounds the hotel. The moonlight is beginning to break through the clouds overhead, blanketing the area once again in the blue-tinted glow of night — yet none of it seems to be penetrating the trees between the hotel and the dunes.

"I don't see anyone, do you?" asks Sarah.

"No, but that doesn't mean they're not out there. If they were on the other side of that seawall, I don't think we could see them." He points to a concrete wall that sits about one hundred feet from the hotel, almost completely hidden by the rolling dunes and pines.

"So what do we do?"

"We could try to make it home by walking along the beach, that would probably be the fastest way — but if anyone is out there we'll be sitting ducks."

"What about the highway? We could just go back the same way we came..."

"The highway has a million places to hide, for us and for them. I think the beach is our best bet."

"I'm ready," blurts out Matt, standing in the middle of the room with a fresh change of clothes on. He has his backpack slung over his right shoulder, nearly dragging him onto the floor from the weight of it — a sight that almost makes Curtis smile.

"I think we'll leave our packs behind," says Curtis.

"But all my stuff is in here..." argues Matt.

153

"Alright, you can take your packs, but only the essentials. If it's not survival gear, it doesn't come with us. We don't want anything slowing us down."

As the kids tear apart their packs to sort through all of the unnecessary crap they decided to bring, Curtis sets two chairs in front of the window and takes a seat in one of them, then motions Sarah into the other.

"I take it we're not leaving right away...?" she asks.

"We should watch for a while, see if there's any pattern or timing we can take advantage of."

"We can't wait too long."

Looking at his watch... "We still have at least eight hours until full sun-up."

They watch the storm outside for several minutes, each of them haunted by the events of the last few days. Sarah can't decide if the last two hours have gone by quickly or not, it all seems like a blur from the moment she first heard footsteps on the floor above them. One thing she knows for sure is that her nerves are absolutely shot. She keeps hearing and seeing things that prove to be figments of her imagination, like movements in the corner of the room, or a faint thumping coming from a hallway she knows to be empty. Other things she can't be completely sure of though, like what appears to be shadows moving among the pine trees just beyond the wall, or the occasional glimmer of light coming from the direction of the beach. Curtis tells her that the latter is probably just phosphorescence from microbes in the ocean, a phenomenon that causes plankton to glow in the dark. For some reason these lights seem different though, and something in her gut tells her that the beach is crawling with whatever these people have become.

"Are you ready?" Curtis asks, startling her. "I don't see anything out there."

154

Although she has every symptom of anxiety and stress imaginable, Sarah tries her best to look strong when she turns to Curtis. "I'm ready." As they step away from the window, Sarah takes one last look at the beach, her mind still conflicted as to whether this is the right decision.

What she can't see, and what neither one of them have noticed all night, is a man standing beneath the sprawl of a spruce tree just inside the wall. He's been waiting patiently all night, watching their every movement, his sense of reason and rationality slipping away with every passing second.

CHAPTER 16
THE PACIFIC OCEAN

Since leaving Neah Bay, the mood on the boat has changed dramatically — partly from knowing that somewhere beyond the heavy rain and rolling waves is a man hell-bent on killing all of them, and partly because of the horrible effect that the ocean is having on their equilibriums. Beth has been out on the open sea before, but it was a lifetime ago when both her and Larry were small children. To this day she remembers vividly how violently ill she felt when the boat began to roll.

Jake has never been on the ocean, and after this trip he's beginning to doubt that he will again. With every mile they travel, his worries and fears of what still awaits them are starting to slip away, and sickness is taking their place. He begins to envy the dead, the fortunate souls who no longer have to experience the wretched symptoms of seasickness.

Other than feeling miserable, Jake was assigned a single task by Larry during their trip south — to keep the water in the bilge below the three bullet holes that Sean left in the side of their boat. Even with the help of two pumps, this one seemingly simple job has proven to be difficult. The hatch leading to the bilge area is barely big enough for an adult to squeeze through, especially one wearing a survival suit. Larry insisted they all wear one in case something went wrong. The stainless-steel ladder was an issue as well — despite having a roughened texture, the wet metal surface is still prone to slipping. He's been removing water for hours now, five gallons at a time, nauseous from both the rocking of the boat and the exhaustion that

156

he feels — but he's also grateful that he hasn't heard any news from Beth concerning Sean.

Sitting next to her brother in the pilothouse, and staring at the water behind them through binoculars, Beth tries her best to carry out the only task she seems qualified for. She doesn't have the endurance or strength to carry buckets of water, and she certainly doesn't have the skill necessary to operate the boat — but she does have the ability to see what's coming after them, or at least that's the idea. Watching the ocean at night is both terrifying and beautiful. Most of the time all you can see of the waves is a thin silver outline at the crest, which seem to dance as the waves roll across the water — but between each of them is a black abyss, which only serves to remind you of just how cold and deadly the current really is.

Of the three jobs on-board, Beth's is the worst when it comes to seasickness. Although the idea is to spot Sean's boat before he gets too close to them, she welcomes the times when she loses sight of the horizon — it's only then that her mind forgets how much the boat is rising and falling on the swells of the water. In fact, the only thing that's keeping her from either throwing up or falling asleep is the constant barrage of thunder, lightning, and rain. The latter is coming down in massive sheets that wrap around the boat every couple of minutes, making Jake's job below that much more difficult.

Beth turns to Larry, intending to say something to him — but she's forced to wait a few moments as the boat climbs over a roll and starts a rapid decent over the other side, making her feel as though her intestines are going to crawl up and out of her throat.

"Have you ever been in weather like this?" she asks, yelling over the strained engines and crashing waves.

"A few times, but never around here. I just hope to hell it's not like this when we get to Astoria."

"And what if it is...?"

157

"Then we sit and wait. If you think you feel sick now, wait until we stop moving forward."

She cringes at just the thought of it, then focuses her attention back through the binoculars.

"What do you see? Anything?" asks Larry.

"This is just a waste of time. If he were twenty feet behind us I don't think I could see him."

Her field of vision is suddenly blocked by something, and when she looks up from the binoculars she finds Jake standing directly in front of her, soaked all the way to the bone.

"We have to talk," he manages to force out, both breathless and exhausted from working himself to the breaking point.

Larry turns around with a grim look on his face. "About what?"

"I can't keep up with the water anymore. For every bucket that I take out there's at least two more that come in from up top."

This is the worst-case scenario for Larry. He knows they can't make it all the way to Astoria as long as they're taking on water, and even if they did make it there, the boat would end up sinking shortly thereafter.

"Did you close the hatch?" he asks Jake.

"Yeah, it's sealed."

"How long do you think we have?"

"It's hard to say. Maybe an hour, maybe a few hours — it's already above the second hole."

"What's the closest marina?" Beth asks Larry.

"I'm not sure exactly where we're at... Probably Westport, but without any lights it's hard to say."

Jake steps between the two chairs and pulls the chart in front of him, dripping water all over the teak dash panel. The only light available comes from the gauges on the instrument panel, making it difficult to read the already worn-out charts. "That might not be a bad

158

idea... We might be able to throw Sean off our track."

"He followed us into Neah Bay, what stops him from following us there?" asks Beth.

"We won't go into Westport, we'll go on into the bay — maybe to Aberdeen."

"That's not a good idea," Larry says dismissively. "Do you have any idea what it's like crossing over the bar at Westport?"

"No, I don't," answers Jake.

"It's not a lot different than Astoria. It'd be suicide in weather like this."

"I don't really see what choice we have. It's either that or we take our chances sinking farther south, and that's only if Sean hasn't caught up to us in the meantime. Whatever decision we make, we have to assume he's right behind us."

Larry stays silent for a moment, frustrated by the two horrible choices facing him. The opening to Grays Harbor is a thin, turbulent passage nestled between two towns — the fishing village of Westport to the south, and the tourist town of Ocean Shores to the north. Beyond that sits the harbor — a body of water fed by the Chehalis River, and lined with the once-industrious cities of Aberdeen and Hoquiam.

"Jake, check the tide chart on Westport," Larry finally says.

He fumbles through the booklet, trying to decipher the tide levels, and trying to remember exactly which day it was. "It looks like high tide is at 12:17AM."

"What time is it now?"

"11:32"

"That doesn't give us much time." He takes another look at the GPS, which is tracking them at least fifty miles off-course. "I wish this fucking thing worked." Disgusted, he reaches up and turns it off, then turns the charts toward his seat, always keeping one hand firmly on

159

the wheel. "If we're gonna do it, it has to be now. If we wait much longer we'll miss the window."

"I say we go for it," says Jake, who then looks at his wife for her opinion. She simply nods at both of them.

"Okay, go down and tie any essentials to the life rings, but don't put too much weight on each one. You can also use the cushions from the chairs and couch. Then tie everything together and leave the bundle on the deck."

As Jake makes his way down the ladder, Beth starts to follow him.

"Beth, not you. I need you up here with me."

She turns around and sits down in the seat next to him again, wishing she were helping Jake do something that sounds productive. "What am I doing?"

"See if you can spot the water tower, or any other building that might look familiar. They should be somewhere in front of us."

Larry has a few lights turned on to find their way, but the only thing she can see are one or two waves in front of the boat before they move out of sight. Occasionally a flash of lightning illuminates the surface of the water, and even then the visibility is limited by the downpour of rain. Between strikes, the area they're heading into is a vast scene of nothingness, marked only by the spray of saltwater on their windshield as they're confronted by an endless assault of rollers.

"Aren't the waves getting bigger?" she asks.

"We're just at a different angle, I'm turning into the west. Things are gonna get a little hectic when we get closer to the harbor."

Trying to stay focused on the horizon, and not on the swells directly in front of her, Beth decides to give up the binoculars and rely solely on her naked eyes instead. Then she sees it, a square-shaped outline that looks vaguely like a building.

"I see something over there, to the left a little bit."

Larry concentrates on the area she's pointing to, but he can't see

160

whatever she's seeing. "What does it look like?"

"Like apartment buildings."

"Light colored?"

"Yeah, I think so."

"That's Ocean Shores, we need to be a little bit farther south to line ourselves up. Go tell Jake to hurry up — once we start on the approach it doesn't take long, especially with these tailwinds."

Larry knew the odds were against them from the moment they decided to enter Grays Harbor. He told himself that they probably had a fifty-fifty chance of making it across the bar in one piece, but deep down he knew it was much worse than that. Before turning the boat toward the harbor he reminded himself that despite the terrible odds, it was actually their best chance — running farther south was completely out of the question in weather like this. Within a relatively short period of time the boat will sink, there's no doubt about that now, and having that happen on the open ocean seems like certain suicide. At least this way they would go out fighting.

As 'Larry's Obsession' moves closer to the entrance of the harbor, objects begin to gradually appear in the distance — most of them looking like smudges in a poorly executed painting, bobbing up and down with every rise and fall of the boat. By the time they reach what Larry calls 'the point of no return', the objects reveal themselves as the darkened buildings of both Westport and Ocean Shores. Both towns look alarmingly close to Beth as they position themselves into the narrow channel of the waterway.

Despite seeing dozens of cities and towns along the way that were covered in a veil of darkness, it still seems strange to Beth to see places she knows so well that now look so different — even if she'd

161

never viewed them from the water before. Directly ahead of them, only fifteen or so miles to the east, the skies should be lit by the largest coastal urban area in the Pacific Northwest — and now that they're finally on their way there, she's beginning to have second thoughts about traveling into an area that was once home to so many people. When the epidemic first started she wanted nothing to do with other people, aside from her husband and brother of course — but as the days turned into weeks, and the sickness changed into something that resembled the apocalypse, her feelings began to shift. She missed her morning walks through her old neighborhood, and her monthly trips to Seattle with the friends she once felt so close to. More than anything she wants to find a place untouched by all of this, a place where life continues as it did before — but with every passing day she's beginning to doubt that such a place actually exists, and based on the black skies in front of them, that place almost certainly isn't Aberdeen.

Since there are only two chairs in the cramped pilothouse, Jake has managed to wedge himself into the corner beside Beth, his eyes shut tight against the constant assault from the weather outside. Occasionally he does open them for a moment or two, each time half-expecting to see Sean's boat closing in on them — but the view is always the same, a never-ending string of rolling waves that quickly overtake the boat, thrusting them upward with each pass.

The current of the ocean runs east, toward the shore — but the river they're aiming for runs directly into the oncoming waves, causing larger-than-normal waves to appear in the inlet passage to the bay. Even in calm weather these rollers will outrun a boat, but during storms they run fast and violent, hitting the vessels with enough force to knock them sideways every time they hit. Worse yet, they come at you from behind with no pattern or regularity, forcing the pilot of the boat to make crucial life and death decisions with no warning whatsoever.

Beth wants to close her eyes like Jake, to block out the stress and terror that she can't help but feel, but for some reason she can't look away, not even to see how Larry is handling it in the seat beside her. Every ten to fifteen seconds the next wave reaches them, lifting them nearly two stories before dropping them on the other side of the swell — the boat landing perpendicular to the current almost every time. Whichever way they do land, Larry has only a few seconds to right their position before the next roller comes in behind them. If they're hit from the side, the wave will simply wash right over them, taking the boat under the surface as it passes, and likely taking the lives of all three people on-board.

As they reach the crest of one of the largest swells, Beth thinks she sees something up ahead, a shimmering on the water that looks out of place. Each time they're lifted up she tries to get a better look at what it is, but by the time her eyes find it they start dropping again. Finally, on the fourth roll, she recognizes what it is that she's looking at. Up ahead, probably a few hundred yards or so, the force of the river is creating large whirlpools on the surface of the water. While the swirls of water themselves probably don't pose much of a threat to them, the debris caught in the middle of them certainly does. They look like scattered piles of trash spread out across the passage.

"Larry, do you see..." Beth says, pointing out the windshield.

"I know, I can't worry about that right now..."

"But..."

"We'll deal with it when we get there," he says abruptly.

The words of concern manage to wake Jake from his self-induced coma next to Beth, encouraging him to finally pull himself to his feet to see for himself what all the fuss is about. As he braces his feet against the floor and adjusts his eyes to the scene directly ahead, he finds that they're sitting on the very top of a roller, looking out at the

163

darkness of Grays Harbor. The only thing standing in their way is a collection of driftwood, garbage and what looks like hundreds of human remains floating amongst the rest of the storm wreckage.

"Do you..." Jake says, pointing out the windshield.

"He sees it," responds Beth.

CHAPTER 17
WESTPORT

Sarah thought that she knew what extreme fatigue felt like, but she was wrong. She'd given birth to three kids, the first of which took a day and a half to arrive — she'd run marathons, taken part in endurance obstacle courses, stayed up for days at a time while studying for exams... but none of those came close to how she felt at this moment. The aching muscles and heavy exhaustion were familiar, but there was something different, something wasn't right. It had nothing to do with the virus, she felt perfectly healthy in that sense — but her strength was beginning to slip away somehow. She was starting to give up.

It started out feeling like apprehension, like something horrible was about to happen and she'd forgotten what it was. Then little by little everything around her began to feel hopeless, her family's efforts to survive futile. It was at that point that she realized just how low her resolve had sunk.

It took every ounce of energy left in her body to get to her feet and walk toward the door to the hallway, but one look at her boys standing next to their father gave her the extra push she needed. The same line keeps running through her head, over and over... 'They have to make it, no matter what the cost'. Whether it's the stress of the situation, or some primal form of maternal instinct, she begins feeling something inside of her change — a building determination and anger against the people waiting outside the hotel. She suddenly realizes that her sympathy for them is now gone, and some form of resentment and hatred was now taking its place.

"Do you remember what the plan is?" Curtis asks Matt and Ben. Instead of an answer, the two of them simply nod. "Tell it to me then..."

"We sneak out and run down the beach," answers Matt.

"Which way?"

"To the left."

"And then...?"

"We go back to the cabin and lock the door."

Curtis almost laughs. The part about locking the door wasn't included in the plan, but it seems only logical. At least he's thinking ahead. "Right, we head to the cabin and we don't stop until we get there. Do you remember how to find our trail from the beach?"

Ben pipes up this time. "We look for the anchor."

"That's right, you find the anchor and then cross the highway."

In reality, it isn't a real anchor that they're looking for, but rather a large piece of driftwood that looks somewhat similar to one from the right angle — if you squint just right, and maybe turn your head sideways. Regardless, each of them know exactly what it looks like, and it seemed the best landmark to use to find their way home.

"Are you guys ready then?" asks Curtis.

Another set of nods.

"We're ready," replies Sarah.

He holds up his hand as a signal for his family to stay back, then quietly opens the door and steps out into the hallway, glancing momentarily at the door down the hall where he watched a man choke to death only a short while ago. Confident that the coast is clear, he motions for Sarah and the two kids to join him.

As Sarah steps out across the threshold, her first reaction is to shield Ben's eyes from the blood splattered all over the floor and walls, but she holds back instead, and allows him to take it all in. To her surprise, he carefully and casually steps over a pool of it in front of the door, then checks his shoes afterward to see if he got any on them.

With his gun at his side, and his family walking only a few feet behind him, Curtis creeps slowly toward the stairs at the end of the hall, their footsteps filling the hotel with the sound of creaking floorboards. His hands are shaking so badly that he has a hard time holding onto his flashlight, and after about twenty feet he decides to place his gun in his pocket just to be safe.

"Curtis..." Sarah whispers from behind.

He turns around and sees her pointing at something on the floor, lying beside one of the pools of blood. When he gets closer he can see what it is, a detached human finger.

"Is it from the guy you saw?" she asks.

"I don't know, I didn't notice." He honestly hadn't noticed if the guy was missing a finger, but he knows for certain that this finger didn't belong to the man. It's small and slight, likely belonging to a woman or a child. He gently tugs at Sarah's coat. "Let's keep moving."

When he finally reaches the staircase, he motions for the others to stay back again — and after noticing that the area is already partially lit from the moonlight, he switches off his flashlight and peeks around the corner, then quickly pulls himself back into the hall.

"Shit..." he mutters under his breath.

"What did you see?" asks Sarah.

"They're outside the front door." He waits a few seconds. "I think I can hear them..."

Sure enough, Sarah can hear a faint rattling sound coming from the lobby below, as well as the sound of muffled voices. She moves up beside Curtis, then turns her own light off before glancing around the corner.

It's hard to tell how many there are. There could be a half-dozen, or there could be a hundred, it's impossible to say as dark as it is

167

outside.

"Is there another way out?" she asks Curtis.

"I think I saw an exit in the kitchen."

He peers around the corner again, watching them walk back and forth in front of the glass doors and windows, trying to figure out why they're acting the way that they do. Most of them are just wandering aimlessly, occasionally bumping into somebody else as if they had no idea they were there.

"But we have to go through the lobby to get to the kitchen, right?" asks Sarah, breaking his concentration.

"I wonder why they don't just break the windows...?"

"I don't know... but we have to figure out a way back to the beach — after that we can think about everything else," responds Sarah, recognizing his lack of focus. "Curtis... are you listening to me...?"

Instead of responding, Curtis waves his hand forward, then steps onto the middle platform of the staircase — his flashlight by his side, but still turned off. The boys follow behind him as Sarah takes the rear, all three of them staying two or three steps back.

The people outside don't seem to notice them, at least not yet anyway. Every minute or so someone comes to the main door and jiggles the handle, then after finding out that it's locked, they turn around and walk back down the sidewalk. One woman in particular keeps coming back, at least three times now from Sarah's count. She's wearing pajama bottoms and a tee-shirt, and apparently no shoes — a common trend among the infected it seems. The woman is also completely soaked to the bone, her body shivering uncontrollably as she circles around yet again, this time placing her hands and face against the window beside the door.

While watching the activity outside, it occurs to Sarah that the carpet under her feet is squishing with every step, as if it were soaked with water — or something worse. Thinking that she might be

168

walking in blood, or God only knows what else, she moves over to the side until the sensation goes away. Then, with only a few more steps to go until the bottom, Curtis suddenly stops in his tracks. She hears a voice in front of him, extremely faint and rattling with congestion, like they were drowning.

"Please... help me..."

Curtis moves to the side, exposing a man stretched out on his back lying on the bottom steps, his head resting on the marble floor of the lobby. His clothes are blotchy and stained, but it's too dark to tell whether or not it's blood. Curtis takes another step down, positioning himself directly beside the man. As he starts to bend his knees slightly to get a better look, Sarah grabs Matt and Ben's shoulders and pulls them closer, then slowly backs up the stairs, bringing the boys with her.

"Please..." the man says again, raising his right hand into the air as he pleads.

Without saying anything, Curtis reaches into his pocket and pulls out his pistol, aiming it at the man's head.

"What's your name?" he asks the man in a whisper.

"Please..."

"I asked your name. What is it?"

In a flash, the man reaches his hand into the air again, this time grabbing for Curtis' jeans. Sarah and the boys take a couple more steps back as Curtis kicks the man's arm away — his foot landing harder than he intended though, sending the sound of cracking bones and tendons echoing throughout the room. The man's body is thrown onto his side, his front now facing away from Curtis.

"I'm sorry, I..." Curtis begins, then the man slowly rotates onto his back, facing him once again — a wicked smirk plastered onto his face as he begins to laugh in a low, raspy voice. Curtis looks down at the man's arm, which is obviously badly broken, then up at Sarah, who is

169

waiting several steps up the stairs, her face filled with terror and disbelief.

"Come on down, just keep to the left." he tells her.

"What if he does something?"

"He's not going anywhere. He's all busted up."

She starts down the stairs again, this time taking the lead ahead of Matt and Ben. When the man sees her he stops laughing and begins speaking nonsense instead — a jumbled mess of rhythmic gibberish that sounds like the ramblings of a madman. She finally reaches Curtis and stands next to him, then allows for the two kids to safely pass behind them, her eyes fixed on the man's face as he continues his speech.

"Sarah, let's go," says Curtis, who is still pointing his gun at the man's forehead.

As Sarah steps down onto the lobby floor, Curtis finds himself conflicted on what to do with the guy. He's clearly insane, and in all likelihood dying, but he's still a human being — and kicking him like he did is only making the thought of leaving him that much harder.

"Are you coming?" asks Sarah.

"What should we do with him?"

"We leave him. What else are we going to do with him?"

The man stops talking for a few seconds and simply stares up at Curtis with a menacing look in his eyes — his one working hand still struggling to reach out despite being pinned underneath his body. Placing his gun back in his pocket, Curtis joins his family on the stone floor below, and they make their way toward the hallway that leads to the kitchen in the back of the hotel.

Halfway across the lobby, just as they finally lose sight of the staircase, they hear a horrible scream coming from behind them — the same blood-curdling cry they heard earlier in the night. Curtis stops in his tracks as Sarah looks at the front entrance to their left, spotting dozens of people walking toward the door and windows, some of them already looking frantically around the lobby for the source of the scream.

"Nobody move," says Curtis.

"We have to get out of here!" replies Sarah, trying to keep her voice as quiet as possible.

"We're in the shadows, they can't see us."

Most of the people still aren't doing much aside from peering in through the glass — and then a woman comes to the door, the same woman that Sarah has seen repeatedly, this time pounding her hands against the pane right above the handle. Several of the others start following her lead, slamming their fists and forearms into the windows on either side of the door. Although their movements are slow, and their strength appears to be weakened, Curtis can still see the panes of glass moving with every hit.

"Come on, let's go — but quietly, we don't want them to see us."

Once they're in the hallway and out of sight from the people outside, Curtis turns his flashlight back on, worried that they might run into somebody else before reaching the kitchen. Instead, the place looks to be completely deserted.

The empty rooms of the hotel give Curtis the creeps, and he has to remind himself that they would be even creepier if they were full of people. As they pass in front of the dining area, a large room filled with Native American artwork and absolutely no tables or chairs, the group stops for a moment when they hear something breaking behind them.

"Keep moving," Curtis tells them, picking up his pace to almost a jog.

When they reach the kitchen, Curtis immediately spots the exit door on the other side of the room, a room that looked much more cheerful and inviting when they were searching for food only hours

171

before.

Its layout is simple — cooking surfaces on the left side, prep surfaces on the right side, which also happens to be the back exterior wall of the hotel, and a long stainless steel island running down the middle. The exit is on the opposite wall from them, on the south side of the building.

Sarah notices that the air is cold and humid down here, with a slight musty smell that gets worse the farther into the kitchen they go. As she follows Curtis down the aisle between the prep counter and island, she grabs a small paring knife that's been left by the sink, an act which catches Curtis' eye.

"Are there anymore of those?" he asks her.

Sarah looks around, but can't see any others. The room is mostly bare, with only a few pots and pans hanging from a rack above the main island. There are no other knives or silverware to be seen.

"I don't see another one."

"Keep an eye out, they might come in handy." he says, walking down the main aisle between the cooking surfaces and the island.

"Don't you have one?"

"Just my pocketknife."

"Why don't you give it to Matt..."

Without stopping, Curtis reaches into the pocket of his coat and grabs his knife, handing it to Matt who's following behind him. Matt waits until both his dad and mom aren't looking, then hands the knife over to Ben, who seems more than happy to take it.

They continue on, finally making it to the door that leads to the south side delivery entrance, a door which thankfully has a window in the upper half of it. Curtis peers through it, looking for any sign of movement outside. The clouds are obviously clearing overhead, allowing the moonlight outside to shine brightly on the sidewalk and parking lot on the other side of the glass. Other than a few trees moving in the wind, and the occasional leaf or branch blowing by the window, nothing else can be seen.

"Are you guys ready?"

"Yeah, let's get out of here," answers Sarah.

Curtis grabs the handle and turns it, then pulls the door toward him — but it doesn't move. Thinking that it might swing out, he tries pushing on it instead, but that doesn't work either.

"What's wrong?" asks Sarah.

"It must be locked."

He looks at the deadbolt and sees that it's the type without a lever to unlock it, you need a key instead. He raises his arm to break the glass with his elbow, but then he hears a sound coming from behind them, a thump that sounded like it came from just outside the kitchen. Curtis immediately shuts his flashlight off, then pulls Sarah to the floor with him.

"Matt, Ben, are you on the floor?" Curtis asks.

"We're right next to you," answers Matt, his voice shaky. "I can see them."

Try as he may, Curtis can't see anything in the kitchen beyond the island cabinet in front of them. He carefully stretches himself out to place himself directly next to Matt, but he still can't see anything except for darkness.

"How many are there?" he whispers into Matt's ear.

"Just one. He looks drunk."

"Why does he look drunk?"

"He's walking funny, and he keeps running into stuff."

"Is he walking in our direction?"

"Yes."

"Okay, don't say anything more. Just be ready to run if I say so..." Curtis turns to Sarah, then holds his hand out. "Let me see that knife..."

She hands it to him, then asks... "What are you gonna do?"

The sound of pots and pans crashing to the floor startles both of them, then they hear the subtle taps of footsteps coming their way. He must be halfway across the room already.

"I don't know yet, but I can't shoot him without the others hearing it." He then pulls the pistol from his pocket and hands it to Sarah. "Move under the island, he might not see you guys under there."

"What about you?"

"He won't see me either."

Watching his family scramble to wedge themselves beneath the island, Curtis crawls on his hands and knees down the opposite aisle, trying to get as close as possible to the man before confronting him. He can barely see anything on the other side, and the farther he gets from the windows, the darker the room becomes — but then he spots something moving directly across from him, a muddy slipper that's dragging along the cold tile floor in spastic jerks. Beside it he can see his other foot as well, also muddy, but bare with no protection whatsoever. It finally dawns on Curtis that most of the people they've seen tonight aren't wearing any shoes, or even clothes in some cases.

He considers moving against the man right away, maybe by grabbing his legs and pulling him under the island — but he decides to let him walk ahead just a few feet before making his move. As he squeezes through the open-sided island and carefully pulls himself to his feet on the other side, he tries to build up courage to do what needs to be done. He's now standing right behind the man, knife in hand, knowing that in just a few seconds one of them will be dead.

The thought of contagion has crossed Curtis' mind, and the last thing he wants to do is contract the same disease that's clearly sickened this guy. Time is not on their side, however, and any minute there could be a dozen or more people wandering in from the lobby — some of them in much better physical condition than this guy.

174

This one seems manageable. Besides his odd choice of footwear, he's wearing blue jeans that are obviously put on backwards, a simple t-shirt that's completely soaked through, and an arm that's dripping a large amount of blood all over the stainless steel counter-top beside him.

Curtis follows behind him, trying to match his footsteps to conceal the sounds of his own. This proves to be difficult though. His gait is unbalanced, muffled by the soft cushion of his slipper every other step. Feeling that the time is right, Curtis holds his breath, tightens his grip, then lunges forward at the guy, nearly stumbling to the ground as his left foot catches on something hard. He regains his composure almost instantly, but when he looks back up, he finds himself staring into the man's eyes. They look dead and uncaring, the eyes of a madman. Worried that he might trip again, he glances down at the floor and spots a large pot. The man lets out a pathetic moan, then reaches for Curtis, grabbing hold of his collar and weakly tugging it in his direction. Curtis takes a swipe at him with the knife, which does nothing but remove the guy's grasp, then pushes him away with his other hand, causing the man to fall back onto the floor.

Curtis picks up the pot up from the floor, then stands over the man's semi-conscious body. The pot is surprisingly heavy and uncomfortable to handle, even empty. Taking a few deep breaths to steady his nerves, he swings it as hard as he can at the man's head, smashing it against the hard tile surface of the floor beneath. He drops the pot immediately, then checks himself for any sign of blood splatter that may have gotten on him. Confident that he's clean, he turns his flashlight on again and looks around at the aisle behind him, seeing several pots and pans that were also knocked down. As he bends down to pick another one up, he hears another set of footsteps in the distance, and he runs back to the locked door and motions for his family to get up.

175

"Hurry up, we're getting out of here."

Sarah, Matt and Ben climb out from under the island just as Curtis smashes a pot into the window above the door, sending glass flying everywhere. After removing as much debris from the opening as possible, he takes off his coat and covers the bottom of the newly-formed hole, then grabs a chair from the corner of the room and places it under the opening.

"Sarah, you first..."

Sarah steps onto the chair, then pauses as she hears the sound of metal and tile colliding only a short distance across the room. She can hear several footsteps coming toward them.

"Go!" Curtis yells as he pushes her through the window, paying no attention as to whether or not she landed safely. He grabs Ben next and lifts him through the opening. As he turns around to help Matt onto the chair, he can see movement coming down the aisle. As Matt sticks his head out, Sarah's arms help him through to the other side, leaving only Curtis in the room to deal with the unwelcome visitors. After jumping onto the chair and reaching out to Sarah, he feels something grab hold of his pant leg in the kitchen. He kicks his leg out, freeing it from their clutch, then pulls himself through, falling onto the concrete sidewalk outside the hotel.

When he gets to his feet and looks back at the window, he sees a young woman with a fresh wound in the middle of her forehead staring back at him. She's trying desperately to pull herself through the window, but she keeps catching herself on the jagged shards of glass around the opening. Curtis can't imagine the amount of pain she must be in from all the cuts and scrapes, but her face shows absolutely no sign of discomfort — and although her attempt is obviously hopeless, she continues to struggle anyway.

Realizing that his coat is still draped over the door, Curtis contemplates whether or not he should try to grab it — but before he

176

gets a chance, the woman pulls it inside. He glances over at Sarah, who looks terrified, then back at the woman, who's still stretching out as far as she can in order to reach him, despite the fact that the glass is piercing into her stomach with every thrust.

"Curtis, lets go," Sarah pleads.

He realizes that this is the first time he's been able to safely approach one of these people. She's stuck, but it seems she's completely unaware of it. He wonders what could possibly be going on in her mind to make her do such a thing. Curious, he turns on his flashlight to get a closer look, but when the beam hits her eyes she screams and pushes herself back inside, leaving part of her flesh hanging on the opening. As soon as she disappears from sight, another person, this time a teenage boy only a few years older than Matt stands in front of the window. His face is without any form of expression either, and even though he's looking in Curtis' direction, you'd swear he was looking right through him.

"Curtis! Come on!" Sarah screams.

It takes him a second to respond, and when he finally does, he sees his wife and sons already running down the sidewalk toward the beach. As he starts to jog down the sidewalk himself, he turns around and shines the flashlight at the kid. His eyes come alive in an instant, and a madness appears, like a rage that's been building up inside of him for years. Then, just like the woman before him, he drops out of sight.

CHAPTER 18
WESTPORT

He's been waiting for what seems like an eternity, although what he's waiting for he can't be certain. Lately his mind has been muddled and foggy, and for days he hasn't been able to focus on anything for more than just a few seconds — that is, until tonight.

When he first spotted the two boys walking with their parents into the Regency, he was surprised to see anybody moving around in the daylight, especially as carefree as they seemed to act. He, along with all of the others in town, had given up on that long ago, choosing instead to travel at night after the burning light of the sun had disappeared from the skies.

Some days he actually misses it — seeing the rays of light shine through the leaves of the trees, or the way it glistens off the breakers in the early evening. For the most part he doesn't miss his life before the sickness though, back when everything seemed miserable and hopeless — although looking back at it now he can't imagine what seemed so bad. He had a job, and a wife, although he can't remember what he did or what his wife's name was. In fact, he's not entirely sure if she's still alive. Probably not though, few are it seems. Truth be told, he's not even one-hundred percent confident in what his own name is.

It wasn't long ago that he still felt fear, and pain. Now he feels nothing but distrust and anger. The agony of not knowing who he is gets easier by the day, and as the memories fade away they're replaced with a flood of unorganized and mostly senseless thoughts that help to fill the emptiness inside of him. More than anything, he needs focus now, something to slow down the disturbing thoughts and images running through his head. Why this family will be any different from any of the others he doesn't yet know, but they're clearly from out of town, and they don't act like everybody else does. As he watches them climb out of the window and onto the sidewalk, he can feel the compulsions start to take over again — this time stronger than before. Hatred begins to course through his veins, with images of their lifeless and mangled bodies taking ownership of his thoughts. Soon they'll be dead, and the voices and fever that's ripping his mind and body apart will die with them.

Running down the sidewalk toward the beach, Curtis can still hear the people behind him as they attempt to scratch and claw their way through the door. By the time they left, the woman who had grabbed his leg was joined by at least two others, both of whom were just as frantic to follow them. Forced to leave his coat behind, he has only a heavy buttoned-down shirt to protect him against the driving rain coming from the direction of the beach.

"What about your coat?" Sarah asks Curtis.

"I'll get another one."

"You're gonna freeze to death before we get back to the cabin, especially out on the beach."

"I'll be fine. We'll start a fire when we get back." He points across the parking lot toward the dunes, where a large thicket of blackberry bushes and scotch broom threaten to choke out the forest of pine trees. "Over there, the seawall is just on the other side."

"I can see the wall ahead of us," Sarah tells him, pointing directly ahead.

The wall is made out of concrete, and thick enough to hold back

179

the tidal surges that occasionally make their way across the dunes. The section of the wall behind the hotel blocks any view of the ocean beyond, and separates the parking lot from the sand and surf on the other side.

"It's too visible, someone might see us there."

After making it across the parking lot without seeing anybody, they finally make it to the thicket just as the rain begins to fall again. Under the pines it stays relatively dry, but the droplets of water cling to the brambles and bushes in between the trees, and only a few feet into the brush Curtis is already soaked from brushing past them.

Their surroundings are turning darker as they travel farther in, no doubt made worse by the clouds that are now blocking the moon once again. Sarah is following from the back, keeping an eye out behind them as they try to avoid the sharp thorns and tangled vines of the blackberries. The only thing that makes it even somewhat bearable is the cushioning sensation from the sandy pathway — a welcome feeling after the miles of torture their feet have been forced to endure over the last three days. As she reaches up to move another vine out of the way, she hears a crack somewhere close-by, like a branch breaking.

"Wait..." she whispers. Curtis and the boys both stop.

"Did you hear something?" asks Curtis.

"I thought I did."

"I heard it too. I think it came from up the beach." They wait another minute or so, but they hear absolutely nothing but the raging ocean in the background, and the wind and rain thrashing against the pines. "It must have been the wind knocking a branch down or something. Let's keep moving."

When they finally approach the wall, the shade from the larger trees that grow on either side of it start to choke out the vines and brush, leaving nothing but a bed of wet needles covering the ground in front of them. The wall itself isn't quite what Sarah expected it to be. She was picturing something substantial, something you would fear to climb over. In reality though, it rises only about six or seven feet above the ground, depending on where you're standing.

"I'm going up first. I have to make sure the other side is clear," Curtis whispers.

"Do you have the binoculars?" Sarah asks.

"They were in my coat."

"I have some," Ben tells him.

As Ben fishes through his backpack for the binoculars, Curtis waves Sarah off to the side, barely out of Matt and Ben's earshot.

"What is it?" she asks.

Curtis hardly looks at her, keeping his eye on the two boys at all times. "Somebody is following us. I heard another crack, and when I looked up I saw someone jump into the shadows."

Sarah reaches into her coat pocket and pulls out the revolver, handing it to Curtis.

"I don't really have a pocket anymore..." he tells her.

"I don't even know how to shoot it."

"Yeah, that makes two of us."

She looks up at him with a puzzled expression on her face.

"I bought it a few months ago, I've never actually used it," he explains.

"You've shot a gun before though..."

"Just a pellet gun. It's not exactly the same thing."

Ben walks up and taps Curtis on the arm. "Dad, I found it."

"Thanks son."

After looping the binocular string around his neck, and placing the gun in the back of his jeans, Curtis steps onto a large boulder and pulls himself up onto the wall, the top of which is covered by a thick coat of moss and algae, giving the surface a slimy feel under his feet.

181

Once he stands up, he finds that the view isn't exactly what he'd hoped for. The rain is obscuring what little visibility there is, and the beach is still hidden behind dozens of sand dunes, none of which look particularly inviting. Worse yet, the ground is several feet lower on the other side, with huge boulders stacked next to the wall along the entire length. There's no way they can jump down safely, at least not here. Curtis drops to his stomach and reaches his arms down the wall toward his family.

"Ben, grab my hands, I'll pull you up."

One by one he helps them onto the wall, feeling safer somehow being away from the thicket.

"We have to walk down the wall a little ways until we find some place to jump down," he tells the others.

The trek isn't an easy one, despite having a wide, somewhat flat surface to walk on. The wall was built to hold back storm surges that from time to time cause extensive damage to the structures along the coast — but it also blocks some of the low moving wind from pouring into the streets of Westport. Every few steps a gust of wind comes out of nowhere, nearly knocking them off of the wall. After being forced to finally crawl on their hands and knees through the onslaught of it, Curtis stops and leans over the edge, noticing that the rocks below are mostly buried in sand.

"Figures," Curtis says, his voice raised over the storm.

"What figures?" asks Sarah.

"The end of the seawall is right up ahead of us," he says, pointing directly in front of them. "We might as well jump from here though, it's hard telling what it's like up there." He wipes some of the slime off of his hands, then motions for Matt to come closer. "I'm gonna jump down. After I do, go ahead and throw all the backpacks down to me. Got it?"

Matt gives him a thumbs up.

182

"Curtis!" Sarah screams.

"What?"

"Where is Ben? Did he jump down already?"

Curtis turns his flashlight on, frantically shining it around on the sand below — but there's no sign of him anywhere. He moves over to the inside of the wall, but all he can see are fallen branches and brush — and then he spots something moving, twenty or so feet from the wall.

"Ben! Is that you?" he yells, but there's no response. He turns to Sarah, who's now searching with her flashlight as well... "I'm going down, keep looking for him."

When he jumps, his right foot lands on a small rock, rolling it over onto his ankle — but he stays upright, refusing to acknowledge the pain. It takes him only seconds to make it to the area that he saw from above. What he finds isn't Ben though — it's a man that's hunched over, looking around at the ground frantically, as if he's lost something.

"Hey!" Curtis yells.

"What?" Sarah answers from behind him.

"Not you. There's a guy down here." The man stands upright, looking at Curtis with a dazed look in his eye. "Have you seen a boy around here?" he asks the man.

"A boy..." the man replies.

"Yes, have you seen a boy around?"

Instead of answering, the man raises his right hand, revealing a large butcher knife.

"Oh God..." Curtis says to himself.

As the man begins staggering toward him, scuffing his feet through the sand and needles with every small step, Curtis aims his gun at the man's head and pulls the trigger twice. The first bullet lands just below his eye socket, ripping a hole in his face before dropping the man to

183

the ground. The second bullet flies past him and into the woods beyond.

"Ben! Where are you?" Curtis yells over the wind.

"Curtis, what's going on?" screams Sarah, who's still on top of the wall behind him.

"I'm alright, just wait up there for a minute."

Curtis approaches the man's corpse carefully, half expecting to see his body come alive and attack. What he finds is more disgusting than terrifying though — a gaping wound pouring blood and brain matter onto the ground, and a dirty and dull knife lying next to him. The only positive thing is that the knife seems to be free of any blood, meaning there's a chance that Ben is still alive.

After Curtis helps Sarah and Matt off of the wall, the three of them search the area thoroughly, but find no trace of Ben anywhere. Feeling sick to his stomach with worry, Matt shines his light up onto the wall, feeling somewhat foolish that he half-expected to see Ben staring back at him. What he sees instead are several bloody scratch marks in the moss and algae below the spot where they were standing.

"Mom, Dad..." says Matt, pointing at the marks.

Sarah gasps and places her hand over her mouth, frozen with fear.

Curtis walks closer and examines the scratches. They're fresh, that much he can tell right away — and big, whoever left them had enormous hands. "These scratches are too big for Ben's hands, that guy must have pulled him down."

"So where is he now?" asks Sarah, her voice shaken.

"He might have ran off, I don't know..."

"Do you think that guy could have dragged him off someplace?"

"I don't think so, he could barely walk."

They stand in silence for a moment, none of them sure what to say, or what to do. Their world, which had started to feel like it was closing in on them, suddenly felt bigger than ever. Ben could be anywhere, and all of them feel helpless to do anything about it.

Sarah starts to walk toward the brush and away from the wall. "We have to do something, we have to go look for him. I can't imagine how scared he must be..."

Curtis wraps his arms around Sarah as she passes by him, and she breaks down in tears, overwhelmed by the stress of the last few hours.

"We will, we'll find him — but we have to split up."

Sarah's heart sinks at even the thought of separating, especially at a time like this. She pushes herself away from Curtis, staring at him with a look of uncertainty. "What do you mean?"

He opens the gun up and replaces the two bullets with fresh ones from his pocket. "There's only two places Ben could have gone — he's either hiding somewhere close-by, or he's already making his way to the cabin. One of us has to stay here and look around..."

"And that means Matt and I are going back to the cabin... without you..."

"I don't see that we have any other choice..."

Curtis extends his hand out to Sarah, and at first she thinks it's to comfort her, until she notices the gun. She takes it without hesitation, placing it in the side pocket of her parka.

"It should only take you a few hours to get back to the cabin as long as you keep moving. If you can help it, don't yell out for Ben, you might attract attention that you don't want. Besides, if he's on the beach he shouldn't be hard to spot."

"And what if he's not at the cabin... what then?"

"Turn off all the lights, stay as quiet as you can, and find the other gun. Ben and I will follow right behind you as soon as I find him." He embraces her again, this time pulling Matt in as well. "Whatever you do, try to stick to the beach, and don't come back to town, no matter what."

CHAPTER 19
COHASSETT BEACH

Hoping that Ben might have come this way, Sarah decides to walk the entire length of the seawall rather than cross it. She's still optimistic that he's running down the beach at this very moment, and that she and Matt will find his footprints in the sand that will lead them directly to him. As they come around the corner of the wall and step foot onto the sandy path that leads to the beach, they can see tracks in the sand illuminated by the moon overhead, but they're not Ben's — at least not all of them anyway. The pathway is well-used, and recently by the looks of it.

"We might want to stay off the trail..." Sarah tells Matt, who nods in agreement.

After studying the footprints and landscape in front of them, they finally settle on what looks like an older path that winds through a grove of pine trees and grass-covered dunes. As they climb to the top of the first dune, the rain finally tapers off to a light shower, then gradually stops altogether, leaving only the gusts of wind for them to deal with — and even that seems to have warmed up over the last several minutes.

Sarah's legs are aching miserably, tortured by the soft, unstable sand under her feet, not to mention the three grueling days of non-stop walking they've endured. The strange thing is, if not for her legs, and the gut-wrenching feeling in her heart, this could actually be a pleasant walk for this time of the year. The air feels warm, the moon is shining bright in the sky, and the sounds and smells of the ocean are starting to overwhelm her senses.

186

She never spent as much time on the coast when she was a child as Curtis did, but she does remember the stormy weekends spent in Seaside with her parents, when they would wake her up in the middle of the night so she and her sister could run on the beach. Those memories of exhilaration stay with you, and there's something in the air tonight that reminds her of back then. The air feels refreshing and crisp.

"Mom, do you think Dad will find Ben?" Matt asks her, bringing her back to reality.

"We might find him first..."

"But if we don't... Do you think he'll bring him home?"

"Of course he will. If Ben is still in town, your dad will find him."

It was a line delivered with as much confidence as she could possibly muster, but it felt like a lie. Westport is a big area, and if Ben ran in any direction besides the beach, it's hard telling where he might have ended up at. It could take Curtis days or even weeks to thoroughly search the town, even if it were empty — and although her mind isn't yet ready to deal with it on a conscious level, deep down she wonders if she'll ever see her son and husband again.

As they reach the top of the next dune, they quickly realize that it's the last one. The only thing between them and the water is one-hundred yards of wet, flat sand and a few scattered pieces of driftwood that were no doubt brought in by the storm.

"Mom, look..." says Matt, pointing down the beach.

Silhouetted against the iridescent waves in the background, Sarah can see two people walking near the water. At first glance she can't tell if they're sick or not, but they're walking up the beach in their direction.

"Lets wait here a minute, we don't want them to see us."

They crouch down, then watch as the two figures make their way up the coastline only twenty feet apart from one another, each one

187

seemingly unaware that the other exists. The one nearest the water keeps falling down as the waves come crashing in, but their struggles don't draw the least bit of attention from the other. The one falling down seems unfazed as well, showing no signs of changing course to prevent another wave from crashing into them.

"Why does he keep doing that? Why doesn't he move?" whispers Matt.

"I don't know sweety. I think they've gone crazy."

"From the virus?"

"I think so."

Sarah watches as the waves finally overtake the one figure, their body vanishing as the water is sucked back into the undertow. Hoping that Matt hadn't noticed it too, she tugs at his shirt.

"Come on, lets stick to the dunes for a while. It's gonna be all night before the other one passes by."

They walk south across the dunes, always staying within view of the ocean. All around them they can see flashes of lightning, filling the air with the muffled sound of thunder in the distance. The trees to their left have now disappeared, and in their place they can see the beach-houses that make up the southern portion of town, a mixture of new and old homes clustered uncomfortably together. In the distance behind them is a series of wind turbines in the hills east of the city, their propellers locked in place and glowing bright white against the dark skies. They walk in silence for a while, both of them exhausted, but unable to shut out the thoughts running through their heads. Then after about twenty minutes, Matt finally speaks up.

"Things are never going to be the same, are they?"

"The same as what?"

"Before the virus. Like they were when we still lived at home..."

"No, things will never be the same."

"Do you think there's anyone out there like us?"

"You mean people that aren't sick?"

"Yeah."

"I suppose so."

"Do you think they'll find us?"

"Maybe someday, after the virus has run its course."

Matt returns to silence again, which Sarah is perfectly fine with. She knows he has questions, but she doesn't know how to explain to him that there are no answers, at least none that she knows about.

"Get down!" Sarah whispers, pulling Matt down to the ground with her.

"What?"

"Do you see something over there, in front of that farthest dune?"

She points ahead of them and slightly to the west, where they can barely see a hint of movement where the sand flattens out.

"Yeah, I see them."

"How many do you see?"

He begins to softly count out loud, making Sarah nervous as the number continues to grow.

"It looks like fourteen, but there might be more behind them. I can't see that far."

"We need to move, they'll pass right next to us if they keep walking in the same direction."

She starts looking around for places they could hide, but the dunes have flattened out in this area, and the trees were cut down years ago to provide views for the homes and hotels along the highway, leaving them completely in the open. The only place close-by that she can see is an older single-story house that sits less than a hundred yards from where they're hiding.

"Come on, lets try to make it to that house up there..."

As they run across the dunes, their heads slouched low to the ground, they can start to make out the faint noises coming from the

189

group on the beach. Some of it sounds vaguely like conversation, but most of it is unintelligible moans and hollering.

When they reach the house, Matt ducks behind an old half-painted rocking bench that looks as though it hasn't been used in years, then makes room for his mother. After making sure they haven't been followed, Sarah reaches up and tries turning the door handle, hoping that it's unlocked like so many other homes they've been to over the last two days. When she finds that isn't the case, she starts to move across the covered deck to make her way to the front, motioning for Matt to follow — but just as she steps away, she hears a clicking sound coming from the door, followed by squeaking hinges as the heavy wooden door slowly opens. She looks at Matt, then at the beach, where she can see the hazy outline of people making their way across the dunes.

"What do you think, should we risk it?" she asks Matt.

"You should get the gun out first."

With the gun held behind her back, she slips through the doorway and into a large living room. The temperature inside is surprisingly warm, and then she spots the small wood stove crackling in the far corner. The room is also heavily decorated in a nautical theme, complete with glass floats on the coffee table, netting on the walls, and even an anchor hanging precariously over the couch — an oddly dangerous place to put one, Sarah can't help but think. It would be cozy other than the fact that something smells horrible, something that Sarah can't quite place through the array of other scents assaulting her senses. It's not the woodsmoke, or extensive amount of perfume that seems to be coming from everywhere — this is something foul. Whatever it is, it's strong enough to nearly send her running back outside just to get away from it. What she doesn't see, or hear, is the person that unlocked the door for them.

As soon as Matt enters, she shuts the door behind them, once again immersing the room in nearly total darkness — the only light coming from the dim flames of the wood stove. Making sure that the blinds on the windows are sufficiently tight, she turns her flashlight on and looks around the room — but she still doesn't see anyone.

"Hello? Is anyone here?" she says in a normal volume, but still nothing. "Thank you for letting us in. We don't mean to intrude, we just wanted to stay for a little while..." Matt steps casually into the room a couple of steps, but Sarah pushes him next to the door again, shaking her head at him.

"Were you followed?" comes a voice from somewhere in the room. It sounds like a woman, but her voice is slightly raspy.

"No, but there are people on the beach," answers Sarah.

"You can stay for a while, but you have to turn your light out first."

"I'm not sure that I'm comfortable doing that."

"I can light a candle if it makes you feel better — but no flashlights."

Sarah considers arguing with her, but this *is* her house, and the woman certainly doesn't sound like the others they've come across. Instead, she shuts off her light as the woman requested, knowing that if she keeps her talking she can still track her location in the room.

"Are you alone in here?" Sarah asks her.

"Just me and my husband," the woman replies from across the room.

"Oh, I hope we didn't wake you up... I know it's late."

"No trouble at all. I was still up myself." Sarah hears drawers opening and closing, this time coming from the next room.

"It's quite a storm we're..." Sarah stops mid-sentence as the woman enters the room from the kitchen, holding two candlesticks, each one holding three burning candles. She's older than Sarah pictured her. If she had to guess, she'd probably say she was in her mid-eighties to ninety, but it's hard to tell in the dim lighting.

191

"Come in and sit for a while. You can hang your coats up by the door," she says in a grandmotherly tone.

Sarah slips the gun into the pocket of her parka, then moves cautiously into the room, keeping a close eye on the woman as Matt and her sit down on a couch near the wood stove. The woman sets both candlesticks down on the table in front of them, and then stands on the other side and looks the two of them over. Sarah can't help but notice that her clothes are filthy.

"You don't want to take off your coats? They look like they're soaking wet..."

"Thank you, but we'd rather keep them on if it's okay with you."

The woman looks at her suspiciously, and then a warm smile suddenly comes across her face as she sits down in a badly worn-out chair that faces them.

"As long as you're comfortable."

The next several seconds feel like hours as the three of them sit in an awkward silence. Sarah wonders to herself what exactly is appropriate to talk about in a situation like this.

"Where are the two of you from?" the woman asks, breaking the silence. "I haven't seen you around before..."

"We're from Portland. We moved here a couple of weeks ago."

"My husband was originally from Portland, lovely city."

"Is your husband asleep? I don't want to wake him up."

The woman gives her another warm smile. "So it's just the two of you, all by yourselves out here?"

Sarah can't help but feel that she's avoiding the question, and just before she asks the question again, it finally dawns on her what the smell is that's permeating the house — someone in the house is dead.

"My husband is back at the house with our other son," Sarah replies. She smiles at the woman, then reaches into her pocket and grips the gun in her hand, just in case. "Are you doing okay here? Do

192

you still have food?"

The woman laughs. It's a soft, kind-hearted laugh, but it's followed by a weak cough that sends chills up Sarah's spine.

"What a strange question to ask... Of course I have food," the woman answers. "Why on earth would you ask me that?"

Sarah hesitates, not sure of how to respond. "I uh... you know, considering what it's like in town... I just figured you might be running low, that's all."

"Oh, what's going on in town?" she asks innocently.

Sarah glances over at Matt, who's looking at the woman with the same level of skepticism as she feels.

"We really should get going, I'm sure my husband is probably worried sick by now." Sarah stands up and starts to step away from the couch, with Matt right behind her. "Thank you so much for letting us in."

With a scowl on her face, the woman stands up out of her chair, blocking the only clear pathway to the door. The only other way out is to jump over the couch and the table that sits behind it, something that Sarah briefly considers.

"Let me get the door for you," the woman says. The smile returns, but it's different somehow. Her eyes have a wicked glint in them, like she knows that something horrible is about to happen.

She walks to the door slowly, her steps frail and unbalanced. Sarah is hoping that it's due to her age and not the illness, but she has her doubts. When she finally gets to the door, she places her hand on the knob and pauses, then reaches up to the deadbolt and locks it.

Sarah immediately takes a quick step back and pulls the gun out of her pocket — but instead of aiming it, she keeps it at her side, hoping that the woman is simply confused.

"Ma'am, I think you just locked the door..."

At first she doesn't respond, she just stands there looking at the

193

doorknob — then she turns around and looks at Sarah, her smile even more evil than before.

"I wish you wouldn't go, you only just got here..." Her voice is still pleasant sounding, even charming.

"We can come back soon, but we have to get home before it gets too late."

"I'm afraid that's not going to happen, dear."

Sarah aims the gun at the woman's head and cocks the hammer, bracing her feet against the floor just as Curtis showed her.

"Open the door, now!" she yells at the woman.

The woman looks at her with a confused look, then begins walking toward them in small, delicate steps.

"Don't come any closer!" Sarah screams at her, taking another step back.

"Mom, shoot her!" Matt yells.

Before Sarah can react, the woman lunges forward with surprising speed and throws her hand at Sarah, hitting her first in the leg, and then in the arm that's carrying the gun. The blows were thrown so hard that the woman ends up falling to the floor, landing flat on her back.

Initially Sarah thinks the woman merely smacked her, and then she notices the blood running down her arm. It's only then that she looks down and spots the knife in the woman's hand.

"Mom, the gun!" Matt yells, pointing to the floor.

She scans the floor, looking for a gun that the woman must have dropped — but it's not the woman's gun that she sees, it's her own. She must have dropped it somehow in the attack without realizing it. When the woman sees it herself, she reaches out for it — but Sarah is able to kick it away just in time, sending it gliding across the hardwood and underneath a dresser on the other side of the room.

The old woman is now furious, slashing at Sarah with the knife as

194

she attempts to stand-up. As Matt chases after the gun by jumping over the couch, Sarah picks up a large picture book off the coffee table and smashes it over the woman's head, knocking her out instantly. When she looks up, she sees Matt standing on the other side of the woman with tears running down his face, and the gun aimed squarely at the woman's head.

"Matt, don't!"

"Why not? She tried to kill you!"

"I know, but you can't shoot her, it'll make too much noise. Give me the gun..."

He keeps his distance from the woman as he walks around her, and then hands the gun back to Sarah. After taking it, she aims it at the woman's head herself.

"Go see if you can find something we can tie her up with."

"Why don't we just leave?"

"I don't think we can. I can hardly feel my leg."

Matt had already seen his mom's bleeding arm, but in all the chaos and confusion he'd somehow missed the gash right below her knee, a cut that was now spilling blood down the front of her jeans and onto the floor. With a new sense of desperation, he makes his way toward the kitchen, a feeling of determination building inside of him as he passes in front of the hallway beside the kitchen — and then he stops.

"What's wrong?" asks Sarah.

"I thought I heard something."

And then she hears it too.

A thump.

Coming from down the hall.

CHAPTER 20
WESTPORT

After a night of shivering and numbness from the cold, damp air and wet clothes that cover his body, Curtis starts to feel a little better now that he's walking down the highway in the direction of town.

He'd searched every foot of the pathway leading back to the hotel, and then backtracked and followed yet another trail that twisted through a narrow forest of thick, overgrown shrubs and trees — eventually making his way back to the highway only a couple of blocks from the Regency. Throughout all of that searching, he never found a single trace of Ben.

As deeply concerning as all of that is, he considers his newly found comfort level just as troubling. There's no logical reason for him to feel warm, not on a night like this, and certainly not when you're soaking wet and wearing nothing but a tee-shirt and jeans. He knows that he's developing hypothermia, and if he doesn't find a place to dry off soon, his search for Ben could very well end with his body lying in a mud puddle or leaned up against a building in the middle of town. He can't let something like that happen, not as long as his wife and sons are still at risk.

He keeps to the other side of the road as he passes by the front entrance of the hotel, trying to stay in the shadows of the towering fir trees overhead. At least a dozen people are still outside, most of them still staring through the windows as they slam their fists against the glass — all of this despite the front door sitting wide-open for all to see.

Madness has taken every last one of them, and for a moment he

196

wonders if the same thing will eventually happen to his own family —
their minds slowly slipping away, pushing away what little sanity is
still left. These people have become something less than human, less
than even wild animals.

As he tries to shake the thought from his mind, he finds himself
standing once again in the middle of Forrest Street with the center of
town directly in front of him, unsure of where to go or what to do
first. The fact that he's standing in plain view of everyone in town
doesn't even cross his mind.

Walking down the road, his arms crossed to preserve what little
heat he has left, he starts yelling out for Ben, not caring if anybody
else hears him or not. And then he sees something, a flash of
movement coming from an alley beside a local tavern. He stops and
watches the alley, calling out for Ben at the top of his lungs before
heading in that direction, his legs beginning to buckle from the lack
of blood-flow to his nerves.

He gets almost to the front steps of the tavern before he realizes
that the movement he saw didn't actually come from his son, but
from a young man in his teens or early twenties instead. The look in
his eyes and the expression on his face are just like the others Curtis
has seen, cold and vacant, but somehow filled with hate at the same
time. As the man begins walking toward him, Curtis hears the sound
of rustling leaves and crunching gravel coming from behind him.
Turning around, he can see dozens of people emerging from the
storefronts and alleyways up and down Forrest Street, all of them
with the same bloodthirsty look, and every one of them drawing
closer.

Although they're approaching him from seemingly every angle,
none of them are moving with any sense of urgency or speed. Seeing
only one graveled side street with nobody in it, Curtis takes off in an
uncoordinated run that still manages to out-pace the people

following him.

The street, which is little more than an unpaved alley, is also covered in darkness, shadowed by the old brick buildings on either side of it. Deep potholes and standing water from the rain earlier in the night cover at least half of its surface. Even though Curtis can't see anything through the obscurity of fog behind him, he can hear the crunching of footsteps over loose gravel as the people move closer.

"Over here..." someone whispers from the shadows to his right.

Worried that the mob behind him might soon catch up, and knowing that none of the people he's encountered so far seem capable of talking, he decides to take his chances by following the voice. Walking in silence, he can hear their faint footsteps as they lead him to an unmarked doorway that's been left open just a crack. Before entering, he takes one last look behind him, where he can barely make out a stream of featureless silhouettes only twenty feet away. All of them are passing by without a glance.

Once he steps inside the building, the door slowly creaks shut again, engulfing the room in total darkness.

"Who's there?" Curtis calls out.

"Shh, they'll hear you..." comes a small, frail voice. It sounds like the voice of a child.

They both keep quiet for a few minutes as the mob passes by outside the door. Curtis doesn't really know what to expect from whoever he's standing next to, but whoever they are, he's glad they cared enough to risk their life for him. He can't say that he would've done the same thing if the roles were reversed.

"Okay, I think it's safe again," the voice says.

"Can I turn my light on?"

"Not here, come with me..."

He feels a small, warm hand grasp his own, pulling him farther into the room and then down a long, dimly lit corridor. As they pass by the rooms on either side, each of them looking like sparsely decorated bedrooms, Curtis suddenly knows where he's at. This building was once used as a sanitarium during the smallpox and Spanish flu outbreaks almost a century ago. After that it sat abandoned for decades, serving only as a tourist attraction for the few people that enjoyed seeing such things. Curtis remembers taking the tour as a kid with his father, but it looks different somehow, like people had actually started living here again.

Curtis can tell that whoever is guiding him is short, and probably quite young. When they reach the end of the hallway, they stop and turn around, letting go of his hand as soon as they do. "Okay, we're safe here. You can turn on your light."

When he does, the first thing that he sees is the reflection coming from a large butcher knife, the handle of which is held tightly in the hand of a young girl standing in front of him. She's wearing an unbuttoned black winter coat over a heavily-stained white laced dress that looks like it could be homemade — and her long black hair almost covers her entire face. On the side of her cheek, just under her left ear, is what appears to be a spot of dried blood. When he glances down at the knife in her hand, he sees the same thing covering most of the blade.

"How old are you?" he asks her.

"Twelve."

"Are your mom and dad around?"

She hangs her head slightly, then shakes it. When she looks up at him again, she speaks to him so softly that he can barely understand what she's saying. "You look cold..."

Curtis smiles. "Yes, I am cold."

"I saw clothes in some of the drawers..." she points inside the closest room, where Curtis spots a small upright dresser beside the bunk-beds.

199

"Thanks. I'm Curtis by the way." He holds out his hand.

"I'm Amanda," she answers back, shaking his hand.

As Curtis sits on the edge of a bed with a blanket wrapped around his otherwise naked body, Amanda is busy digging through the dressers of the various rooms, piling items of clothing onto the mattress next to him. He's trying his best not to fall asleep — but between the warmth of the room, the hypothermia he's still suffering from, and the almost complete lack of sleep he's had over the past few days, he's finding it more and more difficult not to lay his head on the pillow next to him and crash for a day or two.

Determined to stay awake, he decides to focus on what to change into from the mountain of clothing options lying beside him. As he starts picking through them one by one, he discovers that every single piece belongs to women. Not one mens shirt, jeans or underwear is anywhere to be found.

Then he remembers.

Last time he was in town, which was a few years back, he'd noticed that the building had been converted into a home for battered women. A fitting purpose for a building that had seen its fair share of unfortunate souls cross its threshold.

"Amanda?"

In just a few seconds she pops her head into the room, carrying a fresh pile of clothes in her hands. "Yes?"

"Did you notice that all of these clothes are for women?"

"Yes."

"Have you seen any for men?"

"No. Did you want me to stop looking?"

"These will be fine. I'll find something that'll work."

200

After finding a pair of thick sweatpants and a more or less gender-neutral sweatshirt, he turns his flashlight off again to change his clothes — hoping that Amanda couldn't see as much in the dark as he feared.

"How long have you been alone?" he asks her.

"I don't know."

"Have you been eating?"

"There's cereal in the cupboards, and the house across the street has cans of fruit."

"What about water?"

"There's a barrel down the street."

Curtis stops dressing himself for a minute, surprised to hear that she walks around the neighborhood.

"You go out there by yourself?"

"Sometimes."

As much as he wants to know everything that she knows, Curtis worries about pressing her for too much information — but after talking to her over the last few minutes, he's amazed at how well she's handling all that's happened. Maybe it's just shock though. Either way, he decides to turn on the flashlight again and push a little farther...

"Did people become like that all at once, or did it happen a little bit at a time?"

"A little bit at a time."

"Are there any others like you in town?"

She shakes her head.

"Do you know how many sick people there are?"

She shrugs.

He knows it's a long-shot, but has to ask her anyway. "Have you seen a boy in town? He's a little younger than you..."

This time she nods.

"Can you describe him?"

201

"His name is Ben."

Instantly his heart starts pounding, and then the room starts to spin as he processes this new information. Eventually his more rational side begins to take over though, and he starts to doubt everything she's said. Maybe he already mentioned Ben to her, and he's just forgotten about it. Maybe she's only playing games with him now. Or maybe she heard him yelling his name out on the street earlier. At this point anything is possible.

"Do you know what he looks like?" he asks, trying not to sound over excited.

"He has a green backpack, and a yellow coat."

Now he knows it has to be Ben. That's exactly what he was wearing.

"When did you see him? Did you talk to him?"

"He's hiding in a building down by the harbor."

"Did you hide him there?"

She nods.

"Can you take me there?"

She nods again.

Curtis stands up, feeling just how weak his legs have gotten for the first time, then turns the flashlight onto Amanda to get a better look at her. She doesn't look the least bit sick or scared, just tired. Everything she does though, whether it's carrying clothes or buttoning up her coat, is done with the butcher knife squeezed tightly in her hand, her constant companion.

She reminds him of his daughter Annie when she was younger. Her hair is the same jet-black color, running perfectly straight almost down to her lower back, and the way she carries herself, as if she's merely observing the world around her, and not actually taking part in it. The only thing that's unlike Annie is how much she talks. Amanda doesn't, at least not very much.

Still, he can't imagine what she's probably been through over the last few months, living in a practically deserted town that's overrun by lunatics hellbent on killing anyone they make eye contact with. Also, considering that these same lunatics used to be the residents of the town, she might actually know some of them — or at least she used to. Pity doesn't even begin to describe what he feels for her.

"Did your parents get sick?" he asks her.

She nods. "And my brother."

"And you never did?"

She shakes her head.

"Did you want to come and stay with my family?"

She doesn't react at first, she just stares at him — and then finally she gives him a slight nod.

Curtis smiles, then strokes the filthy mess of tangled hair on top of her head. "Good, that's settled. Now lets go find Ben so we can go home."

As the two of them make their way out of the shelter, Amanda leading the way, she takes him on a winding course through the streets, staying in the shadows almost the entire trip.

"Ben said that you live in Cohasset..." Amanda says out of the blue, after staying completely quiet ever since leaving the shelter.

"Not too far from there. We have a cabin up in the woods."

"My mom is in Aberdeen, Ben said he would go with me to find her."

Curtis isn't sure what to say, the idea is obviously ridiculous. "Maybe once we're back together, we'll see about finding your mom, all of us."

Without reacting, Amanda stops and waits inside of a shadow, then peeks around the corner of the building to get a look at the street beyond. Then she draws back and stands beside Curtis.

"Did you see something?" he whispers.

"No, not yet." she says in a normal voice.

Curtis isn't sure what she means by that, but he decides not to question her any further about it. She might be young, but so far she seems to be far better at concealing herself than he is.

"Did you see us walking around earlier this afternoon?" he asks her.

"Yes."

"Why didn't we see any of these people? Were they hiding?"

"They don't come out in the day. The sun hurts their eyes."

As strange and fabricated as her explanation sounds, it actually makes sense in a way — they've yet to see anyone walking around during the day. Some form of stupid, clumsy vampires sounds more plausible than anything he's been able to come up with.

"I'm still trying to figure out why Ben didn't go back to the cabin like we talked about. He must have gotten turned around..."

"He tried to go back, but I talked him out of it."

"Why?"

"The beach isn't safe. Not at night."

A desperate feeling of doom washes over Curtis as he thinks about Sarah and Matt walking down a beach covered with the infected souls of Westport. They never should have split up.

"Okay, I think it's safe now." Amanda tells him after peeking once again.

They walk right around the corner and stop in front of a beat-up sliding garage door that has 'Leo's Auto Repair' scrawled across it in faded red ink. Amanda reaches inside of her coat and pulls out a key, and then opens the padlock on the latch and turns the handle.

"He's inside," she tells Curtis.

"Aren't you coming in?"

"No, I'll wait out here."

"Okay, but leave the door open, just in case..."

She nods.

Turning his flashlight on again, he slides the door open just far

204

enough to squeeze through, trying not to make too much sound, then sticks his head through the door and looks around.

"Where is he at exactly?"

"Upstairs."

He pushes himself through the door and walks quietly across the concrete floor, the smell of gasoline so strong in the room it burns his eyes. Then he hears a rumble coming from behind him, and he looks back just in time to see Amanda's small frame closing the door — and then a click as the lock snaps shut.

"Amanda!" he hollers, running back to the door. "Amanda, can you hear me?" As he tries to open it again his flashlight falls to the floor and goes out, leaving only the pale light from the moon visible through the small windows. Despite putting all of his body weight against it, the door won't budge. "Amanda!" he screams louder.

"I wouldn't yell so loud," he hears from the other side of the door.

"Open the door Amanda, this isn't funny."

"They'll hear you..."

"Who will hear me?"

"The people upstairs."

CHAPTER 21
GRAYS HARBOR

The idea of dying at sea had never really crossed Larry's mind before. Although he'd spent most of his adult life working on fishing boats from Alaska to California, he'd never been placed in a position where he truly felt his life was at risk.

Tonight, however, was different.

Attempting to pass over the Westport bar during a heavy winter storm has always been considered a long-shot, even to the most experienced of pilots — but doing so when your only real source of propulsion is the storm surge at your back was almost certain suicide. He felt foolish for risking his own life, and guilty for risking his sister's.

Of all of his experience up and down the Pacific coastline, he'd never actually crossed the bar at Westport before, and he'd never crossed any bar during conditions like tonight — especially with a boat that was sinking lower into the water with every passing mile. By the time they reached the meeting waters, where the eastbound currents of the ocean and the westbound currents of the harbor converge, the controls were getting sluggish, almost to the point of being unresponsive.

Larry wasn't alone in his assessment of the situation. Mortality was on all of their minds as they grew closer to the harbor — and every time the next surge would lift them into the air, time seemed to slow down ever so slightly, giving all of them a feeling of surreality that was only intensified by the weightlessness they felt when the boat would drop back down only moments later.

206

When they finally enter the swirling currents just inside the bar, instead of rushing full-speed into the debris field like they feared, the boat actually slows down, hampered by the movement of the river-fed harbor under the surface. It then gently bumps its way through the mass of logs, kelp and who knows what else, until at last the current begins to flow westward against them. As the boat slows further and straightens itself into the wide channel in front of them, Larry lets out a huge sigh of relief, knowing that can only mean one thing — they've officially entered Grays Harbor, a body of water that in only a short time will become the final resting place for 'Larry's Obsession'.

Whether they wish it or not.

As the storm surge fades away into the mouth of the harbor behind them, Larry eases up his grip on the wheel slowly, his arms and hands shaking from the physical and mental stress of the last several hours. Then he turns to Beth and Jake, giving them a slight smile before returning his gaze back the harbor.

"Is it over?" Beth asks him.

"Not quite. We're still sinking," says Larry, who switches off the few lights they still have on, leaving them in darkness once again, except for the subtle glow from the moon overhead. "I'm gonna try to get to the marina in Westport, it's our best bet."

"Is that it over there?" Jake asks, pointing to a large marina barely visible to their right.

"Yeah, that's it."

"There's something moving on the docks..." Jake says, squinting at a cluster of dark silhouettes on the closest dock.

"It's people," responds Beth. "A lot of them."

As Larry guides the boat straight ahead and past the town of Westport, Jake and Beth watch out the side window as dozens of people stream out of the darkness and onto the wooden decking of the marina, all of them seemingly staring directly at them.

"What do you want us to do?" asks Jake, who's glancing through a small window behind him, aware once again that Sean is still following them. He doesn't see any sign of him though. Instead, he sees the breakers they crossed over just moments ago, crashing against the outgoing water, their tops glistening a bluish-white sparkle from the moonlight overhead — and behind them, barely visible, is another bank of thick, black clouds rolling toward them in the distance.

"Why don't you guys go down below and make sure everything is still ready to go. I'm gonna try to make it to the docks up the harbor a few miles," replies Larry.

With the worst of it now behind them, Jake and Beth step down onto the lower deck, exhausted and anxious at the same time, both of them still uncertain as to what the future holds in store for them. The last time they spent an entire night on land seems like a lifetime ago, and the thought of sleeping in a house, even if it was somebody else's, seemed almost too good to be true.

As they both try to untangle the mess of floats and seat cushions thrown around during the voyage, Beth hears something splashing in the water over the side, like they're dragging something. Looking overboard, she sees an image that will forever haunt her.

A string of corpses, a couple dozen of them in all, are tangled in a ball of kelp that's now hanging off of the side of the boat. Most have been dead a long time, half-eaten by fish and whatever else happens to be in the water — all but one that is. The closest body looks recent, a young boy with blond hair whose vacant gaze is aimed directly at the sky above. Beth can't help but stare at him. She wonders who the boy is, and where he came from. Most of all she wonders how he ended up all the way out here, tossed out like a piece of trash. Just the thought of it sends a chill down her spine.

When Beth finally looks away, she sees Jake standing beside her, also looking down at the boy — his face pale and withdrawn. Then, without saying a word, he wraps one arm around Beth's shoulder and squeezes it. There was really nothing to say, nothing that makes sense anyway.

Looking down once again, and trying not to look at the bodies, Beth clears her throat enough to speak, hoping that her voice sounds confident. "What should we do about this?"

"There's nothing to do. We're sinking, let them sink with us."

"Where do you think they came from?"

"I'm not even sure I want to know..."

"Did you notice how dark it is over there?"

"Over where?"

She points slightly ahead of them, where the hills to the north look as black as night. "Do you know what's over there?"

It suddenly dawns on him what she's talking about. "Yeah, Aberdeen."

He's right — just beyond the North Bay, almost the entire north shore of Grays Harbor is taken up by the twin cities of Hoquiam and Aberdeen — both of them major population centers for the central Washington coast. Normally the lights can be seen for miles around.

"You'd never know they were even there, would you?" she asks.

Jake doesn't say anything, he just stares at the dark void beyond, still clutching his wife closely. He can't help but think about his brother, Mark, who was still in Anchorage last he'd heard — and their mother Susan, who had moved to San Francisco only a few months ago to work for a marketing firm there. The last time he'd talked to either one of them was shortly before the virus struck. Now, looking over the cold, dark waters of the harbor, toward a city that now lies silent and empty, he knows deep down that his brother and mother are most likely dead.

209

Realizing this for the first time, he should feel something. He should be overcome with grief and heartache, knowing that his entire family is likely gone, but he doesn't feel any of that. Too much has happened in too short of a timespan to feel anything but fatigue and hopelessness. He's tired of running, tired of searching for something or someplace that he knows doesn't exist. The world has gone mad, and he figures the sooner they come to terms with that fact the better off they'll be.

Jake feels something else as well, just under the surface, something he hasn't mentioned to Beth or Larry. It's a strange sense of mental or emotional numbness that seems to get worse with every passing day. He wonders if that's how the virus begins, by slowly robbing you of your humanity, before finally turning you into the mindless shells that they've seen wandering around on the streets. Or maybe it's shock, and it's merely his brain's way of telling him that all of this is too much to handle. Whatever it is, his natural instinct is to fight it, an instinct that's beginning to lose the battle.

"Jake..."

He turns to see Beth staring behind him, pointing toward the sandbar they just crossed, a look of terror intensifying in her eyes. He turns and looks in the same direction, but he doesn't see anything.

"What is it? I don't see any..."

And then he sees it, a black spot silhouetted against the moon, and the occasional glint of light reflecting off of its front windshield as it bobs up and down across the harbor. He immediately shuts off his flashlight, then motions for Beth to do the same.

"Do you think that's him?" asks Beth.

"It could be someone from Westport... or maybe some sort of patrol from Aberdeen."

"I'd better tell Larry."

Beth climbs up the ladder and into the pilothouse, where she finds

210

Larry starting to nod off at the wheel. She can't blame him, not after everything they've been through.

"We've got a situation..."

Larry straightens up, startled and slightly embarrassed. "What is it?"

"Someone is behind us, with no lights."

"Are they following us?"

"I can't tell, but they seem to be heading in the same direction."

"Take the wheel for a minute..."

As Beth takes his place at the helm, Larry grabs a pair of binoculars and stands in the doorway, looking out at the harbor beyond. It doesn't take him long to see the boat, a small cuddy cabin that's heading directly toward them.

"Do you see it?" asks Beth.

"Yeah..." he replies, still looking through the binoculars.

"Can you tell who they are?"

"It's Sean," he says in a matter-of-fact, almost calm voice.

Beth has to remind herself to breathe as she processes what Larry just told her. "What do we do?"

"I think he's gaining on us, I can't tell for sure." He glances down at the instrument cluster, and at the blinking red light that indicates that the boat is taking on too much water. He knows what they have to do, but he's having a hard time saying it. This boat was supposed to be his life.

"Larry! What are we supposed to do?" Beth asks again, her voice becoming desperate.

"We have to abandon the boat, it's our only chance."

"Should I stop?"

"No, we'll keep the boat running, it might buy us some time. Just hold course for a minute."

He drops the binoculars down to his chest, then grabs two bungee

211

cords from the floor and places them on the steering wheel. He stretches each one to either side of the cabin, locking the wheel in place.

"Let's go, we don't have much time," he tells Beth.

As they both climb down the ladder, Jake can tell from the look on Beth's face that the news isn't good.

"We're leaving," Larry tells him.

Jake doesn't need to hear anything else. He bends over and grips the tangled mess of netting, supplies and safety rings in his hands, lifting one end of the heap over the side of the boat. Larry and Beth grab the other end, and the three of them slowly lower the supplies into the water, careful not to let go of them just yet. "Beth, go ahead and jump in," Larry tells her.

As she makes her way onto the side of the boat and slips into the frigid water below, Larry and Jake drop the supplies all the way overboard. Only seconds later, as Beth swims for the brightly colored safety rings in front of her, Jake jumps in and starts to make his way toward her. When she reaches the closest ring, she loops her arm through it, afraid of letting go of everything in the world that they still possess. She looks up and sees Larry standing on the side of the boat, trying to tie an extra life preserver around his waist — then she hears a loud crack from somewhere in the distance, and she watches as Larry's body falls into the ice-cold water below, leaving behind a trail of blood streaming down the side of the boat.

"Larry!" she screams at the top of her lungs. As she starts to scream again, Jake grabs her from behind, covering her mouth with one hand, while using his other to control her struggling body.

"Shh, we don't want him hearing us..."

She forces herself to settle down once again, as her nerves begin to go numb from the shock of the near-freezing water of the harbor. As Jake watches for Sean's boat to appear somewhere through the mist,

212

Beth looks in the other direction, hoping for a sign that Larry is still alive. All she can see, however, is their own boat disappearing into the fog, like some sort of ghost ship fading away into the darkness.

"Duck down," Jake whispers.

They both lower their heads into the water as Sean's flashlight scans the area above them. When it finally goes away, they reemerge again, seeing just a glimpse of Sean's boat following 'Larry's Obsession' farther upstream in the direction of the Chehalis River.

"Come on, we need to get to shore..." says Jake.

"What about Larry?"

"Beth, he's dead. You saw the blood..."

"We have to find him!" she cries out, her voice quivering from the cold.

"We need to get out of the water before we freeze to death."

He searches through the bags tied to the tangle, finding two backpacks that he removes and ties to his arm instead. Then he turns around and faces the shore, surprised to see the outline of downtown Aberdeen from where they're at. It looks unreal, like a drawing sketched by a madman — a dark gray silhouette of buildings and streets that are barely visible, and a single light, barely visible on the hill behind the town.

213

CHAPTER 22
COHASSETT BEACH

Matt can hear the thumping even clearer now than before, sounding as though it's coming from a room halfway down the corridor in front of him. There's no rhythm to it whatsoever, it's just a random bump, followed by a faint scratching noise that sends chills up his spine — like fingernails slowly making their way down a chalkboard. As he takes a step into the hall toward it, he hears his mother from the other room speaking to him.

"Wait, come here," she whispers, barely loud enough for him to hear.

He had a feeling she wouldn't approve of him going to check it out alone. She still thinks of him as a kid, her baby boy, but he feels different now — more mature. As much as the last few days seem like a blur in his mind, the years preceding them seem even more distant, almost as if the memories of his childhood had happened to someone else.

As he makes his way back into the living room, fully intending to argue with her over whether or not he was ready for something like this, he's surprised to see her holding the gun out for him to take.

"You might need this..." she tells him. "But be careful."

Matt reaches out and takes the gun from her, placing it at his side like his father had shown him. "I will."

As she watches him turn around and walk away, she whispers... "Don't use it unless you have to, and hurry up."

Matt nods at her, then rounds the corner and enters the hallway, mindful to keep his unsteady finger off of the trigger of the revolver.

With his hands shaking, he turns on the flashlight, instantly questioning whether that was a good idea or not, but he decides to leave it on anyway.

There are only three doors in the short and narrow space, one on the end and one on each side. The noises are coming from the one on the left, and he can tell immediately that something doesn't look right, the door looks different somehow. When he reaches the middle of the hall it becomes obvious what it is — someone has crudely nailed a fence board to either side of the opening, then tied a rope between the board and the doorknob, creating a primitive but effective barricade. As he approaches the door, a floorboard under his foot creaks, alerting his presence to whatever is on the other side. Now, in addition to pounding and scratching against the hollow-cored door, they begin to frantically twist the knob, pulling it against the rope in a futile attempt to escape.

Their breathing sounds slightly labored, but not raspy like the other people in town, and he can hear them speaking faintly — words that are almost loud enough to make out, but not quite. The voice sounds deep and masculine.

Matt carefully backs up, not wanting to arouse too much attention from whoever they are, then he heads back into the living room again, where his mom is busy tying the old woman up with a white cord. She has her sitting in the chair, her wrists fastened to the arm cushions, and the back of the chair bound to an antique dresser in the corner of the room just in case she tries tipping forward. She also has a long scarf wrapped around the woman's mouth, blocking most of her face.

"You found something?" Matt asks her.

"Telephone cord," she replies, holding up the end of it, where the phone is still attached.

"Will it hold her?"

215

"If it doesn't, we'll shoot her."

She finishes the knot, then scoots across the floor on her butt and leans back against the couch, admiring her handiwork.

"What'd you find down the hall?" she asks.

"I think it's a guy, he's locked in one of the rooms."

"Can he get out?"

"I don't think so."

Sarah grabs the couch behind her and pulls herself up onto the cushions, wincing in pain from the cuts on her leg and arm. Matt rushes to help her, but almost passes out when he sees the blood start to flow again.

"You didn't happen to see a bathroom did you?" she asks him.

"I think there's one across the hall from the uh... the guy."

"Good, go see if they have a first aid kit. I'll keep an eye on her." she says, pointing to the gagged and tied-up elderly owner of house. If the circumstances were any different, the scene would look absolutely horrible.

Matt returns in only a few minutes, carrying in his hands an entire drawer full of medical supplies, including gauze, tape, scissors, bandages — and best of all, painkillers. While his mom tends to her wounds, Matt sits down in front of their hostess and stares at her, noticing in particular the open laceration on top of her head.

"Do you think she'll die?" he asks his mom.

"She might, I hit her pretty hard."

Matt had already noticed the lack of compassion in his mom's voice when discussing the woman. He can't really blame her though, he doesn't necessarily feel anything for the woman either, especially after what she tried to do to them.

"Do you think Dad will find Ben?" he asks her.

Sarah stops unwinding the gauze, finding it hard to answer the question. She wants to break down and cry every time she thinks

216

about either one of them, but she knows she can't allow herself that privilege, not yet anyway. Besides, Matt deserves an answer, even if it's not a good one.

"I don't know sweety. I know he'll try his best."

She goes back to wrapping her leg while Matt sits in silence, still glaring at the woman intently. Then he turns around and looks up at Sarah.

"Dad said that everyone in town was probably dead... but they aren't, are they?"

"No, they're not."

"I wish they were dead..."

"So do I."

She cringes as she hears the words escape her lips, and part of her feels as though she should be scolding him for saying something so incredibly ruthless — but he's right, everything would've been perfectly fine if the rest of the residents in town had been killed in the plague. Instead, what they've turned into is something unnatural, something entirely evil.

"Mom, she's waking up."

Sarah looks up from her bandaging to see the woman starting to squirm in the chair, frantically shaking her head from side to side in an attempt to free herself from the crude blindfold that covers her face. When her soft moaning grows louder though, and her arms begin twisting in an attempt to free herself from the wire shackles, Sarah takes the gun from Matt and hands him the scissors.

"Cut the scarf off, it might calm her down — but keep your gloves on, and be careful. You don't need to catch whatever she has."

The woman's body goes still the moment Matt touches her head, and the panicked moaning slows down to a whimper. As he begins cutting through the fabric, trying not to nick her oily and knotted hair, the woman starts to whisper quietly — words that Matt can clearly hear at this distance, but can't understand. It sounds like another language.

After he takes the scarf off and tosses it on the floor beside her, he moves her hair from in front of her eyes, revealing a kind and gentle face underneath. She smiles at him, and then at Sarah as Matt moves back to the couch next to his mom.

"It happened to me too, didn't it?" the woman asks in a hoarse voice, her smile turning into a look of concern.

"What do you mean?" Sarah replies, thinking the woman has clearly lost her mind.

"I was really hoping that it wouldn't..." she responds, barely loud enough for Sarah to hear.

"What exactly do you think happened?"

"Would the two of you like something to eat? I have some canned peaches in the cupboard... They're wonderful." And the kind smile returns.

"Do you have a name?" Sarah asks her, purposely ignoring the question. The woman has either gone completely mad, or she's more diabolical than Sarah realized. She's beginning to think it might be both.

"Oh, I'm sorry, where are my manners? My name is Clara Embree. And yours is...?"

"Sarah, and this is my son Matt."

Matt gives a sheepish wave, feeling embarrassed for having done it.

"It's very nice to meet you Matt," she says, sounding very sincere.

"Is this your house?" asks Sarah.

"It was built by my father just before the war. I still like to think of it as his."

Sarah looks down at the painkillers in the drawer beside her, wishing that she could take some of them to ease her discomfort —

but she can't afford to lose control of her senses, not until they're back at the cabin anyway.

"Do you know what happened in town?" she asks Clara.

The warm smile and sparkle in Clara's eyes disappear as she contemplates her answer.

"No, not really. We didn't go into town much after everyone started getting sick. We couldn't risk coming down with it ourselves, not at our age." She looks away, then lowers her head, a look of shame washing over her face. "After a few days, people started coming to our door, asking for help, or wanting us to take their children in before it was too late, but we couldn't..."

"I'm sorry, that must have been difficult..."

"Some of them were neighbors that we've known for years."

"Did the people in town disappear quickly after that, or did it take a while?"

Clara lifts her head again, looking directly at Sarah, tears running down her cheeks. "Disappear? They never disappeared..." The woman cocks her head to one side, looking at Sarah with a look of suspicion. "You really don't understand what's happened, do you?"

Sarah wants to respond, but she doesn't know quite what to say. The woman is right, they really don't know what's happened, not beyond the few shreds of evidence they've picked up over the past forty-eight hours anyway.

"We're all going to die — all of us, one by one," Clara continues in a calm, soothing voice. "We thought we were immune too, my husband and I, but he came down with it weeks after we isolated ourselves."

"Is that your husband in the bedroom down the hall?" Sarah asks.

She nods. "A couple of weeks ago Carl tried to... force himself on me." Her words become quick and defensive. "He's not like that, he never has been. It's the disease, it makes you do things, terrible things... evil things..."

219

"So you locked him up? By yourself?"

"Fear can make you do incredible things, Sarah, even an old woman like me..."

The comment and its tone sound more like a threat than an answer, and as Sarah sits there, staring at the woman's stern demeanor, she starts to wonder if the woman has been feeding her husband or giving him water all this time — although in all honesty she really doesn't care enough to ask.

The room and all of the memories that it contains are sad to look at, even if you don't recognize any of the people or experiences. Judging from the photographs on the walls, this woman was probably a loving wife and mother at one time, and Carl a perfect husband and father. They both built a life here on the edge of the ocean, a life which has now been shattered and destroyed.

None of those things matter today though — they can both rot where they sit as far as Sarah is concerned. They've become carriers of the plague, a scourge to the rest of humanity, and the sooner they're gone the better off her family will be.

"When did you realize you were sick yourself?" Sarah asks her, only half-interested.

Clara grins slightly, the evil glint appearing in her eyes once again. "I wasn't aware I am..."

CHAPTER 23
WESTPORT

With his eyes burning and his lungs desperate for fresh air, Curtis takes a quick look around the garage, hoping that Amanda's warning was just a lie — and that the only thing in the garage of concern was the overwhelming smell of gasoline. After waiting only a few seconds, however, he knew it was no bluff — he can hear someone else in the building with him.

Although the room is poorly lit after he dropped his flashlight, he can see oil stains and trash completely covering the floor. It has a ceiling that extends all the way to the roof, but the back of the building is broken into two floors, the top floor being only accessible from a rickety wooden staircase barely visible in the far right corner. Whoever is in here with him sounds like they're behind the door at the top of those stairs. He can hear their footsteps, slow and heavy, and always moving. He can't really tell how many there might be, but it sounds like there could be several of them.

Crouching down, he feels around for his light, his hands blindly searching the greasy concrete floor — and then suddenly he stops. He can feel skin, human skin — someone's face and neck. It's ice cold to the touch.

His first and only thought is Ben, and whether or not Amanda is playing some sort of a sick game with him.

Knowing that the flashlight rolled in that direction, he carefully runs his hands around the edge of the body, and finds the light resting against their arm. To his surprise, when he presses the button it actually comes on, its beam aimed squarely at the face in front of

221

him. It's the body of an older man, probably in his seventies. Most of his clothes have been ripped off and thrown to his side, revealing a corpse covered in dark bruises and bloody abrasions. He also has bite marks on his face and arms. Whoever this man was, and whatever was done to him, they took their time doing it — dead bodies don't bruise.

Curtis stands up and turns his attention back to the door he entered through, which despite its weathered look seems to be quite sturdy. As he searches it more carefully he spots a knothole, and looking through it he can see Amanda walking casually away from him and into a building across the street. He wants more than anything to scream at her, to demand that she unlock the door — but he knows it wouldn't do him any good. There's obviously something wrong with her, and it may have nothing to do with the virus.

Instead, he decides to find his own way out, and that means searching the entire building — with the exception of upstairs of course. The front of the room is lined with grungy windows, which unfortunately have thick steel bars covering them. Underneath one of them is a cluttered workbench covered with a variety of different tools and scraps of metal, which Curtis decides is probably his best bet for finding something that can pry open the door. After carefully weaving his way through the garbage and spilled chemicals on the floor, he reaches the workbench just in time to hear something from behind him, from the direction of the stairs.

A click, like a door opening, followed by the creaking sound of rusty hinges.

Without even glancing back he turns off his light and crouches down behind two 55-gallon drums that sit only a few feet away. Then he waits, trying not to move, his legs burning intensely from all the abuse they've taken recently. For a moment he considers dropping to his knees, and then changes his mind when he hears the first footsteps coming down the staircase. A few seconds later he can hear another

222

set, and then another. After that he loses count. Then suddenly they stop, and the only sound left in the room is heavy breathing.

After waiting a couple of minutes with no activity, Curtis peers around the drums and through the darkness to find what appears to be five people standing at the bottom of the stairs.

He looks around on the floor, hoping to find something he can use as a weapon, but all he can see are empty plastic jugs and soiled shop rags. Then finally he spots something — resting on the edge of the workbench is a large wrench, just within reach. Keeping as low to the floor as possible, he extends one hand out and grips the handle, trying not to let it drag across the surface of the bench. The weight of it, however, is more than he imagined — and just as he begins to lift it, the wrench tumbles to the concrete floor and lands with a hard crash, the sound echoing loudly throughout the room.

Curtis freezes, fully expecting the people on the other side of the room to confront him, or to at least react — but instead they do nothing. Knowing that his cover is blown, he grabs the wrench and stands up, keeping it hidden behind his back. The people, who he can clearly tell now are a woman and four men, are still standing in the same place, all of them staring at Curtis. Even in the dim moonlight he can see that they look absolutely filthy, as though they haven't changed their clothes or brushed their hair in months. Just like several of the others he's seen in town, two of the men are wearing pajama bottoms and t-shirts. In what appears to be a normal trend, none of them are wearing shoes either.

"I'm not looking for any trouble..." Curtis tells them, his voice as calm and soothing as possible. "I'm just trying to get out of here..."

No response.

"Do you know if there's another way out? The door is locked."

Again, no response. They simply stare back at him.

He waits for a moment, listening, trying to determine if there

223

might be others that are still upstairs — but all he can hear is the wind howling outside, and the rusty steel sign out front swinging in the breeze. If he could get past them and up the stairs he might be able to barricade himself on the other side of the door, but he also knows there's a possibility he could be trapped up there.

He tightens his grip on the wrench behind his back, then slowly steps out into the open, the five sets of eyes following his every move. As much as he wants to believe that these people can be reasoned with, he knows full well that they were the ones that mutilated the man at his feet. Ordinarily he would simply run away, but that doesn't seem to be an option. The only choice he can see is violence, or at least the threat of it. As he brings the wrench out into full view, hoping that the sight of it will intimidate a few of them, the moonlight in the room begins to fade away, swallowing most of the room in darkness.

The moment the room turns dark, he hears something. Footsteps in front of him, coming his way.

"Stay back!" he yells, turning his light on. All five of them are closer, only about ten feet away, but they've stopped moving once again. The expressions on their faces haven't changed at all, but in the bright light he can see that their eyes are severely bloodshot. The men turn and look away, all four of them staring in the direction of the window over the workbench. The woman continues to gaze at Curtis' flashlight, seemingly mesmerized by it.

When he glances over at the window himself, he sees Amanda staring back at him, a slight smirk visible on her face. Then she raises a short piece of iron pipe, her hand and arm shaking from the effort, and smashes it against the glass, leaving only the steel bars between the two of them.

"Amanda, you have to let me out of here! Just unlock the door, okay?" he pleads, shifting his eyes between her and the other people.

She drops the pipe on the ground, then rests her arms on the window trim — a look of sadness on her face. "You shouldn't worry about Ben, he'll be safe with me..." She glances behind her, smiles brightly, then looks back at Curtis with a reassuring look on her face. "When we get home my mom will know what to do."

Curtis steps toward the workbench, trying to see what, or who, is behind her — but it's too dark outside to see anything. "We can all go to Aberdeen together, the entire family. We'll take care of each other. Wouldn't that be better?"

"They're getting closer..." she says, casually pointing behind him.

When Curtis spins around, he sees that two of the men have edged a few feet closer. "Amanda, open the door..." he says, keeping his eyes on the men.

"I'm sorry, I really am." She sounds sympathetic, her voice sounding as innocent and pure as her age.

Then the moment after the words leave her mouth, he hears the characteristic ripping sound of a match, and he turns his head to face her. She looks determined, almost menacing. In her right hand is a long stick match, its flame flickering in the wind.

"Amanda... don't..."

"I'm sorry, but this is going to hurt."

It all happens in slow motion, and for a moment everything seems like a dream, or a nightmare. Curtis watches as a massive fireball engulfs the center of the room. All four of the men are consumed immediately, their feet already standing in the pool of gasoline on the floor. The woman falls onto her back, then manages to stumble to her feet again before climbing back onto the stairs. She looks down at Curtis, and for a moment he thinks he catches a glint of fear in her eyes, almost as though she were expecting him to help her. Then, just as quickly, her eyes return to the cold and vacant look they had before.

225

Curtis looks back at the window, expecting to see Amanda watching them — but she's no longer there.

His mind should be paying attention to the events around him — the fire that's spreading across the floor toward him, the shrieks of pain coming from the four men that are now throwing themselves against the walls. He doesn't see or hear any of it though. His mind is now focused on only one thing... the fact that his son is now with Amanda.

By the time he finally begins to move the flames have reached the far end of the workbench, near a shelf filled with chemicals and various oils and additives. Noticing that the woman is still finding her way up the stairs, he decides that even in her questionable state of mind, she probably has the best idea. He quickly works his way around the untouched edge of the room, past the still-moving body of one of the men sprawled out on the concrete, his face now unrecognizable. When he reaches the stairs, the woman screams at him, clawing at the air with her hands.

"Stop, I'm not going to hurt you!" he yells.

It doesn't do any good, however. She takes a step down, toward Curtis. As she reaches for his face, he swings the wrench directly at her chest, hearing and feeling several of her ribs breaking as he makes contact. Even then, she doesn't seem to be fazed. Continuing down the stairs, she reaches out for him again with both hands, one of them briefly grabbing hold of his sleeve. Curtis jumps back to avoid contact, then lunges forward again, driving the wrench directly into the middle of her forehead. Her body immediately crumbles to the steps, then rolls past Curtis before finally ending up on the landing below.

As he makes his way to the second floor, Curtis can hear the crackling sound of wood behind him as the building's frame begins to break apart. By the time he enters the room at the top of the stairs the

226

smoke has become unbearable. When he walks in and locks the door behind him, he spots two windows on the back wall — and much to his relief, neither of them have bars on them. After finding out that both of them drop straight to the alley below, he opens the closest one and leans out. The moment he does, the fresh, moist, salty air blowing in from the ocean fills his lungs — and causes a long coughing spell that sends him back into the room again before finally catching his breath.

Smoke has begun rising between the floorboards and from around the door. He can feel the oddly comforting heat coming through as well, and the orange glow filtering in from every crack and knothole in the floor. He knows the building won't last much longer. Leaning out the second-story window once again, he sees a mostly empty alley below, one that looks like it's been recently paved. A couple of doors down he can see a couple of dumpsters, but there's nothing directly under the window. More importantly, he sees no sign of people. As he starts to climb out, the rain begins to pick up, coming down in massive sheets that are pooling up on the surface below. The window is a tight fit, but he manages to squeeze through, landing safely on his feet once he reaches the pavement. After waiting a few seconds for the pain in his feet and calves to dissipate, he runs to the end of the alley and rounds the corner toward the main street. When he reaches it, he looks around for Amanda or Ben, but there's no sign of either of them. He considers looking for their footprints, but the street looks more like a river than a road in the downpour of rain, washing away any mud or dirt that may have been left behind.

Huge clouds of smoke are pouring into the night sky from the garage in front of him, and the glowing coals that used to be the building's frame are now sizzling as the cold rain hits them. Curtis backs off as the roof starts to collapse and the walls begin to buckle. After looking around for a few minutes, letting the burning garage

227

light up the buildings around him, he starts walking south, never looking back at the building, and wondering if it might be a good idea to take shelter until the rain tapers off. In the end, however, his desperation prevails — and he convinces himself that he'll catch up with them just down the road.

There will be plenty of time to rest once his family is together again.

CHAPTER 24
COHASSETT BEACH

After spending nearly thirty minutes closing drapes, lighting candles, locking doors and tightening the telephone cord fastened around Clara Embree, Matt collapses next to his mother on the couch. Both of them are exhausted, mentally and physically — and for the first time tonight, Clara has been silent, leaving the house mostly quiet aside from the occasional bump from the bedroom down the hall. Even while he was securing the rope between her arms and the chair, she never opened her mouth once. Instead, she simply stared straight ahead, her eyes unfocused and blank.

"Do you think we'll catch whatever she has?" Matt asks his mom.

"I don't know, hon — but I think it's a good sign that we haven't caught anything up until now..."

"Yeah, I guess." He squirms a little, fidgeting with his fingers. He's not sure about asking this next question, and he's not entirely sure if he wants to know the answer. "Is everyone like this?"

"I think most people probably are, the ones that are left." She puts her arm around his shoulder and squeezes, then kisses him on the forehead.

"Do you think they'll get better?"

"Maybe, I don't know."

She looks up at Clara, and finds the old woman looking back, her eyes focused once again. The same sinister grin that she had on her face earlier is back, and her hands are clenched so hard they've turned white.

"Matt, hand me the kitchen knife," Sarah says.

229

He hands her an old knife with a nine inch blade that he found on the kitchen counter earlier. He still has the gun, but he now keeps it in his pocket.

"Doesn't the front door have a window in it?" she asks him.

"Yeah, I covered it with some sheets."

"Why don't you go see if you can peek through... see if anybody is out there..."

A look of fear immediately takes over Matt's face. Sarah knows that he must be terrified, but she can't allow him to stay in the room — not for the next few minutes anyway.

"They won't be able to see you if you stay still and keep quiet," she reassures him.

"What about her?" asks Matt.

"She's not going anywhere, you made sure of that."

Reluctantly, he stands up, crosses the room, then looks back at his mom, hoping that she'll change her mind.

"Just for a bit, nobody will see you as long as the room is dark," she tells him.

Besides the fear of being out of sight of his mother, Matt is reminded of the other reason he hates the front room the instant he enters it. The smell is overwhelming — rotten food and human filth permeate the air. This is obviously a room that Clara spent very little time in. He carefully feels his way around the cluttered furniture and knickknacks until finally reaching the front door. It takes his eyes a few moments to adjust to the darkness, but when they do he finds that he has a clear view of the highway only about fifty feet away. The wind is still blowing hard, sending leaves, branches and litter flying through the air. He can just barely make out the cars lined up on the road, and the longer he stares at them, the more certain he is that some of the shadows in front of them are moving. He tries telling himself that it's only a figment of his imagination, or that it's the swaying branches of the trees in the front yard — but it soon becomes clear that a small group of people are slowly walking down the road. He thinks of his dad, and of Ben, knowing that whatever route they take to get back to the cabin, they're certain to run into someone along the way.

Sarah waits a few minutes, making sure that Matt is in the front room and out of earshot. Then, still holding onto the knife, she grabs the armrest of the couch and drags herself to her feet, then reaches down and picks up the pillow that she's been resting against.

"Is there any way your husband can get out of the bedroom?" Sarah whispers to Clara.

Clara looks up, her face innocent, and perhaps a little confused. "No, I don't believe so."

"Has he ever gotten out?"

"Once, but that's been a couple of days ago."

"Has he eaten since then?"

Clara looks away, pursing her lips as a sign that she refuses to talk about it.

"There was someone else in the house with you too, wasn't there?" Sarah asks. "Someone who didn't make it..."

"I don't want to talk about it," Clara answers back, still refusing to look at Sarah.

"Are they in there with your husband?" She waits a while, then when it becomes obvious that she's not going to answer, Sarah approaches the old woman, then moves directly behind her. She sets the knife down on a small table next to the chair.

231

"Clara..."

"What?" the old lady answers back, clearly agitated.

"What was your husband's first symptom?"

"Coughing, that's the first sign."

"Did you start coughing too?"

Again, no answer. Sarah begins looking around at the house, wondering if there might be a better place to hide while her leg heals enough for the journey home. She worries that if they spend too much time here that Curtis and Ben might come searching for them, leaving them vulnerable to others just like Clara — or worse. It'll probably be days until she's ready to travel though, and this house has nearly everything they need to survive. Food, medicine, even dry towels in the hall closet. There might be other places that could work, but they're already here, and even standing for these few minutes has made the pain in her leg almost more than she can handle. Moving would be foolish.

Gripping the pillow in both hands, she quickly places it over Clara's face and tightly wraps it around her head. The old woman struggles as best she can, but with her feet and arms tied to the chair she really has no ability to move. Sarah turns her head and closes her eyes, trying to block out the moaning and head jerking, and praying that Matt doesn't walk in to see this. Eventually the movements begin to soften, and then stop altogether. The moaning stops shortly afterward as well, but Sarah keeps the pillow held securely over the woman's mouth and nose, and instead watches her hands and feet as confirmation that she's passed.

Holding back tears, Sarah finally releases her hold after she notices that Clara's hands have gone completely limp. She stuffs the pillow in the corner behind the chair, then covers the woman's body with a blanket that had been draped over the back of the couch. Wiping her eyes dry, she limps over to the doorway that leads to the front room,

232

and sees Matt crouched down in front of the door, still peering out the full length window.

"Matt..." she whispers.

He crosses the room carefully, trying to be as quiet as possible, but also concerned about why his mom is calling him. Before he reaches her, Sarah turns around and sits back down on the couch, then pulls a small antique table in front of her, using it to elevate her injured leg on top of two pillows.

"What's wrong?" asks Matt.

"I think Clara is dead. She stopped breathing a few minutes ago."

"Should we do something with her?"

"No, it can wait until morning." She pats the cushion next to her, motioning for him to sit down. "You should get some sleep, we'll have to take turns keeping watch."

Matt lies down on the other end of the couch, resting his head on his mom's lap. She reaches for the blanket on the back to cover him, then realizes that she used it to cover Clara's body.

"There are people outside, walking down the road," he whispers.

"Did they look sick?"

He nods his head, and both of them stay silent for a while. "Do you think the others are crazy like her?" he asks, pointing to Clara in the corner.

"We have to assume they are. We can't trust any of them — do you understand?"

He nods.

"How many people did you see outside?"

"I couldn't really tell, but I think there were a lot."

As Sarah begins slowly stroking Matt's hair, her mind wanders to Curtis and Ben, and the hope that they've found someplace to hide for the night. No matter how hard she tries, she can't bring herself to fully recognize what's happened to her family over these last couple

233

of months. All three of her kids are separated, and her husband is still out there somewhere, with absolutely no idea where they've ended up.

"Matt, are you still awake?"

"Yeah."

"The world is going to be different from now on. It's not the same place it used to be."

"I know Mom."

"We're going to have to be brave, and do things we wouldn't normally do..."

He nods slightly, then closes his eyes, falling asleep immediately.

Feeling something against her side, Sarah reaches down beside her and pulls out a magazine that had been stuffed between the armrest and the cushion. It's a travel magazine, addressed to a Mrs Clara Embree. She starts to flip through the pages, which are filled with people partying, scuba diving, gambling, hiking, you name it — all of them with smiles on their faces, having the time of their lives. Normally this would probably be a magazine that she would enjoy — but tonight, as she quickly scans through the pages, a single thought crosses her mind... All of these people are dead, and the incredible places they're enjoying are likely as deserted as Westport.

Disgusted at the idea, she drops the magazine on the floor, then leans her head back and closes her eyes — certain that she wouldn't be able to sleep even if she wanted to. As her thoughts begin to wander into areas where only anxiety thrives, she's brought back to reality once again by a loud bang. It happened so suddenly that she wasn't able to figure out what it was or where it came from. Then it happens again — someone is knocking on the front door.

234

CHAPTER 25
ABERDEEN

As Jake and Beth step out of the icy waters of the harbor, dragging their supplies onto the rocky shore beside them, they both stand silent and take in the view of Aberdeen, a city that was once the heart of Grays Harbor. Tonight, the streets are dark and empty, with only a few parked cars scattered here and there. The docks just to the north of them, which are usually filled with both ships and smaller boats, looks mostly deserted as well.

The city looks like it's been through a war, with broken windows in almost every building they can see, even on the higher floors. Trash is being blown around in the street just ahead of them, carried by a stiff wind that whistles overhead as it passes by the buildings. They can smell something burning too, very faint, but they can't tell exactly what it might be. Only a few blocks are visible with any kind of clarity — beyond that the thick fog moving in from the harbor obscures the view.

"We need to find some shelter. We'll have to leave everything but our packs behind for now," Jake tells Beth, handing her one of the backpacks he'd tied to his arm earlier.

"What if somebody finds our stuff?"

He points to the east, where they can just barely make out a glimmer of light rising over the horizon. "The sun will be up soon, and we've never seen them out in the daylight. We'll come back and get everything in the morning." He points to a small three-story building across the street. It has a sign out front indicating that it's a barber shop. "Let's check that place out..."

235

As they walk across the empty roadway, the wind blows against their wet clothing and tired legs, leaving Beth feeling more exhausted than she's ever felt in her life. Her feet have gone numb, along with her hands and face — and she's finding it difficult to remember the last time she'd slept.

"Did you see that light on top of the hill?" she asks Jake.

"Yeah, any idea what that was?"

"It looked like it was coming from the hospital. You don't think it's open do you...?"

"I don't know, we'll have to check it out tomorrow."

Just before they reach the entrance to the building, both of them stop and turn their heads down the street. There's a scraping sound coming from just around the corner, and it's getting louder.

"Quick, get inside!" Jake whispers to Beth.

Jake is the first one to the entrance, which fortunately is already opened just a crack. After pulling his wife through, he closes the door quietly and then locks it — both of them standing off to the side, barely hidden from view, but still able to see the sidewalk on the other side of the door.

The sound becomes louder with every passing second, until at last they see a man walking past the building, his movements stiff and slow. Following right behind him are two others, a man and a woman. The man in the back is dragging a long piece of tangled netting from his foot, and several aluminum cans have been caught in the mess. Once they pass by, Curtis taps Beth on the shoulder, then points to a large counter that's near the back wall of the shop — one that's completely out of view from the floor to ceiling windows in the front.

After removing their wet survival suits, they both sit down behind the wooden counter, leaning against one another, shivering from the cold that's run clear to their bones.

"Sean is still out there..." Beth says quietly.

236

Jake doesn't say anything at first, then finally answers... "I think we have more serious things to worry about right now."

"What could be more serious than that?"

"We need to get out of the city, find someplace without so many people — a place where we can rest for a while."

"After we check out the hospital. We have to do that first..." she says sleepily, the words barely making it out of her mouth.

"You need to get some sleep, I'll take first watch."

As his wife sleeps beside him on the hard tiled floor, Jake pulls his pistol from its holster and holds it in his hand, listening as more people walk by in front of the shop. This time they sound like they're headed in the other direction, and in a hurry. Although his mind is too tired and numb to feel much of anything besides fear, he knows that tomorrow, and probably for the rest of his life, his heart will be filled with guilt and regret. Although he can never let on to Beth — he saw the bullet hit Larry, and he saw him shortly after he landed in the water. The round hit him in the upper arm, not necessarily a fatal wound. Whether or not he's still alive he can't be certain, but he could still see him struggling in the wake of Sean's boat as he pulled Beth away from the area. He tries telling himself that he made a tactical decision, that it was necessary to leave Larry behind in order to save the lives of Beth and himself — but the guilt he's beginning to feel tells a different story. He was scared, pure and simple — and it grows worse with every person that passes by.

CHAPTER 26
EAST OF COHASSETT

Walking through the overgrown forest just to the east of town, Curtis knows he's likely losing precious time catching up to Amanda — but he can't risk being seen by people on the highway. He's almost certain that Amanda has taken the same route, having already found a fresh pair of shoe prints in the mud that matched hers only about ten minutes ago. The fact that he didn't see any other footprints alongside of hers was unsettling to say the least.

He has to be careful as he makes his way around bogs and downed trees, he can't do anything that draws attention to his whereabouts — either from Amanda or anyone else. From time to time he catches a glimpse of the coastal highway, its pavement still filled with abandoned cars and the supplies they carried that never proved to be useful to their passengers. Shadows of people are visible too, moving back and forth against the filtered moonlight. Mostly though, it's quiet, eerily quiet. Besides the occasional owl, or gust of wind in the trees overhead, only the rushing sound of the ocean in the distance can be heard. To the east, he can see the first sign of daylight making its way through the needles of fir and spruce.

It's nearly thirty miles from here to Aberdeen, a long stretch of road for a frail girl to walk without slowing down considerably, especially in conditions like this. Although the rain has tapered off to only a light shower for the time being, the wind still continues to blow in from the west — and last he saw, Amanda wasn't exactly dressed for the elements. With any luck, he'll catch up to them within the hour — which will give plenty of time for himself and Ben to make their way back to the cabin sometime in the afternoon, even if he has to carry him. Amanda, and what to do with her, is his biggest problem — one that he really doesn't want to think about.

It's taken Amanda and Ben over an hour before they finally reach the highway interchange that leads to Aberdeen, both of them soaked to the bone and covered in mud. Ben's feet are killing him as he steps onto the pavement, and he feels fortunate that Amanda insisted that she carry both his backpack and her knife. Without her, he's sure that he wouldn't have survived the night.

"We have to walk on the road from now on," Amanda informs him.

"What about the scourge?" Ben responds.

'Scourge' is a term that Amanda came up with to identify the infected, a name she remembers her father using shortly after the outbreak began. She's not completely sure what it means, but she liked the sound of it.

"The sun is coming up. They won't be out for the rest of the day."

"Why not?"

"You ask a lot of questions, don't you?" she says, smiling.

He turns red from embarrassment, reminding himself not to talk so much.

Amanda begins walking again, glancing through the car windows as she passes by, which are becoming few and far between this far outside of town. "My mom will know what to do when we get there, you'll see."

"And then we'll find my family, right?"

"Right."

Ben feels inside of his pocket, running his fingers across the knife that Matt handed him the night before. He pulls it out of his pocket,

239

then holds it out to show Amanda. "Look at this..." he says proudly, but when he looks up at her, he notices that she's no longer walking, and instead is simply standing in the middle of the road.

"Amanda, are you okay?" He places the knife back in his pocket, then faces the girl. She looks as though she's in a daze, her eyes blank, her mouth hanging half-open. "Amanda!" he cries, shaking her slightly. With that, she snaps out of it.

"What?" she asks, confused.

"You did it again."

She smiles at him, then begins walking again. "I'm sorry, I must've gotten distracted." She holds out her hand, inviting Ben to do the same, and the two hold hands as they make their way toward the sunrise. "Did you ask me something before?" she asks.

Ben looks up at her, noticing that her eyes look different somehow, like they belong to someone else. "Nah, it wasn't important."

Curtis had hoped to catch up to Amanda somewhere along the highway shortly after sunrise, but looking up at the deserted road ahead of him, he had a horrible feeling that she might actually be gaining ground on him. He still had no idea whether Ben was with her or not, but shortly after reaching the paved highway he begins seeing clues along the way that tell him that she isn't alone. For one, oftentimes there are now two sets of footprints visible alongside the road, both of them small enough to belong to children. He also found two candy bar wrappers and two empty cans of soda, all of which had been recently consumed.

After being half delirious the night before from both hypothermia and pure exhaustion, the temperature has greatly improved today, and the rain that fell throughout the night has been replaced with sun

240

breaks and only the occasional sprinkle. The exhaustion, however, is still there, and it's getting worse with every mile that he travels. The aching feet and sore leg muscles from the hike the day before were bad enough, but the lack of sleep over the past few days is beginning to take a toll on his concentration and alertness.

The cars are scarce along this part of the highway, a stretch that's mostly lined with muddy bogs and thickly overgrown evergreen forests covered in long hanging gray moss, the last of which is kept alive by a year-round supply of fog coming off of the harbor. The smell coming from the bogs is strong — a putrid mixture of rotting vegetation and stale saltwater. When he does come across a vehicle, he takes a few minutes to look it over, hoping to find one that still runs — but so far none of them do.

Just a little after noon he comes to an old general store that sits only a few feet from the highway. The name on the sign says 'Diller's Market'. Curtis remembers stopping at the store every time he came to the beach with his parents, back when John Diller still owned the place. In recent years it's remained a store, its new owners changing little or nothing about the place — even the name. Curtis takes a quick walk around the outside of the building, taking time to check out the few cars sitting in the parking lot, then walks in through the open door in the back. The place smells moldy and wet, and the stench of spoiled food and rotten bait have permeated virtually everything inside, including the county road maps that Curtis slips into his pocket. He also comes across a couple of breakfast bars and a bag of potato chips behind the counter, along with an insulated winter coat that's about four sizes too big. While the shelves in the main market are almost completely empty, in the next room he finds floor to ceiling wire shelving filled with canned goods and boxes of dried food — enough to feed his family for a few months if they were careful. Lying on the floor in the middle of the room, however, are

241

two bodies, a man and a woman — both of them badly decomposed.

His first thought is to take off the coat, fearful that it might be contaminated with whatever killed the two people in front of him. Then he sees the gun. Sitting next to what's left of the man's outstretched arm is a semi-auto pistol, dried blood still splattered on the side of it, and a gaping hole in the temple of both individuals. Whether dying from the virus, or fearful over what's happened to the world around them, these people obviously felt that their life as they knew it was over.

As Curtis reaches out for a container of sanitation wipes sitting on the shelf, he hears a noise from the room behind him — like the closing of a car door. Hurrying, he opens up the wipes and cleans off the gun lying on the floor, then takes another and disinfects his new coat the best he can. He pops the clip out of the gun and looks closely at it, still eleven bullets left.

When he walks back into the store itself, he spots an older man outside in the parking lot, siphoning gasoline out of a car. Curtis stands off to the side and watches the man, letting the shadows hide him from sight. The guy goes quickly from one car to the next, searching the inside of each one of them before moving on. Finally, once he's done with the last one, he looks over at the store and begins walking to the front door. He lays down the can of gas and pulls out a gun before reaching for the doorknob. Knowing already that the front door is locked, Curtis stands still with his own gun aimed at the doorway. The man jiggles the lock, at first carefully, and then more forceful. Just as he prepares to break the window out with his elbow, Curtis yells out at him.

"I wouldn't do that!"

The man stops, startled — then he looks in through the window to see who spoke to him. "Who's in there?" he asks.

"You got your gas, now move on..."

242

"Listen, I don't mean any harm, I'm just hungry," the man claims, placing his gun back into his side holster.

Curtis wants to believe him — but desperate people, even healthy ones, can be dangerous and unpredictable in times of despair. "Which direction did you come from?"

"Johns River, to the east."

"You didn't happen to see anyone else on the road did you?"

"I'm afraid not, are you looking for someone?"

Curtis places his gun into his pocket, then unlocks and opens the door before moving back out of the way again. When the man steps through and he gets a good look at him, he knows he has to be at least eighty years old — maybe more.

"Did you walk all the way from Johns River?" Curtis asks him.

"It's not far, just a few miles down the road." the man replies, moving farther into the room.

"Where're you headed?"

"Westport, I have a son that lives there. I haven't been able to contact him for weeks."

"I just came from there, I'm afraid it's overrun."

"Overrun with what?"

It's clear to Curtis that this guy has no idea what's going on, but he doesn't have the time or energy to explain everything to him. "Is it just you out here?"

The expression on the man's face changes somewhat, and a look of sadness suddenly appears in his eyes. Whatever it is, he looks away for a moment, toward the empty street out front. "Yeah, something like that." When he looks back at Curtis, it seems as though he wants to say something else, but nothing actually comes out. Whatever the guy has been through, it obviously hasn't been easy.

"Have you heard any news from outside the harbor?" Curtis asks.

The old man reaches into his pocket and pulls out a half rusty flask, then takes a swig. "No, not for a while. You...?"

"No, nothing."

He holds the flask out to Curtis, offering him a drink, but Curtis only shakes his head in response — wondering to himself if this guy is the least bit worried about the virus. The man takes another drink before putting it back in his pocket, then walks behind the counter and takes a seat on a rickety stool that sits in front of the cash register, looking around the room at the nearly empty shelves.

"Not much left, is there?"

"There's food in the back room, along with a few supplies."

"Good to hear, the pantry is getting a little bare back at the house."

"I saw you siphoning gas out front, do you have a car?"

"Sort of, it doesn't run. So far I haven't found one that does."

"I've noticed the same thing. The batteries all seem to be dead."

"Yep, that's what I've run across too."

Curtis can tell the man is tired, maybe even more than he is. "Listen, I'm gonna be coming back through here in a day or two — why don't you rest up here for a while, and I'll check on you when I get back...

"No, I'll be fine. I'm just gonna rest my legs for a while."

Curtis approaches the counter, and without thinking holds out his hand for the man to shake — a strange custom considering the risk of contamination. The man smiles, then reaches his own hand out and shakes.

"My name is Curtis by the way..."

"Nice to meet you Curtis, my name is Peter."

Curtis begins to leave, then turns around. "Stay away from any of the cities, Peter, especially Westport."

Peter nods, then asks... "Can I ask where you're headed?"

"Aberdeen. Have you heard anything from there lately?"

"No, but my place overlooks the harbor, so I look right across at it

244

— it's a ghost town. Maybe you should follow your own advice..."

Curtis makes his way down the road toward Aberdeen, and as he glances back at the gas station he sees Peter walking in the opposite direction, toward Westport. As tired and drained as he is, he still can't help but feel sorry for the man. Maybe he should have warned him more forcefully, let him know what actually lurks in the shadows of Westport when the sun goes down — but in the end he decides to say nothing at all. Every passing minute places his own son in greater jeopardy from Amanda, and right now there's nothing more important than returning him safely to their home in Cohasset. He can only hope that Sarah and Matt have managed to find their way back.

Continuing his journey east, it takes him about thirty minutes to reach the southern shore of Grays Harbor, where the highway finally leaves the bog-infested forests and begins paralleling the coastline. The views of both Aberdeen and Hoquiam across the water are breathtaking. The snow-capped peaks of the Coastal Range rise up behind the two cities, dwarfed only by the much larger Olympic Mountains farther in the background. In other circumstances Curtis would appreciate the sights, and would wish that his wife were here to witness it herself. All he really notices this time, however, are the multiple plumes of black smoke scattered around the cityscape, with both small and large fires burning throughout the area. He keeps walking, at first keeping an eye on the towns, hoping that he spots some form of normalcy on the other side of the harbor. After a while he stops watching altogether though, and a disturbing realization begins to finally sink in — whatever has happened, it seems to be everywhere.

Looking up into the sky, he can see that the sun is already moving into the west, dragging the darkness of night behind it — and with every passing mile his thoughts turn to hindsight and regret.

He should have never allowed his family to leave Cohasset, he knows that now. They were all blissfully ignorant only a few days ago, their greatest fear being that they were the only human beings left on earth — an idea that doesn't seem so bad when compared to the actual truth.

The shock, stress and exhaustion of the past few days has taken its toll, leaving Curtis in a dreamlike state of consciousness where nothing around him seems real. In some respects it feels like a nightmare — his wife and son somewhere behind him, trying to find their way back to a cabin that might not be as safe as they assumed it was. His other son is somewhere ahead of him, escorted by a young girl who is either severely infected or mentally ill, and perhaps both.

As he searches for a way to stop his mind from over-analyzing everything, something from out of the corner of his eye catches his attention. He sees something along the shore, something light-colored that's resting among the rocks only about fifty feet from the road. Jumping the guardrail, he carefully makes his way over the rocks, driftwood and garbage that litter the beach until he gets close enough to see the object.

Stacked on top of one another, and stretched out along the shore to the east as far as he can see, are the remains of people. There must be hundreds of them, maybe even thousands — of every age, race and level of decomposition imaginable. Most of them are practically skeletons, but a few look recent, some of them very recent.

He turns around and starts walking back to the road, his mind trying to block out the image and smells that are behind him — and then suddenly he stops, finding himself directly in front of a man that's sitting next to a large piece of driftwood, his eyes fixed on the

246

harbor. Curtis places his hand in his coat, his fingers wrapped around the pistol he swiped from the store.

"Are you okay?" he asks.

No answer. The man just stares straight ahead. His clothes are soaking wet, and a life ring is still clutched in his right hand. At his feet is a large duffel bag that's zipped shut.

"Hey, are you okay?" he asks again, this time louder than before.

This time the man snaps out of his trance, gazing directly at Curtis with a bewildered look on his face.

"How long have you been out here?"

"I, I don't know..." the man says, still confused.

"Are you sick? Do you have the virus?"

"No, I'm not sick. I'm just tired."

Curtis considers leaving him behind. He's supposed to be finding his son before Amanda does something terrible, and so far all he's accomplished is offering his help to two strangers. On the other hand, whatever is waiting for him down the road might be easier with two people. Besides, other than being wet, the man doesn't look sick. "Do you have a name?"

"Yeah, Larry, Larry Gossman."

"Nice to meet you Larry, my name is Curtis Lockwood."

CHAPTER 27
COHASSETT BEACH

In the first few moments after waking up, before her eyes had fully adjusted to their surroundings, Sarah thought she was back home nestled comfortably in her own bed. Her bed in Portland that is, not the musty, worn-out mattress that occupies the cabin in Cohasset.

As the seconds pass, however, reality begins to seep in, until eventually the nightmare of the last twenty-four hours starts to truly sink in. One by one the memories creep into her consciousness — their trip to Westport, the terrifying night spent at the Regency Hotel, her son Ben disappearing without a trace, and then somehow she ended up here, sleeping on a couch that once belonged to a woman that she killed with her bare hands only hours before.

And then there's the pain... Clara's knife attack in the night has left her with a significant wound on her leg, an injury that despite taking painkillers earlier in the morning, continues to disrupt her sleep.

The house looks different than it did last night, no doubt partly due to the filtered sunlight that's coming through the curtains and illuminating every cluttered corner of the small living room. The nautical theme is more evident than ever, but only in the light of the day can Sarah see the true decrepit state that the house is in. Peeling wallpaper, cracked drywall, large water stains on the ceiling, and various-colored stains on the floor — some of which are Sarah's own blood from the attack. One thing that hasn't changed is the smell. A putrid, vile stench still hangs in the air — and with Clara's body still slumped in the corner of the room, the foul odor isn't likely to improve anytime soon.

248

"You're awake."

Sarah looks toward the kitchen, where she sees Matt standing in the doorway. "Barely. How long was I asleep?"

"About an hour." He walks into the room and sits down on the couch next to his mom, placing his head against her arm. "How does your leg feel?"

"It's really sore, but it's not throbbing anymore. That must be a good sign."

"The people outside are gone, even the ones out front."

Her and Matt had decided the night before that they would take shifts keeping watch, but neither of them were really able to sleep with all the commotion. The man down the hall, while still a concern, had been quiet for most of the night — only occasionally trying to open the barricaded bedroom door. The people outside, however, were anything but silent. Every few minutes throughout the night, an endless parade of people attempted to come in through one of the doors or windows. Most of them simply wiggled the handle for a few seconds, or quickly tapped on the glass before moving on — but a few of them were more relentless. At least one woman stayed for most of the night, moving from one window to the next, never doing anything more than rubbing her hands across the glass panes. Sarah had an idea early on that they might be attracted to the candlelight emanating from the living room, but after extinguishing every last one of them, the drove of people kept coming in from both the beach and the highway. Eventually, as the first sign of light appeared from the east, the people began disappearing into the shadows, with only a handful still visible after daybreak.

"What about the guy down the hall?" Sarah asks. "Anything going on in there?"

"I haven't heard him for a while." He looks over at the wood stove against the wall, seeing only a small ember of charcoal still glowing through the soot-covered window in the door. "Should I put more

249

wood in the stove?"

"No, the smoke might attract too much attention. Besides, it shouldn't get too cold in here today."

She shifts her position on the couch, trying to sit up straight as much as she can, and trying not to let on how much pain she's really in. While it's true that the bleeding and throbbing has stopped, the sharp pains are worse than they were last night.

"Are you hungry?" she asks him, trying to distract herself from the discomfort.

"Not really."

"Well, you need to eat. Both of us do. Why don't you get a couple of energy bars from your bag..."

He gets up and crosses the room, digging through both of their bags, apparently looking for something, then he holds up a single bottle of water that's only about half full. "Mom, was there anymore water?"

"There should be, did you look in my bag?"

"Yeah, that's where I got this one."

"Bring them over, let me take a look."

It takes her all of about ten seconds to go through both bags thoroughly, only to find a couple of empty bottles rolling around in the bottom of each of them. Then she gets a sinking feeling in her stomach as she remembers what happened.

"Ben has the water, remember?"

"All of it?"

"Your dad might have some too."

"What're we gonna do?"

"You'll have to search the house. Clara had to be drinking something."

Having already searched the kitchen and bathroom the day before looking for bandages and pain killers for his mom, Matt starts looking for water or anything else that might be useful in the front room. The outside wall of the room faces east, toward the highway, and the sun is still low enough in the sky to come directly through the windows on either side of the front door. For whatever reason, these windows have no curtains covering them, and the smeared mud on the outside of the glass look like some kind of primitive hand paintings.

The only place in the room to search for anything is the coat closet just inside the door, but all that he finds inside, besides coats and shoes, are totes filled with Halloween and Christmas decorations. In the laundry room he does find a dozen or so mason jars filled with what looks and smells like dirty water, but only pure desperation would ever allow him to entertain the idea of drinking it.

Finally, the only rooms left in the house are the two bedrooms, one of which is occupied by someone that Clara deemed so dangerous that she went through the trouble of fortifying the door. Entering the second bedroom, he looks in the closet first, finding nothing but clothes and old boxes. The dresser and nightstand next to the bed aren't much better, filled mostly with newspaper clippings and magazines — both of which can be used to start fires at the very least.

Turning around to leave the room, he sees something on the bed, the outline of a person under a large, tattered quilt. His legs begin to buckle a bit as he realizes there might have been another person living in the house this entire time without them knowing it. He walks backward as quietly as possible back to the closet, never taking his eyes off the bed, then reaches in and grabs a broom he remembers seeing only moments before. Then he stands next to the bed again, the broom in one hand and the revolver in the other — not

251

completely sure of which one to use. He reaches the broom out, his hand shaking, and nudges the lump lightly with the end of the handle — but there's no response. After several attempts, each one harder and more aggressive than the last, he finally decides to use the broom to pull the covers down from their face — an act he regrets immediately.

To say the body is decomposed would be an understatement — it looks more like a mummy than anything, with the skin appearing dry and stretched.

He uses the broom to move the quilt back over their head, still unsure of whether it's a man or a woman, then walks back into the kitchen to take a final inventory of food that's still left in the cupboards and pantry. In the middle of the floor there's a large pile of discarded wrappers and empty cans from food that Clara had already eaten, but after an exhaustive search, Matt discovers that she's nearly out of anything else that might be edible. He takes the half-dozen cans of fruits and vegetables, and the few boxes of dried pasta that are still left into the living room where his mom can examine them.

"That's it?" she asks.

"Yeah, except for whatever is in the fridge."

"Well, there's some water in the cans of fruit, but it's not enough. We're gonna have to go outside and see if there's some rainwater we can collect."

"I can go by myself, you shouldn't be walking around that much."

Sarah knows that he's right, but she can't stand the idea of him out there by himself — especially considering the crowds of people wandering around outside the house only a short time ago. "Are you sure?"

"I'll be careful. Besides, I don't see anybody out there anyway."

He takes the empty water bottles from his bag and walks to the back door, then peers out the small window, carefully looking around

252

the backyard for any signs of people — but everything seems to be quiet.

"The sun is out, it looks warm."

"Don't be too long, just find the water and get back. Okay?"

"Okay." He opens the door and steps through, and a welcome blast of fresh air comes blowing in around him. Then he turns around and faces his mom. "Oh, and there's another body in the other bedroom. I think they've been dead a long time."

Not wanting to hear an argument about whether or not he should be doing this alone, he shuts the door and disappears around the corner before she has a chance to respond.

From the back porch it's impossible to see the ocean with the number of dunes that are in the way, but the pathway that runs in that direction looks worn and well-traveled. As Matt makes his way around the house, looking for any source of water that doesn't appear contaminated, he notices another pathway that leads south through a small stand of trees. Although he can't really see what's at the other end all that clearly, it appears to be some type of structure. After searching around Clara's house with no luck, he decides to walk down the path to find out where it leads. As soon as he discovers that the structure on the other end is actually another house, however, he takes the gun out of his pocket and aims it directly in front of him, wishing that his dad had showed him how to use it properly before they left the cabin.

He sneaks up on the house as stealthily as he can, hoping not to arouse any attention if the house turns out to be occupied — but the second he spots a rain barrel sitting underneath a gutter downspout, all of his fear and apprehension turns into excitement in an instant.

253

He takes one of the bottles and dunks it into the barrel, then holds it up to the sunlight, admiring the clarity and cleanliness of the contents. He dips the next bottle into the water, then brings the full one to his mouth to take a drink, tasting a slight tinge of saltiness that he figures must have been brought in from the nearby ocean. As he screws the cap back on the bottle, he catches a glimpse of something out of the corner of his eye — something inside the house.

He screws the caps back onto both bottles, places them into his bag, then walks up to the window and looks inside. The house looks like a mess on the outside, with badly peeling paint and missing trim boards — but none of that can even begin to compare to the chaos that's on the inside. There's no flooring, no wallboard, wires and pipes are hanging from everywhere, garbage is strewn across the moldy and stain-marked sub-floor — and at the very far end of whatever room this is, a young man wearing an orange-colored stocking cap is staring at a bare wall, swaying back and forth as if listening to music. As strange as it all seems, especially after what he and his mom dealt with all night, the oddest part about the scene isn't the house or the bizarre rhythmically-challenged swaying — it's the look on what he can see of his face that truly frightens Matt to his core. It's blank, absolutely void of any emotion or presence of mind. If not for the movement, he'd swear the man is already dead.

CHAPTER 28
ABERDEEN

After a long, restless night of trying to sleep on a hard tiled floor, with the sound of rapid gunfire coming from somewhere nearby waking them up in the middle of the night, Beth and Jake decide to wait until the sun is fully up before venturing from behind the barber shop counter. When they do, they find themselves looking out over a scene of trash covered streets and burned out cars — and somewhere through the fog, a view of the tranquil waters of Grays Harbor in the background. As they open the door and walk out onto the sidewalk, the silence of the once-busy city is almost deafening. There's no sign of anybody, living or otherwise, and no sounds of cars or machinery of any kind. Only the screeching coming from the seagulls sitting on the docks, and the lapping of waves against the shore in front of them.

"Did you want to check out the hospital?" asks Beth. "See if that's where the light was coming from?"

He glances down to the shore, making sure their bags are still lying in the same spot they left them in. "Let's get our supplies inside first. They should be safe in there for now."

Jake looks to the west, toward the neighboring city of Hoquiam, where a massive cloud of black smoke is rising from a group of structures near the river that runs between the two cities. There should be sirens and flashing lights, or at least an alarm of some kind, but there's nothing.

"Jake, look..."

He turns around to see Beth pointing toward one of the docks only

255

a block to the east. Tied to the end of the it is a single boat, identical to the one that Sean had been using to follow them.

"He's still alive..." she whispers, her voice full of fear.

Seeing what looks like a body on the sidewalk directly in front of the dock, Jake immediately recognizes that it has Sean's bulletproof vest on. Despite the possibility that it might be a trap, he decides to check it out anyway. "Stay here for a minute."

He pulls his gun out and moves cautiously toward the body, and when he gets to within about thirty feet of it, he can tell without question that it's Sean. He can see his dark blue jacket underneath his vest, and the poorly hidden flask in his front pocket. A few feet away from him, lying in the street gutter and covered in blood, is his rifle. His pistol with an attached silencer is only inches from his hand. With his gun aimed directly at Sean's head, Jake kicks the pistol away from his reach, and then moves around to get a look at his face — or at least what's left of it. If not for a scar just below his hairline, even Jake would have a hard time recognizing him for certain. Someone, or multiple people, have beaten his body so severely that his face has been literally caved in. Chunks of flesh from his throat and limbs have been ripped off as well, and are lying on the sidewalk next to him. Noticing empty shell casings all over the sidewalk, Jake kneels down and picks up Sean's pistol and checks the clip. Just as he thought, it's empty. Whatever happened here last night, Sean put up a hell of a fight, and lost. No other bodies are anywhere in sight.

"Is he dead?" asks Beth from across the street.

"Yeah, he's gone." He stands up again, then turns around and faces Sean's boat — which looks more or less in one piece. "Let's check his boat out. He might have some supplies we can use."

Beth joins him, purposely not looking in Sean's direction as she passes by — then bends down and picks something up off the pathway to the dock.

256

"What's this?"

Jake takes it from her, examining it. "It's a locater device. The son of a bitch must have been tracking us."

After throwing the locater into the water, he walks down the pathway and onto the floating dock. "Is it me, or is that boat listing to one side?"

"It looks that way." The closer they get, the more clear it becomes that one side is sinking into the harbor more than the other. "You know, you shouldn't have thrown that thing into the water. It could have come in handy."

"I doubt it. The more time that goes by, the less accurate those things will become."

"Why is that?"

"Nobody is around to correct the satellites. They're moving off-course, that's why the GPS doesn't work anymore."

When they finally reach the boat, it's obvious to both of them that it's the same one that Jake set fire to in Neah Bay. The entire bow is charred and partially melted from the gasoline dumped onto it. They climb onto the back and enter the cabin, hoping that the off-kilter position is due to the supplies that Sean has on-board, and not just a leak in the bottom. Inside, they find a couple of bags filled with food and a first aid kit. A tote sitting right next to them has an assortment of medications and bottles of alcohol.

"He must've gone into one of the towns to get this stuff," Jake says as he reads the labels on the prescription bottles.

"I wonder how many of these people he killed..."

"These aren't regular prescription bottles, these are the bulk bottles that the pharmacies use."

Beth searches the cabinets in the small kitchenette, finding nothing of any value, then moves onto the bedroom in the bow. The bed is big enough to sleep two people, but one side of it is full of guns

257

and ammunition. There must be at least a dozen rifles, and probably twice as many pistols.

"One thing you have to give him credit for, he's been busy."

Jake looks over her shoulder and sees the guns, then smiles for the first time in weeks. "I just checked the bilge, and it's taking on water. We have to get all this shit into the shop before it sinks."

It takes them over an hour of walking back and forth between the boat and the barber shop, and another two hours working to barricade the door without making too much sound — but after they're done they have the small bathroom in the back of the shop almost completely filled with guns, ammo, medications and a variety of other supplies and food.

After pocketing a couple more of the pistols and one of the rifles, Jake follows Beth out of the room, then looks back at their newly found possessions. "We have to figure out a more permanent home for this stuff. Someplace without a wall of glass looking out onto the street."

Beth looks at her watch, then looks out the window to make sure the weather looks decent. "It's still early enough in the day to search the hospital. Maybe we'll find somewhere more secure inside."

"We need to get out of this city as quickly as possible."

"So what do you want to do?"

"We'll check out the hospital, then first thing tomorrow morning we'll try to find a truck or boat to get us out of here."

The street that leads to the hospital is uphill most of the way, passing by an endless number of rundown buildings that look as if they were abandoned and forgotten long before the viral outbreak. Aberdeen has always had a reputation for attracting the very worst that society has to offer, and the standing of its neighboring city of Hoquiam isn't much better. Whorehouses, illegal gambling and drugs all represent the foundation upon which both cities were built on. Although some might argue that logging and fishing have been the heart of the area's economy, the more sinful occupations have certainly proven to be much more resilient over time.

"It looks like a ghost town," remarks Beth, looking down a street lined with cars and knocked over garbage cans on the curb waiting to be picked up — but still no people anywhere, not even dogs or cats.

"If last night was any indication, I'm sure they're here somewhere. That's why we need to be someplace safe before sunset."

Beth looks to the west, where from this elevation she can see Hoquiam with more clarity. "That fire over there is spreading. Do you think it'll jump the river?"

"Probably." he responds, not bothering to look for himself.

As they approach the hospital, Jake guides them into a building across the street, and after searching it for people, he stands in the front window and watches the hospital entrance with binoculars for any sign of movement. Everything inside is dark, but the glass covered walls of the first floor seem to be intact.

"I wonder if that light has some kind of backup generator hooked up to it...?" Jake wonders aloud.

"Do you see anybody inside?"

"No, everything looks quiet."

"I thought there might be other people here that saw the light, just like us."

"You would think that, wouldn't you..."

Placing the binoculars back into his pocket, he exits the building

259

and begins walking toward the hospital, Beth following closely behind him. When he reaches the front entrance, he looks inside closely and makes sure there's still no activity before trying to open the door. There's no activity to be seen, but the door is also securely locked.

"Should we break it down?" asks Beth.

"No, we might need it intact. Lets check around the other side for a window."

They start circling the building, looking for any possible way inside, and eventually end up finding a small office window that's been closed, but left unlocked. Jake shines his flashlight around the room, takes a pair of latex gloves out of his bag and slips them on, then opens the window and climbs through. The hallway outside the room is dark and quiet, with no sign of people anywhere. There's litter everywhere, similar to the police station in Dungeness, but with fewer papers and a hell of a lot more dried blood. The floors and walls have it smeared everywhere, most of it by hand from the looks of it.

"What the hell happened in here...? whispers Beth, trying not to step in any of it.

"Whatever it was, it happened a while ago."

"Do you think we should be here? Don't you think this blood is probably infected?"

"If it's airborne, then we're already infected. Just don't touch anything without gloves on."

Jake continues down the hallway cautiously, his gun held in front of him ready to fire. When he finds the entrance, he unlocks the door, explaining to Beth that they might need a quick escape route. After searching the main lobby and various hallways without finding anything of use, they start searching the rooms one by one. In every one of them they find pretty much the same thing, a chaotic mess of supplies and linens being tossed around as if someone was looking for something. Some of the rooms have blood smeared just like the

260

hallway, but throughout the entire search they never actually come across a body — not even a body part. The pharmacy looks ransacked just like every other room, but nothing seems to be missing. All of the bottles are still there, some of them on the floor, but all of them still have medicine inside. All of the doors leading to the stairs, however, are locked and barricaded somehow, making it impossible to open them — despite Jake's failed attempt at breaking them down.

Sitting in one of the waiting areas, as Jake looks over an emergency exit map of the hospital for any other ways to the upper floors, Beth stares out the window at an older house across the street. To her surprise, the front door opens slightly, then sways back and forth a few inches.

"Jake, someone just opened that door..."

He looks up from the exit plan and watches with her as the door continues to sway, then slowly it opens wider, and a young man emerges from the doorway and onto the porch. For a moment he just stands there, then he begins making his way down the steps and onto the sidewalk, his movements stiff just like the others they've seen.

"Why is he out so early?" Jake asks.

"It's those dark clouds rolling in — it's like dusk out there."

He looks down the street, and sure enough, more people are outside wandering around the neighborhood.

"Fuck, we'll have to spend the night here I guess."

"To be honest, it won't really bother me sleeping in an actual bed tonight. That concrete floor last night was horrible."

After looking around at the different rooms available, they decide to sleep in one of the cleaner patient rooms that's near the front entrance. It also has the added benefit of having two doors, minimizing their chances of being trapped. As night approaches, they carefully remove the blanket and sheet off the bed, then flip the mattress before climbing onto it to test it out, neither of them

261

minding the small size.

"Is the front door still unlocked?" asks Beth, suddenly remembering it.

"Shit, I forgot about that. I'll be back in a minute." He gets out of bed and starts walking to the door.

"Shouldn't we both go?"

"No, it'll just take a sec."

After he leaves, Beth lies back down and closes her eyes, her mind racing too quickly to ever fall asleep. She thinks about Larry, and whether or not he survived the shooting the night before — and even if he did, whether or not she'll ever see him again. As much as she agrees with Jake that they need to leave the city in order to stay safe, she also knows that any chance of ever seeing Larry will also disappear if they do. Then, just as her mind begins to slip into sleep, she hears a noise coming from the hall. Thinking that it's just Jake returning, she ignores it and lets her mind relax again — and then she hears something else, a scratching on the walls just outside of the room. It gets closer to the door, then passes over it before continuing down the hallway. She turns on the flashlight and listens carefully, then opens the door and shines the light down the corridor, a slight smell of smoke drifting down the hall coming in on a draft of cold air. Almost to the next room, a woman is walking away from her, dragging her nails down the wall as she stumbles forward. Then she stops and begins to slowly turn around toward Beth — but before she turns all the way around, Beth steps back inside and locks the door, expecting at any moment to hear the woman trying to open it.

Sitting alone in the dark, worried that her flashlight might be seen through the cracks around the door, she begins to hear sounds coming from all directions from inside the hospital, even on the floor above her.

262

CHAPTER 29
HIGHWAY 105

It takes a few minutes for Larry to get onto his feet and steady himself, which makes Curtis seriously reconsider his decision to take him along to Aberdeen. The last thing he needs right now is to be slowed down by a stranger that may or may not be injured — or worse. After Larry gets up and starts moving, however, his pace quickly improves, and before long the two of them begin making good time down the highway.

They walk in silence for a while, both of them wishing the wind would change direction and blow the stench coming from the harbor someplace else. If there's one constant on the Pacific Northwest coast, however, it's the endless flow of air that washes straight in off the Pacific, and today is certainly no exception.

"Were you headed to Aberdeen too?" Curtis finally asks, tired of listening to his own internal thoughts.

"Yeah, my sister and her husband are there."

Curtis still isn't sure if this guy knows the full magnitude of what's happened to the world around them. In truth, neither does he — but he knows enough not to get his hopes up that Aberdeen will be in one piece. "When was the last time you heard from them?"

"Last night."

Surprised at the answer, Curtis waits for more details, but none are given. Apparently his new travel companion isn't much of a talker. "I'm headed there to find my son."

"Has he been there long?"

"No, as far as I know he's still on the highway, on his way there.

263

They could be right ahead of us."

"Is he with somebody else?"

"A young girl."

Larry can tell that they both have secrets they're not willing to share at the moment. Although he hasn't asked a word about it, he doesn't really want Curtis to know that the wound on his arm was from a gunshot, or that the man who pulled the trigger might be waiting for them farther on down the road. He can only imagine what the man walking next to him has been through, what hardships and agony he's endured over the past few months — every man, woman and child still alive probably have similar stories.

Curtis looks past the scattered and mangled corpses along the shore and out to the waters of the harbor beyond, where cormorants and seagulls are floating on the surface, their lives completely unaffected by the destruction and chaos that surrounds them.

"I used to love this view," Curtis says, still looking at the harbor. "I can't believe everything has changed so quickly. I keep expecting to see a plane in the air, or hear some message on the radio telling us to hang in there just a little longer."

"Yeah, but I wouldn't hold my breath. The fact that we haven't even seen military aircraft isn't a good sign."

Larry notices a lumber ship sitting about halfway between them and Aberdeen on the other side of the water. He stops for a moment and takes out his binoculars, bringing the ship into focus.

"Do you see anything?" asks Curtis.

At first he sees nothing but an empty deck on top and peeling paint down the sides that's giving way to the inevitable decay of rust. Then something else catches his eye, a group of seagulls gathered near one of the doorways just outside of the crew quarters. They're picking at whatever is left of a skeleton, or several judging from the number of bones that appear to be scattered across the deck.

264

"Looks like everyone on-board is dead."

The road ahead of them begins to curve away from the harbor, a welcome circumstance considering the rotting filth that lines the shore — and shortly after that there's an overgrown mobile home park on the north side of the highway, bordering the water.

Curtis turns and begins walking down the gravel driveway of the park, with Larry following right behind him. "Let's see if we can find a car in here that runs."

Most of the parking spaces in front of the homes are occupied, which most likely means that the people who once lived here never left. After checking a few of the newer cars for keys, Curtis politely knocks on one of the doors and waits, then eventually kicks it in after receiving no response. Inside he finds a set of keys hanging on the wall of the entryway, and two corpses resting in the next room — both of them little more than dried skin stretched over skeletons. He finds the car under a carport beside the mobile home, but when he sticks the key into the ignition and tries to start it nothing happens, just like every other car he's come across north of Cohasset.

Larry bends down, noticing the lack of lights on the dash. "Pop the hood, let me take a look."

Curtis releases the hood latch, then waits as Larry enters a nearby shed — coming out only a few minutes later with a short piece of wire. He takes the wire and places it between the two terminals on the battery.

"The battery is shot."

"I've tried a few dozen cars along the road, but none of them would run either."

Just past the mobile home park, on the other side of a narrow

265

stream that flows into the harbor, they come across a small town that looks as though it was mostly abandoned even before the virus struck. The only two businesses, a gas station and a general store, both appear neglected and empty. A few dozen houses are clustered together on the harbor side of the road, with only a swamp on the south side.

"I was hoping to make better time," Curtis says, looking back at the sun that's getting dangerously close to the horizon, and is now partially blocked by a dark bank of clouds coming in from the coast.

"If you need to go faster, I understand. I'll catch up eventually."

"No, it's not you. I can't move any faster than this anyway."

"Well, we need to find someplace to sleep before it gets dark — before those things come out."

"I was gonna to ask you about that, but I couldn't figure out how to the bring it up. You've seen them too?"

"Yeah, we saw them in Port Angeles first, then again in Sequim and Neah Bay."

"I saw them in Westport."

"How many?"

"It's hard to say — dozens, maybe more."

"There were hundreds in Port Angeles, maybe more. I can't imagine what Aberdeen looks like at night."

Not wanting to think about what Larry just said, Curtis looks at each of the houses along the road, trying to decide which one might be the safest to spend the night in, and wondering if Ben and Amanda might already be inside one of them. "Did you have a preference for which house we stay in?"

"I think I'd rather stay in the store or gas station. Sleeping in the same house as a dead body isn't high on my list of things I'd like to do."

"Sounds good to me."

266

They look inside the buildings, and decide that the store looks the cleanest of the two. That, and the fact that it still has a bit of merchandise left on the shelves. Not wanting to break the front door down, they end up finding an unlocked window in the back of the building that's just big enough for Larry to squeeze through.

Besides the usual array of travel gadgets and air fresheners seen in most small town stores, the latter of which actually comes in handy to block the foul odor from the harbor, the only item they find that's edible is a travel-sized box of saltine crackers. Curtis opens the box up, then hands Larry one of the two small bags inside.

"They only expired four years ago," he tells him, reading the box as he pops one of the stale crackers in his mouth.

"Hey, I'm not complaining."

Curtis sits down on a stool behind the counter, then turns around and gazes through a window that looks out onto the harbor. He can just barely make out the outlines of the buildings across the water through the smoke and fog, which are getting thicker as the night closes in on them. "It doesn't seem real, does it?"

Larry stands beside him and looks in the direction of the bridge, which is almost completely obscured. "No, it doesn't."

"I thought it was horrible a few days ago when I thought that everyone was dead — but I think this is worse..."

"Did you live around here? You know, before...?"

"No, we lived in Portland. We came here to get away from everyone."

"Was it bad there too?"

"Like this? I don't know. There was a lot of looting and destruction going on. People were burning cars and houses, and it didn't do any good to call the cops. We were the last ones to leave our neighborhood."

"We were on our way to Astoria, although I'm not really sure why

267

anymore. It just seemed like the place to be."

"We drove through there on our way up the coast, but that was before everything really went to hell."

"There's no way we're getting there now, not without a boat. It's probably just as well anyway though."

"Yeah, I'd imagine those things are everywhere by now."

"Things?"

"The people that lived. Whatever they are, I don't think they're human anymore."

"What does that make us?"

"Lucky I guess."

Larry had never thought of himself as being 'lucky'. After losing his wife to the illness, becoming suicidal because of it, then becoming separated from the only two people that he knows in the world — that's the last description he'd ever use for himself. All things considered, however, he might be right. He woke up this morning on a beach surrounded by the bodies of those who weren't so fortunate.

"How far is it from here to the city?" he asks Curtis.

"The bridge is only a mile or so up the highway. Downtown is right on the other side."

Both of them stare out the window, watching as the fog rolls in from the entrance of the harbor and over the town of Westport in the distance. Little by little the buildings of Aberdeen across the water begin to disappear into the darkness and haze, and then a faint white light appears on the hill right behind the town.

"Do you see that light?" asks Larry.

"Yeah, I thought I was seeing things."

CHAPTER 30
HIGHWAY 105

Ben can't imagine a worse pain than the way his feet are feeling at the moment. This is the third straight day he's been walking, and the only sleep he got last night was for a brief time at the Regency Hotel with his parents.

The past twenty-four hours have been a roller coaster of emotions for the ten-year-old boy. After being separated from his family, Amanda became his savior, rescuing him from certain death at the hands of an angry mob of people outside the hotel. She was kind to him, giving him shelter from both the people and the weather outside — but even in those early moments of kindness, something seemed off, something that he couldn't quite figure out until early this morning. At first he thought she might be sick like the others, that she'd lost her mind somehow — but she didn't seem to have any of the other physical symptoms that he'd seen in all of the other people in town. It was when they started walking through the woods that he really knew something was wrong — that was when he first heard her conversations with Aaron, her older brother. She was carrying on both sides of an angry argument while standing in the middle of the trail — her eyes glazed over and unfocused, and her hands shaking slightly. Even then, however, part of him was glad that she was with him. He felt safe around her, safe from the 'scourge' that she seemed to know so much about.

Earlier this evening, that all changed. He'd noticed two people following them earlier in the day as they walked along the shore of the harbor, both of them walking down the middle of the highway

269

without a care in the world as to who saw them. Amanda told him that there was obviously something wrong with them, and that walking along the rocky beach was clearly the safest route to Aberdeen, despite the bodies and filth that lined the shore. A few hours later, as the sun began to set into the west, he could see without question that one of the men was his father. In any normal circumstance he would've blurted out his excitement to her, but with every passing minute his fear of her was growing — he'd seen her do things to people, full-grown adults, that made him sick to his stomach. She didn't just kill them, she enjoyed it.

It's now dark outside, and he has his eyes closed, pretending to be asleep on a stranger's couch while his travel companion watches something outside that she clearly doesn't want him to see. He knows that it's his dad that she's watching, and that he's staying somewhere nearby — the only problem is finding him without Amanda knowing about it.

He opens his eyes just a slit, unsure of whether or not she can see him in the subdued lighting of the living room. She's about twenty feet away, still sitting in front of the dining room window, her stained and tattered white dress outlined by the faint moonlight coming through the glass. He waits a few minutes for his eyes to fully adjust to the darkness, then quietly swings his legs off of the couch and stands up. After a quick glance in Amanda's direction to make sure she didn't hear him, he sneaks across the room and into the kitchen, where he can barely make out the back door on the far wall. His shoes, still wet from the mud and rain earlier in the evening, squeak slightly on the linoleum floor as he crosses it. When he hears the sound of a chair being moved in the other room, followed by footsteps in his direction, he runs to the door and tries to open it, forgetting that she'd locked it when they arrived. As he fumbles with the deadbolt, finally managing to get it turned, he suddenly gets the feeling that he's not alone.

"What are you doing?" he hears Amanda say from behind him, her voice angry. "Get back in bed."

He considers responding to her, not knowing if he should simply lie and tell her he had to go to the bathroom. Something deep inside tells him otherwise though, that he needs to get as far away from her as humanly possible. He slowly takes his hand away from the lock and onto the handle, his entire body trembling from fear.

"Don't do it..." she warns him.

Ignoring her, he turns the handle and runs out into the wind and rain, closing the door behind him. As soon as he steps off of the wooden deck and onto the ground below, he slips and falls onto the muddy ground. He can hear the door open as he gets up and keeps running, eventually making his way onto the gravel driveway beside the house. The area in front of him is wide-open, making him an easy target for Amanda to spot — and then he sees a small woodshed on the side of the neighboring house, the inside of which is hidden from the dim glow of the night sky.

He ducks inside the shed and wedges himself into the far corner, then realizes that there's only one way in or out of the place. Just as he considers moving, he sees the beam coming from Amanda's flashlight on the driveway. She's walking slowly, the gravel crunching lightly under her feet, the light aimed only a couple of feet in front of her. At first Ben can't figure out what she's doing, and then he realizes — she's looking for footprints. She walks about ten feet down the driveway, and then stops, shining the light around her. He hopes that the rain has washed away any trace of his prints, but then he notices the wet and muddy marks left on the entrance of the shed. As she shines her light all around the area, he holds his breath as the beam comes into the shed and lands right over his head — but then it moves away after only a few seconds, and she begins to slowly walk farther down the

271

driveway toward the highway.

Peeking out from the doorway, Ben waits until she turns and walks toward the front of the house, then he exits the shed and runs in the opposite direction, toward a car that's sitting in front of a gas station only a couple of doors down. When he makes it to the car, he crouches down behind it, trying to spot Amanda's light again — but he doesn't see it anywhere. As he reaches up for the door handle, he sees two figures walking down the highway in his direction. At first he ducks down out of sight, and then he begins to wonder if it might be his dad and whoever he's walking with. He stands up slowly, careful not to make his presence known just yet, but he can't quite tell exactly who they are. As they get closer, he watches their movements closely, trying to determine if they're walking like all of the other infected — but their gait looks normal as far as he can tell.

He steps out onto the edge of the highway where they can easily spot him, and then waits for them to get closer. It doesn't take them long to begin walking directly toward him, and when they're only about ten feet away, Ben can hear the labored breathing and wheezing coming from both of them. By the time he sees their faces they're only a few feet away — and neither one of the men is his dad. He turns around, intending to run, but instead he feels a sharp pain in the back of his head, and then his eyesight fades away as he loses consciousness.

CHAPTER 31
COHASSETT BEACH

For whatever reason, shock, denial, or otherwise, Matt hadn't given a lot of thought about the people outside, until tonight that is. Seeing the man next door changed the way he thought about them. He no longer saw them as some sort of monster or creature from a comic book or film — these people were much worse than that. Whatever made them this way also destroyed his life as he knew it, separating him from his father and siblings. Every time he comes near them, or touches anything they might have had contact with, he worries about catching their disease and becoming whatever it is that they are. Monsters aren't contagious, at least not any that he's ever read about.

Earlier in the evening, after the cloud bank covered what little sun was still visible, some of the people started passing by the house again — only this time they were mostly traveling in the opposite direction as the night before. He and his mom had wondered why almost everyone was walking toward town, with only a few going against the tide. Tonight they came to the conclusion that there's no reason for anything that they do, they simply react to whatever is in front of them at the time.

Whether due to the increased traffic earlier in the night, or possibly the heavy rain and wind that's coming in from the ocean once again, the numbers outside are down dramatically from yesterday — so much so that Matt is having a hard time staying awake. He keeps coming up with new ideas to stay alert, like naming the other students in his class, or reciting the impossibly long list of rules that his father had written for them at the cabin. Sleep, however,

273

seems inevitable — and shortly after midnight, Matt's eyes begin to close, leaving his mind in a state somewhere between reality and the dreamworld. He hears something rhythmic in the background, still unsure of whether or not he's dreaming — and then suddenly he opens his eyes.

Despite being fully conscious, the rhythmic sound is still there, this time clearly recognizable as footsteps coming from somewhere in the room. He can feel his mom sleeping next to him, and he can see Clara's dead body still propped up in the corner of the room — which only leaves the man in the other room. He reaches to his side and grabs the revolver, then lifts his head up, aiming the gun toward the footsteps. Just as his eyes start to adjust to the darkness of the room, he sees the silhouette of someone as they open the back door and step outside, slamming the door behind them.

"What's going on?" Sarah asks, awoken by the closing door.

"I must've fallen asleep for a few minutes."

"Was someone in here with us?"

Matt stands up and aims the gun at the door, then starts walking toward it. "Yeah, they just left." The house is creaking with every gust of wind that hits it, pelting the window with rain and pine needles, causing Matt to flinch every time it happens. When he finally reaches the door he quickly locks both the handle and the deadbolt, then backs up without looking behind the curtain, afraid of what he might see. "I know I locked this..."

"You should check the front door, and make sure the guy down the hall is still there."

He has to will himself across the floor toward the hallway — fear has taken control of almost every part of his body. He takes his flashlight out of his pocket and shines it down the hall, relieved to see that the door is still barricaded the same as before. Then it occurs to him — if it wasn't the man in the bedroom, then who was it? Still not wanting anybody to know that they're inside the house, he turns his light off again and proceeds through the kitchen and into the front room, half expecting to see someone else waiting there for him. All he finds, however, is another unlocked door.

After locking the door and checking the house once again for any intruders, he sits down next to his mom on the couch, now wide-awake despite the minuscule amount of sleep he's gotten lately.

"Did you figure out how they got in?" she asks him.

"No, I checked all of the doors and windows last night."

"We should both keep watch for a while, just until we know it's safe..."

Nearly an hour has passed by since the intrusion into their temporary home, and both Sarah and Matt are huddled together on the couch, frightened by every breaking tree branch or piece of debris that hits the side of the house. Every so often a flash of lightning illuminates the room for a brief second, followed quickly by the booming sound of thunder from overhead. Sarah is almost certain that on two occasions she spotted people walking by the window when the lightning hit, and she wonders what sort of psychosis would make somebody want to walk around in weather like this.

"We need to get back to the cabin tomorrow, we can't keep living like this," Sarah whispers.

"What about your leg?"

"You'll need to find a car or something. There's bound to be one around here that we can take."

"I don't know how to drive though..."

"I'll show you, it's not that hard. Some of the dumbest people I

275

know are still capable of it." She looks over at him, hoping to see a smile on his face, but even in near darkness she can tell something is distracting him. "What is it?"

"I thought I heard something."

"Like what?"

"A clicking."

Immediately after the words come out of his mouth, they both hear a door shut in the front room, followed by a slow set of footsteps making their way into the kitchen. Sarah rolls off of the couch and onto the floor, pulling her son down with her — and then they both crawl into the far corner, hiding behind the chair that Clara's body is tied to.

They can tell that he's still in the kitchen by the sounds of crashing pans and breaking dishes. Then everything goes quiet, and the only sound that can be heard is coming from the storm outside. After what seems like an eternity passes by, they finally hear the familiar footsteps once again, this time heading down the hall and into the bathroom across from the barricaded bedroom. They only stay in the bathroom briefly, but when they come out, they stand and stare at the bedroom door, their position in plain view of Sarah and Matt's sight. It's a man, that much is obvious, and when he first approaches the door and tries to open it, the rope around the handle does its job and keeps the door closed.

Anybody with half a brain could tell with a quick glance how to remove the rope from the knob, but this guy doesn't seem capable of figuring it out. He tries again and again, each time growing more frustrated and angry, until eventually he begins throwing his fists against the door — but even then it stays shut. It's only when he begins walking away that his hand brushes against the rope, making it fall from the knob, and causing the door to open just a crack — but he either doesn't see it, or doesn't care, because he continues walking

276

into the living room where Sarah and Matt are hiding. He turns toward the back door, then stops and looks around the room, sniffing the air like an animal. Then he continues on, messing with the doorknob for an absurd amount of time before finally getting the door open. As the door swings inside, a gust of wind catches it and smacks him in the face, nearly sending him to the floor. Once he regains his balance, he forces himself into the driving rain and leaves the door open behind him.

Matt jumps up and runs across the room, then struggles to close the door against the storm. He sees the man standing just outside, staring in the direction of the ocean, the pine trees swaying violently in the wind. When he finally gets it closed and locked, he starts to run toward the front room, then stops when he hears his mom's voice.

"Matt, don't bother locking the front door, he obviously has a key. You need to make sure the bedroom door is shut."

For a moment he forgot that the bedroom was even open. "Can you see anything in the doorway?"

"I can't see inside the room, but the hallway is empty."

Matt creeps around the corner, his gun in his hand once again, and then very carefully makes his way down the hall until he reaches the bedroom. He extends his hand to reattach the rope, and then takes a step back when he looks through the now open doorway.

"Mom, you have to come here..."

CHAPTER 32
HIGHWAY 105

With the world feeling as though it's literally spinning out of control, and the room too dark to see anything but vague shadows and outlines — Ben wakes up confused and in pain, scared to move his body even the slightest. The last thing he remembers is standing out on the street, trying to get away from Amanda, and then the two men that approached him, one of which he had hoped was his father. Closing his eyes again, he hears two male voices in the background, both of them sounding far off, as if they're in a tunnel.

"It's only a matter of time before she finds out where we're at..."

"She already knows — she's probably watching us right now."

"Is she sick?"

"I don't know, it seems hard to believe that a girl as young as she is could be that twisted all on her own. She doesn't look sick though."

"What about the kid?"

"I don't know, he was hit pretty hard."

The voices stop for a minute, and then Ben suddenly feels a cold hand on his forehead. Without meaning to, he flinches, then tries to lie as perfectly still as possible, hoping they hadn't noticed.

"He's awake."

Ben listens as both men gather close to him, their breath feeling warm on his face.

"It's okay, you're safe now. Nobody is going to hurt you."

The voice sounds familiar. He opens his eyes slowly, still unable to make out much detail. He focuses on one of the men at his side, who he doesn't recognize, but he looks friendly enough. Then he hears the other man speak...

"Ben, look at me..."

Although his voice still sounds strange, he instantly knows that the other man is his dad — even without looking at him. He turns his head and smiles at Curtis, then closes his eyes again as the room begins to spin.

"Go ahead and keep your eyes closed, it's okay," says Curtis.

"What about Amanda?" asks Ben.

"She's outside somewhere, don't worry about her."

"And the two men, what about them?"

"They're both gone."

"Where are..."

Curtis cuts him off mid-sentence. "Shh, no more questions for now. You need to get some rest."

He watches Ben for another couple of minutes, and as soon as he falls asleep again, Larry motions him to the other side of the room.

"Look outside."

Curtis looks out the rain-spattered window at the street beyond, where he sees a couple of dozen people gathered near the bodies of the two men.

"You shouldn't have tried to shoot her, it made too much noise," Larry whispers.

"I wanted her out of our lives."

"I thought you said that she saved both of you..."

"It's complicated. There's something seriously wrong with her."

"Yeah, well, it's too bad. She made a mess out of those two guys she killed. Someone like that could come in handy."

They watch the small crowd of people outside as they move slowly around one another, all of them soaking wet from the wind and rain. Only a few of them are wearing jackets. One of the men kneels down in front of the corpses and just stares at them for a moment, looking

279

at one and then the other, his body rocking back and forth. Then he places his face to the middle of their torso and just stays there. Almost immediately the others do the same, their hands ripping at the men's clothing.

"Are they doing what I think they're doing?" asks Curtis.

"We saw a bunch of them eating a dog in Sequim. There was nothing but bones when they were done." Larry replies, turning around to face the room again.

"Did you ever see them do that to one another?"

"They don't seem to discriminate. They eat whatever they can find."

Curtis watches them for a while, horrified and curious at the same time, until he sees one of them look up with blood covering their face and arms. Then he turns around and faces his son, who at the moment seems to be the only glimmer of hope he has left.

"Any idea what you're going to do after this, where you'll go?" Curtis asks.

"Not a clue. Somewhere quiet I guess — if there is such a place."

"You could come stay with us at the cabin if you want. It'd be nice to have someone else around to help out with things."

"I appreciate the offer, but it would be a little crowded, wouldn't it?"

"There's an old house on the next property, I doubt it's occupied." Curtis looks across the room at the window that faces Aberdeen, and notices that the fires in the city are casting an orange glow on the window sill. "Those fires must be getting worse over there." He waits for a response, but gets none. "Are you sure you want to go there tomorrow? You could come back with us in the morning, we could be there by evening."

"Would you leave your son behind if you knew he was over there?"

"No, I wouldn't." Curtis turns back around toward the street, seeing that only a few people are still on the ground eating what's left of the

280

bodies. If this is what it's like in a small community outside of town, he can't imagine what it must be like in the city itself. "Can I at least draw you a map of where to find the cabin?"

"Sure, that'd be great."

Staring out at what's left of the cities across the harbor, Larry wonders whether or not Curtis is right about the dangers of crossing over the bridge. He can only see a small portion of it from the store window, and every once in a while he spots a group of people walking across it, most of them heading south in his direction. The streets, alleys and buildings in Aberdeen must be crowded with them, their deranged minds now seemingly filled with nothing but anger and violence.

He glances back at the table behind him, where Curtis and his son are sound asleep, and he feels both relief and sadness at the same time. It was only a couple of months ago that he and his wife were discussing having a child of their own. They hadn't planned on it when they first got married, but as time went on both of them felt as though their lives might be incomplete without one. Looking at Curtis and Ben, however, he wonders if the opposite might actually be true. While he realizes that the most important things in Curtis' life are his children, the added pressure and stress of having to protect them in whatever is left of the world seems overwhelming. It might be true what they say, that it's different once you have them, that some profound paternal instinct takes over and gives you whatever strength is necessary to keep going — or perhaps it only serves to deepen your desperation. Either way, Larry doesn't feel it, and he's fairly certain he doesn't want to.

He looks back out the window at the amber reflection in the water

281

from the fires, telling himself that he needs to get some sleep if he's going to make the trip tomorrow — whether it be across the bridge, or back to Cohasset with his new friends. He stands up from the stool and starts to look for a decent place to lie down, then he hears something from the other side of the room — the sound of radio static. As he crosses the room and heads toward his bag next to the front door, Curtis sits up and whispers to Larry.

"What is that?"

"It's my radio, I didn't think it still worked," replies Larry. He unzips the bag and pulls out a handheld radio that's still damp with saltwater.

"*Jake, are you there? Please answer me... I'm worried about you...*"

"Who is that?" asks Curtis.

"It's my sister. Jake is her husband," Larry responds, his voice filled with excitement as he answers the radio. "Beth, can you hear me?"

"*Jake, is that you?*"

"No, it's Larry. Can you hear me?"

"*Yes, I hear you — where are you?*" she answers, her voice filled with tears and emotion.

"I'm on the other side of the bridge. Where are you?"

"*I'm in the hospital up on the hill.*"

"Okay, I'm going to come and get you, but I have to wait until morning — it's too dangerous at night."

"*Jake went out to lock the door a couple of hours ago, and he hasn't come back — and now there's people all over the hospital.*"

"Are you someplace safe?"

"*I think so.*"

"Okay, turn your radio off until morning, you have to save the battery."

"*What about Jake?*"

"We'll find him when I get there. Don't leave whatever room you're in, okay?"

282

"*Okay, I won't.*" Then her voice turns to a whisper, barely audible. "*I have to go, someone is outside my door again.*"

Larry listens to the radio static, his mind filled with every conceivable scenario that ends badly. Then he switches the radio off, knowing that the batteries have to be nearly drained.

"We'll wait for you," says Curtis. "We can all leave together the next morning — if that's what you want..."

Larry looks to be in shock, not responding at first. Then finally he faces Curtis. "You don't have to do that, you should get back to your family."

Curtis glances down at Ben, who's still asleep. "He's in no shape to travel anyway, he needs at least another day to rest."

"Thank you, you have no idea how much I appreciate this."

"You need to get some sleep, you have a pretty good walk ahead of you. I'll keep first watch."

Larry nods, then places the radio back inside of his bag. Before he lowers himself to the floor, he takes another look out at the street, expecting to see the same people wandering around — but they aren't there. Instead, he sees a single person facing the store, a young girl in a blood-stained tattered dress and black coat, and a large kitchen knife held tightly in her small hand.

CHAPTER 33
COHASSETT BEACH

Sarah slowly makes her way across the living room and down the hallway, leaning on Matt as she looks through the open doorway of the bedroom. Lying on the floor in nothing but a t-shirt and underwear, covered in filth and grime, with his hands and feet tied with rope and his mouth taped shut — is the withered body of an old man, his eyes frightened at the sight of strange people. Sarah takes a glove that she found in the kitchen out of her pocket and slips it onto her hand, then reaches down and pulls the tape off of his mouth.

"Can you talk?" she asks him. He starts to speak, then coughs so badly that he begins to choke. "Matt, give him a little water — carefully."

Matt reaches down and pours a small amount of water from his bottle, just wetting the man's mouth.

"Thank you." the man manages to say.

"What's your name?"

"Carl, Carl Embree."

"Embree? Is Clara your wife?"

The man nods, then sits up and rests his back against the dresser behind him.

"Did she do this to you, tie you up like this?"

"Yes."

"Why would she do that?"

"I wish I knew the answer to that, I really do."

"So you're not sick?"

"No, I'm not sick." He looks down at the floor, and a deep sadness

284

takes over his face. "She's dead, isn't she?"

Sarah looks down at Carl's arms, and notices several large bruises on his forearms — then she notices the same type of bruises on his legs just below the knees. They look like defensive wounds. "Did she do that to you? Did Clara hurt you?"

He nods, then looks Sarah in the eyes. "Is my wife dead?"

"I'm afraid so."

He looks back to the floor again, then shifts his hands around to make the ropes tying them together more comfortable. In the dim luminescence of the flashlight, Sarah can see red bands under the ropes where the skin has been scratched off and replaced with raw flesh. "How long have you been locked in here?"

"Four days."

"And you've been without food and water this entire time?"

"Yes," he replies, nearly choking once again.

Sarah suddenly feels awful for knowing that he was in here this entire time, and yet she did absolutely nothing about it. She also wants to be cautious of his story though, and take whatever he has to say with a grain of salt, but she also realizes that there must be other people like her and Matt out there, people that for whatever reason have never contracted the virus. To allow one of them to simply perish feels wrong on every level.

"Are you well enough to walk?" she asks, wondering the same thing about herself. The pain in her leg is excruciating.

"I don't know, I can't really try with my legs tied together like this."

She holds out her hand to Matt. "Give me the gun, then cut his ropes off with a knife from the kitchen." She then looks down at Carl with a menacing look as Matt hands her the revolver. "If you try anything, I'll put a bullet in your head — understand?"

285

After freeing Carl of his restraints, and finding that he could barely walk with the assistance of a cane that once belonged to his wife, Sarah and Matt return to the living room while Carl cleans himself up in the bathroom with half of their drinking water. As much as Sarah hated the idea of having only a liter of water once again, she also couldn't imagine spending time around Carl with the smell of filth so heavy in the air. When he finally comes out of the bathroom with clean clothes on and most of the grime removed from his body, he glances into the corner where the body of his wife rests, then quickly looks away after realizing what he's looking at. He finally sits down in a chair on the other side of the room.

Sarah and Matt spin the couch around to face him, then she sets a burning candle on a small table between them, more as a gesture than anything else, considering she can already see the first sign of light coming through the window curtains.

"Do you know who the person in the other bedroom is?" Sarah asks him.

"That's our son, Samuel."

"Did you know that he's..."

"Dead? Yes, he died a few weeks ago."

"I'm sorry, I really am."

"Thank you."

Sarah can tell that he's exhausted, and she can't imagine the stress that he's feeling, but she needs answers before she feels comfortable letting her guard down. Even Clara seemed somewhat reasonable for a short while. "My name is Sarah by the way, and this is my son, Matt."

"Yes, I heard you introduce yourself to Clara last night. I wish we were meeting under different circumstances."

"How long had she been sick?"

"She first started showing symptoms shortly after Samuel passed

286

away."

"What kind of symptoms?"

"Just strange behavior at first, and then she developed a cough a couple of days later."

"Why didn't you leave?"

"She's my wife, I couldn't just let her die."

The room falls into an uncomfortable silence, and then Matt finally speaks up.

"Did your TV work before the power went out?"

"Yes, why?"

"Did you see anything about the rest of the country?"

The question surprises Sarah. She wasn't even aware that he wondered about such things, let alone worry about them.

"The last thing I saw was a report from New York. They said the city was being overrun."

"With what?" asks Sarah.

"They didn't say exactly. I assumed they meant the sick — you know, the ones who don't die."

As the words leave his mouth, the doorknob on the back door begins to jiggle, and Sarah quickly aims the gun at the doorway. All three of them hold their breath as they watch the door, expecting at any moment to see it open — but it never does. Eventually the doorknob settles down, and the person on the other side of it apparently moves on.

"The man that unlocked the bedroom door earlier, do you know him?" Sarah asks.

"His name is Jacob, he's the neighbor's son."

"Does he have a key?"

"His mother did."

"I assume he's sick?"

"I thought he was dead for a long time, he came down with the

287

virus early on."

Sarah knows in her heart that she only has two options — either kill Jacob, or somehow try to get back to the cabin where she was hoping to find Curtis and Ben already waiting for them. Getting there, however, was the problem. There's no way in hell she can walk that far, and the road out front is completely impassible due to the cars lined up for miles. The only alternative left is the beach.

"Do you have a car that runs?" she asks him.

"There's one out front in the driveway."

"Does it run?"

"It should, but I haven't tried starting it for a while."

"Do you mind if we borrow it?"

"As far as I'm concerned you can keep it — as long as you take me with you..."

Sarah starts to say something in response, and then they freeze as they listen to the front door open once again. All three of them drop to the floor, and Sarah keeps an eye on both the entryway into the room, and on Carl behind her. She still doesn't completely trust him, and now would be the perfect time to try something. They wait another couple of minutes, and then they hear the sound of the door as it closes — and then silence.

"Is he gone?" whispers Carl.

"No, I can hear him breathing."

CHAPTER 34
HIGHWAY 105

"Curtis, wake up..."

Curtis opens his eyes and sees Larry standing in front of him with a duffel bag in his hand. The room is dimly lit from the sunlight outside, telling him that it's either very early, or the skies are heavily overcast. He glances down at Ben, making sure he's still asleep, then carefully rolls off of the table and walks to the other side of the room.

"Are you taking off?" asks Curtis.

"Yeah, it's light enough out that those people should all be indoors."

"Any sign of Amanda?"

"No, I don't see her anywhere."

Curtis holds out his hand, and the two men shake before Larry turns around and heads for the door, neither one of them knowing what else to say. Then, right before he opens the door to exit, Larry turns around. "If I'm not back by tomorrow morning, consider me dead. Take Ben and find the rest of your family."

Curtis nods, then watches him walk out the door.

Having already spoken to Beth shortly after leaving the general store, and finding out that things at the hospital were still more or less the same as last night, Larry steps onto the bridge that spans the Chehalis River and begins his trek into the heart of Aberdeen. The fires to the west of town, where the city borders Hoquiam, have grown overnight, and the thick black smoke emanating from them has now

289

enveloped large sections of both cities.

As he passes by the dozens of abandoned cars along the bridge, the scenes inside of them seem eerily similar to the ones that Curtis told him about in Westport. While many of them are empty, others contain horrible sights of rotting corpses inside, both human and animal — and all of them well decomposed. He wonders at first why someone would allow themselves to die like that, why they wouldn't at least try to walk to safety — and then he notices the locked doors, and the fingernail scratches on the outside of each of the cars. Someone, or something, was trying desperately to get inside. He figures that he'll likely never know exactly what happened here in those first few weeks after the infection, and if the scenes in front of him are of any indication, he'd rather keep it that way.

As he reaches the other side of the bridge and starts up the hill toward the hospital, he notices through the smoky haze that the streets are filled with broken glass and litter, but very few bodies. Only the occasional skeleton lying in the gutter or an alleyway can be seen, and even those have been picked clean of any trace of flesh. The entire town looks like a wasteland — dead and defeated. Looking up the hill, he can't help but recognize how much the buildings ahead of him look like massive gravestones in a crowded graveyard — even more so with the smoke rolling through town and obscuring the streets below them. He can't imagine how many of the infected are inside each of them, waiting for darkness to encroach the city.

About halfway up the hill he walks into the massive plumes of smoke coming from the fires, each one filled with an ungodly mixture of horrid scents and limited visibility. He covers his nose and mouth the best he can, but he can't do a thing to protect his eyes from the burning gasses. Finally, with the hospital only a block ahead of him, the smoke begins to dissipate, leaving him a clear view of the front entrance. Both of the glass doors are wide-open.

Larry stands on the sidewalk outside the doors and takes a look inside, making sure that at least the lobby is clear. After he's relatively certain that it is, he pulls out his radio and switches it back on. "Beth, are you still there?"

"*Yes, I'm still here. Where are you?*"

"I'm right outside the hospital. I'll see you in a few minutes, okay?"

"*Okay, what about Jake?*"

"Don't waste your battery, we'll talk when I get there. Room one-twenty-seven, right?"

"*Right.*"

He glances down at his watch, which reads almost 10AM. He left the store over two hours ago, which is actually making decent time, but it also doesn't give them a lot of time to search for Jake before the sun goes down.

As soon as he steps over the threshold and into the main lobby, he can instantly hear the sounds of people moving in the corridors all around him. Their raspy breathing and coughing are the loudest, but it's the faint sound of slow footsteps that bothers him the most. He's never seen them active in the daytime before, but then again, he's never seen them in a darkened building either. He shines his flashlight at the signs visible at the beginning of each hallway, finding that room one-twenty-seven is to his left.

As he walks farther into the building and away from the daylight, he moves his flashlight cautiously around, making sure that nobody gets close to him, his gun at his side in the other hand. Every corridor that he passes by has at least a dozen people standing near the end, and some of the spaces appear to be half-full. The floors are slimy and sticky under his feet, but Larry purposely doesn't look down to find out what's causing it — he'd rather not know. Finally, after making it nearly halfway down the hallway, he reaches the room number that Beth gave him. He taps lightly on the window three

291

times, then shines the light onto his face to make it easier to recognize him. Just as he hears the door click and begin to open, he hears another sound coming from farther down the hallway — the sound of clumsy footsteps walking quickly across the linoleum.

"Beth, come on! Somebody is coming..."

The door opens and Beth steps out, tears running down her face. "Who is it?"

He shines the light in the direction of the noise, and sees a man in a ripped and tattered suit walking straight toward them, both of his eyes bloodshot and bright red. When the light hits him he nearly falls to the floor, then manages to get to his feet again, shielding his face with his arm as he starts to inch forward once again.

"Does your light work?" asks Larry.

"Yes," Beth answers, quickly turning it on.

"Aim it toward the lobby, make sure nobody is in the way. I have to keep mine on this guy."

She moves the beam of her light toward the lobby as he asked, seeing nothing but the bloodstained floor she saw the night before. "It looks clear."

Both of them start walking down the hallway as quickly as they can, the sounds of footsteps heard all around them. They become even more active once the man following them starts screaming. Larry is forced to walk almost backward, keeping his light directly on the man, and making sure he doesn't start to gain on them. Then right before they reach the end of the hall, Beth pushes against him, stopping both of them.

"Wait!"

"What's wrong?"

"There's somebody in the lobby, they're standing right in front of the door."

"Keep moving, I'll take care of them."

292

As they move farther into the lobby, and the light level begins to grow, the man following them slows down, then starts to make his way around the edge of the room where the shadows are the heaviest. Larry turns around and faces the man standing in the doorway, aiming his gun directly at the back of the man's head — then watches as the man calmly walks outside and turns the corner, never bothering to look back.

While still keeping an eye on the man with the bloodshot eyes, Larry nudges Beth through the doorway, and the two of them step out onto the sidewalk and into the safety of daylight — or at least what's left of it. Between the smoke and the black clouds rolling in from the ocean, the skies are beginning to darken considerably.

"Where'd he go?" Beth asks.

"Who?"

"That guy that just left. I don't see him anywhere."

Larry takes a quick glance around, not seeing a trace of anybody, then turns back around and closes both of the hospital doors, tying them together with a short piece of rope that he pulls out of his coat.

"What about Jake?" she asks frantically, finally noticing what he's doing.

"Beth, if he's in there, there's no way we're getting to him. I'm sorry."

She looks stunned, and heartbroken, but when she looks back through the lobby doors and into the dark room beyond, she sees dozens of people flooding into the lobby from every direction — all of them heading straight toward the doors.

Larry puts his flashlight back into his bag, but keeps his gun in his right hand as he crosses the street and heads toward the harbor.

"We have to get across the bridge before sunset," he tells his sister, who's following right behind him, still in shock.

"Why can't we wait around here for a couple of days? Jake might

293

still be in there."

"We can't stay here, it's just too dangerous."

As they pass by an abandoned building, one of many that were empty long before the viral outbreak, something catches Beth's attention in the window. She sees a woman facing her, and for a moment she assumes the woman is inside the old storefront where it's still dark — and then she realizes that it's merely a reflection, that the woman is actually outside, standing on the other side of the street from them.

"Larry, there's a woman in the street over there..."

He looks over at her, making sure that she doesn't start following them — then he looks back up the hill in the direction of the hospital. A few other people are walking down the middle of the road, but none of them seem to be paying any attention to him and Beth.

"We need to stop somewhere for just a minute," says Beth quietly.

"We don't have time."

"It's on the way. Jake and I spent the first night there, and if there's even the slightest chance he made it back...

"Okay, okay, we'll check it out — but just for a minute."

Only a few blocks farther down the hill, the skies open up and begin pouring rain down on them, turning the street gutters into small streams — and while the rain serves to partially clear the air of the horrible smoke, the sound of it falling loudly onto the cars and puddles also limits their ability to hear anything that might be around them. Every block they pass, watching their every step to prevent a fall or twisted ankle, they see more and more people coming out of the buildings and alleyways and onto the streets. A few of them glance in their direction, but most look unaware that they even exist.

"They seem kind of quiet," Larry says, as he watches a woman hitting her fist weakly against a storefront window.

"It's early, I'm surprised any of them are even out. The worst ones always come out after dark."

Larry then realizes that he really doesn't know that much about them — he only took watch for a single night while they were in Sequim. Not long after his shift started, he looked through binoculars at downtown and saw the people pouring out onto the streets, where angry mobs attacked and mutilated one person after another — some of the mobs even turning on each other when there was no one else around to brutalize. The moment that some of the crowd began stalking a young child, whether a boy or a girl he couldn't tell, Larry put the binoculars down and refused to watch any further. From then on he kept his eyes and mind focused on the entrance to the marina, making sure the boat and his family were safe. Part of him now wishes that he would've paid more attention to them, learned more about their behavior and habits.

"When you say the worst ones, do you mean violent?" he asks.

"They're worse than violent — they're inhuman."

When they finally reach the waterfront road where the barber shop is located, Beth looks down at where they found Sean's body just the day before, but it's not there now — only his shoes and a ripped up shirt are left.

As Beth opens the barber shop door and steps into the small room, she doesn't really expect to find her husband waiting there — she knows that he would never leave her inside the hospital alone. She had to check though, if nothing else than to free her of the burden of always wondering 'what if'.

"Jake, are you in here?" she yells out, heading straight to the bathroom in the corner of the room.

"Beth, we should go. He's obviously isn't here."

"Come here, we should grab some of this shit before we go."

Larry walks up behind her and sees the room filled with supplies, most of it guns and ammo. They fill his bag to its limit with a variety

295

of things, like medications, matches, energy bars, bottles of water, and a couple of pistols with ammo. Beth grabs another bag and fills it with somewhat the same items, with more emphasis on the ammunition, knives and guns. On the way out, she takes an AR-15 semi-auto rifle leaning in the corner and swings it onto her shoulder, then heads to the entrance of the shop, looking back at Larry to see what's holding him up.

"What're you doing?" she asks, seeing him reach into his bag.

"Finding this." He holds up a piece of paper and then sets it down on the counter. "It's a map of where we're going. If Jake is still alive, he might come back here and find it."

Beth looks out the window, seeing more people spilling out into the street from the nearby buildings and docked ships. A group of seven of them is chasing what appears to be an old woman down to the shoreline, nearly catching her by the time they slip out of Beth's sight.

"Maybe we should stay here for the night. They're getting restless out there already," says Beth.

"You said Sean's boat is still afloat?" he replies, clearly ignoring her suggestion.

"Barely."

Larry stands next to her, appraising the situation for himself, then opens the door quietly when it appears that nobody is looking their way. As they both step out onto the sidewalk, Larry turns and whispers into her ear. "If anybody gets in your way, try to walk around them — but if they won't move, shoot them in the head until they drop. Got it?"

"Got it."

They move along the sidewalk slowly, trying to stay hidden against the sides of the old brick buildings they pass by — but the number of people on the street next to them is growing by the minute, and after only half a block it becomes painfully obvious that at least some of them are now watching their every move. Beth glances up at the road in front of them, and sees two older men in filthy clothes staring at them intently, almost as if they recognized them from somewhere. As they get closer, Beth can see the red tinge in their eyes.

"Those guys ahead of us are really sick, look at their eyes."

"I see them."

The men begin to walk toward Larry and her, each step looking stiff and painful. She turns around to see if they can still get back to the barber shop, and sees a small group of a dozen or so people almost to the entrance and coming their way.

"We have to do something..." she whispers to Larry, her voice shaking with fear.

He grabs her hand and steps off of the sidewalk and onto the roadway, crossing to the other side where the marina is only a short distance ahead. The men ahead of them start crossing the street to cut them off, and when Larry looks back at the group of people following, he notices that they've fanned out, and are now completely blocking the road behind them. Whether operating by instinct or intelligence, or perhaps a little of both, it's obvious that he and Beth are being hunted.

"We might have to make a run for it," he tells his sister.

"We can't even be sure the boat is still there."

"Just be ready."

Still staggering somewhat, the two men speed up their advancement and make it across the street, and have now stopped directly in front of them, blocking their way to the marina only fifty feet ahead. Larry notices that the others behind them have stopped as well, and that the people to their side have closed in and sealed the street off, leaving the harbor to their right the only way out. He feels Beth tug on his hand as she begins to move toward the water, but he

297

pulls her back onto the sidewalk next to him.

"Aim for their torso, just like Jake showed you..."

Beth feels his hand let go of hers, then watches as he aims his pistol at one of the men in front of them. She slides her rifle off of her shoulder slowly, trying not to make any sudden movements, then pulls the charging handle back in a quick motion to cock it. The people behind them and to their side are still about thirty feet away, but the two men are only about half of that. Turning to face the crowd to her side, she lifts the rifle up and aims it at the chest of a young man who appears to be in his early twenties. She feels horrible doing it, and for a moment she wonders whether or not she's even capable of pulling the trigger and killing another human being — and then the man smiles at her. The grin is almost mischievous, but the red-tinged teeth underneath tell her that there's something much more dangerous about him.

When Larry's gun goes off behind her, it startles her enough that she almost drops her rifle. When the second round is fired, and the people surrounding them quicken their pace to close in on them, Beth begins firing her gun at each of them, trying her best to keep her composure and not waste ammunition. In only a fraction of a minute, she pauses and looks around, seeing nothing but bodies lying on the ground, all of them either dead or writhing in pain.

A few of them are moaning loudly, or screaming in agony. Then she hears a rattling noise, and after looking down she realizes that it's coming from her own gun, and that her hands and legs are trembling.

"Beth..."

She turns around and sees Larry pointing up the hill, where huge crowds of people are making their way down the pavement from seemingly every street.

"We need to get out of here, now..." he tells her.

They both grab their bags and begin running down the sidewalk and onto the walkway that leads to the marina. About halfway to Sean's abandoned boat, they feel the floating dock suddenly shudder and sway, the wooden side supports cracking loudly as it sinks farther into the water. Beth glances back quickly, seeing a large swarm of people running onto the dock from the street, filling every square inch of the decking.

"Hurry, they're gaining on us!" she yells.

Larry can tell from here that the boat is taking on water, but the fact that it's still floating is a huge relief. When they finally reach it, he throws his bag onto the deck and starts untying the rope from the dock. He can hear the hundreds of footsteps getting closer, and the splashes of water as they push one another into the harbor. Fearing that he's running out of time, he grabs a large knife from the bag and starts cutting his way through the rope — both of them pushing off from the berth as soon as he's finished, and just in time to see the first people reach the end of the dock. Still only a boat length away, Larry and Beth watch as dozens of people are pushed into the water from the masses right behind them. Within a few minutes, the surface of the harbor is filled with struggling bodies, all of them grabbing onto whatever is close by in order to stay afloat.

As the fog and smoke moves in around them and completely blocks their sight, Larry and Beth are left with only the sounds of splashing water and screaming, and the occasional clawing at the boat's hull.

CHAPTER 35
COHASSETT BEACH

Sarah listens to the labored, congested coughing emanating from the next room, and the slow sound of footsteps as the man walks across the tiled kitchen floor toward the living room. She points her gun in the direction of the intruder, and then feels a tug on her sleeve.

"Mom, shouldn't we hide?" Matt whispers to her.

She looks over at Carl, whose withered body is pushed as far into his chair as humanly possible, a look of fear and disbelief on his face as he stares at the doorway to the kitchen.

"No," says Sarah. "We're not going to hide — not anymore."

They can hear him in the other room going from cupboard to cupboard, spilling their contents across the already filthy floor, then dragging his feet through the trash as he makes his way closer to the entrance of the living room. Sarah almost pulls the trigger the instant that she sees his face. Even in the pale light of the room, she can clearly see the bloodshot and almost lifeless eyes, and that his skin is covered in dark colored blotches that seem to take up most of his face. Upon entering the room, he looks at each of them only briefly, then begins looking through the bookshelf that rests against the wall next to the hallway.

Sarah looks at Carl again, who looks petrified with fear. "Carl, say something to him..."

"Like what?"

"Anything, tell him to get out."

Carl looks back at Jacob, who's now removing every book off of the shelf one by one. "Jacob, can you hear me?"

300

No response.

"Jacob, look at me!" he says more forcefully. This at least causes the young man to stop what he's doing for a moment and turn around briefly, but all Carl gets in response is a hostile glare and muttering under his breath. Carl stands up and takes a couple of steps toward him, prompting Jacob to turn around and scream something unintelligible at him.

"Carl, stand back..." Sarah tells him.

Carl takes a step back just as Jacob lunges forward and takes a swipe at his face — his dirty, overgrown fingernails coming inches from his cheek. As he falls back into his chair and covers his head from any further attacks, Jacob turns around and faces the bookshelf again — pitching the books and knickknacks to the floor.

"Hey, get the fuck out!" Sarah yells at the man, aiming her gun directly at his head. Jacob grabs a book and turns around, then throws the hardcover at her, the corner of it hitting her left shoulder hard enough to nearly knock her off of her feet. After steadying herself, she aims the pistol at his head once again as he stumbles across the living room toward her and Matt, his eyes not only bloodshot, but glazed over with a milky-white substance as well.

"Don't fucking move!" Sarah yells at him — but he keeps clumsily inching his way forward, trying to get around or over the couch that sits between them. As he reaches his right hand up in the direction of her gun, she fires a single shot into his chest, knocking him back a couple of steps — but after only a few seconds he looks down at the red-stained spot on his shirt, then smiles at her and begins to move forward once again. She fires another shot into his chest, and then another, but none of them seem to faze him in the slightest. Finally, as he reaches up once again and grabs for her gun, she pulls the trigger twice more before the gun runs out of ammo, hitting him once in the throat and once in the forehead. He immediately drops to the ground and begins to shake, blood pouring from the holes in his head in thick, streaming pulses.

"Go lock the door," Sarah says, looking at Matt. For a moment he just stands there, his ears still ringing from the gunshots, and his mind numb from what he just witnessed. Then, as the ringing begins to fade away, he hears the light tapping of rain on the metal roof overhead, and his mother's voice beside him. "Matt, do what I said — before someone else comes in." As Matt heads to the front room, she looks over at Carl, who slumps back into his seat in disbelief at what just happened. "Carl, where are those keys?" He doesn't answer, he just stares at the body of Jacob on the floor. "Carl!"

"What...?"

"The car keys — we need them."

"Right, the keys... They should be in the kitchen hanging on the wall beside the fridge." He watches as Sarah spreads a quilt over a part of the couch that's been soiled with blood. After she's done, she nearly collapses onto it, her face filled with pain.

"Is it your leg?" he asks.

"I'll live." She looks at the gun, then cleans a few spots of blood off of the barrel. "I'm out of ammo."

"Do you have anymore?"

"No, it's all at the cabin. I wasn't even in favor of bringing it."

"Well, it's a good thing you did."

Matt enters the room again, carefully stepping around Jacob's body and the mess that its left on the floor. After checking the back door and making sure that it's secure, he sits next to his mom on the couch.

"Should I clean this up?" he asks her.

"No, we're not staying. We're going back to the cabin."

"How? The road is blocked..."

"Yeah, but the beach isn't." She props her legs up onto a small table,

302

then carefully inspects the bandages to make sure none of them have come off or moved. "Did you happen to look outside to see if anybody was out there?"

"Just a few out by the road."

"Okay, hopefully they'll be gone by the time the sun comes up all the way."

"It already is, it's almost nine o' clock."

She looks at her watch, and he's right, it reads 8:54am. "Why are they still out?"

Matt shrugs. "It's still really dark out."

Sarah looks at Carl, who's struggling to stay awake in his chair. "What do you think? Should we leave now, or wait until this afternoon?"

He glances down at the floor, where the body of his neighbor is bleeding out onto the hardwood — and although he knows that his wife's body in sitting in the far corner of the room, he still can't bring himself to actually look at her. "I'm for leaving as soon as possible, if it's alright with you..."

As the front door closes behind them, and the fresh ocean air brushes across his face and fills his lungs, Carl is left with conflicted feelings about leaving his home. It's not just a house that he's walking away from, it's everything that ever gave his life meaning. He knows that in all likelihood, every person that he's ever known is now gone, and with each of them it feels as though a small part of him has disappeared as well. Loneliness can't even begin to describe the way he feels at the moment.

"Carl...?"

He turns to Sarah, who's making her way down the steps. "Yes?"

"Are you okay? You look a little lost."

"No, I'm fine. Just haven't been outside for a while, that's all."

"Do you want Matt to drive?"

He looks over at Matt, who looks excited and scared at the same time. "No, I think I can drive."

Sarah looks around for any other people that might possibly cause a problem, but the only ones she can see are still standing out on the road — their clothes and hair absolutely soaked from the heavy rainfall that's still coming down.

Matt opens the rear driver's side door of the newer model sedan and starts to climb in.

"You sit up front with Carl. I need room to stretch my leg out," Sarah tells him.

At the end of the driveway, as Sarah climbs into the backseat and closes the door behind her, the two men that were out in the road begin to make their way toward the car. With Carl and Matt already inside, she decides not to point out the danger they might be in if the car doesn't start — figuring the pressure might get to Carl, causing him to do something stupid. As he fiddles with the keys, she reaches into her pocket and pulls out her pistol, opening the cylinder as quietly as possible — then she checks the inside of her other pocket and pulls out a single bullet that she's kept hidden, loading it into the gun and closing the cylinder.

By the time Carl finds the right key, the two men are only about a car length behind them and closing in fast. He turns the key and the engine instantly roars to life. As he puts the transmission into reverse and presses his foot against the gas pedal, Sarah looks behind them as the car peels out on the gravel and runs over the two men.

"Did you see those guys?" she asks.

"I saw them."

He places the car into drive once again, everyone bracing

themselves as the tires make their way over the two men, then he steers the car onto an old dirt drive that runs alongside the house. Sarah can hear the tall uncut grass as it brushes against the muffler underneath them, and the constant chattering of wet sand being thrown from the tires once they reach the dunes. She feels a sense of relief for the first time in days as she sees the house finally disappear from sight.

"How far is this place?" asks Carl.

"You should be able to take the southern approach road — it's only a couple of minutes north of there."

She leans forward, seeing nothing but rain and fog ahead of them. Behind them she sees a faint glowing light coming from the top of one of the buildings in town, and the silhouettes of a few people far to the north.

"Have you ever seen that light before?"

Carl quickly looks in the mirror, then slows down slightly as the fog ahead of them becomes thick. "No, but it looks like it's coming from the top of the coast guard station."

Sarah looks up at the dashboard as he slows the car even further, and sees that he's only doing about ten miles per hour. The visibility ahead of them is virtually nonexistent. She looks out the side window to the east, where there should be houses lined up along the dunes, but all she can see are clouds of moisture and rain. Just as she starts to turn her head to the other side, something flashes by right outside of her window — something big.

"Did you...?" she starts to ask. Then she sees it again, something that looked like a child passing only a few feet from the car. Gripping the gun in her hand, wishing it had more than a single bullet inside, she feels the car suddenly swerve toward the ocean as Carl attempts to miss a crowd of people walking down the beach. The car jumps and nearly stops as they run over a few of them, providing an opportunity

305

for one man to slam his fists against the rear window.

"You need to speed up!" she yells at Carl.

"I can't see where I'm going!"

He moves his way through the mass of people slowly, trying to keep the vehicle between the soft sands of the dunes, and the even more dangerous sands near the surf. The people outside look worse than they did in town, with deathly bluish-white skin and sunken faces that look as though they've already died. He takes a quick glance next to him, where he sees Matt staring straight ahead at the carnage outside. He'd hoped that the kid hadn't seen any of it. There's a reason these people are out here, why they've decided to cluster together in the middle of a rainstorm on a beach so far from town — Carl had a feeling that they would be here. Littered across the sand, from the high-tide mark all the way to the surf is the wreckage from a container ship that ran aground nearly a month ago. Most of what's made it to the shore is whatever garbage that happened to be on the deck at the time — that and whatever is left of the crew members. It's the latter that interests the citizens of Cohasset and Westport, but not for charity or pity.

"Don't look at it," Carl tells him as they pass by yet another body lying in the sand. A group of people are kneeling beside it, their hands and faces covered in blood.

After they pass by the last remains of the crew, the people outside start to thin out, and then disappear altogether. Only a few moments later, the fog lifts and leaves only the rain and dark skies to obscure their view — and with Matt still hiding his face to the world outside, the rest of the trip to the access road goes smoothly.

When they reach the highway and turn north again, only a few blocks from the cabin they now consider home, Sarah has a hard time believing that it's only been four days since they left — it seems like a lifetime ago. The pain and throbbing in her leg somehow seems to

306

fade away into the back of her mind as they turn off of the highway and pull up behind the pickup truck that still sits in the same place they left it. She looks up at the chimney, hoping to see smoke billowing up from the fire in the wood stove — but everything looks exactly as it did when they left. Carl stops the car beside the truck and shuts it off, looking around them for any sign of activity.

"You're kind of in the middle of nowhere here, aren't you?" he says, looking back at Sarah. "Still, we need to be careful."

"Do you think Dad and Ben are inside?" Matt asks her.

She stares at the front door, knowing that every second that passes by without the door opening means there's less of a chance her husband made it home. He certainly would have heard them drive up.

After the initial shock and heartache of finding a cold and empty cabin, Sarah sits down in her chair and watches as a sliver of sunlight appears in the sky just as the sun moves below the horizon. Carl fell asleep shortly after they arrived, and Matt finally succumbed after tossing and turning for nearly two hours. Sarah could hear him sobbing quietly off and on through the evening, and was tempted to climb into bed with him to comfort him — but something inside of her resisted. She feels emotionally numb, as if nothing in world could possibly touch her — but she knows that it's only temporary, she felt the same way the moment she realized she would never see her daughter again.

For right now, all she can think about is keeping an eye out for anything suspicious that might be lurking around outside. Every branch that moves in the trees overhead, or wild animal that passes by the front porch — she wonders if it might be her husband and son, or possibly one of the sick bastards who drove them away from her. No matter what happens from this day forward, she's aware more than ever that their lives will never be the same — that the world as they once knew it, is gone.

CHAPTER 36
HIGHWAY 105

"Is she still out there?" Ben asks his father, who's staring out at the street through the grime covered semi-transparent glass of the front window.

Curtis turns around and gives him a reassuring smile. "I don't see anything." He hopes the answer will ease his son's mind, even if it's a lie. The truth is that Amanda has been hanging around the small community all day, moving from building to building, but always staying within sight of them. Now that the sun is beginning to descend into the west, however, more people have begun moving in from across the bridge — for what purpose he can't even begin to imagine. Their presence has sent Amanda into hiding once again, although he knows without a doubt that she's still keeping an eye on them.

"Is it still raining?" asks the boy.

"Yeah, it's still coming down pretty good." He takes one final glance up and down the street, then walks away from the window and sits next to Ben. "How is your head feeling?"

"It still hurts, but not as much."

Curtis places his arm around his son and gives him a gentle squeeze, not knowing what else he can do. He feels helpless and alone, wishing that Sarah was here to help him figure out what to do.

"Dad?"

"Yeah?"

"If they're not back by morning, are we still leaving?"

Curtis hears the sound of unsteady footsteps in front of the store,

309

their feet splashing loudly in the mud puddles of the parking spaces. Unfortunately it's not the first time that it's happened this evening. At any minute he knows the doorknob will begin to jiggle, and he'll hear the sound of someone's hands slamming against the glass panes of one the front windows as they attempt to get inside. "We'll wait as long as we can, but we're leaving tomorrow."

"What about Amanda? Won't she follow us?"

"She might try, but there's no reason to worry about her. She can't hurt us anymore." Another lie, but he can't figure out a good way to explain to his son that the little girl who saved both of their lives only a day before is now hunting them like wild animals.

"Do you think she's like the others?"

"What others?"

"The sick people — is she sick like them?"

"She's sick, but I don't know if she's like them."

They both sit quietly for a few minutes, listening to the door handle start to rattle, and the door itself creaking under the stress of being pushed against. Ben's hands begin to shake slightly as Curtis looks up at the window and sees the glass steaming up from someone's breath, their fingers making a slight squeaking sound as they drag them slowly across the pane. He looks down and notices Ben staring at them. "Don't look, just ignore them."

"What if they get inside...?

"They can't, everything is locked." He watches as Ben looks away, averting his eyes to the floor instead — but it's obvious that his attention is still focused on whatever is happening outside. "Hey, do you remember those three big trees behind the cabin?"

"Yeah."

"What do you say we build a tree house in them when we get back?"

"I guess," Ben responds, sounding a little less than enthusiastic.

310

"I'm sure there's enough lumber lying around." He hears more footsteps out front, like several people are walking by the store. The door begins to rattle again, this time more forceful than before. "Maybe we can even spend the night in there sometime."

"All of us?"

"Sure, why not?" With the doorknob still shaking violently, some of the footsteps outside begin to make their way around the side of the building. Curtis can see dark shadows moving quickly across the windows that look out over the harbor, surrounding them on all sides.

"How long are we gonna stay at the cabin?" asks Ben, who Curtis hopes is now oblivious to what's going on outside.

"I don't know, we might be there for a while."

"If we stay long enough..." He stops mid-sentence, listening closely to something.

"Do you hear something?" The words fall out of Curtis' mouth just as a light thump comes from what sounds like the other side of the room.

"There's someone in the other room..." whispers Ben.

Curtis slides off of the table and onto the floor, then turns around and grabs Ben, placing him behind a nearby desk. "Don't move, and don't say anything." he whispers. He kneels down and aims his gun at the open doorway on the other side of the room that leads to the storage room. Remembering that the room has a back entrance to the store, he listens for the sounds of footsteps or door handles jiggling — but all he hears is the sound of his own heart thumping loudly in his chest. His mind races, trying to remember if he'd checked the lock on the back door earlier in the evening — and even if he had, was the door strong enough to keep one of them out.

He hears the sound of very faint voices as they get closer to the room, their words too muffled to understand.

"Curtis... Are you in here?" he hears softly from across the room.

311

Turning his flashlight on, Curtis aims it toward the doorway, where he sees Larry standing in front of a woman that he assumes is Beth. They're both soaking wet, and visibly shaking despite the heavy raincoats they're wearing.

"What happened out there?" Curtis asks Larry, who's sitting on the table beside his sister, both of them wrapped in a dirty blanket that Ben found hanging in the backroom.

"We took Sean's boat... then tried to get back here," Larry says, his voice shaking horribly. "It sank..."

"How long were you out there?"

"We weren't in the water that long, the boat went down right off the shore."

Curtis turns the flashlight off, and then sits down on the desk across from them. "You guys should get some sleep, you'll need it for the walk tomorrow. I'll keep watch for the rest of the night."

With Ben sound asleep on top of the store counter, Larry and Beth both lie down on the table and close their eyes. Beth, already exhausted from the complete lack of sleep the night before, goes out shortly after her head hits the table. Larry's mind, however, is too active to do anything but replay the nighttime images of Aberdeen after the smoke and fog cleared. At first, the only thing they paid attention to was the turbulent water in an otherwise calm marina, as dozens, or maybe even hundreds of people struggled helplessly against the frigid temperatures. Most of them drowned within minutes. As the scene grew quiet, and their boat drifted farther out into the dark harbor, their eyes were drawn to the streets leading up the hill toward downtown — a sight that he knows will haunt him forever.

312

"Curtis?" he whispers.

"Yeah?"

"We can never go back to town, not even the smaller towns."

"Why is that?"

"I don't think the virus killed as many people as we thought. I think most of them survived it."

"What do you think killed them?"

"I don't think anything did — I think they're still alive."

"You mean alive, but sick..."

"They're worse than sick, Curtis. I don't think there's a word that describes what they are now." Somewhere off in the distance they see a flash of lightning, followed by the rumble of thunder across the sky. "The way it's raining out there, you wouldn't think those fires would stand a chance."

"After high school I used to work in the woods fighting forest fires in the summer. You'd be surprised the amount of rain those things can ignore when they have enough fuel."

The sound of the wind and rain outside is suddenly joined by someone knocking softly on the front door. Curtis stands up and pulls his gun out, pointing it at the door as the handle slowly turns from side to side.

"I thought you said they couldn't get in... What's with the gun?" Larry asks him.

"I don't think that's one of them." he whispers as he moves quietly across the floor. He stands in front of the door, listening closely, but hearing nothing — then he carefully bends over and peers out the window next to it. It takes his eyes a moment to adjust, and even then he has a hard time seeing much of anything. Then he sees something on the ground — the dark outline of a body lying in the mud. Looking around, he spots at least two more of them — one of them still writhing around in a pool of mud, water and blood. He bends

313

over farther to see who's standing at the door, but all he can see is a faint figure walking in the other direction.

Curtis sneaks back to the desk, watching the windows on the back side of the room for any signs of movement. He kneels down next to Larry, who is still shivering beneath the blanket, but is now also holding a pistol in his hand.

"Was it Amanda?"

"I think so. Whoever it was killed the group of people that were out front."

"Maybe she's trying to help us..."

"No, I think she's eliminating the competition. She wants us for herself."

CHAPTER 37
HIGHWAY 105

With no further signs of Amanda, or anyone else for that matter, Curtis unlocks and opens the back door of the grocery store shortly after the first rays of sun appear on the harbor. Although he realizes that Ben has seen dead bodies before, he feels more comfortable avoiding the ones lying by the front entrance.

Enjoying the dry conditions, and keeping an eye on the dark clouds resting over the ocean to the west, the four of them walk along a path that parallels the highway between the buildings and the harbor, until it finally ends on the west side of the small community, bringing them back to the long and winding stretch of road that leads to Cohasset.

"How long do you think it will take us?" asks Beth, who can feel every part of her body aching after a night spent in the harbor, fighting the frigid currents that are constantly moving toward the Pacific with the flow of the river.

"We should get there sometime this afternoon as long as those clouds don't get any closer," replies Curtis.

To the west, where the harbor empties into the ocean, and to the south, where miles of forests and wetlands climb into the coastal mountain range, the scenery still looks exactly the same as it did before the sickness came. The views to the east and north, however, tell a different story. They could see Aberdeen when they first left the store, or at least what was visible through the smoke — but the neighboring city of Hoquiam was kept hidden from their sight. As they come to a bend in the road, however, and see the sun shining

315

down on what's left of the city, every member of the group stops in the middle of the road and stands in silence, shocked at the surreal scene in front of them.

To say the city of Hoquiam is in ruins would be an understatement — there's really nothing left of it. The streets are still more or less there, although seeing them through Larry's binoculars they can clearly tell that the heat has likely done massive damage. The same can be said of the few older stone buildings that are scattered across the newly formed wasteland. Everything else is unrecognizable, even the vast network of industrial docks at the port have vanished overnight. And while the fires have mostly burned themselves out on the west side of the Hoquiam River, they're still raging up the hill on the Aberdeen side, leaving only the buildings along the waterfront free of any damage — at least for now anyway. Larry and Beth can't help but think of the thousands of people still left in the city, and they find themselves conflicted as to whether or not they should feel sorry for the ones that don't make it out alive.

"It probably looks like this everywhere," says Beth, who then looks down at Ben, regretting that she said it in front of him.

"If it doesn't already, it soon will," answers Curtis, who begins walking down the road again.

Following behind the others, Beth looks back and tries to catch at least a glimpse of the hospital where she last saw her husband, but the smoke has blocked most of the hill behind the city, leaving its fate a mystery.

About a mile east of Johns River, where Curtis is hoping the cache of food still exists at the general store, the dark bank of clouds finally moves far enough inland to block any hint of direct sunlight, leaving the landscape around them shrouded in its shadow. Along with the clouds, the first hint of drizzle begins to fall as well, the mist so fine in the air that it's just barely noticeable.

316

Larry looks behind them, glancing only briefly before looking forward again, trying to look as normal as possible. "Everybody act calm," he tells the others, in a voice as soothing and relaxed as he can muster. "Keep walking and don't look back."

"What is it?" Curtis asks.

"Our friend is behind us."

A feeling of dread washes over Curtis, who was beginning to believe that they'd finally lost her for good. "Are you sure it's her?"

"In that dress? It has to be."

Curtis stops and turns around, spotting Amanda walking down the middle of the road about a quarter of a mile behind them. He pulls out his gun, cocks it, then aims it at her.

"Don't shoot, it's hard telling who might hear you!" Larry yells at him under his breath.

"I'm not going to shoot her, I just want to scare her off."

He wants to pull the trigger, to finally end the misery that she's brought to his life — but he doesn't. Instead, he keeps his finger off of the trigger and keeps the gun aimed at her, unsure of whether or not she's seen him yet. Then, while still walking, she lifts her arm up and points her finger at him, her hand roughly in the shape of a gun.

"Crazy bitch..." Curtis mumbles to himself as he turns around and continues walking, placing his gun back into his pocket.

Beth gives Larry a disapproving look, a look of worry and disgust at what she can only assume is abhorrent behavior on Curtis' part — but Larry just shrugs in response. To Beth, she looks like any other young girl, but Larry came to the conclusion a couple of days ago that Amanda was no longer a child, and deserves none of the sympathy or protection you would ordinarily give one.

For the next mile they walked in silence, each of them occasionally looking back to see what progress Amanda had made — and to their dismay, it looks as though she might be gaining on them, although it's

317

difficult to say for certain with all the bends and dips in the road.

"That's the store just ahead," Curtis tells them, pointing at the small building only a hundred yards ahead of them. "There was quite a bit of food inside when I came by a few days ago."

"Maybe we should just keep going," Beth says. "If we stop she's just gonna catch up. At least with some distance between us we might be able to lose her in the woods."

Curtis turns around and sees that a curve in the road has them hidden from Amanda's sight — but only for a few minutes. "I've got a better idea..."

The group makes their way toward the general store through the woods that run alongside the highway, and they finally catch a glimpse of Amanda right before reaching the back entrance. Once inside, Beth and Ben start gathering canned goods and medical supplies off of the shelves in the back room, while Curtis and Larry position themselves by the front window, each of them with a gun in their hands. They told Beth that they were hoping that Amanda would simply pass them by and keep walking toward Westport, while they slipped their way to the south behind her — but in reality, the plan they had in mind was much more violent.

"As soon as we fire a shot, it's hard telling what kind of attention we'll attract," Larry warns Curtis.

"I'm more afraid of her than I am a dozen of those other things."

Curtis leans forward and looks both ways down the highway, but sees absolutely no sign of the girl. "She should have gotten here by now... Don't you think?"

"Larry!" they hear Beth yell from the back room.

They both run into the back room, where they see Beth aiming her gun at the small window that looks out at the woods behind the store.

"She just walked past the window..." she tells them, her voice filled with fear.

"Did she see you?" asks Curtis.

"She looked right at me and smiled. Her face..." she trails off.

"What about her face?"

"It's covered in blood."

Curtis cocks his pistol, then cautiously looks out through the window, seeing nothing but a small set of bare footprints in the mud.

"Beth, I need you to stay here with Ben."

"Where're you going?"

"Larry and I are gonna search for her outside." He opens the door quietly, letting Larry and the AR-15 out first. "Lock the door behind us."

"What if she has a gun?"

"She doesn't, she prefers her knife."

As soon as they're both outside, Beth shuts and locks the door, then stands next to Ben in the far corner of the room, the decomposed bodies of the two store owners only inches from their feet.

"I'm scared," Ben whispers.

"It's okay to be scared sweety, I'm scared too."

They both flinch as they hear a gunshot from somewhere outside — then two more coming from another gun. A few minutes later the sound of crunching gravel can be heard as someone approaches the back door. Beth points the gun at the door, then watches the window for any signs of movement.

"Beth, open up — it's us," she hears Larry say.

She unlocks the door, and Larry motions them outside.

"Did you find her?" she asks, leading Ben out the door and onto the

319

pathway.

"No, we couldn't find her," Larry responds.

"What were the gunshots then?"

"We found someone else. Come on, we should get going."

Beth keeps walking toward the parking lot out front, not really wanting to hear anymore details about what happened. As they reach the highway and start moving west again, she spots something lying on the ground next to the store. She's almost certain that it's a woman, but with their face embedded in the gravel path it's difficult to tell for sure — and she's not really interested enough to ask.

Besides looking over their shoulders, waiting for Amanda or anyone else to suddenly ambush them, the next two hours of walking is rather uneventful — that is until they reach the intersection where the highway meets the Pacific Ocean, and splits off to the north and south. To the south is the outskirts of Cohasset, and the cabin — and to the north is Westport and the rest of Cohasset. Beyond the normal carnage of abandoned cars and litter on the roadway that they've all come to expect, Curtis notices that the doors are now open on almost every vehicle on the roadway. He knows that they weren't like that when his family came by only a few days ago, which means the hordes of residents from Westport have made it at least this far from town.

As the group turns and starts heading south, they walk right by a fresh, partial skeleton that's been picked clean lying in the middle of the highway, with a pair of brown pants crumpled next to it. Curtis is the only one that recognizes who it is, although it takes him a minute to remember his name. Peter — the old man he met briefly at the Johns River general store. It's hard to say what happened to the rest of his body — it could have been coyotes or wild dogs, or maybe even the people who no doubt attacked him. Whatever it was, part of him feels bad for the guy, and another part of him is worried that this

320

happened so close to their cabin.

About a half-mile down the road, the cars that have been opened and looted come to an end, and eventually the cars disappear altogether, leaving only an empty stretch of asphalt all the way back to the overgrown driveway of their home. As the four of them approach the cabin, Curtis feels a sense of relief when he sees a thin wisp of smoke coming from the chimney. That relief, however, quickly vanishes the moment he looks through the open doorway.

"We're never going back home again, are we?" Matt asks his mom as they walk along a path in the woods behind the cabin, both of them carrying pieces of firewood for the stove.

"I really don't think there's anything to go back to."

He really wants to ask her about his sister, Annie, and whether or not they'll ever see her again — but he knows that the subject is too painful for his mom to discuss. "Is Carl going to live with us from now on?"

"If he wants to I suppose. Maybe we can find him someplace close, a nearby house or something." She reaches down and picks up another piece of dried wood, part of a branch that probably came down the winter before. "We should start thinking about gathering enough wood for this winter — that way we won't have to make trips like this in the freezing rain."

"We should put something over the windows first."

"For insulation?"

"No, in case the people find us."

After their walk in the woods, a part of Sarah had almost forgotten about the people in town, and the fact that many of them are lurking right down the road from them.

321

Walking down the last part of the trail, they hear what sounds like a door slamming shut, but they figure that it's only Carl waking up from his nap — and then Sarah spots a woman peering into the pickup truck before moving toward the front door of the cabin. She lays the firewood onto the ground softly, then motions for Matt to do the same. Reaching into her coat pocket, she pulls out the .38 revolver and begins moving slowly toward the back of the cabin, trying to stay clear of any of the windows that might possibly give away her position. When they come to the front corner of the building, Sarah crouches down and peeks around the bend, seeing the woman standing right outside the open door. The woman is clearly upset, making quick glances inside the doorway, then looking away down the driveway.

Sarah stands up and moves into full view, aiming her pistol directly at the woman's head. "Who are you?"

The woman looks startled, backing up a couple of steps. "My name is Beth."

"Carl, are you okay?" Sarah yells. She looks at the doorway, hoping to see Carl appear from the opening, but instead sees the face of her youngest son, Ben. Seconds later, Curtis and Larry both emerge from the cabin as well.

"Sarah, drop the gun, these are friends," Curtis pleads.

She falls to her knees, letting the gun slip out of her hands and onto the ground, then holds her arms out to Ben, grateful to see him alive and healthy.

Larry and Beth stand back, letting the Lockwood family have their moment — but after a few minutes of hugs and tears, Larry interrupts them for something more urgent. "Curtis, the guy..."

Curtis turns and faces Larry, and the smile on his face instantly disappears as he looks back at Sarah. "Do you know the guy inside?"

"Yes, his name is Carl. He helped us make it back here."

322

"Was he alive when you left the cabin?"

A panicked look appears on Sarah's face as she turns toward the cabin and attempts to enter it, but Curtis grabs her and holds her back.

"Don't go in there, you don't want to see him like that."

She throws Curtis' hand aside and steps through the open doorway, seeing Carl sprawled out on the hardwood floor, a trail of fresh blood running across the floorboards from a gaping wound in his throat. She turns away and embraces Curtis, horrified at what might have happened while they were away.

Larry steps forward, a look of genuine sympathy in his eyes. "Why don't you guys wait outside and visit... We can clean this up."

Sarah forces a smile and holds out her hand to him. "I'm Sarah, and that's Matt," she says, nodding to her oldest son.

"Nice to meet you, my name is Larry, and this is my sister, Beth."

"And is that your daughter?" Sarah asks, pointing behind them.

They all turn around, confused as to who she might be talking about.

"Who?" asks Larry.

"The little girl, she was standing there just a minute ago."

CHAPTER 38
ABERDEEN

The moment Jake wakes up and his eyes begin to focus on his surroundings, the room begins to spin uncontrollably. With a great deal of effort and pain, he manages to sit up from the bed he's lying in without passing out, the back of his head throbbing horribly.

The room he's in is mostly dark, with only a hint of light penetrating the blinds covering the window beside him. There's also a strong smell of smoke in the air. He starts to reach into his pocket for his flashlight, then realizes that he's not wearing his own clothes — but a hospital gown instead. Sliding his legs carefully off of the bed, he stands up slowly and walks to the window, pushing the blinds aside to let some light into the room.

Almost blinded by the intense sunlight coming through the window, it takes a moment for his eyes to adjust to the brightness — and when they finally do, he almost doesn't believe what he's looking at. From what he can tell, he's at least six floors up from the street level, looking out over most of downtown Aberdeen — or at least what used to be downtown. Virtually all of the city is gone, reduced to a series of gray and black piles of ash and brick, with only a small portion of the waterfront that still looks to be more or less intact. He can see the hollowed-out bodies of vehicles lining the melted and deformed asphalt streets, and the remains of chimneys sticking up through the rubble like trees in a forest. The only thing in this part of town that seems to be untouched is the hospital itself, apparently mostly due to a wide section of green lawn that circles most of the building.

Focusing once again on the room behind him, he spots a mirror on the wall and decides to check himself out — and immediately sees the reason for his massive headache. The back half of his scalp has been shaved cleanly of all of its hair, and replaced with tightly wrapped bandages that look fresh and expertly applied.

He leans down and opens the single dresser drawer below the mirror, and inside he finds his clothes, flashlight and backpack — everything he'd been carrying when he entered the hospital, minus his gun and radio. He grabs the flashlight and then attempts to open the door, but it's obviously been locked from the outside. Hearing the sound of approaching footsteps in the hallway outside the room, Jake hurries into the small bathroom on the other side of the room and hides behind the door. After listening to the rustling sound of locks, he hears the door open, and a man's voice calling out to him.

"Jake...?

The fact that he knows his name means nothing to Jake. After all, the man has already seen his wallet.

"I know you're in here... There's nothing to be afraid of, I'm not going to hurt you," the man continues. "Listen, I'm gonna leave your door unlocked, come find me when you're ready..."

With the flashlight still in his hand, more useful as a weapon than anything else right now, Jake comes out from behind the door and enters the room again — and sees a man only slightly older than himself standing next to the open door, wearing a white coat and green scrub pants.

"Glad to see you've joined the land of the living." the man says with a warm smile on his face.

"I assume you're a doctor...?"

"A nurse, the only one on duty I'm afraid. My name is Mike Garrett, but you can just call me Mike."

"Are there any other doctors or nurses?"

"Nope, it's just you and me."

325

"What about Beth, my wife?"

"Why don't you sit down and rest, you've had a rough go of it..."

Jake clenches his flashlight more tightly in his hands, answering back with more assertion in his voice, bordering on hostility. "Where is my wife?"

"She left the hospital with another man the day after you were injured. There were too many of the sick for me to get to her."

"How long ago was that?"

"Four days ago. I'm really sorry for all of this, I really am."

The room starts to spin again as Jake processes everything, causing him to lose his balance and stumble just a bit. Mike steps forward and grabs his arm, helping him get back onto the bed.

"You really should stay in bed another day or two. You had a pretty good concussion."

"I appreciate the concern, but I have to get back to my wife. I can't leave her alone out there."

"I already told you, she left with another man. Besides, the streets still aren't safe, even after the fires wiped most of them out."

Jake closes his eyes and takes a minute to gather his thoughts. "Am I the only person you've come across?"

"The only person not infected, yes."

"Then you should come with me, get the hell out of this shit-hole."

Mike looks out the window at the wreckage that used to be a city, then turns around and faces Jake again. "I can't leave. Believe it or not, this shit-hole is still my home, and if there's any chance at all that people actually survived the past couple of months, this will be the place they'll come to for help."

Jake nods, thinking that the man is an idiot, but at least an idiot that means well.

"Were you ever exposed to the illness?" Mike asks.

"From the looks of everything, I can't help but think we all were."

"Yeah, maybe so."

Jake eases off of the bed again, then walks to the dresser and starts changing back into his old clothes. "Can I ask you a question?"

"Sure."

"Do you know what the first symptoms are?"

"Early on we thought they were just similar to the flu or cold, but then we discovered a second type."

"And what are its symptoms?"

"Insanity, delusions, paranoia, just to name a few. I'm pretty sure those are the ones still walking around." He notices a strange look on Jake's face, as if his mind is somewhere else. "Are you okay?"

Jake snaps out of it, then finishes putting his clothes and backpack on. "I'm just worried about my wife, that's all." He walks to the doorway, then turns around and shakes Mike's hand. "Is there any chance I can get my gun and radio back?"

"Sure, no problem. The radio is broken though. It must've happened when you were attacked."

After taking a secured emergency stairway down to the ground floor, Jake manages to sneak his way past the few people still left in the main lobby and out onto the street in front of the hospital. Smoke is still billowing up from a few of the buildings in the area, but for the most part the only obstacles Jake faces as he makes his way down the hill are the sinkholes scattered across the paved roadways.

The only place he can think of to find Beth is the barber shop where they hid Sean's cache of weapons. When he finally gets to the waterfront and enters the barber shop, he knows instantly that she isn't there. Sitting on the counter, in plain sight, is a piece of paper with his name on it. It tells him that Beth and Larry are both safe, and

327

that they're making their way to a cabin near Cohasset with another group of survivors. Below that is a map detailing exactly where the cabin is located.

Jake sits down on the floor, feeling a sense of dizziness and confusion come over him once again. This time was a bit different though, he could feel his mind beginning to slip away from him — and a deep, boiling rage that he was struggling to keep under the surface. He hadn't felt right since they'd reached Grays Harbor, but he told himself that it was only the severe stress that they'd all been living under that was to blame. With his hands shaking slightly, he raises the letter up into the air, and then takes a lighter out of his pocket and ignites a corner of it. He watches as the map vanishes, knowing that Beth's life will be safer without him knowing where she is.

Once the letter has completely burned, and the strange mixture of chaos and numbness in his mind is still somewhat under control, he leaves the barber shop and walks out to the edge of the harbor, watching the sun as it sets over the town of Westport in the distance. Although it's partially hidden behind a hazy layer of clouds, the brightness still causes a sharp pain in his eyes — as if he were being stabbed with a handful of needles. Little by little he can feel his sanity slipping away, and his life from before the outbreak fading away into the back of his mind. The only thing he can concentrate on is getting to a cabin somewhere near the beach.

He remembers vividly how to get there, and that it's important that he does — but all of the other details have somehow vanished from his mind.

As he begins walking toward the bridge, his thoughts now singularly focused — the madness begins filling his mind with grotesque images of death and mayhem, and two people that for whatever reason, he feels compelled to kill.

66342075R00180

Praise for the first edition

"For some reason we imagined that just the 'thinking life' would elicit and feed the Christian spirit. The soul is fed much more by the 'symbolic life' too, where action and contemplation meet, where the inner and the outer learn to operate as one, where words become flesh, where God is no longer just an idea but the heartbeat of life itself. This marvelous book gives you many avenues by which to live such a full and enfleshed life. Phileena tells you to stop 'thinking about it' and to try it! That is when it works."
Fr. Richard Rohr, O.F.M., Center for Action and Contemplation, Albuquerque, New Mexico

"A courageous and groundbreaking effort to build a bridge between those two communities of Christians, still largely unknown to each other, where the heart of Christ burns so brightly: the evangelical and the contemplative."
The Rev. Cynthia Bourgeault, PhD, Episcopal priest, author and retreat leader

"*Pilgrimage of a Soul* is a delightful book that engaged me every step of the way. I was engrossed with Phileena's journey as she entwined her personal story with the account of a pilgrimage in Spain and theological insights she gained along the way. I heartily recommend it to all who are searching for a deeper commitment to God and to the contemplative way of life."
Christine Sine, author, contemplative, activist and executive director of Mustard Seed Associates

"Part memoir, part guidebook for the contemplative activist, *Pilgrimage of a Soul* reads like a good conversation with an old friend. Heuertz's honesty about her own struggles created a space for me to see how wisdom from a host of spiritual guides speaks to my life. It's a gift to all of us, but especially to a guy like me who needs the graciousness of prophetic women like Phileena. I finished the book and felt refreshed, eager to enjoy a walk around my neighborhood."
Jonathan Wilson-Hartgrove, author of *New Monasticism* and *God's Economy*

"Weakness, inferiority, absence and death are turned upside down in these pages, as Phileena Heuertz engages the reader's holy imagination with Christ's good gifts of strength, mutuality, presence and life. Prepare to be transformed."
Margot Starbuck, author of *The Girl in the Orange Dress* and *Unsqueezed*

"In *Pilgrimage of a Soul*, Phileena Heuertz does something quite countercultural: she goes on pilgrimage to the tomb of St. James in Spain and then on sabbatical in Durham, North Carolina. However, this is a travelogue like no other. Her journey becomes ours as she accompanies us through important landmarks of the spiritual journey: awakening, darkness, transformation, union and points in between. In doing so, she provides a wise and helpful guidebook for the spiritual life. I've heard it said that the best writing is so individual that it has a universal appeal. And Phileena's book has just that!"

Albert Haase, O.F.M., author of *Coming Home to Your True Self* and *Living the Lord's Prayer*

"Contemplation is the meditation of the soul. *Pilgrimage of a Soul: Contemplative Spirituality for the Active Life* urges contemplation as part of a healthy spirituality, connecting the conscious to the subconscious. With plenty of discussion on faith and thought, *Pilgrimage of a Soul* is an intriguing and intellectual read for any Christian studies collection."

James A. Cox, *Library Book Watch*, September 2010

"As a codirector of Word Made Flesh, an international community of Christians who live and serve among the poor, Phileena Heuertz understands active faith. In *Pilgrimage of a Soul: Contemplative Spirituality for the Active Life*, Heuertz describes her transforming journey into another aspect of faith—learning to rest in and surrender to God."

Sojourners, September–October 2010

REVISED EDITION

Pilgrimage of a SOUL

CONTEMPLATIVE SPIRITUALITY FOR THE ACTIVE LIFE

Phileena Heuertz

Foreword by Shauna Niequist

IVP Books

An imprint of InterVarsity Press
Downers Grove, Illinois

InterVarsity Press
P.O. Box 1400, Downers Grove, IL 60515-1426
ivpress.com
email@ivpress.com

Second edition ©2017 by Phileena Heuertz
First edition ©2010 by Phileena Heuertz

InterVarsity Press® is the book-publishing division of InterVarsity Christian Fellowship/USA®, a movement of students and faculty active on campus at hundreds of universities, colleges, and schools of nursing in the United States of America, and a member movement of the International Fellowship of Evangelical Students. For information about local and regional activities, visit intervarsity.org.

All Scripture quotations, unless otherwise indicated, are taken from the Inclusive Bible, The First Egalitarian Translation™ Copyright © 2007 by Priests for Equality. All rights reserved.

"Poetry" translated by Alastair Reid from Selected Poems by Pablo Neruda, published by Jonathan Cape. Reprinted by permission of the Random House Group Ltd.

Lyrics to "Hey Little Girl" and "Stronger Than Death" from Kate Hurley, Sleeping When You Woke Me *(Worship Circle Records, 2006), quoted by permission.*

Excerpts from Moving in the Spirit *by Richard J. Hauser, SJ, Copyright ©1986 by Richard J. Hauser, S.J. Paulist Press, Inc., New York/Mahwah, NJ. Reprinted by permission of Paulist Press, Inc. www.paulistpress.com*

While any stories in this book are true, some names and identifying information may have been changed to protect the privacy of individuals.

Design: Cindy Kiple
Images: pair of shoes: ©tacojim/iStockphoto
*   tree line: ©Michael-Tatman iStockphoto*

ISBN 978-0-8308-4635-1 (print)
ISBN 978-0-8308-8933-4 (digital)

Printed in the United States of America ♾

Library of Congress Cataloging-in-Publication Data
A catalog record for this book is available from the Library of Congress.

P *25 24 23 22 21 20 19 18 17 16 15 14 13 12 11 10 9 8 7 6 5 4 3 2 1*
Y *38 37 36 35 34 33 32 31 30 29 28 27 26 25 24 23 22 21 20 19 18 17*

For Chris

*Thank you for believing in me. Your passionate love,
unwavering support and enduring companionship
are my greatest treasures.*

And for my godchildren:
Adina, Toby, Cora, Kirby, Nevan,
Elliott, Amani, Ada

*May your life's journey always be marked with freedom
to live into the fullness of who you are.
Your lives echo immense love and boundless possibilities.*

Contents

Foreword
to the Revised Edition

SHAUNA NIEQUIST

IN THE LAST SEVERAL YEARS OF MY LIFE, God has used spiritual practices like centering prayer, silence, solitude and sabbath to enrich and, in many ways, rebuild my interior spiritual landscape. Essentially, for many years my central spiritual practice was *doing*—working, writing, pushing, performing. The way I experienced my spirituality was through my own effort. Even now as I write that, I can see the myriad problems with that way of living, and I experienced them acutely: exhaustion, isolation, numbness, profound inability to connect with God when I wasn't wearing myself out in his name.

On the path back to connection, to prayer as relationship, to a spiritual life that felt more like *life*, I met Phileena. She taught me about centering prayer, invited me to practice it—awkward and difficult as it is when one begins. She invited a small gathering of us to place our feet solidly on the ground, to fill our chests roundly with breath, to gently bring our minds back to prayer again, again, again. And then later that night we gathered with other friends in my home—people on the couch and on stools around the kitchen island, little groupings here and there, telling stories, sharing experiences. I'd imagine we ate bread and cheese and blueberry crisp, and I'd imagine there was both red wine and sparkling water—on Sunday nights, those are the usual suspects.

What I do remember from that night is that Phileena sat at the center of a small circle, feet tucked under her, answering questions with a quiet voice and generous spirit. We were a group of learners, and she was a guide. We were Christians just tiptoeing into a more contemplative way of faith, and she'd walked further along this pilgrimage. And it was apparent. And it was inspiring.

Phileena lives and writes and speaks and leads with a marriage of groundedness and lightness that draws people toward her; it draws me toward her. When I'm with her, and when I read her words, I know that she knows some things deep in her bones, in her cells. She has listened and walked and prayed and struggled through into a new way of living, and when you're with her, you want to do the same.

I'm thankful for this book, for this journey, for this invitation. There are so many of us who are still just starting out on this contemplative pilgrimage, and I'm so profoundly thankful for this wise and honest guide.

Foreword
to the First Edition

PHYLLIS TICKLE

THERE ARE SEVEN ANCIENT DISCIPLINES—more commonly referred to nowadays as the seven ancient practices—that have shaped Christianity and Christians from before the days of our very beginning. That is to say, the seven shaped, and still shape, Judaism just as they shaped the earthly life of our Lord and of the disciples from whom we received the faith.

Three of them—tithing, fasting and the sacred meal or feast—govern the work and pleasures of our bodies. The other four practices—fixed-hour prayer, the keeping of sabbath, the observance of the liturgical year and pilgrimage—monitor or sacramentalize time, that other dimension in which we live while here. Pilgrimage—the seventh and last of the ancient practices—governs and informs and, indeed, sacramentalizes the largest unit of human time—the span of one's individual life on earth.

As Phileena Heuertz makes very clear in these pages, one of the unfortunate (necessary at the time, but subsequently unfortunate) changes that the Protestant Reformation effected was the more or less active suppression of the practices. While emphasizing the keeping of the sabbath and tithing, Protestantism merely tipped its hat at fasting while energetically discouraging overmuch concern with the sacred meal or feast, the daily offices, the close observation of the liturgical year and, of course, that most dangerous discipline of all—pilgrimage.

Pilgrimage was dangerous, in the minds of early Protestant reformers, not so much for religious or spiritual reasons but for political ones: pilgrimage within the West was inevitably made to Roman Catholic sites. (There were, in point of fact, no other real options, unless one considered that Jerusalem had retained some degree of non-catholicized Christianity; but that too was a highly debatable question.) And thus it was that pilgrimage became, in many ways, the greatest victim of the new ways; formation in the faith went from lived and physically disciplined experience to reasoned and intellectualized understanding. But the times, they are a-changin' . . .

Or more correctly said, the times they have changed. Now younger Christians are looking at the seven ancient practices and wondering aloud whether the abnegation of them can even be justified now—wondering, aloud and in books like this one, about how we can not only return to our formational heritage, but how we can also blend that heritage with the heritage of reasoned theology and intellectual rigor that has come to us from our more recent forebears in the faith. What we get, when younger and devout Christians—of whom Phileena is most certainly one of the more articulate—ask these questions, is often startling and even agonizing.

In this particularly startling, agonizing book, Phileena explores the sacramentalization of time, drawing from her experience on pilgrimage in Spain and on sabbatical in North Carolina. But even these very special physical settings are, for Phileena and for all of us really, in some ways better understood as windows into a more interior journey—the soul's pilgrimage through time.

The special grace of the journey that Phileena leads us on in this book entails the reconciliation of each season of life with the next, and the hope that accompanies the agony we may experience as we exit one season in order to enter another. We are guided by Phileena in this book, but she ably reminds us that in our soul's pilgrimage we are guided by one whose ways are higher than ours.

Enter gently, then, for this is a tender book, even while at the same time it is a sinewy one. There is a candor here that makes one want to whisper, and there is a vigor of faith and a determination to live *Christian*! that makes one want to shout. If anyone among us yearns to see what post-Reformation, twenty-first-century Christianity is leading to, then let him or her follow Phileena on El Camino de Santiago in Spain and, after that, to the Rose Cottage in North Carolina.

But go easy, and follow softly, for there is much pain here as well as much glory. Five hundred years of interruption are ending and new ways are blending in with the power of old ways. What we shall be and what we shall become as a result of that reunion are whispering here.

Listen.

Listen and hear.

"POETRY" by Pablo Neruda

And it was at that age . ... Poetry arrived
in search of me. I don't know, I don't know where
it came from, from winter or a river.
I don't know how or when,
no they were not voices, they were not
words, nor silence,
but from a street I was summoned,
from the branches of night,
abruptly from the others,
among violent fires
or returning alone,
there I was without a face
and it touched me.

I did not know what to say, my mouth
had no way
with names,
my eyes were blind,
and something started in my soul,
fever or forgotten wings,
and I made my own way,
deciphering
that fire,
and I wrote the first faint line,
faint, without substance, pure nonsense,
pure wisdom
of someone who knows nothing,
and suddenly I saw
the heavens
unfastened
and open,
planets,
palpitating plantations,
shadow perforated,
riddled
with arrows, fire and flowers,
the winding night, the universe.

And I, infinitesimal being,
drunk with the great starry void,
likeness, image of
mystery,
felt myself a pure part
of the abyss,
I wheeled with the stars,
my heart broke loose on the wind.

Introduction

DARKNESS. IF YOU'VE EXPERIENCED IT, you know what I'm talking about. Darkness sets in long before we're old enough to recognize it. It begins with anguish. We've been hurt, sometimes tragically, and we don't know what to do with that injury. The safest thing seems to be to hide the pain, perhaps behind a mask. We seek to be safe by any means necessary. We learn to cope. And we achieve for ourselves a form of love, security or power that the wounded part of us desperately needs. But these coping mechanisms rob us of fullness of life. To really thrive in life, our soul needs to be transformed—over and over again. This is the work of the spiritual journey. Exercising the courage to embark on the journey postures us for radical transformation.

Many of you who are reading this book are probably persons of faith. You may feel as if you've been on the spiritual journey for quite a long time. But the spiritual journey is subtly different from our faith conversion. According to Father Thomas Keating—a Cistercian monk—at the time of conversion we orient our lives by the question, "What can I do for God?"[1] Seems appropriate, right? But when we begin the spiritual journey our life is dramatically altered toward the question, "What can God do for me?" This isn't a narcissistic, exploitative question toward a disempowered God. It's the exact opposite. This is the central question of a humble person who has awakened to their true self and to the awe-inspiring adoration of an extraordinary God.[2]

One of the things we desperately need God to do for us is to transform us from what we are today into what God intends us to be. In a world where leaders of nations are making war and preparing to defend their sovereignty by proliferating nuclear bombs, where religious fundamentalists kill innocents under the guise of righteousness, and where the average American citizen contributes daily to the destruction of our ecosphere, it is clear that we are a people in need of transformation. All of us are subject to self-deception. We commit evil and call it good. We commit violence and call it social justice.

Like the blind man Bartimaeus, when we awaken to the reality of our desperate condition we can hear Jesus asking us, "What do you want me to do for you?" (Mark 10:46-52). If we surrender and cry out, "Jesus, have mercy on me!" we have begun the spiritual journey.

Whether or not we've realized it in the depths of our being, we are people who need to ask what God can do for us. *You* are a person who needs to ask God, "What can you do for me?" The spiritual journey invites us into the process of radical transformation, and nothing prepares us as adequately for transformation as Christian contemplation.

The Christian contemplative tradition navigates our path toward a posture of receptivity to the One who can save us from our chaos and destruction—whether that is on a small, personal and social scale or on the grand landscape of global politics. All we have to do is submit to the process. That's it. Submit. Surrender. Dare to approach God with humble adoration. But since the beginning of time, it seems that surrender is the most difficult of postures for humanity. We much prefer self-sufficiency and self-righteousness. In our attempt to "fix" ourselves, we prefer to order, direct and define our own spirituality. In contrast, contemplative spirituality carves the posture of surrender into the fabric of our being, making us most receptive to the transformation that we cannot obtain for ourselves.

This book illuminates how I stumbled into the Christian contemplative tradition and how contemplative prayer facilitated and supported a personal awakening. In these pages I attempt to map this part of my spiritual journey against the metaphor of pilgrimage, drawing narrative from an actual pilgrimage I made in Spain. Through the vulnerability of the unfolding story, this book attempts to illuminate contemplative spirituality for the active life. The "active life" is the life all of us live. We are made to work, play and be in relationship—all very concrete ways of active living. The active life is the life fully engaged and interacting with the world. But to define what is meant by "contemplative" threatens to obliterate the essence of the concept. If we approach the meaning of the contemplative life cerebrally, with the need to analyze, dissect and define, we have missed the gift altogether. The starting place for the contemplative life is surrender. We let go of being in control. We are rendered powerless. To be contemplative is a state of being, a posture more than something concrete of which to grab hold. Even the greatest of mystics tend to use elusive language to describe the contemplative life. Contemplative spirituality is experiential and intuitive. But that doesn't mean it is only for certain personality types. Contemplative spirituality is the portal to the direct life-giving presence of God. When rooted in contemplative spirituality we are more receptive and supple in the hands of God; the life of Christ flows more freely through us.

Rather than dichotomize the active life from the contemplative life—as if it were adequate to choose to live one way or another—the abundant life brings balance or union to the active and contemplative dimensions of life. If we consider the wheel as a symbol for life, contemplation will be found in the centermost axis and the active life extends out in the spokes, as all the while the wheel is turning, progressing forward.[3] But without the center axis, the spokes lose their anchor and are unable to support the forward motion of the wheel. Without the spokes, the center axis is deemed irrelevant. When we are least connected to our contemplative center, our life is most tense and chaotic. When rooted in contemplative spirituality, the active life reflects greater peace, purpose and effectiveness.

Over the years, the following practices have supported the contemplative dimension of my life:

- "Phileena Fridays"—At first I made time and space for contemplation through rest, reflection and recreation one day per week.

- Private retreats—"Phileena Fridays" morphed into regular private retreats lasting a couple of days, four times per year, when I would force myself to be alone with self and God. I was free from the external demands of others and could battle out the internal ones.

- Sabbath—Honoring a weekly sabbath by committing to do only that which rests and nurtures my soul and is a gift of self offered back to God.[4]

- Contemplative prayer—Regular centering prayer (a minimum of two twenty-minute silent prayer periods per day). Consenting to the action of God within me through centering prayer leaves no room for hiding. When we willingly abandon ourselves to God, God calls out to our deepest self and dismantles our illusions. The true self grows in knowledge, awareness and courage.[5]

For nearly twenty years, I was a part of organizing the movement of Word Made Flesh—an international community of Christians who serve among the most vulnerable of the world's poor. We were compelled by the vulnerabilities of children of war, children with HIV and AIDS, abandoned children, children living on the streets, women and children enslaved in the commercial sex industry, and widows abandoned by their families. As a community we entered these dark and desperate realities and surprisingly discovered the reign of God. Driven by our faith, youth and idealism, we established compassionate communities of justice in thirteen cities in the Majority World. Youth, of course, lasts only for a moment; idealism in the context of poverty, injustice, oppression and violence was challenged daily. It was our faith that remained the anchor for our service.

My faith and inevitable need for spiritual formation in the context of social activism motivate the telling of my personal story. After years of laboring with my community among the world's poor, I was in need of a calm and grounded center that could withstand the buffeting of a world full of injustice and unrelenting demands. Contemplative prayer became an oasis in an active life that was becoming arid, and it taught me how "to be," how to surrender my anxieties, compulsions and the suffering of my friends into the hands of God. Contemplative prayer taught me how to find rest in God. But the grace of contemplation also eventually led me into a life-altering dark night of the soul. The experience of internal darkness and subsequent transformation became a wellspring for my active life.

At the heart of Christian faith is the invitation to die and be reborn. During our lifetime we may be invited into a number of deaths and rebirths. The paschal mystery of Christ serves as a model for contemplative spirituality and spiritual formation: at any given point in life we may find ourselves identifying with the passion, death and resurrection of Jesus.[6] Throughout these pages I detail my experience in the paschal mystery and hope that the telling of my story might encourage you to stay true to your own journey.

This is a story of following God, losing sight of God, seeking after and ultimately being renewed by God. This is a story of prayer as a centering, tethering event—an infusion of contemplation into a lifestyle of activism. This is a recurring human story, one of death and rebirth. It is a story of how God awakens a soul to new life.

During a retreat at St. Benedict's Monastery in Snowmass, Colorado (home of Thomas Keating), I had the privilege to be drenched in the silence of God. For ten days I met with twenty-five other retreatants from all over the world. In grand silence (silence of the eyes as well as the voice) we met together seven times per day, for a total of four hours each day, to pray. We prayed a prayer of surrender beyond words, thoughts, imagination and feeling. Together we consented to the action of God within us, growing acquainted with God who is immanent as well as transcendent. But adapting this prayer posture as a way of life isn't easy. Surrender as an active ingredient of the spiritual life invites us into a rude awakening.

Father Thomas explains the complexity of the human story in our attempt to embark on the spiritual journey:

> When we are converted to a new way of life, to service or to a particular ministry, we often experience a wonderful gift of freedom and a radical change of direction. Perhaps you have made enormous sacrifices in your business or profession, maybe even in family life, to be able to begin a journey into the service of the Gospel. But watch out! All the emotional "programs for happiness," over-identification with one's group and the commentaries that reinforce our innate tendencies have sources in the unconscious as well as in the conscious. That is why St. Paul could say, "What I want to do, I don't do. And what I don't want to do I find myself doing" (Rom 7:15ff). If we don't face the consequences of unconscious motivation—through a practice or discipline that opens us to the unconscious—then that motivation will secretly influence our decisions all through our lives.[7]

We are asleep to our unconscious motivations, and these motivations mask our true self. In essence we are hiding. And the wound in our soul remains unhealed, infecting every aspect of our lives. We are so asleep to our reality that we don't know we are hiding behind the masks of our false self. In our slumber we are unable to distinguish between what is true and what is false. These masks become so familiar to us, they become a part of our very identity.

When I awakened to the presence of masks in my life, I knew not at first what was truly me and what was a false version of me. What was a mask and what was authentic, beautiful me? Only time would tell. This is a story of what is possible when we prayerfully dare to remove our masks. And Christian contemplative spirituality provides a way to make this authentic journey through life.

In the following pages we will explore seven movements of the spiritual journey. In doing so I will draw from various experiences in my life, most extensively from my first sabbatical: on pilgrimage in northern Spain and at The Center for Reconciliation at Duke Divinity School in North Carolina.

In this new edition, you are better supported to uncover your own pilgrimage of a soul with reflection questions followed by a spiritual practice at the end of each chapter. I hope that these additions to the book serve you well.

SEASONS OF UNDIVIDED ATTENTION

My husband, Chris, and I make our home in Omaha, Nebraska. In 2007, after a combined twenty-five years of service among our impoverished friends, we received the gift of sabbatical. For the first part of our sabbatical, we determined to make a historical pilgrimage that would stretch almost five hundred miles. For thirty-three days we walked the ancient path of El Camino de Santiago. The Camino is one of three primary Christian pilgrimages—Jerusalem and Rome being the other two. For nearly twelve hundred years pilgrims have made this third-most-sacred passage, whose destination is the legendary burial ground of the apostle James, the son of Zebedee, also known as James the Great.

Pilgrims across the centuries have walked the Camino, Spanish for "way," for all manner of reasons. In one way or another, most people walk it to find themselves or to find God. Curiously, by walking this historic way most are propelled further into their lifelong search for both. With each passing day I awakened more and more to the gift of my life. As time progressed I came to realize that the true essence of my being is rooted in the love of God.

Pilgrimage can be understood as a long journey in search of moral significance. It is a *way* or *passage* from one point to another. Pilgrimage is a metaphor for growth and transformation. To grow is to progress from one place to another; to be transformed is to transition from one form to another; to embark on pilgrimage is to leave where one is and arrive where one is not yet.

Pilgrimage can be a metaphor for the spiritual journey. Even the transition from sleepfulness to wakefulness is a kind of passage. Whether we are walking to a holy site or being mindful of our spiritual life, in both cases we can willfully embark on the journey or not. The choice is ours: either we decide to journey in hope of growth and change or we resign to life as it is.

When made intentionally, pilgrimage offers the gifts of detachment from that which is unhealthy or false and reorientation toward health, wholeness and truth. The way of pilgrimage is a contemplative presence-of-being. By posturing ourselves toward contemplation, our awareness is heightened and we can more easily submit to the process of pilgrimage—progressing from one place to another and responding with grace to the world around us.

Pilgrimage speaks to both the internal and external reality of our lives. As human beings we have the capacity to engage the world in meaningful ways through our actions. We are also able to reflect on our actions. A life characterized by pilgrimage brings union to action and contemplation. With this posture, the human condition is poised to ask questions and find answers.

For the second part of our sabbatical, following the pilgrimage, Chris and I relocated to Durham, North Carolina, as visiting practitioners of The Center for Reconciliation. For five months we were invited to cease our normal, active lives of service and find refuge within the embrace of Duke Divinity School. This long stretch of sabbath—characterized by detachment, rest and relative stillness—was a welcome cocoon for my active self.

The "Rose Cottage" became our home away from home. This small one bedroom house provided all the comforts we would need. As the temperature turned cooler we enjoyed the fireplace and outdoor hot tub. Pine trees towered around the house, suggesting I look up and remember the One who cares deeply for me as well as for my friends suffering in a world of cruelty. The backyard, screened porch and hammock were quiet places where I could rest from all the things I had been doing for God ("What can I do for God?") and hide away with God, whom I would come to know intimately as the Lover of my soul ("What can God do for me?"). Long, lingering walks, working with my hands in the garden, visits to the seaside and delighting in music marked my days in Durham. And gracious new friends entered my life, who became welcome companions in the journey.

The purpose of sabbatical, as dictated in the Hebrew Scriptures, took on new meaning for me.[8] An ancient practice of the early nation of Israel has profound relevance for us today. After thirteen years of social activism, sabbath and sabbatical revealed themselves as crucial gifts for my spiritual journey. This season allowed me to give my undivided attention to the movements of my soul.

SEVEN MOVEMENTS

Throughout these pages we will explore the gifts of contemplative spirituality as the central anchor for the active life, service and mission. Transformation is what the spiritual journey postures us to receive and is supported by the active-contemplative continuum. Within this dynamic we find movements or rings that illuminate growth.

Awakening is the first movement in the spiritual journey. Six movements follow: longing, darkness, death, transformation, intimacy and union. Picture seven three-dimensional rings all interlocked. Each ring represents a movement or season in the soul's development. During a process of formation, the soul moves throughout these rings at various times, in no particular order. The spiritual journey is more cyclical than linear. Each moment in a certain movement or ring provides a necessary experience for personal and spiritual growth and development. At times we may progress from one ring to another, only to find ourselves revisiting a former ring for a deeper work in our ever-expanding soul. The following pages attempt to bring to light these hidden mysteries and wonders of the spiritual life.

This is my story. But in many ways it is *our* story. It's a story of awakening, darkness and transformation. It's a story of being born. It's a story of striving to be free. As a Christian it is a story of ongoing transformation in the image of Christ. As a Christian *woman,* it is a story of feminine awakening as central to spiritual formation—a story that cries out to be heard by women and men alike. This is a story of questions and doubt, sorrow and grief, death and love. Embracing these realities is the essence of the spiritual journey. As you enter into my journey, let these movements burrow deep into your soul, so that your own story might emerge with more clarity.

Whether you read this book on your own or with a group, consider me to be present with you, cheering for you in the process of awakening and becoming who God intends you to be. There's no time to waste. The world needs you to be fully you.

1

Awakening

It is never too late to be what you might have been.

GEORGE ELIOT

WHEN I WAS A CHILD my mother would wake me in a most delightful fashion. She'd come in and draw open the shades and sing,

Good morning, good morning, good morning.
It's time to rise and shine.
Good morning, good morning, good morning.
I hope you're feeling fine.
The sun is just above the hills
and all the day's for us to fill.
The day is calling just for you
and all your dreams are coming true.

Though my husband, Chris, hasn't adopted this way of waking me, eventually I do rise and attempt to shine. Usually I rise before him anyway, though on occasion he has been known to grace me with "the morning dance." Only a few have been so lucky as to witness him strutting around like a proud peacock or "old school gangster," as he puts it. In this fashion he sets the tone for a day full of joy and laughter.

You know how it is when you wake up from a long, deep sleep? At first it's a struggle. I often find myself in this "somewhere in between" space, not quite sure where to land. Sometimes the dream I was having was so nice I want to continue it. Or at times the dream feels more real than the life waiting for me when I wake. Do you ever experience that psychological quagmire where you wonder if reality really is dreamland and what you presume to be your waking state, fantasy?

When it's time to wake up, I find myself wavering between going back into the dark state of slumber that feels comfortable and familiar, and giving in to the pull to open my eyes and transition into the realness of the day. Sleep is comforting. It rests the body and mind and, for a few hours, frees us from the stress and anxieties of life. Maybe it is the stress and anxieties that we're trying to avoid by staying in bed. Choosing to disrupt a comfortable, peaceful state of existence for the unknowns of a day that could include pain seems kind of absurd. Isn't dreamland a better place to be? But sleeping too much is a common symptom of depression. And living life perpetually asleep doesn't seem like much of a life at all. The comatose condition is nothing to be envied.

In our contemporary times, we are so busy that some of us hardly take time to sleep. With the advances of technology, life is fast and very full. Primitive times offered a much slower, calmer pace with more natural opportunities for silence and solitude, in addition to hard physical labor, which is good for the body as well as the soul. Now with electricity we are less in touch with the natural rhythms and cycles of our days, months and years. We can stay up as late as we want with the aid and company of light bulbs, television, DVDs, iPhones, Xbox, Facebook and Twitter. If societies that came before us could see us, they might think we were a bunch of overactive crazies.

Cloaked by overactivity, a typical day in the life of many of us is marked with avoidance and escape. Busyness sometimes serves to help us evade the vulnerable places in our hearts that are wounded and afraid. Perhaps we numb the pain within by filling our lives with commotion and workaholism, we create a full social life to avoid the interior life, or we try to dull the ache by eating, drinking or exercising too much. Others do the opposite—in an attempt to avoid pain they suppress or control it by not eating and by other repressive behaviors. Indulgences of most kinds are often signs that we are avoiding or trying to escape our pain.

Sometimes we resist retiring for the day because it is on our bed at night that everything stops and we can no longer escape the voices in our head or the ache in our heart. The stillness and silence of bedtime is sometimes haunting rather than peace-filled. When we've used so much energy to try to avoid our personal turmoil, and we finally manage to reach dreamland, why would we want to wake up? Another day sometimes threatens us with more avoidance and sedation. And so the cycle continues: we live our days finding ways to sedate our woundedness and, if we're lucky, we find an escape at night through sleep. Inevitably, though, it will be time to wake once again from our slumber and attempt to live the chaos of another day. Day after day the morning comes and the gift of the hours is ours to receive. So we rise. After all, we do have a life to live. And if we remain in a state of perpetual sleep we might as well be dead.

WAKING UP IN ST. JEAN PIED DE PORT

It was a brisk, springtime morning in St. Jean Pied de Port, France. The sun had yet to rise on the foothills of the Pyrenees Mountains. The birds hadn't even begun singing their morning songs. But the promises of pilgrimage stirred in our hearts as we forced our eyes open and stumbled out of bed. El Camino de Santiago stretched out before us and summoned us to our feet. It wasn't long after leaving our guesthouse that we spotted the first yellow arrow to direct our way. All along the Camino yellow arrows mark the path—painted on trees, rocks, streets and buildings. Whether we walked on dirt paths, gravel roads or village streets, the arrows guided our way.

The long flight from Omaha to Chicago to Bilbao in the Spanish Basque region, followed by the winding train that marked the entrance into our journey, culminated on that morning. After decades of service among our impoverished friends, Chris and I detached from our work and determined to walk the ancient Camino.

Just before setting out on our first day's journey we read the following reflection as a prayer for pilgrimage:

> Up early on this first day and not at all sure you want to embark on a journey to some distant, fabled place. Why bother? You would prefer to be asleep, warm within the comfort of your day-to-day routines.
>
> Yet you start on your pilgrimage, unsure of what lies ahead or even why you've chosen to go on such an arduous adventure. You only hope that, drawn forward by the lure of some far-off sacred city, you will find journey's end worth the hardships along the way.
>
> At the same time, you sense a call to some larger purpose, a call that will not be denied.
>
> Knowing that the road flows forward beyond your time of pilgrimage, just as it winds behind you through countless other lifetimes, fills you with a sense that you are part of a great continuum.
>
> You take a deep breath, put your pack on your shoulders, and step out onto the road.[1]

The spiritual journey too is marked with an invitation to wake up. The Buddha is remembered to have said that people live most of their life asleep.[2] Of course he didn't mean that people spend most of their lives in bed, physically asleep. Five hundred years before the time of Christ, the Buddha referenced the spiritual condition of humanity. Jesus echoed this universal truth when he said,

"I came that you might have life and have it to the full" (John 10:10)—in contrast to a "partial" life. The Christian journey begins with an invitation to wake from our sleepfulness. As St. Irenaeus said, "The glory of God is a human being fully alive." It's hard to be fully alive if we stay asleep. By waking up, we determine to embark on the spiritual journey.

Like my mother's morning ritual or my husband's dance, there are spiritual practices that can help us wake up and fully live. The posture of pilgrimage and the practice of contemplative prayer have been vital to my awakening. As I have awakened, I've endured brokenness, confronted the false self and experienced new revelation of the love of God. Awakening is difficult and life altering, but the glory of God compels nothing less.

BROKENNESS

Months prior to setting out on the Camino, I had a sense that I would not be the same when I returned. In a state of awakening, my identity was being shaken and dismantled, and I was entering an internal nakedness. It's difficult to describe this experience. Only in hindsight can I really name it for what it was. I felt like I was losing my orientation for life, relationships and service. During prayer I would often find myself in tears and not know why. (This is an outward sign of what Thomas Keating calls "divine therapy.") I found myself needing to differentiate in new ways from my husband, my community and my work. But that left me feeling very insecure with seemingly no anchor to keep me stabilized. Jesus points to this transformation when he says, "He who seeks only himself brings himself to ruin, whereas he who brings himself to nothing for my sake discovers who he is" (Matthew 10:39 NAB).[3]

In this internally exposed condition I felt vulnerable, insecure and fragile. Symbolized by pilgrimage but realized through awakening, I was finding out that I wasn't who I thought I was. Meet the false self—the shadow of who we truly are, the expression of who we are that pales in comparison to the truth of who we were created to be. The false self is so much a part of our identity that we don't know it is there. We don't distinguish it from our true self.

St. Paul taught about the false self and true self using the language of "old and new creation" in 2 Corinthians. "Therefore, if anyone is in Christ, [she] is a new creation; the old has gone, the new has come!" (2 Corinthians 5:17 NIV). He also described the battle between the two in the process of being transformed into the likeness of Christ. "I don't understand what I do—for I don't do the things I want to do, but rather the things I hate. . . . This makes me the prisoner of the law of sin in my members" (Romans 7:15, 23).

Watchman Nee, the famous Chinese Christian author and church leader of the early twentieth century, expanded on this teaching and spoke of the "old man" and the "new man." Thomas Merton, Trappist monk, spiritual writer, poet and social activist, wrote of this ideology as the "false self" and "true self." Mystics throughout the ages have spoken and written prolifically on this state of our human condition.

The apostle Paul explains in Ephesians the spiritual revolution that we need in order to grow into the life of Christ or our true self.

> So I declare and testify together with Christ that you must stop living the kind of life the world lives. Their minds are empty, they are alienated from the life of God. . . . That is hardly the way you have learned from Christ, unless you failed to hear properly, when you were taught what the truth is in Jesus. You must give up your old way of life; you must put aside your old self, which is being corrupted by following illusory desires. Your mind must be renewed by a spiritual revolution, so that you can put on the new self that has been created in God's likeness, in the justice and holiness of the truth. (Ephesians 4:17-18, 20-24)

Awakening and embarking on the spiritual journey invited me to have a good hard look at reality. I was being invited to die so that more of the life of Christ could live in me. "For to me to live is Christ and to die is gain" (Philippians 1:21).

In those moments, days and months I began to recognize my false self and the ways in which it controlled me and kept me from being fully alive. "False Phileena" let particular cultural and religious expectations define and limit her. I was overly concerned with what others thought of me, and those actual or delusional opinions determined many of the decisions I made and responsibilities I stepped up to. My true self was a "prisoner of the law of sin at work within me." But having embarked on the spiritual journey, my true self was waking up and was a force to be reckoned with.

Reflecting on the gospel message, Thomas Keating says that the first stage of the spiritual journey involves the dismantling of one's worldview and self-image.[4] Over time, I began to distinguish the false self from the true. This is nothing short of a profound grace, for we cannot make ourselves grow. We can only will to wake up and submit to the process.

Waking up and embarking on this journey involved an uprooting and tearing down of my false self and worldview. At times I felt like I was coming undone. Submission to this grace reoriented my life to a deeper degree of truth. The transformative work of Christ is very real. By a mystery that can hardly be explained, the work of Christ sets us free. The true self is free once the false self is confronted and dismantled.

This is Jesus' promise to us—that it would be "no longer I who live but Christ who lives in me" (Galatians 2:20). The false self has to "die" in order for Christ's life to reign in us. This is the spiritual journey—to live into the fullness of Christ's life within us.

But living into our potential is not easy.

All sorts of factors inhibit us from reaching our full potential and divert us instead toward the reinforcement of a false self. For many women, one big factor is patriarchy. Men too report awakening to perils of male domination. Various sectors of society, in both subtle and painfully conspicuous ways, effectively repress the feminine. Male and female alike suffer from this repression.

SUBJUGATION OR MUTUALITY?

Central to my awakening and growth was the breaking or dismantling of patriarchal paradigms that had stifled me from reaching my full potential and had contributed to the creation of the false self. Slowly I began to recognize the effect of patriarchy (male dominance and superiority) on culture, religion, family and my personal life. Rising from my slumber meant examining all sectors of society that repress the feminine. Power and powerlessness were constant companions in this awakening. Power paradigms that communicate a "woman's place" in a limiting and repressive manner came into view. I felt powerless and longed to be empowered.

Awakening invited me to be broken of who I thought I was (the false self) and to submit to the work of the Spirit in me, which enabled me to submit to who I truly was (the true self). Even submission started to take on new meaning. Submission as mutuality was making sense to me, instead of submission as subordination or subjugation. Mutuality is love-reciprocated submission. This was good news to me.

Growing up, the typical model of male-female relationships that I witnessed looked something like this: In church, only the man was allowed to teach from the holy pulpit. Women were not permitted to teach men. Women weren't allowed to pass the offering plate or to serve Communion either. They were consigned to playing the piano, singing in the choir, teaching women and children, and cooking and serving church dinners. And the more revered women became missionaries in faraway places where they could minister more freely (somewhere else).

Though my dad was supportive of my mom and me pursuing our dreams, many of the marriages I witnessed took on this kind of expression: The husband always had to drive the car, even if the wife wanted to. The husband also expected dinner to be made by a certain time and his laundry to be washed. The wife was expected to meet every need of her husband. And if the husband committed an affair, social gossip usually indicted the wife for not being attentive enough to her husband's sex drive.

The woman wasn't even afforded a name of her own. She belonged to her father and then to her husband, most well-noted through her last name. And a woman was subtly defined in relationship to men through her title as Miss, Ms. or Mrs. Obviously, a man is not subjected to such definitions: he is Mr. no matter his marital status.

My mom was one of the more radical women of her day. She is spunky, intelligent and courageous. Raised by her widowed mother, Mom witnessed daily as a child, adolescent and young adult how a woman can be independent, free-thinking, creative and a provider for her family. Throughout her life, Mom could often be found breaking with convention, much to the dismay and ridicule of others. She was the first preacher's wife to wear pants to the church in which I grew up—a subversive act indeed.[5] I remember her telling me this story and how she thought the whole congregation would be scandalized. But it wasn't long before several of the women quietly thanked her and told how they had wanted to be free to wear pants instead of skirts or dresses to church (especially in winter). Though Mom often resisted the status quo, she couldn't escape all the influence of patriarchy. Bright, talented and hardworking, she worked an average of thirty-five hours per week to put herself through college. But Mom did what many women in her day did— she discontinued her college education once she married. She used to joke about getting her "M-R-S degree." In fact, many women in her generation were noted for such an accomplishment. Even twenty years later at the college I graduated from, this tradition was evident. My peers and I witnessed the same phenomenon— women attending class and receiving education but aspiring to their "M-R-S degrees."

To a young girl trying to find her way in the world, the message was clear. Not only am I defined in relationship to my husband and subjugated to him, but my opportunities are limited by him. This message was subtly engraved into my very being, taking shape in the following mental musing.

> You can be anything you want to be in life except a pastor, elder or deacon. Why? Because you are female. You are less. You are a little lower than your male counterpart. Because of no reason other than your gender, you are to submit to male authority. You can attend church and maybe help out in the nursery, but you have nothing worthwhile to share in the company of men, except service of their needs and the feeding of their ego. Though you can be anything you want to be except a leader of men, your highest calling is that of wife and mother, so be satisfied with that alone. And once you obtain this most worthy of callings, your duty as wife and mother is to please your husband and care for your children. Serve your husband and support him and your children even if it means repressing your own dreams. Your identity is found in relationship to your husband and children.

Many of the predominant people in my life as a child, teen and young adult viewed a woman's place in life as reflected in Debi Pearl's book *Created to Be His Help Meet*. Pearl is cofounder with her husband of "No Greater Joy Ministries" and coauthor of the book *To Train Up a Child*. In *Created to Be His Help Meet,* Pearl gives women advice about how to be a godly woman, wife and mother. She sums up well the patriarchal teaching by which I was conditioned. While this view has left the mainstream, it can still be found in understated forms, and its impact on both women and men extends well beyond the fundamentalist churches that still preach it.

In essence Pearl suggests that being a woman is defined by one's role as wife and mother—it is her "created nature."[6] "A good help meet will have a passion to be of service. Her first calling is to be of service to her husband, then her children, and when time affords, her passion of service will spill over to serving others."[7]

At one point early in the book Pearl responds to a woman who sought her advice about her husband's emotional affair with his secretary. In shocking rhetoric that has been widely accepted in Christian circles, Pearl instructs this woman and all those reading her book to exploit her beauty and sexuality and compete with the secretary in order to win her husband's affection and fidelity. "God has provided for your husband's complete satisfaction and deliverance from temptation through you. . . . Your man, like many men before him, is a fool to wink at sin, to play with temptation."[8]

Pearl goes on to explain that, if the woman confronts her husband, calls him to account and asks him to change his behavior, the marriage will end in divorce. She'll be standing on principle, Pearl says, but she'll be sleeping alone. And if she finds another husband, Pearl says, he'll be no better than her first.

> Get down on your husband's emotional level, and make yourself more attractive than that office wench, and do it today! . . . Never demand that a man love you and cherish you because he ought to. Earn every smile and shared moment. Cultivate his love for you. . . . Be creative and aggressive in your private, intimate times. Keep him drained at home so he won't have any sexual need at work. If you feed him well, emotionally and sexually, her cooking won't tempt him.[9]

As I reviewed Debi Pearl's book, which was being read by a number of our friends, I couldn't believe the blatant female subordination and male domination she promotes. Pearl sums up her perception of the biblical mandate of female subjugation by saying,

> There is no loss of dignity in subordination when it serves a higher purpose. God made you to be a help meet to your

husband so you can bolster him, making him more productive and efficient at whatever he chooses to do. You are not on the board of directors with an equal vote. You have no authority to set the agenda. But if he can trust you, he will make you his closest advisor, his confidant, his press secretary, his head of state, his vice-president, his ambassador, his public relations expert, maybe even his speech writer— all at his discretion.[10]

This kind of submission is a picture of power and powerlessness, exploiter and exploited, superiority and inferiority, better and less. Women are not lovable and lovely in and of themselves; they must "earn" the love of others. Submission of this nature is the result of a power paradigm that favors men. Women are created for and expected to serve the sole benefit of men. When women adhere to this view, they are held captive from reaching their potential.

One would think this book was published in the 1950s, but make no mistake—it was published in 2004. This kind of manipulation and self-exploitation disguised as "submission" and "godly" is a widely accepted posture for many women.

In stark contrast to Pearl's perspective, on the Camino I grew aware of a different kind of submission. Chris and I each encountered physical, mental and emotional obstacles that we had never experienced before. At times, I needed Chris to support me and keep me going. At other times Chris needed me to support and encourage him. Mutuality. The presumption I had grown up under—that the woman submits to the man as part of the natural order of things, that to submit means to suppress myself and elevate someone else, not as an act of mercy but as an act of penance for my gender—was being subverted and reshaped as we made our way together along the Camino. We needed one another, and we needed to trust one another.

Mutuality is beautifully expressed in John 13. In this passage we learn of the Last Supper—Jesus' last Passover meal with his disciples before he was crucified. With a totally countercultural gesture Jesus insisted on washing his friends' feet. Here the teacher stooped down to do the job of a slave. One of the disciples, Peter, was indignant and initially refused to let Jesus touch his grimy, first-century feet. But Jesus told Peter that unless he allowed Jesus to do this, Peter would have no part in him. Peter's response was then one of total submission. He asked Jesus to not stop with his feet but to wash his hands and head as well.

Peter's initial reaction to Jesus is similar to our gut reaction. We don't want Jesus to "go there"—to those vulnerable, needy places in us. We want to pretend that we are self-sufficient, capable people who don't need anything from anyone. Peter's submission to Jesus required Peter's own admittance of his weakness, his need. The act of Jesus washing his feet would expose Peter's vulnerability. Submission is about receiving, but sadly society and culture have made it about subjugation. And so a power paradigm is created in which often women are expected to "submit" (subjugate themselves) and men don't posture themselves to receive (submit).

Unfortunately, a lot of Christian women have embraced the posture of "submission" (subjugation) to their detriment. One way this subjugated posture is often endured is by pretending that we as women don't need anything. We can do it all and ask for nothing in return—run the household; birth and nurse the babies; feed, care for and support the husband; maybe work a job to help meet the financial needs of the family; and, if there's time left over, serve in the church, most likely in the nursery. In a world where the woman is intricately connected and subjected to the needs of everyone around her, there is no room for dreams of her own. She exists for everyone else. And she can continue to live that way if she pretends she is not vulnerable and needy herself. Once she admits her own need (to dream, perhaps, and to give expression to those dreams and ambitions), the presumed natural order of family and societal dynamics is thunderously shaken.

In contrast, mutual submission between men and women invites us into true intimacy and frees us to give as well as receive and to live into our full potential. Mutuality between anyone, regardless of gender, is redemptive.

At the church I'm a part of today, Jesuit priests courageously demonstrate the lesson Jesus taught Peter in a foot-washing ceremony on Holy Thursday. With a humility rarely demonstrated by the powerful, these brilliant, dignified men humble themselves in a posture of receptivity and let others wash their feet. In so doing they reveal a central characteristic of an apostle of Christ—vulnerability.

The ones who hold power in any institution are often the most guarded—they are glad for others to reveal their hidden vulnerabilities and needs, but they neglect to reveal their own need. Meeting the needs of someone else may be kind, compassionate and even righteous, but it is, after all, a powerful gesture: *You have a need, and I can meet that need. You need me, but I don't need you.* The reverse is in view during the Holy Thursday ceremony. This isn't an exhibition of the powerful doing something for the needy, but an expression of our common humanity, with the capacity to give and the need to receive. Parishioners are invited to participate as well— parishioners and priests, men and women, giving and receiving with mutual respect. The point of the service is to remember the gift of mutuality—that we need one another, that we are not self-sufficient and that while we do have a lot to offer and give, we also have need to receive. During this grace-filled church service wounds and needs are embraced as avenues for mutual grace and transformation.

Waking up caused my worldview of submission to be shattered, breaking along with it my inferior and subordinate view of self. This was a rather new way of understanding brokenness. Often I had associated the need for brokenness with the sin of pride. Strangely, the brokenness invitation I received was one of being broken of self-abnegation or self-effacing. I was like the woman in the Gospel of St. Luke who was bent over for eighteen years by an evil spirit—Jesus' healing of her meant a strengthening of her spine to stand up straight. She didn't need to be broken of pride but to be broken of what shackled her in a posture of oppression.[11]

The invitation during this season of awakening was "self-assertion"—to be broken free of what was holding me back from being more truly and fully me and to stand up straight with proper confidence. Marianne Williamson articulates the fears we encounter upon awakening:

> "Our deepest fear is not that we are inadequate. Our deepest fear is that we are powerful beyond measure. It is our light, not our darkness that most frightens us." We ask ourselves, Who am I to be brilliant, gorgeous, talented, fabulous? Actually, who are you *not* to be? You are a child of God. Your playing small does not serve the world. There is nothing enlightened about shrinking so that other people won't feel insecure around you. We are all meant to shine, as children do. We were born to make manifest the glory of God that is within us. It's not just in some of us; it's in everyone. And as we let our own light shine, we unconsciously give other people permission to do the same. As we are liberated from our own fear, our presence automatically liberates others.[12]

Waking up allowed me to surrender to the removal of masks of fear, inferiority and subordination. I was coming out from hiding and breaking free of that which kept me from being fully awake, fully alive. Some of what I needed to be liberated from was familial, cultural and religious paradigms of what it means to be a woman. I began realizing just how much I was living my life for other people rather than for who God made me to be. I was realizing how much I put everyone else first like a good self-denying Christian, only to discover how in some of those ways I was *hiding* and pretending that I didn't have needs and dreams. The easier, *broader* way was to hide behind selfless deeds rather than to live up to my potential to influence and to create change, to heal and to lead.

Theologians Reinhold Niebuhr and Carol Lakey Hess help me understand this notion of *hiding* as the sin of self-abnegation, the cousin sin of pride.[13] According to a number of theologians, the sin of self-abnegation is widely overlooked in Christian teaching, yet it has as devastating effects on people and society as does the sin of pride.

Niebuhr suggested that sin takes on two primary expressions. The first is "the unwillingness of [humanity] to acknowledge [their] creatureliness and dependence upon God and [their] effort to make [their] own life independent and secure," which is commonly understood as pride.[14] The alternative form of sin is sensuality (doing what feels good), evasion of self or self-abnegation. Unfortunately, Niebuhr underdeveloped this side and focused most of his work on the first expression of sin. Both expressions are effectively a form of denial. Pride is *the denial of one's need to depend* on God; self-abnegation is *the knowledge of the need but refusal to depend* on God. Pride can be associated with a superiority complex; self-abnegation can be associated with an inferiority complex. Both prevent us from living into the fullness of who God created us to be.

I think of Moses as a good example of one who struggled with self-abnegation. In the Torah, Exodus 3–4 outlines this marvelous story. God calls Moses to lead the Hebrew people out of slavery, but Moses doubts his abilities and tries to wiggle out of the calling. The Scriptures mention four times that Moses responds to God with "what ifs" and excuses. Self-abnegation is seen clearly in Exodus 4:10-14. Moses understands that in order for the people to be liberated, he will have to speak to the king of Egypt to negotiate their release—a tall order, no doubt. Moses seems afraid and doubtful that this is going to work. By way of struggling with the calling and delaying to step up to the responsibility, Moses says that he is not a good speaker:

Then Moses said to the Holy One, "Please, my God, I am not good with words. I wasn't yesterday, nor the day before, nor am I now, even after you spoke to me. I speak slowly, and with a wooden tongue."

YHWH replied, "Who taught people to speak in the first place? Who makes them deaf or mute? Who makes them see, or be blind? Who, if not I, YHWH? Now go! I myself will be with you when you speak. I will teach you what to say."

But Moses said, "Please, my God, please send someone else. Not me."

Then God's anger flashed out against Moses. "If you can't do it, I know someone who can."

How many times have we been like Moses—full of self-doubt and reluctant to step into our calling? Self-abnegation and sensuality are intricately connected, but at first it is difficult to recognize the connection. Often, doing what feels good (sensuality) means hiding or avoiding one's potential. When we are subject to the sin of self-abnegation, we are shirking our responsibilities. Fear is usually a contributor. We fear upsetting the status quo or we fear our abilities or we fear the potential for rejection, criticism and failure—so we hide. Hiding feels safe.

With the support of a number of scholars, feminist theologian Judith Plaskow explains the problematic nature of overemphasizing the sin of pride while neglecting the sin of self-abnegation. Carol Lakey Hess summarizes Plaskow's point by saying that a description of "sin as self-assertion, self-centeredness, and pride speaks out of and to the experience of powerful men. . . . [W]omen are better indicted for such behaviors as lack of self, self-abnegation, and irresponsibility"—the alternative expression of sin that Niebuhr recognized. "When sin as pride is generalized, self-abnegation is deemed a virtue and harmfully reinforced" in the lives of the historically powerless. "A theology that emphasizes self-sacrifice as the human telos functions to further enervate women's struggle for self-assertion. Such a theology may chasten little boys, but hasten the devastation of girls."[15]

In this movement of my soul, I was waking up to the fullness of being created in the image of God—male *and* female God created them. There was something beautiful and divine to be embraced in my feminine identity. I was confronting the sin of self-abnegation and growing in self-assertion rooted in dependence on God. Sadly, a theology that overemphasized self-sacrifice had served to devastate me. Now awakened, I realized that spiritual growth for me meant owning the responsibility to live into my potential to offer my voice, perspective and influence—at the risk of upsetting the status quo and being criticized and rejected. Once awakened, I couldn't turn back. Pilgrimage is not a round trip. The spiritual journey beckoned me further and deeper into the consequences of patriarchal theology and practice.

THE LOVE OF GOD

In her album *Sleeping When You Woke Me,* Kate Hurley beautifully echoes the process of awakening through song. In the track "Hey Little Girl," we hear of a small child and the root of her pain. The pain inflicted at a young age is too much to bear. It is deeper than even tears can express. The child grows up to be a woman only to find that the "little girl" is still within her:

> I see a little girl
> In the back of my mind
> See daisies in her hand
> She's looking to the sky
> She is looking to the sky
> She is sitting on the stairs
> Of her two story house
> And the pain that she bears
> Leaves no tears left to cry

Leaves her no tears left to cry
Where is the reward
For the ones who have been torn
Where is the treasure laid for the
Ones who've known so much pain

Hey little girl
Let me whisper some hope
There's mercy for you that overflows
Everything's going to be all right
Everything's going to be all right
Hey little girl won't you hear me say
There is love enough
To cover your shame
Everything's going to be all right
Everything's going to be all right

And that little girl
So small and so scared
Been near so long
I forgot she was there
I forgot that she was there
Somehow the pain
That she couldn't feel
Passed on to me
A weight too great to bear
Much too great to bear
Someone is standing near
Who will wash away her tears
Someday when she's been found
Her scars will become a crown.[16]

My initial awakening could probably be traced back two or three years before I made pilgrimage in Spain. I had decided to make regular private retreats, and my first was a day spent at the Abbey of Gethsemani in Trappist, Kentucky—former home of Thomas Merton. This was my introduction to the prophetic presence of monastic communities. In the monks' silence, I encountered the penetrating presence of God.

What started out as a few silent retreat days per year turned into a quarterly rhythm of overnight private retreats. Though there are many places that have provided solitude and silence for me, one of my favorites and the place I most regularly return to is a small Benedictine monastery in rural Schuyler, Nebraska.

During one of my visits to Schuyler, Kate's song wakened me to some of the pain in my heart that I had previously been numb to. Her song gave rise to haunting questions and painful doubts within me. I found myself asking, *What is this pain that I feel? Why am I so sad? Who is this little girl in me and what is her pain?*

The descent continued. Questions ran deep as I sat in my little cell at the monastery and cried and cried until I thought I could cry no more. Tears gave rise to words: *Who am I really? Am I lovely? Am I loved? Am I really loved for me? Does anyone see me? Does anyone know that I'm alive? Does anyone care? I have dreams to dream! I have a life to live! Does anyone hear me? Does anyone see me?*

The root of all these questions was an invitation to realize to a deeper degree of faith that God loves me, truly loves me. Thankfully, I grew up in a Christian home where my parents did everything they could to communicate to me the love of God. For the daughter of a pastor who grew up attending church three times a week, this was Sunday school lesson 101: "For God so loved the world, that he gave his only begotten Son, that whosoever believeth in him should not perish, but have everlasting life" (John 3:16 KJV). However, the "love" message got somewhat lost amidst the fear of "perishing." Subtly, the idea that I could do something to avoid perishing became a primary unconscious motivator in my life. Rather than letting the love message sink in, the louder message I absorbed was how to avoid being punished and damned to hell. "God loved the world so much that God sacrificed the Son to save us from hell" didn't get through to me that well. Certainly over time I grew to want to be in relationship with my Creator and with the one who I was told expressed this earth-shattering act of love for me through a crucifixion. But recognizing, realizing and experiencing the *love* of God seemed to evade me. The sentiment that we are "sinners in the hands of an angry God" seemed to subtly underline a lot of the "Christian" teaching I received.

This is simply (or complexly, depending on how you look at it) the human condition that we're all faced with if we awaken to it. We are cut off from our Creator—the one who provides our every need—and we spend our lives trying to return to and live in that all-fulfilling relationship. We long for the Garden—the place that symbolizes the relationship between God and humanity. In the Garden all is right with the world. The true self is free to be expressed in her fullness. Men and women live together in life-giving mutuality. But the sins of self-abnegation and pride ruin this utopia. We are cut off, fragmented, distanced from God and from one another. It is easier to remain asleep to this reality because it can be downright traumatizing to wake up.

Ironically, in the garden story of the Hebrew Scriptures it seems that Adam is the one who fell to the sin of self-abnegation, while Eve succumbed to the sin of pride. When Eve submitted to the temptation to become like God, she sinned by exhibiting "an unwillingness to acknowledge [her] creatureliness and dependence upon God and [her] effort [was] to make [her] own life independent and secure"; while Adam in contrast exhibited sensuality and evasion of self, the sin of self-abnegation.[17] When God asked Adam why he did that which God had told him not to do, he replied, "It was the woman you put beside me, she gave me the fruit, and I ate it" (Genesis 3:12). A little speculation causes me to conclude that either Adam thought the fruit looked good (sensuality) or he didn't think for himself (evasion of self). Either way, the sin of self-abnegation seems clear. Interestingly, one of the consequences of Adam and Eve's sin would be a lack of mutuality and union between men and women. "You will desire union with your man, but he will be bent on subjugating you" (Genesis 3:16).

In our feeble attempts to return to the Garden—which represents union with God and mutuality among humanity—we either appeal to substitutes or we respond to the world in an exploitative manner to get the power and control, affection and esteem, or security and survival that we crave.

Thomas Keating writes and speaks copiously about our estrangement from God. A doctor of psychology and theology, he examines what it means to be human in a holistic way. By understanding the depths of the mind, will and emotions Keating is able to connect the teachings of Christ with the most vulnerable parts of our human condition. In his book *The Human Condition: Contemplation and Transformation,* he outlines three basic "programs for happiness," of which he says that each of us usually over-identifies with one:

- power and control
- affection and esteem
- security and survival

These "programs for happiness" invariably conflict with one another so that the space between us becomes toxic. None of our relationships "outside of the Garden" will offer us power and control, affection and esteem, and security and survival to the extent that we need.

Keating says that these three "programs for happiness" emerge from very basic instinctual needs. It is a natural part of our human development to seek a degree of power and control, affection and esteem, and security and survival. The problem is that in time we over-identify with one set by way of compensating for that basic need which may have gone largely unmet in our childhood; thus, the false self gains fuel for its existence. This intensifies when we over-identify with a particular group or culture. Temperament also plays into the false self. For example, if I am a dominant personality type and I didn't experience the control that I needed as a child, I will be compelled to control my situation and surroundings and in some cases other people. Experiencing anxiety and frustration is often a sign that in the unconscious there is an emotional program for happiness that has just been triggered.[18] Do you ever have an overly emotional reaction to a situation or relationship and later wonder why you reacted so strongly? As we grow in self-awareness we often realize that some of our reactions to present circumstances are actually reactions to past events that are buried in our unconscious. The current situation provides a trigger for the unresolved anguish. When we recognize the agony surfacing, we have experienced grace. This is an invitation to greater wholeness.

"The spiritual journey is a journey of self-discovery since the encounter with God is also an encounter with one's deepest self," says Keating.[19] Thomas Merton spoke of "finding [oneself] in God" and wrote, "In order to find God, Whom we can only find in and through the depths of our own soul, we must therefore first find ourselves."[20] Self-awareness is central to becoming whole and connected to God and others. If God dwells in our soul, then being connected to God within us will allow us to be connected to God who is also all around us.

Experiencing a certain deficit of our particular "program for happiness" causes us to develop an alternative way of living in relationship. This is where the toxicity develops. In essence we develop a mask or a costume to hide behind to try to gratify our need for power and control, affection and esteem, or security and survival. *Maybe if I create a mask I will feel safe and get the attention and acceptance that I want. Maybe the mask will be more interesting than the real thing. Maybe the mask is more lovable than I am.*

Interestingly, the terms *masks* and *costumes* are also used in the field of psychology. Shirley Jean Schmidt, M.A., L.P.C., creator of Developmental Needs Meeting Strategy (DNMS), helps patients heal from unmet childhood developmental needs using the imagery of a costume. As the patient heals and grows, the child-state of mind is able to discard the costume as a sign of wholeness and healing—parallel to shedding the false self.[21]

The human condition is so complex that being cut off from the Maker and Lover of our soul affects our psyche, emotions, spirit, body and relationships. Our relationship to God, self and others, including the earth and all its creatures, is distorted. The spiritual journey is about being restored, returning to "the Garden," returning to the love of God. Restoration to wholeness of self and relationship with God and others is offered on "the narrow way." The journey begins by waking up. Following is a quote from my journal just before starting the Camino. These musings depict part of my experience in the initial stages of waking up and in the struggle to leave the comfort of what is known for what is unknown.

> For the past several weeks I've been a bit emotional thinking about leaving my community for this season. These are my people. This is home. In home we find safety, security, familiarity and embrace.
>
> I'm going on pilgrimage to a place not my home, not familiar, not safe. Will I find an embrace?
>
> I'm going on pilgrimage and the way is unknown and the destination unclear and I think some of the emotion I feel in leaving my community is tied into a deep knowing that I will not be the same when I return.
>
> I'm going on pilgrimage. As I walk, I hope to shed the mold of my false self. Abandoned to all I've known and found security and identity in, I hope to walk more fully into my true self and trust that Christ and the saints that have

journeyed before me will accompany me into these places of the unknown. Their presence, assurance and example will breathe into me the courage that I need to fully embrace me and all of God's dreams and intentions for me.

I'm going on pilgrimage. The Camino is not a round trip. There is a commencement and a benediction. I will walk. And as I walk, I will leave behind. I will journey ahead. And I will arrive at an unknown destination.

And then I will start a new journey. I will not turn back. We will not turn back.[22]

Embarking on pilgrimage mirrors the initiation of awakening. In taking the initial steps to wake up, I began to listen to the voices in my head and the pain in my heart that I had long avoided. As my eyes opened, my false self started to come into focus. As I dared to wake from my slumber, chains of female inferiority and subordination revealed themselves. No longer seeking sedation or escape, I gave ear to the lies in my head that said, *Phileena, you are what others need you to be. You are only as good as you are able to meet the needs of others. You exist for the sole purpose of supporting others and helping others realize their dreams. Those dreams that your mother sang of in the morning hours are not yours to be had. You have no dreams to be realized. You don't need dreams. Your purpose as a godly woman is to elevate others to realize their dreams.*

The lies in my head were the voices of my false self that had secretly dominated much of my life. With deepening awareness the journey progressed.

Pilgrimage certainly isn't a round trip and neither is the spiritual journey. It is a progression from one place to another. We don't arrive at a new place in our spiritual life only to regress to the place from which we disembarked. It's funny though—on the Camino we did encounter a few people who were walking in the opposite direction. They had reached Santiago and were walking back. Practically speaking, after arriving at Santiago there is the inevitability of returning home. For some, especially before the time of mass transit, I guess they would more than likely return home the way they came—the pilgrimage route. But the imagery of seeing one walking in the reverse direction struck me as odd. We have but one life to live and we can't do it over. We live life and we reflect and we grieve and we learn from our experiences, but God forbid that we revert or regress or stay in the place from which we have been delivered. The invitation is to make a passage and, once that passage is made, we are prepared for the next part of our life's journey. Pilgrimage is not a round trip. There is a beginning point and end point. And then we embark on a new journey. We don't relive the old one.

As I mentioned before, the Spanish word *el camino* means "the way." Pilgrimage has become for me a *way* to live. As I walked the Camino I often thought of the words of Christ, "I am the way, the truth and the life" (John 14:6). And, "for the way is broad that leads to destruction, and there are many who enter through it . . . and the way is narrow that leads to life, and there are few who find it" (Matthew 7:13-14).

The narrow way speaks to the way of the spiritual journey. To find authentic life, one has to have the will to wake up and embark on the journey. In so doing one submits to the redemptive, though painful, road of transformation. If this is not acceptable, choose the broad way. It may be comforting and fun—like a jaunt through La Rioja (the heart of Spain's wine country), which I have also thoroughly enjoyed—full of vineyards and bodegas (wineries) to delight the senses. But it can also serve as a numbing agent to keep one asleep to the gift of one's life. The difference is in the posture. Both the Camino and a visit to La Rioja can have transformative or destructive purpose. It's all in how one orients and submits his or her life.

The gospel says, "Jesus is *the way*." The Camino, the posture of pilgrimage, had a way of carving that reality, *the* Reality—Jesus—

into me. Waking up and embarking on the journey provides the way to tap into the tangible love of God.

CONTEMPLATIVE PRAYER HELPS ME WAKE UP

Parker Palmer, the respected writer, lecturer, teacher and activist, says that contemplation is any way that our illusions are dismantled and reality is revealed.[23] After a few years of a regular practice of contemplative prayer, my soul was ready for this life-shattering dismantling of illusions.

In the seventies, like a few other Christian monks around the world, a Benedictine from England named John Main rediscovered the ancient Christian tradition of what is known as "pure prayer." Pure prayer was taught widely by the Desert Mothers and Fathers of the third and fourth centuries, but the practice had dissipated some over time.[24] Main experienced the groundedness and growth in faith that this disciplined Christian prayer offers. And so he devoted much of his life to teaching this form of contemplative prayer. Main said that contemplative prayer is

- learning to stand back and allow God to come to the forefront of life
- the step away from self-centeredness to God-centeredness
- leaving the ego behind
- simply being open to Jesus' being[25]

Contemplative prayer disciplines our soul to be attentive to God. I like the way my husband, Chris, explains it. He says contemplative prayer is a prayer of consent that creates "muscle memory." It then becomes easier and more natural to consent to God in active life. In essence, it is pure faith, abandonment to the Creator and Lover of our soul. It is "not a conversation in words but an exchange of hearts."[26]

In the Gospel of John, Jesus says:

If you dwell in me, as I dwell in you, you will bear much fruit;

for apart from me you can do nothing. . . . If you remain in me and my words dwell in you, ask what you will, and you shall have it. This is my Father's glory, that you bear fruit in plenty and so be my disciples. As the Father has loved me, so I have loved you. Dwell in my love. If you heed my commands, you will remain in my love, as I have heeded my Father's commands and remain in his love. (John 15:5, 7-10)

This is contemplative prayer: to dwell, abide, be or remain in the love of God. We desperately need to recognize and be rooted in the love of God. According to Keating, this is the first stage of contemplative prayer.[27]

The essence of contemplation is the trusting and loving faith by which God both elevates the human person and purifies the conscious and unconscious obstacles in us that oppose the values of the gospel and the work of the Spirit.[28]

Contemplation is the development of one's relationship with Christ to the point of communing beyond words, thoughts, feelings and the multiplication of particular acts; it is a process moving from the simplified activity of waiting on God to the ever-increasing predominance of the gifts of the Spirit in one's life.[29] In the broadest sense, I understand contemplation to mean creating sacred space to be still, to rest in God, to attend to the inner life, to simply be with God in solitude, silence and stillness.

St. Augustine said that we are restless until we rest in God alone. Contemplative prayer teaches us to rest in God, and in so doing the soul settles out of its fears, anxiety and pain.

Contemplative prayer is a "divine therapy" that helps us wake up. As we give ourselves over to trying to satisfy our emotional program(s) for happiness we distance ourselves more and more from our true self and our belovedness. The energy that this takes tends to increase over time; it requires a lot of energy to sustain an illusion. As we fight to stay asleep, we go deeper and deeper into hiding. We need divine therapy to wake us from our slumber.

To submit to the divine therapy [in contemplation] is something we owe to ourselves and the rest of humanity. If we don't allow the Spirit of God to address the deep levels of our attachments to ourselves and to our "programs for happiness," we will pour into the world the negative elements of our self-centeredness, adding to the conflicts and social disasters that come from overidentifying with the biases and prejudices of our particular culture and upbringing.[30]

Even some of our best deeds can be laced with violence that we are asleep to. Contemplation purifies our actions. Through contemplation we are able to confront the darkness of our personalities and the emotional investments we have made in false "programs for happiness."[31] As a result we open ourselves to the possibilities of experiencing

- interior freedom instead of pursuing power and control
- divine love instead of craving the affection and esteem of others
- presence of God instead of clinging to security and survival

Growing acquainted with the presence of God through the discipline of silence, solitude and stillness makes way for contemplation. But this discipline takes courage. Whoever we think we are, we find out we're not. Contemplative prayer provides a way to wake up from our illusions and to live into the gift of our life—fully awake, fully alive.

TRYING TO UNDERSTAND THE HUMAN CONDITION

The spiritual journey is an invitation to know God and to be known by God, which presupposes that one finds and knows one's self. Awakening allows for the initial stages of distinguishing between the false and true self. In relationship with God, grace reveals false parts of ourselves and invites us to embrace what is real. We have to abandon what is false for continued growth in wholeness and authentic relationship with God and others. As we press into deeper acquaintance and friendship with God, what is false in our preconceived notions of God, the world and our self burns away. Ancient Christian wisdom calls this experience purgation—a process of spiritual cleansing. As I began my journey, through the grace of contemplation I was waking up. The light of Christ was shining in my darkness and I began to let go of false parts of myself with their hidden motivations and distortions. Jesus was inviting me to greater transformation and freedom.

Keating says that because Christ lives in us, we need not go anywhere to find God; we simply need to stop running away and to be attentive to the One who is within us.[32] Surrender to the spiritual journey, aided by the practice of contemplative prayer, is central to personal growth in attentiveness to the presence and love of God.

Like a person waking from a deep sleep, the soul too is invited to wake up. Jesus spoke of this by inviting Nicodemus to be born again (John 3). The invitation is to embrace the world through the eyes of a child, the child-state of innocence that represents Adam and Eve before the Fall. The Christian invitation is to return—return to the essence of who we are and to the purpose for which we were created. There is a state in our human condition that is pure and innocent and that knows she is full of God, in God, aware of herself and of the paradise of God's creation.[33] Christ's invitation is to return to the Garden—the place that symbolizes perfect relationship with God and humanity—to be born anew and to wake up from our state of slumber to enter fullness of life. But when we wake, the light may shine so brightly that all will seem dark. Longing for truth helps us navigate the darkness.

QUESTIONS FOR REFLECTION

1. The spiritual journey begins by waking up. But it's too easy to stay asleep. Ignorance is bliss. So instead of waking up to the gift of our life, we all too easily numb out with the help of digital distractions and addictions to food, alcohol and other substances or habits. In what ways have you been numbing out?

   What is required for you to wake up?

   How is the still, small voice of God nudging you out of your slumber?

2. "Awakening and embarking on the spiritual journey invited me to have a good hard look at reality. I was being invited to die so that more of the life of Christ could live in me. 'For to me to live is Christ and to die is gain' (Philippians 1:21)." In what ways are you being invited to die so that you can live the abundant life Jesus calls you to?

3. When we wake up, we realize the ways in which we've been living a lie. The old and new creations within us come into focus. And we have a choice to take responsibility for our life: to live into the new creation or let the old creation rule us. Twentieth-century Christian mystic Thomas Merton referred to this psychological dichotomy as the true and false self. Unlike the false self, the true self is not defined by what we have or do or what others say about us. The true self is characterized by personal freedom combined with clarity of purpose. In what ways has the false self dominated your life?

   The false self over-identifies with power and control, affection and esteem, and security and survival. Which of these "programs for happiness" do you tend to over-identify with?

   How do you see this hindering your freedom?

4. Part of my awakening included waking up to the ramifications of patriarchy and the personal sin of self-abnegation. In what

ways do you or don't you identify with the experience of female subordination and male domination?

In what ways would you like to live into more mutuality between women and men?

5. We all have differing degrees of identifying with power, given our race, social class and economic status. In some cases it may be different depending on the setting. In what ways do you identify with experiences of being powerful in a family, church or society?

In what ways do you identify with experiences of powerlessness or forced subjugation?

How has your lived experience shaped your view of self and relationships to others?

6. Given your lived experience, does the invitation to humble yourself resonate with you, or does the invitation to stop hiding, stand up straight and assert yourself resonate more?

Share how this particular invitation applies in a specific situation in your life.

PRACTICE

Spend some time journaling about Thomas Keating's programs for happiness: power and control, affection and esteem, security and survival.

Which do you identify with more? Do you notice one being triggered more often than the others?

How do you know when a particular program for happiness has been triggered?

2

Longing

My soul is restless until it rests in you alone O God.

St. Augustine

On THE THIRD DAY OF PILGRIMAGE Chris and I walked thirteen miles in five hours from Zubri to Pamplona (famous for its annual running of the bulls)—a day that will always be remembered as the "Phileena Shuffle."

As we started out in the morning I didn't know how I would be able to do it. The previous two days we had walked a total of thirty-two miles, down the backside of the Pyrenees. Given that I was unconditioned and carrying a much-too-heavy pack, my neck, back, hips, knees, ankles and feet were completely overused. I didn't want to complain, yet I was in so much pain. After a cocktail of Tylenol and ibuprofen set in, I began to regain some hope that I could make it through the day's journey. Even though Chris's body also ached, he was incredibly patient and encouraged me. He seemed to have more stamina and determination than I at this stage. We tried to find the mystical path in the midst of our physical distractions of pain. By the last couple of hours, I was literally hobbling because of the pain in my calves. I was moving so slowly—

terribly humbling when people ten-plus years older passed me with such ease. In my humiliation, I hobbled into the city of Pamplona where the cheers of the passersby hit me to the core: *"Buen Camino!"*[1] In light of my condition I thought, *Can I really have a good Camino? Will I really make it to Santiago?* "Hope deferred makes for a sick heart" (Proverbs 13:12). I hoped beyond hope that the Camino would get better for me. Starting out, I wondered if I would make it to Pamplona, let alone walk out of Pamplona the following day. Santiago seemed like a far-off dream.

During pilgrimage, as the road stretched on ahead, a longing crept up within me. With each ache in my tired body I longed to reach Santiago. Engulfed in physical pain, I desperately wanted relief and to experience the joy and peace of attaining my destination. I wondered if I would truly make it. *Would I really reach Santiago? Could I persevere?* There were countless moments when I lost faith and doubted that I would get to Santiago by foot. Many pilgrims end up opting for transportation because of injuries. Less than 5 percent who start in France make it all the way to Santiago by foot. But I didn't want to compromise my journey. I wanted to make it step by step. I cried out to God for assistance.

In spite of the pain and suffering, *walking* to Santiago was important for me. So I put one foot in front of the other day after day, moment by moment. With each agonizing step the voice of God was calling me to greater dependence. I longed to make it.

CHILDHOOD LONGINGS

Longings are like growing pains in that their origins can be difficult to trace, and yet they give indication of something deep and profound, something immediately true of us. In that respect, noting our longings and looking more deeply into them can function as a sort of "thin space," in which God pierces our desires and then redeems them with a more devout understanding for how we can live in relationship to God, one another and all of creation.

I can remember as a young child longing for the school year to end and summer to begin—a transition from one stage of life into the next. I remember feeling like the years would drag on before I finally turned sixteen and got my driver's license—such a milestone in a North American teenager's life. I remember the longing that grew within me once I was first cognizant of a call to mission. I was in fifth grade and the teacher asked all the students what they wanted to be when they grew up. Being in a public school and thinking that most of my peers were not Christian, I was embarrassed to say that I wanted to be a missionary. Their responses seemed much more glamorous than mine: Doctor! Lawyer! Astronaut! But clearly in my heart of hearts I knew I was called to mission. From that point on I secretly longed for that dream to be realized.

I grew up in a lower-middle-class family in Indianapolis. My father was the third son of a simple farming couple from central Indiana; my mother was the only child of a struggling widow from Columbus, Ohio. Though the church where my father ministered for sixteen years did not provide adequate salary or benefits for a family of five, my father frugally managed what little we had to provide for our basic needs. Extras were extremely hard to come by, but Dad made sure we always had proper medical and dental care, good shoes, clothing and supplies for the school year, and a decent, modest family automobile.

Mom and us kids were well taken care of on my father's limited salary and personal sacrifices; we always had the basic necessities even if it meant my father would have to go without. The cost of ministry was felt deeply by him and our family, but we knew that counting the cost was a part of the Christian journey. We may not have had the latest material goods, but we were a family rich in character and integrity—due largely to my father's example. I can remember him praying with me each night before I'd go to sleep. And every morning, I'd find him reading the Scriptures and praying before he'd start his day. Though the church didn't provide for his and Mom's retirement, Dad's wisdom and discipline found a way to put back a little each year to plan for their future. Because of my father's thoughtful, frugal lifestyle they will manage to live out their golden years with adequate provision.

As a family in these circumstances, we struggled to dare to dream, let alone to imagine our dreams could be realized. Together with my older and younger brothers, our collective aspirations as a family were to have enough money for food and clothes. It was a rare but delightful Friday night when we could afford carryout pizza—which I remember enjoying occasionally while watching *The Dukes of Hazzard* as a family. (As conservative as my family was, it's a bit surprising to me that we were allowed to watch that show considering Daisy's "immodest" short shorts. This and *Hee-Haw*'s farm beauties were shocking images of female beauty to behold in our family room.) My family had such meager economic means that we rarely ate meat unless my grandfather butchered a cow and could share some with us, or—my friends get grossed out when I tell them this—if we purchased the occasional can of Spam. I have only fond memories of Spam, though I have never bought it myself. My mom could make a mean fried Spam sandwich!

As a kid I longed for scrumptious food like carryout pizza, instead of make-it-yourself "Chef Boyardee" pizza from a grocery store box; and steak was a rarity that I thought was reserved for the rich. This childhood longing has been made sacred in more recent years. Rather than eating meat with every meal, today I gladly choose to go without it most of the time. Most of the commercial meat produced for consumption in the United States comes at the exploitative cost of the poor and the environment. And the treatment of animals in the meat and poultry industry is generally horrific. As I grow in contemplation, I find myself learning to revere all of creation; every bit of food I eat is a sacrificial offering. But my dietary commitment didn't have such lofty origins; the simplicity of my childhood created a longing that made way for a sacramental view of food that finds its origins in the Scriptures.

> But turn to the animals, and let them teach you; the birds of the air will tell you the truth. Listen to the plants of the earth, and learn from them; let the fish of the sea become your teachers. Who among all these does not know that the hand of YHWH has done this? In God's hand is the soul of every living thing; in God's hand is the breath of all humankind. (Job 12:7-10)

Physical longings are not so unlike spiritual ones. Longing is a necessary movement in the progression of the spiritual journey.

LONGINGS OF A YOUNG ADULT

Growing up under these conditions built character but made ambitious pursuits, like crosscultural mission, hard to realize. Most of the members of my parents' families didn't wander far from their birthplace. Life was simple and pragmatic—love God, love your neighbor and pay your taxes. The furthest I traveled while still living at home was to Florida for a family vacation to Disney World and the beach when I was in eighth grade. This was the beginning of my love for the seaside. My father scrupulously saved pennies for years to give this gift to his children. (Thanks so much, Dad!) Unlike many of my peers, I didn't have a college fund and therefore doubted I'd be able to go to college. When I was accepted to Purdue University I didn't know what to do. I was anxious about how we would pay for it. At that point I had decided to pursue a degree in education. I figured if I ever realized the dream of crosscultural mission, a teacher's training would be practical. But then I felt a call to a different university that would require even more faith: Asbury College, which cost almost double the expense of a state university. Named for the founder of American Methodism, Bishop Francis Asbury, Asbury College is a private Christian liberal arts school located in the Mayberry-like town of Wilmore, Kentucky.[2] The institution was established in 1890 by a Methodist evangelist, the Reverend John Wesley Hughes.

From the moment my mother and I stepped foot on campus we had a strong sense that this would be a good place for me. We left incredibly inspired for me to attend college there. A longing grew within me to arrive as a student in autumn, but we knew it would take a miracle to convince my father, who had doctrinal views strongly opposing Asbury's Methodist roots. My father grew up in a small country Bible church. His faith tradition supports its own colleges from which it recruits its congregational preachers. My mother, father and older brother all attended the same Bible college based in Cincinnati, Ohio. The thought of sending me to a historically Methodist college was, at the least, a stretch and, at the most, out of the question. But to my surprise, Dad was persuaded without even visiting the campus. I am forever grateful for the countless personal sacrifices he and my mother made to help me pay for my college education. And as if that wasn't miracle enough, amazingly, upon graduation I received the one and only E. Stanley Jones Scholarship, which paid almost all of my school debt, because I was committed to giving my life in service among the world's poor. The scholarship, combined with a few generous gifts from friends, enabled me to be debt free once I joined Word Made Flesh—a rare miracle.

At Asbury, I grew in faith and discovered new and wonderful aspects of God's character. It was at Asbury that I experienced a profound encounter with the grace of God's acceptance and received further direction for my initial call to mission.

DISCERNING A CALL

In college, I remember longing to know what my life would look like post graduation. I eagerly sought God's heart for decisions concerning Christian service and seriously contemplated the possibility that fulfilling a call to mission could mean accepting a call to celibacy. I counted the cost of what it would mean to create geographical distance between my family and me. I sorted through my desires to be married and determined to give up everything and everyone to follow Christ. A mentor at the time encouraged me with Jesus' promise in Mark 10:29-30: "Jesus answered, 'The truth is, there is no one who has left home, sisters or brothers, mother or father, children or fields for me and for the sake of the gospel who won't receive a hundred times as much in this present age.'"

Little did I know then how that promise would be fulfilled.

As time went on, I sought out various mission opportunities until one day I met Chris Heuertz and the call was clarified. Chris was the first person to introduce me to God's heart for the poor, and something in his experiences among the poor in the Middle East and South Asia resonated with my heart's longing—especially the stories of the people of India and his time with Mother Teresa. Mother quickly became for me the most compelling woman to emulate. It wasn't long before the call to mission was merging with a call to marriage—the first miracle of God's provision for family. The call in my heart to respond to a world of poverty weaved with the life of a young man who was also responding to the same call. Over time, it seemed evident that the sacrament of marriage with one another would help us fulfill our dream for a more just and compassionate world. God's provision for family has further expanded—I have countless mothers, fathers, sisters (an added bonus since I have no biological sisters), brothers and children all over the world, on nearly every continent (but only one husband!).[3]

My senior year of college, I prepared to leave the nation of my birth for the first time and visit India. I read everything I could get my hands on about this intriguing and mysterious nation that I felt like I had waited my whole life to find. Amy Carmichael's *A Chance to Die* spoke deeply to me, as did Dominique Lapierre's *City of Joy*. Mother Teresa's *Total Surrender* challenged me to the core. As I read, prayed and prepared, the yearning to be in India grew stronger.

Chris and I spent most of our two years of courtship apart—he in India and I in Wilmore finishing my education. This was before e-mail was widely accessible and international telephone rates were very expensive. So we depended on good ol' fashioned snail mail and would occasionally shell out the expense for a fax. I can clearly remember going to Kinko's and asking the staff to dial a twelve digit phone number which would often be answered by a South Indian with an accent rarely heard in Kentucky or Indiana. Our friend's voice would echo throughout the entire store, and we would have to shout through the speaker, "Faxing! Faxing!" in the hopes that they would hang up before the bill ran too high and we could resend. And boy, was postal mail slow! We'd have to wait between ten days and three weeks to get a letter from one another, and sometimes mail would turn up months after the postage date. Today those letters fill five two-inch deep three-ring binders that my Mammaw (maternal grandmother) and I carefully assembled. The notebook paper, aerograms and postcards intermingled with one another bears witness to the longing within us to be together.

HIRAETH: MORE THAN LONGING

Christopher Webb, an Anglican priest, explains longing with the help of the Welsh word *hiraeth* (pronounced "hear-ithe").[4] One of the places the word *hiraeth* is found in the Welsh-translated Scriptures is Psalm 63:1: "YHWH, my God, you are the One I seek. My soul thirsts for you, my body longs *(hiraeth)* for you."

The word *hiraeth* is not easily translatable into English. It means more than longing. It indicates an all-consuming homesickness. It cuts to the bones, soul and DNA of our being. It indicates a longing for where one belongs.

In John 14:3 we read that Jesus will take us to where he is now. This promise was not spoken to the dead but to the living. And John 1:18 tells us where Jesus is. Jesus is close to God's heart. Jesus lived and suffered his passion so that we might be where he is—close to the heart of Abba God. We don't need to physically die to be there, but we do need to long for this destination. Through longing, thin spaces that separate us from God are penetrated; we are broken and our desire for God grows. The movement of longing makes us vulnerable to and penetrable by the action of God.

What consumes you? What have you longed for with the intensity of homesickness? Longing signifies a desire for more. It stands in stark contrast to the complacent life. Complacency is a stalemate to the journey. Longing propels us forward. It's difficult to sit in the ache of longing, so sometimes we avoid it. But when we embrace that gut-level discontent, we are moving and growing. Because the ache of longing can be so agonizing, it is a consolation to be accompanied by others in the journey.

PILGRIM MIRACLES: GOD'S PROVIDENCE

Discerning one's vocation or purpose in life is not an easy undertaking. In my case, in college, discerning the path for my life coalesced between my faith, my compassion for suffering humanity, my desire to serve in the Majority World and my love for Chris. But these kinds of human desires don't always come together. Often, one has to choose—getting something usually means giving something up. In my case, I chose to give up a traditional life with family. The direction my life was headed meant a certain kind of separation from my parents and brothers. It meant not living in the same town with them and seeing them only once or twice a year. It has been a painful loss that we all grieve, but we do the best we can to support one another in our diverging journeys.

The beautiful thing about being true to the inner Voice directing our path is the provision miraculously given along the way. When we set out to live our life with purpose, the journey can get lonely and difficult. We often face hardships and doubts that threaten to take us off course. It is only the veracity of the inner

Voice and God's provision along the way that sustain us in the midst of the harshest trials.

On the Camino, during trials and obstacles that threatened our journey, Chris and I were blessed to experience God's providence through what are known in Spain as "pilgrim miracles." We had heard about such mysteries through various literature we'd read about the Camino, and we came to know personally their reality.

On a day when I wondered if my knees would finally give out, I was desperate for a walking stick. Other pilgrims had told us that walking sticks absorb more than thirty percent of the shock that the knees naturally take in. There was no question from the pain I was experiencing that my knees, as well as my hips and ankles, had been terribly overused.

On this particular day we remembered hearing about an old Spanish man who was known for crafting walking sticks for pilgrims out of hazel wood—the traditional pilgrim staff.[5] Señor Pablito's home happened to be on our route that day. As we ventured into the tiny, quaint village of Azqueta we took a short detour and found two staffs waiting for us outside the elderly farmer's cottage. We couldn't find Señor Pablito, but there were exactly two staffs waiting for us—and just our size![6] It was like he knew we were coming and made provision for us before we could even ask.

Other pilgrim miracles marked our days. One of our friends prayed before we left the States that we would have a bed every day, and even in the most crowded villages we did indeed have a bed each night. This is no understated miracle. In 2003 more than 65,000 people made pilgrimage to Santiago, and accommodations are in short supply during the busy season. Convents, monasteries, guest houses and hotels provide what is available, but some villages are quite small with few beds to offer. It's not uncommon for weary pilgrims to show up in a town after walking twelve to twenty-five miles to discover that all the beds have been taken. The pilgrim is then left to either walk another ten to fifteen miles to the next village or stay in the open air. At one point, after a twenty-four-mile walk to Santo Domingo, we were tempted to panic because all of the pilgrim houses and hotels were full. But the town took pity on all of the exhausted pilgrims and decided to open up the public gymnasium. We slept comfortably that night on old gymnastics mats.

Further miracles occurred through the lives of fellow pilgrims. In the middle of our journey, when we were feeling lonely for companions, three angels found their way into our lives and hearts: Simone, an Italian nuclear physicist from Paris; Miriam, an Italian pharmacist; and Markus, an East German cardiologist. Their joy, enthusiasm and aid in a number of ways lightened our load and encouraged our spirits. We journeyed together—Simone carried some of the contents of my pack; Markus nursed all of our blisters, even performing very minor surgery in some cases; and Miriam comforted us with her warm embrace and joyful demeanor. Though these miracles supported us in the journey, they couldn't dismiss the longing to reach Santiago that etched deeper into my heart, soul and weary body with each pain-filled step.

During seasons of longing, sometimes miracles occur—walking sticks are found, beds are provided, new friends are made, college education is supplied, the call is clarified, a spouse is met and family is multiplied in unusual ways. Following our dreams is not easy. The longing intensifies the longer we persevere in the journey, and all kinds of obstacles threaten to deviate us off course. God's provision along the way reassures us that we're on the right path and encourages us to keep going.

People like Mahatma Gandhi, Oscar Romero, Martin Luther King Jr. and Dorothy Day bore witness to longing. With their entire being they yearned for that which was yet to be realized. By faith they endured and hoped for the promises of a world that reflects the reign of Christ—peace, justice, equality. By their longing they experienced brokenness—they faced head-on some of the most humbling aspects of their human condition, and they were confronted with their limitations as well as their power. Gandhi, Romero and King were even martyred for daring to yearn for something more.

My community emulates this longing. Together we yearn with our lives for a better world, a world where diversity is celebrated and equality realized—male and female, black and white, rich and poor coming together in a full expression of the God who created us. We long for both the victim and the oppressor to be set free. My friend Taylor, a member of the Omaha nation, echoes this perspective. His grandmother would tell him, "We try to extend our hand to our enemy and the enemy of our most vulnerable friends and remind them that they and we are human—we both have a mother and a father and we belong to one another whether we like it or not."

The international offices for Word Made Flesh are based in Omaha, Nebraska. The name *Omaha* comes from the Native American tribe of the same name and translates as "going against the current." I can't think of a better location for Word Made Flesh to call home. The Omaha tribe is known for its countercultural perspective on tribalism: the Omaha people emphasize common humanity, seeing their enemies and the enemies of the vulnerable in their midst as belonging to one another as members of a common family.

The Word Made Flesh community demonstrates our collective longing for the global family through activism expressed in building communities of justice and compassion. Like pilgrimage, there are times when we feel we can't go on. We grow weary, we are injured along the way, our hope wavers. At times we are desperate for miracles of providence to keep us going. We long for *compañeros*[7] to join us—they are essential in the journey of creating a just world. In, with and through community the dream for a better world is realized.

But the dream takes time. All at once we *long for* and *move toward* the realization of our dreams. At times, it may feel like we're getting nowhere, but the longing is moving us. In this way, we participate in a sacramental lingering or vigil.

Seasons of longing in my life have been some of the most intense experiences. In the yearning, space is made in me for the work of God. I am forced to wait and surrender. And there's a sense of restlessness that foreshadows the rest that is coming. When God is doing a new thing, the restlessness stirs up out of an ache for change, birth and new life. Rest comes when what is longed for is realized.

KEEPING VIGIL

Longing. Waiting. This is a movement of the soul in which one can do nothing but linger.

Do you ever waken in the middle of the night unable to go back to sleep? Do you toss and turn and fight with all your might to will yourself to sleep, to no avail? These nighttime disturbances can be an invitation to vigil. Cistercian monks like the ones at the St. Benedict's Monastery in Snowmass, Colorado, rise purposefully in the middle of the night for vigils. During the deep silence of the moments between midnight and dawn, prayer is an act of keeping vigil, waiting before the Lord. Waiting in this manner bids listening.

Longing is about waiting. Longing *is* waiting. Any mother who has labored and delivered a baby knows what I'm talking about. I don't have children of my own, but on January 2, 2009, I had the privilege of waiting through the night while my sister-in-law labored with her second daughter. We got the call around midnight. Chris's brother Adam and his wife, Winter, were headed to the hospital. Winter's labor had begun, resonating profoundly with the winter of my soul and my own longing to bring forth new life. Chris and I were so excited for them we couldn't sleep. So Chris called Adam to check on them after they were settled and they invited us to come over.

It was the middle of the night, so the maternity ward was pretty quiet save a few crying newborns. At first, Winter was fairly comfortable—tired but comfortable. We talked and walked together periodically. As time went on, the contractions got closer and more intense. As Chris and I struggled to stay awake, Winter moaned and groaned in between restless slumber, reminding me of my own struggle to stay alert to the painful reality I had awakened to in my soul. We waited . . . and waited . . . and waited. In the dark labor and delivery room there was very little we could do. We just entered into moments of waiting for the birth of Claire Jula. The hours stretched into the early morning. Labor progressed and before I knew it, the doctor was coming in to deliver the baby. All the months of preparing for this little one, all the sacrifice that Winter made with her body to develop another, all the long hours of labor were finally bringing forth new life. Winter's birth canal was widening and untold miracles were taking place in her body to prepare the way for the baby.

The season of longing in our lives is a crucial time for listening. We listen to the desires within us and to the voice of God in those desires. We wait and listen and learn the will of God. As we wait, we become more acquainted with the presence of God. As we wait, we submit ourselves to the action of God and thus bring forth new life.

Macrina Wiederkehr, in her book *Seven Sacred Pauses: Living Mindfully Through the Hours of the Day,* reminds us that the quality of our waiting can vary. She writes, "There is a difference between waiting and keeping vigil. Anxious, fretful, impatient waiting is nothing more than waiting. Waiting with purpose, patience, hope and love is *vigilant* waiting."[8]

One of the most common images of vigilant waiting is the caterpillar in her cocoon. Butterflies are celebrated as something fascinating and beautiful, but the process of becoming a butterfly doesn't happen overnight. No matter how much the caterpillar yearns to become a butterfly, she must wait. And the process of metamorphosis is anything but gentle. Rid your mind of light and airy, carefree "Flight of the Bumblebee" thoughts.[9] Vigilant waiting can be one of the most distressing experiences in our soul's journey. Change is agonizing. Waiting can be turmoil.

Thanks to nanoscience we know a bit more about what the caterpillar goes through during the long waiting of metamorphosis. In a lab at UCLA, scientists use high-tech tactile microscopes to read the vibrations inside the chrysalis. Those vibrations are then transformed to audio. At the suggestion of my friend, I listened to those sound waves through a report on *Studio 360*.[10] The sounds are like that of an agonizing cry.

Long waiting is not sheer passivity. The English words "passive" and "passion" are both derived from the Latin word *pati*, which means "to endure." Waiting evokes both passivity and passion. Sue Monk Kidd, in her book *When the Heart Waits: Spiritual Direction for Life's Sacred Questions,* writes,

> [Waiting is] a vibrant, contemplative work. It means descending into self, into God, into the deeper labyrinths of prayer. It involves listening to disinherited voices within, facing the wounded holes in the soul, the denied and undiscovered, the places one lives falsely. It means struggling with the vision of who we really are in God and molding the courage to live that vision.[11]

Longing is essential to brokenness. Brokenness is the realization that our false self is dominating, which causes us to be alienated and isolated from God and one another. Through brokenness we recognize our wounded condition and admit that we cannot heal ourselves. Transformation is possible when we accept our brokenness and long for that which only God can do for us. A circular and interdependent relationship develops between longing and brokenness.

THE LONGING CONTINUES

One night during this intense season of longing for changes in me to be realized—for my true self to be freer to emerge—Chris and I had a spirited exchange. The old Phileena was happy to hide in the background, gladly pushing her husband forward and denying herself at every turn like a good, "submissive" woman. Though Chris completely supported and in a lot of ways called forth the more assertive Phileena, we struggled to know how to make appropriate room for two equal but different self-assertive individuals sharing one marriage. The changes in me toward female self-assertion were bumping up against both of us in new ways. We were colliding with one another. Old patterns for how we related to one another were being challenged and the new creation of our transforming marriage wanted to overthrow the old rule. Chris and I couldn't help but to have been shaped by the patriarchal society and religious culture in which we grew up.

Ancient paradigms rooted in male superiority still pervade the minds and teachings of people today. Throughout history, societies have propagated the notion that people could be owned, including wives. In fact, women have been seen as similar to animals—which is even noted in the Hebrew Scriptures. Frequently, women were listed alongside livestock and servants (Exodus 20:17; cf. Deuteronomy 5:21; Judges 5:30). It's interesting that in a lot of cases animals are treated better than some women—dogs affectionately get the favored title of "man's best friend," while women have often been referred to as the "ball and chain" or demeaned by associations such as "You run like a girl"—enforcing the view that women are untrustworthy and the inferior and weaker sex.

These disempowering notions are steeped into cultures the world over. Particularly, these attitudes permeated ancient Mediterranean cultures, religions and philosophies that have had such pervasive influence on present-day Western culture—most notably

Christianity. Some of the more prominent Christian Fathers demonstrate the influence of patriarchy in their teaching. The faith tradition we call "Christianity" has never existed apart from these influences. These teachings have dominated religion and culture for so many hundreds of years that it can be difficult to determine where the gospel of Christ ends and misogyny begins.

Augustine, a father of Christendom, is highly debated by theologians as one who perpetuated patriarchy. But his writings also illustrate his countercultural perspective. The truth is that early Christians were unable to completely escape the dominant conscience of the time that viewed women as inferior and subordinate to men. Even though Augustine affirmed the ontological equality of women, it can be argued that he perpetuated some tenets of sexism that we are still trying to identify, confess and repent of today. Though a devout follower of Christ, even Augustine was influenced by the patriarchal mindset of his day.[12]

And so the ideology of female inferiority still infects many aspects of religion, culture and society. Though we've come a long way in redeeming the oppressive perspective of women, the prejudices run deep. Women and men both are guilty of adhering to and perpetuating a demeaning view of women. And Chris and I had to come to terms with the ways in which we had both been influenced by this repressive ideology.

In contrast to power paradigms that repress women and rob men of their holy potential, liberation is central to the message of Christ. It seems that personal and systemic liberation is the common, prominent cry of humanity. Whether it is longing to be free to live into our true self or yearning to be freed from systematic oppression like inequality or slavery, the gospel of Christ is about freedom. But for some reason freedom frightens us, and so two thousand years later we are still subjugating ourselves or expecting others to submit to a posture or system of captivity rather than liberation.

In order for our marriage to endure, the changes occurring in me required changes in Chris. Submission as mutuality would require us to learn a new dance, with its own music and rhythm. We needed to learn new ways of receiving from one another. The two of us were being transformed by awakening. Each of us, and our marriage, was experiencing a metamorphosis. In our longing to be free, we cried out at one another in agony. We desperately tried to communicate our different experiences and perspective. We were in turmoil, much like the caterpillar in its cocoon. But we didn't need a high-tech microphone to hear our distress and anguish—the torment was obvious. We wanted to break free from our suffocating cocoons. We longed for the metamorphosis to be over.

The only sure thing we knew was what and who we were before. We didn't know what lay ahead. It seemed easier to me to submit to a traditional patriarchal paradigm of marriage that was ground into me from an early age and reinforced in so many spheres of my life. If I would just accept my "repressive place" as a woman, Chris and I wouldn't fight with one another and we would experience the feeling of closeness—even if it was an illusion. Marriage marked by male-dominant superiority and female-subordinate inferiority has a long cultural and religious history. It is presumed right and fail-safe. But what if our constructs of safety keep us asleep to God's desires?

PERSEVERING IN THE JOURNEY

The temptation at this stage is to abandon the spiritual journey and opt for what is safe and secure and previously known. We are faced with a choice: push through the pain or give up. The story of the Hebrew people illustrates this human tendency. Even though they yearned for the land God promised, they were tempted to go back to Egypt where they originated—the land of their bondage.

During their exodus from Egypt, the Hebrews demonstrated longing. When God rescued them from their slavery, God brought them into a journey to the Promised Land—a long journey lasting forty years. We know from the Hebrew Scriptures that Moses, the leader of this forty-year wilderness-wandering people, most certainly longed for the land God had promised them. The Hebrews ultimately longed not for where they came from but for where they were heading. They ached for something different and better. But during the long wait, there were periods of time in which some of the people actually wanted to go back to Egypt. The journey was long, the way unknown and difficult. And they had no guarantee that they would end up in a better place. All they had was their faith and the trust that God would indeed meet their heart's longing for the Promised Land.

In the spiritual journey we also face moments of temptation to return to the land of our slavery. It's safe, secure and known. Where God is taking us is risky and unknown and requires deeper trust, courage and greater maturity. No matter the nature of our awakening—feminine or masculine—each of us faces aspects of our human condition from which we long to be free. Perhaps the bondage is an addiction or a self-perception, an attitude or a posture. Whatever the shade of our personal slavery, longing forces us to actively wait, thereby keeping us anchored in the journey toward freedom. We long for what we hope for and are certain of what we do not see.[13] This kind of longing keeps us submitted to the transformational work of God in us.

Chris and I continued trying to find our footing together. Longing for transformation in one another and in our marriage anchored us in the journey. In his exhausted anguish that one heated night, Chris said that all of this was new for us, that we didn't know our way, but that we would find our way together. The morning brought renewed promise of transformation as we held one another and tried to not laugh at the absurdity of our behavior the night before.

The invitation in the season of longing is the prayer of faith. The prayer of faith is different from praying *with* faith. In the first, faith is the mode of prayer. In the latter, faith is the object of prayer. The prayer of faith necessitates an experiential relationship with God in which I let go of control and let God be God. I let God introduce God's self to me in an existential way. I come to God in prayer based on pure faith in God's existence within me and beyond me. Preconceived notions of who I think God is are abandoned for the purer, truer Reality that *is* God, revealed by God in God's essence. Prayer of faith is based in relationship with God rather than in what other people say about God. In this posture we believe that God can do for us what we cannot do for ourselves. For months, this in fact was the only prayer I could pray: "God, please do for me what I cannot do for myself." And then all I could do was wait; and the longing within me carved deeper and deeper into my soul, making space for the work of God.

I longed for greater freedom, for new life, and I waited. Like a grain of wheat, death would be inevitable to bearing fruit. Darkness was slowly creeping in.

QUESTIONS FOR REFLECTION

1. Longing has been likened to homesickness—that bone ache for home. What have you longed for with that kind of intensity? A lover? A pregnancy? Perhaps an accomplished academic degree? Describe the experience.

2. Longing propels us toward God. The bone ache or heart ache for something more opens us to the new thing God desires to do in and through us. What is an experience you've had when longing served to open you up to new growth and awareness about God, yourself or others?

3. Consider the state of your family, community, society or the world. Certainly there are some situations that are not as we would like them to be. Describe a situation that you long to be different.

How does longing for things to be different affect you?

In what ways does longing open you up?

In what ways does longing cause you to close up?

Describe what you notice about how God is at work in your longing.

4. Seasons of longing can be frustrating because it seems there's so little we can do to alleviate the ache. We are at the mercy of the unknown, imminent future. Longing is essentially a time of waiting with purpose. And waiting or keeping vigil is a time of listening. What have you heard or what are you hearing during experiences of longing?

5. Consider the imagery of a caterpillar in her cocoon. Like the caterpillar waiting to be the butterfly, we too are invited to yield to God's work of transforming us. But this waiting can be agonizing; the process of change, excruciating. In what ways do you relate to the process of waiting in a cocoon during metamorphosis?

PRACTICE

The temptation at this stage is to abandon the spiritual journey. Longing and waiting are just too difficult. We want a quick fix. However, if we persevere and endure this stage, the hidden work of inner transformation can take place.

This season requires the prayer of faith (p. 75)—prayer that helps us to let go of control. Take time to pray a prayer of faith. Perhaps this one resonates with you: "God, please do for me what I cannot do for myself."

Otherwise, take a moment to craft your own prayer of faith. It may not be with words. It may be with a daily gesture such as lighting a candle or incense as sign of your purposeful waiting, the vigil you're keeping. Take time to listen for what kind of prayer of faith would be most helpful to you at this time—a prayer that anchors you in longing and symbolizes your desire to be open to the mysterious work God is doing in and through you. And then dare to let go and wait.

3

Darkness

A woman's body, like the earth, has seasons
When the mountain stream flows, when the holy thaws

When I am most fragile and in need,
It was then, it seems God came closest. . . .

And God is always there, if you feel wounded.
[God] kneels over this earth like a divine medic,
And [God's] love thaws the holy in us.

TERESA OF ÁVILA, "WHEN THE HOLY THAWS"

OUR FIRST DAY ON THE CAMINO involved hiking the verdant and breathtakingly beautiful Pyrenees. Having never really even day-hiked before (unless you count hoofing it all day through the streets of some of the poorest urban centers in the world), Chris and I had no idea what we were getting into. Our mountain-loving friends Andy and Andrea tried to prepare us, but we ignorantly overlooked some of their recommendations. We were far from what we would later understand as "conditioned." Many people train months in advance, breaking in their boots and bodies by taking long hikes with heavy packs on their backs. Chris and I, however, hadn't trained at all.

In the early morning we rose before daybreak, laced our boots and slung our packs on our backs with eager anticipation. It wasn't long before we found ourselves climbing and descending the lush mountains. We walked through various terrain and even more varied weather—blazing sun followed by dropping temperatures that fluctuated fifty degrees. Our bodies moved us up rocky pathways as we ascended above the tree line and down precipitous descents. Upon reaching the summit, after about five hours of this excruciating physical feat, we found ourselves in hypothermic conditions and ended up in a hailstorm.[1]

During the storm on the peak, when the temperature drastically dropped, I hit my first "wall"— the physical, mental and emotional limit that climbers and athletes describe. Remarkably, the human spirit can break through these walls time and time again. This was my first real mountain-hike experience; my pack was much too heavy and my body was out of shape. Enduring the change in temperature from damp cold to a burning warm sun before the weather plummeted to subzero temperatures was a lot for my body to handle all in one day; I was overextended. My neck, shoulders, back, hips, legs, feet and muscles I didn't know I had ached in a way I'd never known before. Mentally and physically I didn't know how I could continue. I had never hit this big of a wall before.

My body, mind and emotions all reached their limit at virtually the same time. Every muscle, bone, joint and tendon seemed to be shouting for me to stop. To make matters worse, my internal feminine cycle would *not* be stopped. Though much of my body wanted to lock up, yes, on the summit of the Pyrenees—day one of our pilgrimage—my body cried out "woman" in crimson red! My abdomen started cramping and my mind felt foggy. Fatigue was setting in throughout my entire body. The ushering forth of womanly lifeblood caused a drain on my physical stamina. How I wanted to curl up in a fetal position and rest! Though it was counterintuitive to impede our journey, in order to take care of feminine necessities, I momentarily had to.

As soon as Chris and I stopped, we realized how much the temperature had plummeted. Our extremities began to tingle from the cold and our sweaty backs suffered a sharp chill. A Buddhist who had stopped with us anxiously pulled out his gloves and wool cap (we, of course, didn't think to pack those!) and warned us of the dangers of frostbite. He told us to not stop for more than a few minutes. The danger in these conditions was worsened by the fact that our bodies were so warm and sweaty from the ascent; we might not know the effects of the cold before it was too late.

Frantically, I found as private a place as I could behind some rocks and brush and dug through my pack for the Tylenol and other provisions. In the process of attending to the womanly essentials, my bare backside got a stark freeze that alerted me pretty quickly to the dangerously icy temperature.

Once my emergency was hurriedly brought under control, it was time to continue. It felt near to impossible to sling that heavy pack back on my back. Everything in me wanted to find a warm place to rest, but there was no shelter from the elements. We had to keep moving. I couldn't stay there. I had run into a wall and didn't know how I would climb over it or get through it. I felt depleted and defeated, and I'd just begun. But like endurance athletes know, amazingly I was able to keep going. Somehow I managed to put one foot in front of the other and carry on. I overcame the first wall.

As time went on and we had still not reached our destination, emotional breakdown number two hit—another wall. I had already extended and overcome my physical limits once, and my body wanted to rest. The hailstorm had intensified its rage with rain and snow, and the temperature continued to fall. I cried a soft cry of agony and told Chris that I didn't know how I could continue, but there was nowhere to stop and rest and take shelter from the elements. Chris encouraged me and helped me recover perspective, and remarkably I made it through the second wall. If I had stopped we would have surely died of hypothermia.

After this grueling experience of extending my limits for the second time, we finally began to descend. The end was in sight—at least mentally if not physically. The rain and snow continued to fall but the temperature started to rise a bit. Unbeknownst to me at the time, we had gotten off the trail. Chris was carefully navigating our way, but in the storm we missed an important marker and took a wrong turn. We were descending, but off the beaten path. Our destination was still not in sight; we had to keep moving.

The rain began falling harder and harder as we wound our way through trees, brush and muddy earth, lost in a lush forest. Despair started setting in because, after all these agonizing hours, we had no idea how far we were from the end. With one more weary, heavy-laden step I slipped in a mudslide and landed flat on my back. That was it! Emotional breakdown number three with a vengeance! The third wall I hit was even bigger and more intimidating than the other two. Sitting in a stream of muddy rainwater pouring down the mountainside, I was beyond depletion and defeat. My tears mixed with rain and mud, and I knew I couldn't go on. We had descended, so the threat of hypothermia had lifted, and everything in me wanted to stay flat in the mud and pray for another day. Chris turned around to find me in my muddy mess and compassionately said, "Honey, we can't stop here. You can do it. It won't be long." Again somehow I got to my feet. We walked about two hundred yards more and, through the trees, spotted the monastery that would provide shelter, food and a bed for the night.

Eight hours after setting out, following three emotional breakdowns and thinking each time I'd reached my limit and could go no further, we arrived at the ancient monastery of Roncesvalles on the eastern border of Spain. An old, gothic stone hall that held one hundred pilgrims would be our shelter for the night. We marveled at the feat we endured and what we had accomplished together.

Attempting to shower and find dinner with the few hours of daylight we had left, we realized we could barely walk and wondered how in the world we would rise the next morning and set out again. We ached from head to toe and everywhere in between. Sleep never felt so good—even with the cacophony of snorers from around the world sharing our medieval shelter.

In the early morning of the next day, waking to the sound of Gregorian chant, we discovered how remarkable the body is: as we slept, our bones, muscles and joints rejuvenated themselves enough that we could walk again. During the darkness of night, there was a restorative work taking place in the dark and hidden places of the body—a sign of the genius of God's creation. Like a woman's menstrual cycle, I was experiencing the benefits of the hidden and darker elements of life. In the cyclical fashion of menstruation, the body was remaking itself. My soul was experiencing a similar effect from the darkness it was experiencing. The secret work of God was transforming me.

We could indeed walk again—though not without significant pain, a natural consequence of being out of shape and carrying a much-too-heavy pack. The pain of that first morning would become my companion every day on the Camino. What inspired us as a perceived romantic stroll through Spain quickly became a rude awakening to the ancient act of pilgrimage for purification. Chris and I decided to lighten our packs of everything but the most essential items for the journey—a process we took part in several times along the way. It's embarrassing to list the things I packed that I clearly could have done without: a travel-size hairbrush, retractable clothesline, travel umbrella, fleece, fourth pair of socks, and books. As I simplified, I abandoned myself to my limitations and the rules of the road. Pilgrimage would have to be made with simplicity and a desire to be free.

Each morning we set out, we prayed with all of our hearts that God would give us the grace to make it to Santiago. With each painful step, we found ourselves in the company of pilgrims from past centuries who bathed the way before us with their prayers and tears, injuries and sicknesses, pain and joy. In the company of these *compañeros,* we were indeed accompanied with grace. As E. Allison Peers says, "Grace, far from destroying nature, ennobles and dignifies it."[2]

As the days progressed, the Spanish countryside rolled out before us as a grand display—the greenest green and bluest blue were before us as far as the eye could see. The reddest poppies and whitest daisies sprung up to line our path and tickle our senses. When we entered La Rioja, the vineyards spoke to us of life and fecundity found in being connected to the vine. My thoughts returned often to the words of Jesus: "I am the vine; you are the branches. Those who live in me and I in them will bear abundant fruit, for apart from me you can do nothing" (John 15:5).

In a spirit of mutuality, there were days when I leaned on Chris and days when he leaned on me. One day we passed through what seemed like the Hobbits' quiet, rural village. There was a small forest of the most magnificently shaped trees I had ever seen. I really felt we had been transported to another world. As we passed through this magical countryside, Chris was really struggling. The pack on his back weighed down heavily and was causing him a lot of pain. The stamina and determination of earlier days failed him at this point in the journey. He was struggling to find any inspiration to keep going. It's amazing how when one is weak the other is strong. A depth of courage and determination rose within me and I encouraged him to keep going. Every time his eyes would drift down to his feet I would remind him to look to the horizon and to let it pull him forward. I would periodically call out to him, as he had to me, "We're doing this Bebe!"

We walked. Every day, we walked. We alternately supported one another when one was feeling disheartened. Finding the courage and the stamina to return to the Camino each day grew more and more difficult. Our necks and backs ached constantly. The joints in our hips, knees and ankles seemed to rub together and often there would be kinks in them—their overuse was apparent. The chronic pain was like nothing I'd ever known before. I clung to the hope that "though this physical self of ours may be falling into decay, the inner self is renewed day by day" (2 Corinthians 4:16).

DOUBT AND ABANDONMENT: THE BEGINNING OF DARKNESS

When I set out on the Camino, I hadn't fully realized what I was getting into. Darkness came in waves. I couldn't avoid or go around the dark physical and mental feats I faced. I had to pace myself with it and go through it. We can't skip over or outrun darkness; neither can we hide from it in the busyness of life or in a time of extended rest, such as my time at Duke.

After the Camino, as I transitioned from a very active life of service into a long, deep, contemplative rest in Durham, I experienced a necessary yet difficult detachment. Like the experience of the feminine cycle, I was transitioning from one phase and God's activity in it to another. Progressing from one stage to the next is not easy—it is filled with discomfort, pain and disorientation. But it is ultimately life-giving, actually essential to the creation of life.

I was quite familiar with the active, engaging, busy stage of life—the Phileena who jetted across the globe in partnership with her husband to build communities of justice. But I was not at all prepared to explore the deeper, more complex phase that was waiting for me.

On the Pyrenees, as I faced the unknown and experienced feats completely new to me, doubt crept in. *Am I really capable of climbing this mountain—let alone, walking all the way to Santiago?* Similar questions haunted me during the Duke portion of sabbatical as I detached from my life of activism—an experience completely new to me. *If I'm not actively supporting and serving the movement of Word Made Flesh, who am I?* I questioned my identity, abilities and gifts. I was making a gradual descent of the soul.

My experience at the peak of the Pyrenees is a powerful symbol of the spirituality of descent. It's only when we can experience and embrace our deepest pain and suffering that we can emerge transformed. Richard Rohr, a Franciscan friar and founder of The Center for Action and Contemplation located in Albuquerque, New Mexico, wisely highlights the inherent rites of passage unique to the woman. Within her very biology she is given the symbol of blood and the experience of vulnerability from which to draw true courage. At menstruation, childbirth and menopause, the woman is initiated into a passage—from old to new, death to life, weakness to strength. Blood for her is a sign of life. In contrast, a man's blood often triggers for him feelings of death. Perhaps because of the void of this inherent biology, traditionally and historically men have instituted rites of initiation; the symbol of blood and embrace of one's weakness is typically a universal common denominator in these rites. In our modern society, perhaps the lack of such intentional formation creates new challenges for male spirituality.[3]

As the weeks of rest unfolded at Duke, I succumbed to a spiritual descent. I felt like I was in a dark tunnel. I was struggling to find my way. Everything grew dim—my sense of self and my understanding of God. I knew the God who was actively engaged in a world of poverty. I had encountered Christ in the dying, naked man at Howrah Train Station in Kolkata;[4] the child soldier in Sierra Leone; the young mother on the streets of Lima. But who is this God who allows me to rest from a world in need and to engage the beauties of Spain? These questions gave rise to doubt. *Do I really know God at all?*—this God who seems to be suggesting through sabbatical rest that God is interested in me as well as in those I serve. I began to question my identity and what I knew of God.

And doubt gave rise to internal pain that I was not aware of before. I felt like I was in a stone mortar being ground by a pestle. Like the physical pain on the Camino, emotional pain became a constant torturous companion. And because of its presence, I felt abandoned by God. I was left with more questions and seemingly no answers. Anything I had found false security in (the "known")—like my identity in relationship to people and my acts of service—was being challenged and I knew not what the other options would be (the "unknown"). *If I am not what I do, not defined by my relationships with others, who would I be if or when I emerged from this grinding? Would I be anything more than dust?*

For months prior to this dark night experience I prayed daily the prayer of St. Ignatius:

Take O Lord and receive
All my liberty, my memory,
My understanding and my entire will
All that I have and possess
You have given all to me
To you O Lord I return it
All is yours
Dispose of it all according to your will
Give me your love and grace
For this is sufficient for me.

St. Ignatius of Loyola (1491-1556) was the founder and first superior general of the Society of Jesus, also known as the Jesuits. He is marked as one who gave everything to Jesus and who lived a devoted life of prayer and activism. He influenced the movement that became known as the Catholic Reformation[5] and remains an example for how to integrate the contemplative and active dimensions of the gospel.

When we earnestly pray the prayers of saints, I believe we are invited into a treasured storehouse. Praying the prayers of those whose lives are explicitly marked with the life of Christ has transformational power. The saints lived the prayers they prayed. Their prayers made way for a deep inner work of Christ in their lives. When we pray in a posture and attitude related to that of the saint who wrote the prayer, a similar transformation is made possible for us.

Rather than *me praying*, after some time it seemed as if the prayer of St. Ignatius was *being prayed* in me. I found myself asking, *Did I really pray for the "taking"?!* The "taking" was painful and frightening for I knew not what awaited me. Even if what was being taken was ultimately bad for me, it was all I'd ever known. It was familiar. It felt better than the nothingness with which I was seemingly left.

My prayer was being answered, but I couldn't have imagined the experience of how it would be answered. God was taking my liberty in the spirit of the prayer of Ignatius. Even my prayers were no longer my own. Everything was being taken from me at my bidding—my freedom, memory, understanding and entire motivation for life, relationships and service. I was abandoned to the cry of this prayer. And thus I began to be stripped of some of the false parts of myself that were expressed in false identities and false attachments, the parts of me that kept me from faith, hope, love and peace—in essence, from God. Trusting by faith that God truly knows what is best for me, I invited God to take everything from me that would inhibit my growing nearer to God—the destination of my soul. I was abandoning myself by faith to my Creator.

During the first portion of sabbatical, on the Camino, abandonment was doubt's *compañero*. The material abandonment that was required to make pilgrimage in Spain is not so different from what it takes to make spiritual pilgrimage. I had to leave behind everything but what I thought would be essential for the journey. And then even along the way I had to shed a number of items in my pack that were weighing me down and threatening to impede my journey and keep me from reaching Santiago. In the first few days of the Camino I unloaded my pack of what at one time seemed essential, but in reality was cumbersome and even damaging to my body because of the added weight. I was growing in clarity for what truly would be necessary for pilgrimage. Letting go of certain possessions opened me to greater freedom in the journey.

This sort of abandonment invites a kind of darkness. The comfort of my possessions on the Camino provided security for me, like light on a dark road. I had something for every need I could anticipate: books for boredom, a line to dry wet clothes and a hairbrush for vanity. With possessions in tow, my life was somewhat predictable and sure. Shedding some of those things invited a detachment and feeling of abandonment from what was sure and secure. Letting go of several possessions was an act of deeper faith that I would be sustained on the journey beyond what I could do or provide for myself. Being free of certain material attachments meant facing the darkness of the unknown.

During the Duke portion of sabbatical, I spent the first several weeks in deep reflection and prayerful meditation, aided by the therapeutic exercise of gardening. The Rose Cottage—our home away from home—was an answer to prayer and a gift of God. The front and back yards provided an entire landscape in which I could get my hands dirty and reconnect with the earth. As I weeded the overgrown yard, it was as if an internal uprooting was taking place in me.

For those first few weeks, I could hardly do anything other than gardening. One of the prevailing themes that emerged during that time was, "From dust you came and to dust you will return" (Genesis 3:19). If there was no promise of who I was or who I would become, if no promise of a secure self and a guaranteed personal contribution after sabbatical, knowing that I came from dust and would return to dust became surprisingly comforting.

The invitation of the prayer of St. Ignatius is all about abandonment. Willingly, if not fearfully, we can choose to completely leave behind that which we have known and found security in—

everything that we have worked hard to attach to by way of creating our identity. "I know who I am and others know who I am based on what I do, what I like, who I'm friends with, what I read, what I have, how I relate to people, my intellectual musings, what others say about me, my kind gestures." Depending on our experience, upbringing and temperament, the attachments will be different.

As we let go of physical, mental and emotional attachments, we abandon ourselves to God and yield without restraint to God's love and grace—for this is sufficient for life's journey. Knowing and being known by God, relationship with God, is supreme—the source of our identity and purpose. Expressing our truest identity is possible when we are free of false attachments that try to make claim on who we are. These accessories can become quite burdensome and impede our pilgrimage. The spiritual journey has to be made with simplicity and a desire to be free.

In darkness, doubt gives rise to important questions. And abandonment allows us to be free from that which threatens to keep us in slumber. But if we've been asleep, we don't know what it will be like to be awake. All seems dark, unknown and somewhat fear-inducing. Fear is actually the most common response in the brain to the unknown. But studies show that when we face our fears and overcome them, our brain develops and grows; and not only our brain, but our body and spirit as well.

Lee Hoinacki in his book *El Camino: Walking to Santiago de Compostela* says,

> The camino is not a path leading to Santiago, but a way to reach Christ—if one can learn how to walk on it. . . . It is an initiatory exercise, teaching one some elementary truths about stripping oneself bare. The further one progresses in this way, the further one will walk into the mystery of faith, into nothingness, weakness, and darkness.[6]

On pilgrimage I suffered in ways I had never known before. From the first day's mountain climb, my body was ravaged with sore joints and muscles. But by pressing through, I endured a purifying pain in the journey. By overcoming physical, mental and emotional obstacles, I progressed in the journey and received grace upon grace. But the pain I encountered on the Camino was simply a foreshadowing of the inner agony waiting for me. The Camino was indeed an "initiatory exercise." It was preparing me for an inner pilgrimage that would be necessary for transformation. An inner stripping and abandonment was beckoning me.

Following pilgrimage in Spain, when Chris and I relocated to Durham for four months, I stumbled into darkness—a spiritual desolation. I had never felt more spiritually arid, empty and emotionally overwhelmed. I often felt like I was sitting in a muddy mess mingled with tears. I was taken to the depths of my being and identity, but like Chris said in the Pyrenees, Jesus was now saying, "You can't stay here."

IN PRAISE OF FECUNDITY

At the peak of my first mountain climb on pilgrimage—though my body, mind and emotions wanted to give out and give up—a feminine force within me stirred, marked by the onset of menstruation. The red blood symbolizing the capacity to bear fruit from the deepest part of me announced itself as a source of life and energy. The monthly blood flow I experienced at the summit was a symbol of feminine strength within me that longed to be born. This was a birth that required an incubation and gestation period. It would take time. And the delivery of this new life within me would not come without severe trial and anguish—much like a mother giving birth to her child. Darkness was essential for the development of this new life.

Kimberlee Conway Ireton gives some understanding to my experience:

In Western Christian culture, we tend to oppose light with darkness and assume that since light is good, darkness must be bad. But it is not, necessarily. The darkness of the womb and of the soil, for instance, are places of incubation, gestation and growth. Seasons of darkness in our lives are often good and necessary. . . .

Death is a mystery, veiled and dark. We are tempted to fear this darkness, to forget that the good shepherd is with us, guiding and comforting us. In our fear, we can become hasty, rushing blindly and desperately through the darkness in order to get to the light that must be on the other side. But this we must not do. We must remain in the darkness as long as it takes to learn in death's shadow the lessons we can only learn there. We must wait patiently in the darkness, trusting that God is with us and is growing new life in us. For, Jesus says, only if a grain of wheat falls into the earth and dies will it bear much fruit.[7]

Fecundity. I love this word because it means more than being fruitful. It means having the capacity to bear an abundance of fruit. We like the thought of being fruitful, but we rarely examine what it requires of us to be fruit bearing—discomfort, pain, trial, patience, darkness and labor.

Fecundity speaks to the capacity for fruitfulness. Jesus of course understood this concept and explained it perfectly in pointing his disciples to grapevines. Comparing the connection to the vine with a connection to himself, he revealed the secret to being fruitful. The capacity for fruitfulness is found in relationship to him. That connection provides the capacity to bear real and lasting fruit. And if you appreciate a good glass of wine, you know what it takes to produce such exquisite *vino.* The endurance of the grape is equal to the quality of the wine it can produce. Good wine, like good life, requires arid conditions paired with tender care.

The female womb also symbolizes the ability to bear fruit. Fruitfulness doesn't happen without the capacity for it to happen, and the monthly blood loss and pain presupposes a woman's ability to bear a child. The woman's body and feminine cycle is such important imagery for us and it's a shame that we tend to overlook it. Patriarchal systems that divorce us from the feminine rob us of wisdom and perspective that men and women both need. Male and female are both created in the image of God. When we don't allow ourselves to reflect on the feminine nature of God, our understanding of God is deficient. Similarly, our communities are deficient when they exclude women from central places of influence and authority.

In the Hebrew Scriptures God is referred to as "compassionate." The word for compassion is derived from *racham,* meaning "womb." God is "womblike." In Job God refers to God's self as the One who gave birth to the frost: "Whose womb gives life to ice or gives birth to skies filled with hoarfrost" (Job 38:29). Talk about fecundity! One doesn't have greater capacity to bear fruit than God! The whole created world reflects God's feminine facility for bearing fruit.[8]

Male and female created in the image of God have a certain capacity for fecundity which includes the ability, in most cases, to produce children. But a culture that limits fruitfulness to sexual reproduction misses out on the limitless nature of a God whose intelligent creativity and productivity have no bounds.

Having been created in the image of God, the feminine nature of God reproduced in me was stirring. What it means to be fully me, fully woman, wanted to be born and celebrated—making no apologies for my gender, but instead embracing my nature and offering it as a gift to my community and to the world. But this yearning of life was just a seed. It would require a gestation and incubation period. Darkness was necessary.

STUMBLING THROUGH DARKNESS

At the end of the Camino, I found myself in desolation. During this season of life, darkness encompassed me. Having abandoned along the road all I'd known before of myself and of God, I felt as if I had nothing to give the world and I doubted my faith as never before. In the months following I felt the presence of God rarely, if at all.

St. John of the Cross, a Carmelite reformer and doctor of the church from the sixteenth century, refers to seasons like this as "dark nights of the soul." In his profoundly mystical yet straightforward theological work, he illuminates for his disciples the necessary darkness each must endure to live into the light of their life and relationship with God. Both inviting and terrifying, John of the Cross describes in detail the agonizing yet liberating experience of divine grace in the journey toward divine union. The dark night of the soul is understood in stages, distinguishing between the night of sense and the night of spirit. The first is said to come to many, while the latter comes to few. The first is "bitter and terrible"; the second doesn't compare because it is "horrible and awful to the spirit."[9] St. John's *Dark Night of the Soul* explores in greatest detail the night of spirit because, at the time of his writing, there was little communicated about it, in contrast to the abundance of literature on the night of sense.[10]

Mother Teresa's night of the soul has been highly debated—hers being the longest recorded dark night, lasting most of her fifty years of service among the poorest of the poor. Following the release of her most personal letters and diaries in the book *Come Be My Light,* her intimate dark night experience was subjected to harsh analysis and criticism. Most observers, however, are left to marvel at what she endured. After the release of *Come Be My Light,* Chris and I were routinely asked about Mother Teresa's dark night, since we had the privilege to have met her. Friends wanted to know what we thought about her experience, which is explained in despairing detail in the book. Usually we reply that the time we or members of our community have spent in Kolkata has caused us all to despair and doubt.

Kolkata is one of the most densely populated cities in the world, filled with people suffering from extreme systemic poverty and injustice. Home to approximately sixteen million inhabitants, countless live on the streets or in slums. Spending much time at all among impoverished men, women and children in Kolkata necessitates a very honest questioning and wrestling with God and faith. I don't know of anyone who has matched Mother's downward mobility and incarnational ministry except Jesus. Mother had an exceptionally difficult calling to establish a global effort to honor the poor and disenfranchised, and in doing so she pointed millions to Christ. She forged a path, a movement, a presence in the world that can be compared to none. Her long dark night deserves our respect, not our criticism.

Mother's experience can be understood in spiritual as well as psychological terms. Her experience is complex and all-pervasive. And her experience is hers. Amazingly, through the physical, emotional and spiritual desolation, she kept her faith. The transformation and liberation she experienced because of the darkness we are not privy to. But her life and dark night bear witness to the struggle of the human spirit. Her fidelity to Christ serves as a beacon of light for the rest of us when we courageously face our own darkness.

St. John of the Cross offers this exhortation for those who experience the dark night:

> Realizing the weakness of the state wherein they are, they may take courage, and may desire that God will bring them into this night, wherein the soul is strengthened and confirmed in the virtues, and made ready for the inescapable delights of the love of God.[11]

According to John of the Cross and other saints who have gone before us, dark nights of the soul are a way by which the Spirit of

God can penetrate our being, purify us and lead us into deeper faith and more intimate relationship with God. In this way we attain union with the One we were separated from by sin—the disconnection expressly illuminated in the Garden story.

Several years prior to being enveloped by this darkness, I had asked to draw nearer to God. In my naiveté I had no idea that it would mean an internal descent into darkness. As the weeks unfolded into shadows of death, I realized that "emotional junk of a lifetime" (as Keating calls it) was situated between me and God. Intimacy is about honesty and trust. To grow in intimacy with God, I had to face hidden emotional wounds and subsequent "programs for happiness" and let go of them. As much as God may have wanted to embrace me, I was not free to be fully known by such an embrace. And I was not free to know God as God is. Intimacy is not only about knowing the other but being known as well. I was being invited to come out from hiding and into the agony of God's piercing light, to eventually emerge into the "inescapable delights of the love of God." That kind of love could only be experienced through open, honest intimacy. Darkness was an indispensable agony.

St. John of the Cross likens the darkness of the soul to a log of wood being burned with fire. In times of darkness, the Light is actually very near, but our human faculties cannot comprehend this light, so it seems we are in the dark. A friend of mine explains this experience in a different way: Like a sick child with a fever, the caregiver nurtures and tends to the little one all throughout the night, but in severe cases of illness the child is not aware of the caregiver's presence.

Expanding on the image of a burning log of wood, the fire burns in such a way as to cause us the *sense* of darkness. But in fact, this fire or light that causes us to feel darkness is really God's grace—a grace of purgation that heals and makes ready the soul for deeper union with God. John of the Cross writes,

It is well to observe at this point that this purgative and loving knowledge or Divine light whereof we here speak acts upon the soul which it is purging and preparing for perfect union with it in the same way as fire acts upon a log of wood in order to transform it into itself; for material fire, acting upon wood, first of all begins to dry it, by driving out its moisture and causing it to shed the water which it contains within itself. Then it begins to make it black, dark and unsightly, and even to give forth a bad odour, and, as it dries it little by little, it brings out and drives away all the dark and unsightly accidents which are contrary to the nature of fire. And, finally, it begins to kindle it externally and give it heat, and at the last transforms it into itself and makes it as beautiful as fire.[12]

No other explanation helped me make sense of my experience more than the words of St. John of the Cross. After pilgrimage I spent most of my days at the Rose Cottage at Duke. I would wake each morning and venture into the living room to sit for hours in the big, comfy, floral-print sofa chair. I would sit and try to pray and find myself unable to utter any words. Silence and the flickering of burning wood in the fireplace were my only companions. I would sit in contemplation, with no words to utter. I would sit and desperately search for the presence of God, to no avail. For months I had absolutely no consolation or felt sense of the Presence. I would sit *in* silence, *with* silence; and if I was graced with the ability to gesture toward God at all, it came in the form of tears streaming down my face. The purgation seemed to only intensify as time went on.

Like the wood burning in my fireplace, the "moisture" within me was drying out. Before long there were no more tears to shed. Instead, the dark and unpleasant parts of me began to surface and I could hardly bear to face them. As the fire burned, those unsightly, pain-filled, hurting places in me were being driven out.

Though all I could comprehend was desolation, I trusted that I was being healed by darkness and flames. I read *The Dark Night of the Soul* and the complementary book *The Cloud of Unknowing* and took courage.[13] I hoped beyond hope that I was experiencing a *healing* internal fire. The sense of darkness was pervasive, and I longed to sense the light.

As the darkness grew I found myself in a deeper place of fear, doubt and anxiety than I'd ever known.

> Periods of psychological ferment and destabilization are signs that the journey is progressing, not failing. The results can often be horrifying to ourselves. As trust grows in God and practice becomes more stable, we penetrate deeper and deeper down to the bedrock of pain, the origin of our personal false self. In response to each significant descent into the ground of our woundedness, there is a parallel ascent in the form of inner freedom, the experience of the fruits of the spirit and beatitude.[14]

The intense descent to the bedrock of my false self felt destabilizing. It was far from a pleasant experience. I began to face the unknown of my identity and it frightened me. As falsehoods and old affections and attachments were brought to my attention, the invitation was to let them go. Without them I felt as if I had nothing, as if I was nothing. I realized that many of my acts of service were selfishly motivated to fuel a feeling of being loved. If I could meet the needs of others and support them I felt important, needed, wanted, valuable (therefore "loved"). The line between true acts of service or kindness and falsely motivated ones is so thin.

In addition, cultural and religious ideologies that repressed and subjugated "woman" were being stripped away. My very understanding of what it meant to be a woman, what it meant to be "Phileena" was coming undone. Since my previous identity was all I knew, apart from it I didn't know who I was. A more liberated vision of myself was hard to imagine. Needing the identity that the falsehood offers makes its detection difficult. We can be so easily deceived by ourselves. Courageous surrender and abandonment are the keys to liberation for the true self.

The internal descent, like descending the Pyrenees, was painful and despairing. At times I doubted if I could continue the journey, but St. Paul's exhortation encouraged me: "It is no longer I who live, but Christ who lives in me. The life I live in the body I live by faith in the Son of God who loved me and gave himself for me" (Galatians 2:20 NIV).

Through agonizing darkness, I was learning to abandon myself more fully to Christ's life. Faith was the only thing that kept me anchored. By faith I reached out for Jesus' hand and let him lead me through darkness. Most of the time my only audible prayer in addition to tears was, "Jesus keep me." This state of dependency was humiliating and necessary. Recognizing my need and choosing to depend on God was the beginning of liberation from the sins of pride and self-abnegation. Only in this way could the freedom I longed for be realized. My faith was put to the test like never before during this dark night of my soul.

As months went on, with the aid of a few friends and an incredibly supportive husband, I began to find courage in the paschal mystery of Christ. Jesus' passion, death and resurrection became an invitation to intimacy. Before resurrection comes the torment of the passion that includes unmatched darkness and agonizing death. The great Scottish Christian novelist George MacDonald gives word to my experience:

> To give us the spiritual gift we desire, God may have to begin far back in our spirit, in regions unknown to us, and do much work that we can be aware of only in the results. . . . In the gulf of our unknown being God works behind our consciousness. With [God's] holy influence, with [God's] own presence . . .

[God] may be approaching our consciousness from behind, coming forward through regions of our darkness into our light, long before we begin to be aware that [God] is answering our request—has answered it, and is visiting [God's] child.[15]

Like the hidden work of the body's rejuvenation on the Camino, God was mysteriously at work in the dark and hidden places of my soul, remaking me.

A dark night of the soul is not an intellectual exercise but a life-shattering experience. This kind of experience cannot be crafted or sought after—it can only be submitted to. Darkness of the soul, though terrifying, is a profound grace. It is an invitation by the Spirit to transformation.

QUESTIONS FOR REFLECTION

1. Consider the roles you have assumed—for example, child, friend, partner, parent, teacher, pastor, attorney. Share the challenges you've experienced when life has necessitated the shedding of a particular role. Describe what you knew of yourself and God while exercising that role, and the subsequent struggles or darkness that set in when you could no longer find solace for your identity in that role.

2. All great spiritual teachers reveal that growth requires descent. But we resist this necessary pattern. We equate spiritual growth with ascension psychologically and spiritually. Perhaps this is because we have overemphasized God's transcendent presence somewhere up in the clouds, neglecting God's immanent presence with and within us—causing us to relentlessly pursue reaching outward and upward for God.

Expecting the spiritual journey to always be a positive, light-filled experience leads to terrible disappointment and often dis-illusionment when one progresses in relationship with God and experiences the necessary darkness. We often feel lost and alone when struggling to find our way through the dark in the spiritual journey. Few seem able to help us navigate this turning point.

Contrary to much of conventional Christian expectation, wisdom teaches us that the way to God involves descent and darkness, moving down and inward toward the unknown. This requires great personal fortitude, for the hidden labyrinth of the soul takes courage to explore.

In what ways have you or are you being invited by God to descend or go inward and look deeply at your soul?

3. When we begin the spiritual descent, it is likely we'll experience some degree of psychological darkness. We discover that we're not who we thought we were. The spiritual stage of darkness involves questioning our identity and knowledge of God. And this necessarily affects our perception of God. So our sense of self and our sense of God start unraveling. Doubt sets in. But doubt is not the opposite of faith, certainty is. And so we find courage in pursuing the unknown. Describe your own struggle with spiritual descent and darkness.

What role has doubt played in your pursuit of deeper faith?

4. The feminine menstrual cycle and childbirth offer profound spiritual insight for considering the role of weakness, pain and vulnerability in creating and bringing forth new life. How has emotional, mental and spiritual vulnerability been a passage into new psychological and spiritual life for you?

5. Darkness is a necessary condition for gestating new life, whether a seed in the earth or a baby in the womb. The same is true of our spiritual life. What spiritual fruit have you seen come forth from your experience of darkness?

6. During one of my seasons of darkness, it was as if the divine feminine was gestating in me (p. 93). I was longing to live into a

more truthful identity as a woman created in God's image, longing to cease making apologies for my gender. How has gender identity played a role in your relationship with God and others?

7. "Dark night of the soul" is a phrase that sometimes gets used to express a season of trial, discouragement, disappointment or grief. But the sixteenth-century John of the Cross used this phrase as a wise spiritual director helping followers of God as they navigated through the "night of sense" and the "night of spirit."

For John of the Cross, a dark night of the soul is an excruciating experience of being purified of false identity attachments that keep us from greater union with God. It's one way the Spirit works to bring us into a more intimate relationship with God. We eventually realize that the psychological and spiritual darkness is only a "sense" of being in the dark. The Spirit is acting in us like fire penetrating wood. All seems dark to us, but in reality we are surrounded and penetrated by purifying light. When the darkness has done its work, we emerge a more liberated being with greater awareness of being "hidden with Christ in God" (Colossians 3:3).

What is it about a dark night of the soul that intrigues you or terrifies you?

PRACTICE

Spend some time in darkness. Steal away to the countryside at night, find a safe place outdoors and linger in the darkness.

Alternatively, build a fire and observe as it dances on the wood and finally destroys it.

If possible, do both at the same time: build a fire outdoors under the night sky and spend time contemplating what you observe.

Journal your experience.

4

Death

I want to keep my soul fertile for the changes,

so things keep getting born in me, so things keep

dying when it is time for things to die. I want to keep

walking away from the person I was a moment ago,

because a mind was made to figure things out,

not to read the same page recurrently.

DONALD MILLER, *THROUGH PAINTED DESERTS*

DEATH. NO ONE REALLY LIKES TO TALK ABOUT IT. Fewer people embrace it. Death is something we fear and shun. We avoid it at all costs. Our society offers remedy after remedy to help us look young, stay young and prolong life. Death is the last thing most of us want. We avoid it for ourselves and we don't like talking about the death of others.

In contrast, in Kolkata—the city of death—Mother Teresa's Missionaries of Charity have made death a center of attention.[1] They are faithful day in and day out to women and men who are destitute and dying. The ones whom no one can or will look after find a safe and peaceful place to end their lives in Nirmal Hriday,

"Home for the Dying." In this small building attached to the Hindu epicenter of the city, the Kali temple, there are fifty cots for men and fifty cots for women. Men and women from all over West Bengal end up in the Home for the Dying by some of the most extraordinary ways. From the villages surrounding Kolkata, sometimes family members put persons who are desperate for medical attention on the train to the city in hope that they will find the treatment needed. If they have little to no money when they arrive, these ill patients are often forced to beg and are easily manipulated by the underworld of crime that controls the streets. Before long, their health deteriorates even more, and with no one to look after them they begin to waste away, alone. Missionaries of Charity and their volunteers comb the streets and train stations looking for these victims. The lucky ones are found and brought to the Home.

Medical supplies at Nirmal Hriday are in short supply and limited to only the necessities—disinfectant for cleaning wounds, nasal feeding tubes, IV drips for rehydration purposes and a small assortment of pain relievers. Having taken a vow of poverty, the sisters who run the Home use very simple linens and gowns, which are hand washed every day. The most inexpensive tin is their choice of dishware, and this too is hand washed after every meal with a meager blend of soap powder and ash—the soap of the poor.

The patients are invited into these humblest of circumstances that offer a sanitary place to lay their head, the easing of pain and distress through limited resources, and the opportunity to die not alone but in the company of love.

Along the central staircase hangs a large crucifix that reads, "I thirst." Mother Teresa believed that tending to the poorest of the poor—whether materially or spiritually poor—was a way to quench the thirst of Christ in his distress. "Jesus is God," she wrote; "therefore His love, His thirst, is infinite. He the creator of the universe, asked for the love of His creatures. He thirsts for our love. . . . These words: 'I thirst'—do they echo in our souls?"[2]

With similar attention to death, Jon Sobrino writes about "crucified people"—persons suffering poverty and oppression.[3] Sobrino, a Jesuit who makes his home in El Salvador, narrowly escaped assassination by the Salvadoran government during the 1989 murder of his six Jesuit brothers, their housekeeper and her daughter. The Jesuits were targeted because of their outspoken stand for justice and peace during the El Salvador civil war that left about 75,000 men, women and children dead (a majority were civilians). People like Sobrino and Mother bring the world's attention to Jesus in the distressing disguise of the poor, and they invite us to connect with him through the lives of the destitute, exploited, imprisoned and dying. Again, Mother's words are penetrating: "Our life of poverty is as necessary as the work itself. Only in heaven will we see how much we owe to the poor for helping us to love God better because of them."[4]

Rather than attempt heroic feats of modern medicine, which is the privilege of the few, wealthy citizens of the earth, Mother—out of her poverty—gave all she had to the least among her. Mother was often criticized by the rich for her method of ministry to these patients. It seems that the wealthy are usually the most uncomfortable with death, while the poor know that death is an inevitable part of life. The few who have access to all kinds of resources often want to impose their will on the world, thinking they are responding with generosity and compassion; yet in some cases their gestures may be more about themselves, their fears and their needs than about selfless consideration for another. Compassion literally means "to suffer with." But few of us are willing to suffer ourselves, let alone to suffer with someone else.

Committed to a vow of poverty among the impoverished, Mother's mission was pure compassion—to suffer with those who suffer while easing their pain as much as possible and in so doing quench the thirst of Christ in his agony on the cross. An obsession with prolonging life was never a part of Mother's paradigm. Mother was not afraid of death. Her life was marked by dying—dying to her desire to stay near to the mother she loved; dying to her culture and choosing the life of a nun; dying to the safe, protected and predictable life of the cloistered convent and choosing to be a poor Indian among poor Indians;[5] and dying to her desire for consolations in her spiritual life.

In the lives of the most vulnerable of the world's poor, Mother encountered Christ. By suffering with her friends in poverty and accompanying them in their distress, she pointed humanity to life that is stronger than death. In Mother's world, death was not to be feared but embraced.

The first time I entered Nirmal Hriday was the summer of 1995—the hottest time of the year, when temperatures frequently skyrocket over one hundred degrees Fahrenheit and you can cut the humidity with a knife. For a few years I had heard heart-wrenching stories about this mysterious place, and then I suddenly found myself on its threshold. I could hear the moans of the people inside and smell the putrid mix of Detol (disinfectant), curry and decaying bodies. Life and death mingled together. I braced myself as I entered, saying a quiet prayer that God would give me the grace to enter such a place. Turning the corner, my eyes immediately made contact with eyes sunken deep in the skulls of the dying. Nuns and volunteers were quietly, meditatively tending to them. Even the stronger patients were caring for the weaker ones. There was a surprising sense of peace in a room filled with death. Grace filled the room's volume like water. It was dense. Grace was given to me by entering. I didn't need grace to enter; I received it by entering.

One afternoon, as I tried desperately to make myself useful—feeding patients, bathing them, singing to them—one woman gestured for me to sit on her cot and, to my astonishment, she insisted on massaging my arms. Death was creeping at her door, yet she embraced me and tended to me—the one who seemed healthier and full of life being ministered to by the dying. Such a paradox! The dying one offered me more life than I offered that day.

There were other strange encounters during my visits to the Home for the Dying over the years. Sometimes the patients would sing to me. Sometimes they would try to share their food with me. And sometimes they would allow me to tend to their most intimate needs. Death and life intertwined in extraordinary ways.

Though most of us shun it, death is a necessary part of life. Life and death necessarily mingle together.

DEATH BRINGS LIFE

It was springtime in Spain when we set out on the Camino. After a long winter in Omaha, the freshness of a new season was a welcomed gift. How we had longed for the buds of life on trees, to see the new shoots of perennials. Along the road, new life was appearing in colors of green, red, yellow and violet. But the trees and flowers wouldn't have bloomed without the darkness of winter. The darkness of winter is an invitation to death. In order for the trees to bear fruit in the spring, a part of them had to die the previous winter. "For everything there is a season . . . a time to be born and a time to die, a time to plant and a time to uproot" (Ecclesiastes 3:1-2). By dying in season, the plants of spring and summer provide nourishment for the new life that will appear in the following spring. Death brings life.

Humanity is not exempt from nature's cycle of life and death. Most of us accept that eventually we will die—when we are old and gray, and hopefully while we are peacefully asleep. But there are other deaths throughout our lifetime to which we are subject. At birth, we die to the comfort and ease of life in the womb. At adolescence, we die to the innocence of childhood. As adults even the most celebratory moments of our lives—when we move to a new home or city, when we take a new job or get married or have a child—bear vestiges of death and mourning of the lives we've grown accustomed to and must leave behind. At midlife we may grieve the fact that most of our life is behind us. Then in old age, our body and mind begin to falter. And in the Christian tradition, adult baptism offers profound imagery for death and new life; it is an opportunity to die to our old way of being.

Dying at these stages brings the opportunity of experiencing new and different aspects of life—as a baby, the comfort of a mother's breast; as a young adult, leaving home, the delight of passions and dreams and ambitions; at marriage, the wonder of sacred commitment to a human being of our choosing; and in our faith decisions, the mystery of connection to the God of the universe. In such moments we experience a kind of death, even celebrate it, because of the life that extends beyond it.

REDEFINING MARRIAGE

When Chris and I first got married, we were certain we would have children. Chris planned on having six—he is the oldest of six siblings and thought that was a good number. I also wanted children, but being a little more realistic of what it would require of us, I thought it wise we start with two and see what we could handle after that; being careful about not being outnumbered seemed to make sense to me. We were so inclined toward having children that, before we were married, Chris bought a small Indian dress for our first baby girl and a small Nepali jacket for our first baby boy. We still have them. On our honeymoon we made lists of possible names for our future children. Everyone who knows us knows that we love children. So people are usually surprised when we tell them we decided not to have any of our own.

We didn't make this decision hastily or impulsively. We made the decision after years of honest, soul-searching conversation with one another, prayer, fasting and seeking counsel from others. And being sensitive to the maternal instinct, Chris largely deferred to me in the final decision.

As I took inventory of my upbringing and the people in my life, at the time, I couldn't find anyone who had made a decision to not have children, unless they'd also made a decision for celibacy. It seemed to me that a woman's identity very much centered on her relationship to her husband and her children—perhaps even more so in cultures of the East and South. Even after fourteen years of marriage with no children, when I visit some countries I still get asked, "When are you going to have a baby?" And I'm told, "You should have a child." And always, one of the first questions I'm asked when meeting someone new in any culture is, "Do you have children?"

Similarly, women are often pressured to get married. At least in the conservative Christian culture of the United States, if a young woman post university is not engaged or soon-to-be, people start to get nervous. Common questions for a young woman are, "When are you going to get married?" and "Are you dating anyone?" Generally, young men are offered more margin in time before they are plagued with these inquiries. Further, single men and women (at least in the evangelical subculture) are often not nurtured well enough in how to be in relationships with one another as friends and coworkers. The pressure to be an object of potential marriage undermines the exchange of platonic friendship. And this carries over after marriage—men and women struggle to know how to relate to one another outside of marriage. Can we be friends? Or does our friendship have to ride on the coattails of the same-sex friendship of our spouses? Are we so untrustworthy and out of control that we can't exercise restraint in male-female relationships?

Though the tide is slowly turning, a lot of my young, single female friends struggle to make a life for themselves if it doesn't involve a solid prospect for marriage. One young woman was recently heard talking about all the home furnishings she will not purchase until it's time to register for her wedding—she was not even in a dating relationship. Other young women I know struggle to find personal inner drive and ambition for anything other than getting married and having children. If they start a career, it is sometimes commenced as temporary, until marriage. And many women have too easily given up their life ambitions once they do get married under the assumption that this is what a wife and mother is meant to do.

Now please don't get me wrong. I understand that marriage and conceiving and bearing children are some of the most extraordinary experiences a person can have—and in a lot of cases it rightly requires the sacrifices women make. I think marriage is a holy sacrament and I feel really blessed to be married to such an incredible man. And I esteem motherhood (and fatherhood) as one of the highest callings. But I've also come to realize that there can be more to life than being a wife and mother—contrary to what the conservative subculture may suggest. And not being married and not having children can actually be a very fecund thing to do, though traditional Christian teaching has guilted a lot of us into thinking it is our Christian duty to get married and be fruitful and multiply in the form of biological reproduction.

The identity struggle and role tension I see in young women today can be understood from a number of perspectives. Human development theory suggests something insightful for this discussion. According to Robert Kegan in his book *The Evolving Self,* there are six stages of human development: incorporative, impulsive, imperial, interpersonal, institutional and, when fully mature, interindividual.[6]

Contrary to prevailing conservative Christian opinion, human development theory suggests that we don't acquire gender roles inherently alone. Culture also plays a large part in shaping expectations for men and women. And in many cases, women are not nurtured for the institutional development stage. Instead of being encouraged socially, religiously and educationally to develop our personal interests, ideologies, strengths, skills and gifts beyond relationships, they are reared, trained and educated to remain in the interpersonal stage—forced to find identity in relationship to others. Men in contrast are generally afforded the opportunity to develop further into the institutional stage, encouraged to pursue their own interests, ideologies, strengths, skills and gifts toward contributing to society and, traditionally, toward "providing for the family." This easily explains why young men aren't plagued with the same tensions in relationships and regarding marriage and children, and why young women often struggle to develop their identity into the creative stage of institution.

It's the twenty-first century and we've come a long way in recognizing the equality of women and men. But we still have miles to go before women and men are both free to develop their fullest potential, liberated to make free choices that connect to their deepest selves. For some men that might mean that being a homemaker would be the truest expression of who they are, but the pressures of society and culture don't typically allow that as an option.

The most difficult and most mature stage in human development theory, interindividual, is usually a struggle for both men and women. But if one is nurtured through the interpersonal and institutional stages of development, they can also find their way into the interindividual stage where mutuality is more possible: fully actualized men and women expressing themselves through a lovely exchange of persons, where giving and receiving is met with grace and appeal.

Having been reared well for the interpersonal stage, it was an earth-shattering proposition to consider choosing to not conceive children. I really had to wrestle with what it meant to be a woman. If being a woman means being defined in relationship to others—primarily husband and children—and I deny having this most sacred experience, then am I still a woman? I'm married. I can check that off my list. But what does it mean to be a woman if I don't have children? I would imagine that some women who, due to biology, cannot bear children go through similar daunting questions, as well as some women who are not married or are wrestling with the consideration of opting not to marry. If the woman is not Catholic or Anglican, she's really in a quandary since other Christian faith traditions do not offer an esteemed celibate option for people of either sex.

Making the decision to not have children meant I had to die to some of the false parts of myself that wanted to be connected, understood, accepted, and free of judgment and criticism. And most importantly, I had to die to the experience of ever conceiving a child, giving birth, and having reflections of Chris and me to enjoy and cherish for the rest of our lives. Not an easy decision. Not an easy death. There was necessary grieving and mourning involved.

But being available to a world of children who long for the same opportunities I would give my own was both the motivation for and the fruit of my decision. Because of this decision, in addition to being in relationship with a number of these children around the world, Chris and I get to spend our energies investing in an international community who will ensure provision and opportunity for children of poverty for years and years to come. And we get to enjoy and cherish a number of godchildren. Sure, these children aren't "our own," but we have a certain sense of responsibility to them nonetheless. We are committed to them to the extent of sacrificing the opportunity to conceive our own children. We are invested in their well-being, their personal development, their interests, their sadness, their hopes and their dreams.

So what does it mean to be "woman"? Certainly being a woman may include motherhood. There are plenty of happy mothers in the world. Yet what I had come to understand was that being a woman (like being a man) means to be free to be one's truest self (whether or not that includes parenthood). Being a woman (like being a man) means to be free of gender-role expectations imposed by family, religion, culture and society. Being free means that we are not defined by what we have, what we do or what others say about us.[7]

My decision to not conceive children is an expression of how the grace of God moved me from being *defined* by relationships to *having* relationships. A woman who chooses to have children can also achieve the same ends. Both decisions can be the truest expression of who we are. The point is not the outcome—being or not being married, or having or not having children. The point is to move from the interpersonal stage, where we are defined by our relationships, to the institutional stage, where we are free to uncover and be oriented by our ideologies—and to ultimately be free to be in mutual relationships of genuine interdependence (interindividual). Is this not the freedom Christ represented and offered through his friendships?

A woman's growth path often involves healthy differentiation that allows for separateness, while most men have a different experience. Being reared through the interpersonal stage to the institutional stage, they sometimes get stuck in being disconnected from relationships. The growth path for them involves differentiation that allows for connectedness. When men and women move through these paths of growth, they are able to experience relationships of mutuality.

REDEFINING CHRISTIAN FAITH

My decision to become Catholic was not any easier than my decision to not have children. Death was central to this decision, even in how the church designed the rite of initiation. In the early church, martyrdom was such a likely outcome of one's decision to become Christian that a three-year initiatory process was instituted so that one could contemplate the death they would endure by making this decision. We no longer have to wait three years—the Rite of Christian Initiation for Adults that I went through was a period of about eight months. (I added another four months or so onto the beginning of that time during my initial discernment.)

I was brought up to believe that Catholics weren't really Christians. But from an early age, because of a few Catholic friends, I was drawn to the liturgy and ritual of the Catholic faith tradition. As time went on, I received exemplary influence from Mother Teresa and the Missionaries of Charity as well as the Jesuits. But I didn't think leaving the evangelical tradition and becoming Catholic could ever really be possible for me. I didn't seriously consider it. However, after a few years of attending a Jesuit parish I began to take more seriously the prospect of conversion—turning from one way of expressing my Christian faith to another.

When sabbatical ended, I returned to Omaha and went back to my neighborhood parish, St. John's Catholic Church at Creighton University's campus. During the first Sunday mass I attended after my return, I was overwhelmed with emotion. I should tell you that I'm a "feeler." On the Myers-Briggs or Kiersey Temperament Sorter, I rank an F for "feeling." I filter the world through my emotions, and contrary to the rational mind, as a feeler it *is* possible to make decisions based on feelings. It's the primary way we feelers take in and process information. It's quite a remarkable way of interacting with the world. It took me years to accept the feeling part of me—perhaps because in a male-dominated world, the rational mind tends to be elevated as superior, and emotions are seen as inferior. A friend of mine actually said to his soon-to-be-bride when they were sorting out a conflict, "The rational mind is superior."[8] I remember, in college, being at a church service and going forward to the altar (we feelers can often be found at the altar) pouring out my heart to God, tears streaming down my face. The pastor quietly came to me and talked with me for a few brief moments. I apologized for crying and he said, "Never apologize for your tears. Some of us wish we could cry and can't. Your tears are a gift." I've never forgotten that.

So here I was, back at St. John's after being away five months. I gazed at Jesus on the cross and had this overwhelming sense that I had come home. The feeling was that I could find an ecclesial home for my soul (a phrase Chris so eloquently offered me in observing my conversion) in the Catholic tradition. And the invitation seemed to be that becoming a full part of the church with its sacraments and traditions would aid me in continued growth, transformation and intimacy with God. I had already stumbled my way into the contemplative tradition; and no other Christian faith tradition could cradle and nurture the contemplative part of me like the Catholic Church could. As I meditated on the cross, I knew that— for me—joining the Catholic Church would mean greater intimacy with Christ. Realizing this, how could I *not* become Catholic?

But in making this decision I would have to answer to my husband, father and countless Protestant friends—relationships that I often used to let define me. This was an opportunity once again to put to death parts of my false self that wanted to be understood, accepted and free of judgment and criticism. Whether viewed from a psychological perspective or a spirituality perspective, "The self truly dies to the self that was, and the new self that emerges is a kind of rebirth."[9] In the dying I was promised new life, but I couldn't know beforehand what that life would be like, and I had to trust that there would indeed be fruit from such a decision. "I tell you the truth, unless a kernel of wheat falls to the ground and dies, it remains only a single seed. But if it dies, it produces many seeds" (John 12:24).

So I counted the cost, found solidarity with the saints who went before me—and gave their very lives for their decision—and invited key people from my community into discernment. At one point during this season of discernment an article of mine was published in our community's quarterly journal, *The Cry*. In that article there was a photo of memorabilia from the Camino: my boots, walking stick and a rosary. A family member, after having seen the photo, asked my parents, "Has Phileena 'crossed over'?" News of my decision to become Catholic would not be easy or acceptable to a number of people in my life. My father and I had several very difficult conversations—the fruit of those has been greater understanding between us. Whereas before I was somewhat afraid for him to know the real me, I took the risk and invited him in, and he has faithfully stood by me. Other fruit and life has come and is coming from the decision. One of the greatest is unity among believers. Barriers of self-righteousness and judgment are brought under scrutiny when people who have known me for decades are forced to reconcile their condemnation of Catholicism with their appreciation for my faith.

Decisions that stand in opposition to the status quo are not for the faint-hearted; they require courage, honesty and risk. These kinds of decisions release us into our destiny. Abundant life awaits each of us, but we must die to obtain it. The challenge is to understand which part of us must die and which part is dying to be raised to life. Until we have grown sufficiently in self-knowledge, it is difficult—if not impossible—to distinguish the false self from the true. I had to die not only to the status quo but to repressive attachments that shackled me in a posture of inferiority and subordination so that I could live and reflect the truth of who God made me to be. This meant dying to my old way of being so that I could live into the responsibility of proper self-assertiveness.

In order to make the decisions to not conceive children and to join the Catholic Church, I had to die to traditional views of what it means to be a woman; and I had to die to religious paradigms and gender ideologies that threatened my very conscience against responding to God in a way that I knew to be right and good for me. For many men or people of power, what needs to die and what is dying to live will look rather different. I like the way Leo Tolstoy puts it: "The changes in our life must come from the impossibility to live otherwise than according to the demands of our conscience not from our mental resolution to try a new form of life."[10]

For many traditional women or persons of imposed powerlessness, the invitation to die is all the more problematic. From a human-development-theory approach, traditional teaching of self-sacrifice and nonassertiveness when one is transitioning from the interpersonal to the institutional stage only serves to repress one from reaching her or his full potential—or the abundant life of which Jesus so often spoke. Teaching that emphasizes assertiveness, empowerment and self-development aids the transition. I think this is why men traditionally make this transition with fewer impediments. Historically, in most cultures, boys are afforded this support while girls receive a message that reinforces subordination, dependence and self-effacing, which traps them in the interpersonal stage and prevents them from progressing to the institutional stage. Under these circumstances, girls too often grow up to be women without a proper sense of self to freely sacrifice. Rather than force women to choose between self-preservation and the church, can we not imagine a community of Christ where all are free to grow and develop into their full selfhood and unique destiny as people created in the image of God? Why on earth do we want to repress in the institution (the church) what is meant to reflect the reign of Christ?

All of this brings the message of the gospel to new light. Just how exactly are we to understand Christ's invitation for us to die? In view of what we now understand of the human psyche and development, this is not such a straightforward invitation. It requires an incredible degree of faith, trust and surrender so that we can understand the life in us that is called to die and the life in us that is dying to live.

Theology and psychology are not mutually exclusive; each informs the other. Together they enlighten us and help us understand what it means to be human and what it means to be a person of faith. The gifts of psychology and human development theory have given me a great appreciation and understanding for the teachings of Jesus. Through the lens of these disciplines, Christian transformation is tangible.

Remember the caterpillar in its cocoon and the long process of waiting? To live into the new life of a butterfly, the ways and existence of the caterpillar have to die. Can you imagine the absurdity of a butterfly trying to crawl and inch around like a caterpillar, rather than taking flight on its expansive wings? Death of the old caterpillar is necessary to live into the life of a butterfly. And like nanoscience revealed through its tiny microphones on the chrysalis, death is distressing. The artist in the *Studio 360* report said, "It is not so easy to become a fabulous being." The process of transformation requires an agonizing death of the old reality.

Immediately after my niece Claire was born she began to quietly moan—continuously. The doctors and nurses looked her over, put her under a lamp and examined her. After several moments when she would not stop moaning and whimpering, the nurse said, "She's lamenting." They actually have a medical term that explains this phenomenon—"lamenting." Claire was in mild distress. She was mourning. Exiting the body of her mother was no easy thing for this little one. She was mourning the familiarity and comfort of the womb. But leaving existence in the womb was absolutely critical to living the life of baby Claire. It's absurd to imagine a baby never leaving the womb. To live and grow into the fullness of who we are, we must move on no matter how painful and distressing it may seem at the moment. Death in varied forms is necessary.

I can't imagine what it is like for trees that succumb to the measured, arid process of autumn and winter. Slowly, slowly the tree dries out; the leaves begin to turn color, losing their life. Their death is imminent. And surprising to most of us, the beauty displayed in the changing colors of the leaves is a sign of their death. They are dying. But oh, isn't it beautiful? What's to be feared in such beauty and promise of new life in the springtime? And witnessing the birth of a baby! There's nothing like it! It's magnificent! But like Claire reminded me, the beauty of her birth required lamentation. And the caterpillar—can you imagine its experience in the chrysalis? The throngs of people visiting the Butterfly Pavilion at Omaha's Henry Doorly Zoo demonstrate our fascination and intrigue with the process of distress these creatures go through—an indispensable anguish to becoming their astonishingly exquisite self.

THE PASCHAL MYSTERY

In my awakening experience, I opened my eyes and, in some ways, saw myself for the first time. I saw that I was living in a posture of gender subordination that reinforced a perception that not only was I less than my male counterparts, but my sole purpose and design was to serve their interests. Prior to awakening, I didn't realize this was my self-perception; now I saw it for what it was. With eyes wide open, if this was who I was, then I wondered who God was—a God portrayed by people in my world from a very young age as the one who established this very order of nature in which male is superior, independent, autonomous and afforded a grand display of opportunity; and female is inferior, dependent, defined in relationship to others and offered limited opportunity (opportunities defined and provided for by her primary relationships). Who knew that a feminine awakening could include being confirmed into another patriarchal tradition? My decision to join the Catholic Church can only be understood within the paradox of God—a God who often dumbfounds us by choosing "the other."

Waking up to this state of affairs is one thing. Longing for something else propelled me forward. But it wasn't long before darkness set in and death was inevitable. It would take time for the life within me to come to fruition.

Jesus affirmed that abundant life requires a process of dying. The spiritual journey begins with a narrow way and carrying a cross—a symbol of our death. Jesus said,

> You who wish to be my followers must deny your very self, take up your cross—the instrument of your own death—every day, and follow in my steps. If you would save your life, you'll lose it, and if you would lose your life for my sake, you'll save it. What profit is there in gaining the whole world if you lose or forfeit yourselves in the process? (Luke 9:23-24)

This is the Teacher who invites us to die—daily. For a people who flee from death, who can embrace such an invitation? Do we cower from the pain that carrying our cross might impose? Do we trust the one who claims he is the way? Can we follow him, no matter what it might cost? Do we believe his way truly is the way to life? Do we believe the narrow way that means our death will ultimately lead to our being fully alive? The spiritual journey is an invitation to identify with Christ in his paschal mystery.

The paschal mystery—Christ's passion, death and resurrection—is a mystery of participation for us. Christ's identification with humanity and his suffering, death and resurrection provide a way for us to make sense of our lives and find redemption. The cliché that "Jesus saves" is not something to write off as a childish belief. Jesus' salvation act in history is a mystery for us to enter today—Jesus has made a way for us to receive fullness of life and experience the love, growth and freedom that we long for.

Catholic priest and author Ronald Rolheiser explains the paschal mystery in four phases that relate to the events of Jesus' last days on earth and the coming of the Holy Spirit. By his description we can see the stages of redemption that we are invited into by identifying with Christ's mystery:

Passion and death	the loss of life
Resurrection	the reception of new life
Ascension	the refusal to cling, as ascending beyond the old life

Pentecost   the reception of new spirit for the
                             new life[11]

During sabbatical I began to reckon with my own passion and death. I began to understand that there were parts of me that had to die. I was in fact losing a part of my life. In seasons of death, we can take comfort in knowing we are not alone. We are like the residents in Mother Teresa's Home for the Dying—they are dying but they are not alone, and that makes all the difference. In our dying too, we are not alone. We are accompanied by Christ. Through his passion and death he has identified with us and made a way for us to identify with him. The act of dying might be the most profound way in which we can identify with God. Episcopal priest and author Cynthia Bourgeault says, "You do not die on a cross *in order* to 'set up' the resurrection; you die on a cross because the willingness to give it all away is itself the original and ultimate creative act from which all being flows."[12]

The season of Lent in the church calendar has become one of the most meaningful seasons of the year for me. Lent is the long period of forty days prior to Easter and the celebration of the resurrection of Christ. It is observed through prayer, fasting and almsgiving. As we spend forty days in intentional reflection on the passion of Christ, a grace is opened up for us to take inventory of the passion we may find ourselves enduring. Through keeping Lent, Jesus' life and suffering become tangible companions in the difficult seasons of life and death we endure. We receive the graces of patience and long-suffering. And we uncover a new hope in the promised resurrection. The paschal mystery is a grace-filled invitation to be accompanied by God through awakening, longing, darkness and death. The mystery reminds us that death does not have the last word.

Fruit comes from dying, like the grain of wheat; new life comes from death.

WE WANT THE FRUIT BUT RESIST THE DYING

The process a tree goes through during the changing seasons from autumn to winter is slow and dry and brutal to the leaves. The leaves are forced to die. Does the tree resist? Or does it surrender to the process in the hope that new life will come in due time?

We want the fruit, the new life, but we resist the dying. Death is the culmination of darkness. During a season of darkness, I wrestled with God, trying to hold on to that which needed to die—my preconceived notions of who God is and who I am. Much of what my identity had been based in was being shattered and I fought to hold onto the crumbling pieces—having no guarantee of who I'd be without my false-self security blanket. The burning away (purgation) of my false self was a horrible experience. At times, I didn't understand what was happening to me. I was sad and disoriented, and all seemed dark. I was losing grasp on who I was. I questioned all of my life's decisions, wondering which of them had been connected to my true self and which had been motivated by my false self. I was just trying to keep my head above water in the sea of darkness when everything about my identity seemed to be fading away.

Looking back, I can see that this was a necessary purging. To be free to live into my true self I had to examine and reckon layers of my identity that were oriented in a false way. I had very little control over this earth-shattering process. I had consented to the journey. I willed to embark on it, but like the Camino, if I wanted to reach the destination I would have to succumb to the pain and anguish that would get me there. After a considerable amount of time in purgation, death sets in. False self-perceptions and false God-concepts die. But purgation isn't enough. The purging season is a time to separate the false from the true. Once the separation is complete, the false-self stuff has to die to make room for truth. Death provides nourishment for the true-self seed of life that has been incubating in darkness.

The gifts and perspective I had to offer from my true self had to be nourished on the dead leaves and mulch of childhood lies and attachments that suggested that I was less than equal, that I was to remain hidden and that my destiny was determined and limited by my relationship to others, particularly men. No longer could I define myself by relationships; I had to die to that misrepresentation of my true self. Christ was resurrecting my passions and calling forth feminine strength in the dried bones of my diminished sense of self.

But with these deaths came a lament, for my identity was intricately tied to these false perceptions and attachments. Like a drug user, I was addicted to the gratification these attachments afforded. Their effect was momentarily satiating. I craved the affection and esteem these paradigms offered me. And yet, like drug addiction, the very thing I craved was killing me. I longed to be free.

DEATH LEADS TO TRANSFORMATION

In my community, we are blessed to be in relationship with children and young people on the margins of society trying to survive on the streets without a traditional family; for various reasons they either do not have parents or no longer live with their parents. In their resourcefulness they attempt to re-create family through a network of loyal friendships on the street, as well as exploitative relationships. Drug abuse, indiscriminate sex and crime fill these children's world. The adage "You can take a kid off the streets but you can't take the streets out of the kid" is proven over and over again.

Transformation is not easy. Having been abandoned by their parents, either literally or emotionally, our friends have learned to survive on their own and rarely depend on anyone. They are hardened and so, instead of being free to be honest with their real developmental needs and trust another to tend to those, they turn to a quick fix through drugs, sex and crime. It's easier to go into survival mode, rather than to do the hard work of risking trust and relationship. They have reasons not to trust and their hearts have been broken too many times. They often believe the lies that they are unlovable, unworthy and unequal. They often believe they deserve nothing more than the repressive life they've been handed.

Like many of my young friends suffering on the urban streets of the Majority World, I had been living a lie about who I was. And living into the truth of my identity would be easier said than done. The old and new were in conflict with one another, and like oil and water, they wouldn't mix. Like the log of wood that St. John of the Cross so aptly describes, death has to come to the log of our false self so that our true self can burn brightly. After a considerable amount of time in purgation—that wrestling match between the darkness we inhabit and the longing we're cultivating—death sets in.

Death, a life-giving surrender.

The seed of life incubating within me promised another way of being. Like the crimson red, monthly blood flow demanding to be recognized, being me meant being unashamedly feminine, assertive, fecund, confident and bold, purposeful and passionate. Could this promise really be actualized in my life? Like the caterpillar, in order to live into this new, truer essence, the old way of being had to die. At the point of death, what dies, dies. Gone. No one knows for sure what, if anything, will come from the death. That's what makes dying so terrifying. Maybe the tree won't bear any leaves next spring. Maybe the caterpillar will die in its cocoon and never become a butterfly. Wouldn't it have been better to have not entered the cocoon but remained in a caterpillar's existence? Maybe slavery in Egypt was better. How do we know there's really a Promised Land? Maybe the baby won't live if it comes out of the womb. Do we risk pregnancy?

There are no guarantees. New life, growth and transformation are risky endeavors. The spiritual journey requires faith and trust. If we want resurrected life, at some point we have to succumb to our crosses and die.

QUESTIONS FOR REFLECTION

1. Death is a necessary and inevitable part of life. What is it about death that troubles you the most?

2. Using Robert Kegan's stages of development, in what ways have you or haven't you been nurtured beyond the "interpersonal" stage into the "institutional" and perhaps the "interindividual" stage?

   What do these stages mean to you?

3. Think about your primary relationships: with parents, partner, friends, children. At this point in your life are you being challenged to differentiate from key relationships in a way that allows for more autonomy for yourself and the others? Or are you being challenged toward greater connection to others?

   What would interdependence look like in your primary relationships?

   What is inviting about interdependence? What resistance to interdependence do you notice?

4. What does it mean to you to have the freedom and support to develop into your highest potential?

   What changes would need to occur in your life to support your growth and development?

5. In the complex journey of becoming, we die to certain parts of our identity to make room for new aspects of identity. One of the deaths that occurred in my journey was dying to traditional definitions of womanhood. Choosing not to conceive and bear children wasn't an easy choice. It meant letting go of others' expectations and sacrificing the opportunity to experience one of the most fulfilling aspects of being biologically female. But it also opened me up to new aspects of conceiving and bearing new life.

What are some of the ways you have been or are being invited by God to die to certain identity attachments?

"Decisions that stand in opposition to the status quo are not for the faint-hearted; they require courage, honesty and risk. These kinds of decisions release us into our destiny. Abundant life awaits each of us, but we must die to obtain it. The challenge is to understand which part of us must die and which part is dying to be raised to life" (p. 116). In what ways are you dying to be raised to new life?

Is there a part of you that has hung on too long and it's apparent that it needs to let go and die?

PRACTICE

Carve out some time to meditate on death. Consider choosing one of the following methods:

- Read one of the crucifixion texts (Matthew 27:32-56; Luke 23:26-49; John 19). Pray with the text. What part stands out to you? Linger with it. In what ways is that text mirroring back to you an aspect of your own life?

- Find an icon of the crucifixion; there are plenty of images online. Gaze at it. What element of the image are you drawn to the most? Linger there. In what ways is that aspect of the icon mirroring back to you an aspect of your own life?

- Consider something in nature that goes through the process of dying in order to bring forth new life (for example, the leaves of trees in winter, a seed in the ground). Consider how this aspect of nature is mirroring back an aspect of your own life and death.

Draw or journal your reflections.

5

Transformation

Your joy is your sorrow unmasked.
And the selfsame well from which your laughter rises
was oftentimes filled with your tears.
And how else can it be?
The deeper that sorrow carves into your being,
the more joy you can contain.
Is not the cup that holds your wine
the very cup that was burned in the potter's oven?

KAHLIL GIBRAN, *THE PROPHET*

ALONG THE CAMINO, CHRIS AND I laughed and cried, we celebrated and we grieved. Some of the most vulnerable places in our souls emerged to be embraced by the all-consuming grace of God. And by that grace we kept moving forward. Many days our packs weighed us down and the pain in our bodies intensified. Inevitably, the harder it got to keep going on any particular day, the more our gaze turned downward. Staring at our boots on a dirt path was rarely motivating. At those times we would encourage one another to keep our heads up, to keep looking around us and before us. In this way we abandoned ourselves to our surroundings, to the horizon and to God, and found the strength to keep moving.

Often throughout our journey, I returned to the thought that pilgrimage is not a round trip. We begin at one point and end at another. We don't go back and retrace or relive our steps. Each moment is lived and let go. By way of El Camino de Santiago, we made a passage through time and into the next season of our lives. As we walked, our pilgrimage became a transformative passage to new life. Starting out, I had no idea that such a journey would mean so much pain. Neither did I anticipate the depth of joy and love we would experience. Like the Lebanese poet Kahlil Gibran expresses, our joy ran as deep as our sorrow. The pain and trial we experienced carved space in us for untold joy. Indulging our senses with the beauty of creation all around us, finding encouragement in the company of ancient and modern pilgrims, and experiencing many Spanish culinary pleasures filled the empty and dry places in our hearts that had emerged over the past thirty years of our lives. As we walked and embraced both the pain and the joy, we were being changed.

FROM DEATH TO NEW LIFE

Like a caterpillar in her cocoon, or a germinating seed, I was changing—undergoing a transformational regeneration of my soul. After months of sitting with an awakened sense of self, experiencing an internal death and learning to simply be, I was changing. These changes in me were both now and not yet—this is the reign of God spoken about so often in the Gospels. At times, Jesus spoke of the kingdom of God as if it is something to come. At other times he spoke as if it is at hand. Some changes had occurred in me, and others were imminent because of what had been set in motion within me, but living into the transformation would take time.

Most butterflies complete their metamorphosis or maturation within thirty to forty days, but human maturation takes much longer. We have long childhoods. This isn't something to be ashamed of, but aware of. Being ignorant or oblivious to this fact leaves us neglecting a natural phase of life. We force maturity before we have actually reached that stage in our awareness, enlightenment or development. Our culture certainly promotes growing up too fast. Children are confronted with adult choices on a daily basis through mass media and marketing. The retail industry has limited child-style clothing options but provides adult clothes in little sizes. Beauty and fashion industries entice preteens to apply makeup and dress sexy. Visual and audio content meant for mature adults is forced into the worldview of the preadolescent. The days are nearly gone when a kid can be a kid. The time needed at the childhood phase is sorely compromised.

On the flip side, our culture *prolongs* adolescence in the lives of adults, delaying our timely maturation. Juvenile programming is cloaked as adult entertainment. Some grown men can't pull away from their Xbox long enough to be a husband and father or general contributor to society. They are numbed into a virtual reality of perpetual childhood. Our culture also reinforces delayed maturation in the lives of women. The fashion and makeup, fitness and cosmetic surgery industries scream at women to stay young.

We are either tempted to grow up too fast or to sedate our growth and transformation. We are a discontented species who seem to resist the natural rhythms of our life and growth. If only we knew what was good for us. We can learn a lesson from the butterfly. She responds to the invitation for change not a moment too soon or too late, and submits to the process, no matter how difficult and painful it might be.

Fascinatingly, once the butterfly cracks its chrysalis—which takes about five minutes—it waits. It doesn't spring forth and take flight immediately. The newly transformed insect requires about ten minutes to inflate its wings to full size—fluids from the abdomen are forced into the wings to inflate them—and then the butterfly rests for two to eight hours, allowing the wings to harden before it is able to take flight.

Likewise, the transformation I longed for months to experience just wouldn't happen overnight. It was like physical conditioning in pilgrimage: transforming the body to endure the feats of walking five hundred miles happened gradually, day by day. Even once I emerged from a long darkness and death, like the butterfly I seemed to perch on the outside of my cocoon and wait a bit longer. All the while, an inner strength was circulating through me, hardening the modifications within to ensure my ability to live into those changes and take flight.

CHANGE DEMANDS REST

Like butterfly wisdom, sabbatical introduced me to the spirituality of rest and the crucial connection of rest to transformation.

> As I sit in the screened-in back porch of the "Rose Cottage" the soft rain is penetrating the dry and weary land of Durham. North Carolina has been in a season of drought and so the rain is a long-awaited gift. Earlier this afternoon as I was in prayer, I heard the rain begin to fall. I transitioned and took my prayer outside to receive the baptism of fresh autumn, life-giving water. Each day on sabbatical is a gift. How could we have known how spiritual rest could be? My days are filled with renewal for my body, mind and soul.[1]

It was a little difficult to pull away from my community for several months to enter sabbatical. *What would become of me and my marriage outside our usual context? What would come of my relationships? How could I ensure that my friends and I would grow closer and not further apart during this absence?* Fear reared its head and I struggled to let go. *Could this solitude create an emptiness within us that would prove to be the source of our togetherness?* Detachment and solitude were necessary parts of this season of rest and would prove to be essential elements for transformation.

The first month of sabbatical at Duke was transition—spiritually, mentally, emotionally and physically. As the good Puritan work ethic collided with sabbath rest, I spent time pondering and crafting my "rule of life."[2] Thinking a rule of life would help me make the most of sabbatical, I dutifully and diligently put together my rule for rest. Though my intentions were good, I now chuckle at the thought of how contradictory this effort probably was to truly entering rest. I chalk this period of time up to *transition.* I had not really been taught *how* to enter a long rest and, therefore, as I plunged in I had to figure it out along the way.

Sabbath rest is in fact a "revolutionary act."[3] Like making pilgrimage, by receiving time and space to purposefully detach from my active life, I was denouncing the compulsions that our technology-driven, rhythm-defying modern society affirms and indeed demands. By withdrawing and ceasing, I was announcing something countercultural and otherworldly. It would take time to adjust.

At first I found myself unable to be present to the moment, instead fretting that sabbatical would soon be over. In the darkness, I wondered if I would be ready to enter back into my normal life. I was feeling abandoned in the dark, questioning my call, my life decisions, God's work in my life and my very self. Tilden Edwards articulates well the questions that rose in my heart.

Ceasing from work tests our trust: Will the world and I fall apart if I stop making things happen for a while? Is life really gifted and the Spirit moving through it, so that I can truly rest and taste this restful caring? Can I trust that this caring will be the bottom line when I rest, beneath all the suppressed and repressed sides of myself that are likely to rise when I relax my controlling reins? Is there truly a unique image of

God in me that is simply given and rises to obscure awareness in such spacious times, an image that is my deepest
identity? Is there really no such deep self in God, and does
everything really depend on my producing, asserting and
protecting a conscious, managing ego-self?[4]

Edwards also says that when we enter sabbath rest as an escape,
"Sabbath rest is never quite full, because there is a lurking dread that
we may run into something from 'the other side' that will destroy
it."[5] My journal entry during sabbatical describes this struggle:

The constant passing of the hours and my focus on tomorrow
threatened to rob me of present peace and rest. I am becoming newly acquainted with Time, being invited into a different quality of time from my normal life. Time is asking me to
receive it as gift rather than enemy, and asking me to risk facing my lurking doubts, fears and questions.

Unfortunately, this does not happen overnight. This is a
process of healing. This is living the redemption.

Much like yoga, there are times when we accept a position
that hurts a little and stretches us in ways of which we didn't
know we were capable. It hurts, it challenges my limits and
my patience, yet if I sit with that dull pain for a while it
changes me. I may want to not experience that pain or I may
want to cut it short, but then I would not reap its rewards.

In life we sometimes wish our pain would not linger so
long. But for our benefit there is a necessary season of sitting,
walking, living in our pain. When we embrace our pain, own
it, we let it transform us.

"Pain is weakness leaving the body," Chris says remembering his days of football training. An oyster endures the
pain of the pebble in its flesh and that pebble is transformed
into a costly pearl. The pain Christ endured on the cross led
to his conquering of death and resurrecting into new life.

His pain is salvation for the entire world.

I trust that my pain could also bring forth strength, priceless gifts and salvation for others. This is the paschal mystery that we are all invited into—living, dying and being resurrected to new life.[6]

The Jewish tradition of sabbath and sabbatical is a time for waiting on, resting in, receiving from and learning to delight in God. According to the Hebrew Scriptures, sabbath was a day of rest from work and activity in honor of God's seventh day of rest in the creation story. This was a most holy day and was intended to be distinguished as such. Sabbatical was a similar principle, but for a longer period of time—one year set aside every seventh year.

A day of rest set aside weekly and more extensive periods of rest throughout one's lifetime allow for an inner work in our soul that is otherwise left neglected. Sometimes, these restful moments take the shape of apparent movement like pilgrimage, a hike in the mountains, a long walk or even the labyrinth prayer.[7] In these ways, though we are active we are actively *disengaged* from our normal activity. Other times, rest demands a quality of stillness. Rhythms of activity and stillness allow us to make music of our lives.

Our modern society abandoned the more natural rhythms of agrarian culture long ago. And with modernization has come ignorance to the body and soul's natural needs and rhythms. In previous times, our people were rooted to a time and place that lent itself to the more natural ways of being human with our bodily needs and rhythms for work and rest. Before the wonder of the automobile, our ancestors were fairly localized—they couldn't travel far very fast, so they didn't go far from home. Furthermore, our agrarian relatives were tied to the earth for their sustenance; they had to work the land. Any gardener knows you can't be away for long when you have plants to tend to.

My grandparents were farmers. Though they lived just forty-five minutes by car from me as a child, they rarely came to visit. They had cows to milk and chickens to feed and crops to tend to. They were relentlessly tied to their place in time. When the sun went down, they did too. And they would rise with it the next morning and live their life in connection to the living creatures all around them. Their home was quiet, peaceful, simple—much simpler than *Real Simple* magazine, a feeble attempt at reclaiming the value of simplicity in a complex, industrialized society. Achieving simplicity according to the popular magazine means stirring up a discontent in the reader in order to want something more—which leads to buying something more—in the false hope that all will be better once we've spent time calculating all these ideas, planning strategic points of action, purchasing the necessities that will "simplify" our lives—and then cluttering up our already overcluttered homes with yet one more foolhardy remedy to simplify our minds, hearts, homes and lives. And of course, we'll need to add this magazine to our long list of subscriptions in a lame attempt toward simplifying our lives to have more space, more time and more energy—whatever is left after the mass download of information through print, television, Internet, iPod, iPhone and BlackBerry.

I love the way Wes Jackson puts it in his book *Becoming Native to This Place.*[8] Jackson has spent more than thirty years taking on the modern agricultural industry, insisting it must change to sustain both our food production and ecosystem. He has a big dream and will die fighting for it. He's a person who will change the world. In his grand, broad-scope dream for revolutionizing the global agricultural industry, he makes a very simple point about being rooted in time and place. Jackson affirms that we are creatures of habitat with rhythms and connections to the natural world—meant to live in harmony with it, rather than in discord. But our modernity threatens that connection and harmony. In an attempt to regain our equilibrium, we build castles in the sky, sprawling retreat centers, spas and vacation packages, which become new loci for breathless acquisition and busyness. All our bodies and souls really need is a long walk in the woods or along the coast, getting back in touch with our habitat. Primitive agrarian cultures teach us something of the value of becoming native to our place—helping us to get back in touch with the elements of our own nature that thrive on rhythm and balance.

In our modern world, it is much too easy to overextend our limits toward activity and productivity. Stillness, solitude and silence are not valued today like they may have been for our ancestors whose days were filled with these qualities simply by the nature of their life's labor and limitations. We tend to see restrictions to activity and engagement as something to be avoided. But limitations and restrictions can be a grace for us. Within the context of our limitations, God can do for us what we cannot. The caterpillar can't make herself become the butterfly—that kind of change requires confinement, solitude, stillness and receptivity to something bigger than herself. This is how transformation is made possible. Remember, we cannot make ourselves grow; but we can choose to submit to or resist the process. And though much growth takes place in our active lives, all elements of creation are subject to contemplative stillness as an integral part of growth and transformation. The butterfly does not become the magnificent, colorful creature by a fury of activity. She submits to the confinement of the chrysalis—womb-like, tomb-like. She is still. She rests. She receives. She submits to a work more glorious than she could have ever conjured up for herself.

SABBATICAL: MY CHRYSALIS

Sabbatical prompted in me a posture like that of the caterpillar-come-butterfly. I entered my chrysalis by way of an extended period of time confined to a place that was strictly intended for rest and renewal. Sabbatical was a disciplined season of withdrawal, detachment, solitude, silence and stillness.

For more than a decade, Chris and I had engaged a world of poverty—children forced to be soldiers in West Africa, children abandoned because of AIDS in India, women and girls enslaved in the commercial sex industry, victims of war in Kosovo, children living on the streets in urban centers of South America. Wanting to respond to these people who had become our friends compelled me to give everything I could toward building an international community that would bear witness to a better world—a community that would emulate justice, peace, equality and opportunity, a community that would reflect the reign of Christ. In a world like ours where the work seems to never get done and there's always more to do, our community encouraged my husband and me to rest from this labor. It's sort of shocking, isn't it? In a world of extreme injustice and poverty, how could we stop serving and disengage from it all? There's so much to be done.

Leonardo da Vinci offers insight into the need for rest:

> Every now and then go away, have a little relaxation, for when you come back to your work, your judgment will be surer, since to remain constantly at work you lose power of judgment. Go some distance away because then the work appears smaller and more of it can be taken in at a glance, and lack of harmony or proportions is more readily seen.

Again, Mother Teresa teaches us. In her rules she established a rigorous schedule of service accompanied by a thoughtful period of regular rest—one day a week, one week a month, one month per year, one year in every six. Mother knew better than any of us that our labor on behalf of the poor is tireless. But she also understood the value of solitude, silence and stillness. Even throughout an active day of service in the life of a Missionary of Charity, every sister keeps to a routine of prayer interspersed throughout their workday. In Nirmal Hriday, amidst a sea of dying men and women, at particular hours in the day you will find the sisters withdrawing to pray in the upstairs chapel. Mother said, "We need to find God, and [God] cannot be found in noise and restlessness. God is the friend of silence. See how nature—trees, flowers, grass—grows in silence; see the stars, the moon and the sun, how they move in silence. . . . We need silence to be able to touch souls."[9]

And this kind of silence is more about an interior state than it is necessarily about the external. Mother's chapel is built facing one of the busiest streets in Kolkata. I've never been in that chapel when it's quiet. But the nuns who gather there still their minds, bodies and souls for regular, brief moments in their day—even amidst the sounds of blaring horns, diesel trucks and people calling out the sale of their wares. Rest, stillness, solitude and silence are all critical conditions to transformation in our lives and the world around us.

Work—Rest. Service—Prayer. Action—Contemplation. Life offers us the challenge of holding these essential elements of what it means to be human in tension with one another. One without the other leads to either pompous piety or frantic fury. The one who closes herself off from the world under the guise of "prayer" is at risk of becoming out of touch, irrelevant and prone to self-righteousness. In her "prayerfulness" she may succumb to judgment and superiority since she is not connected with the real lives of people around her. True prayer connects us with the compassionate Christ who connects us to all humanity and inspires us toward compassionate service.[10]

Similarly, the one who neglects contemplation is at risk of being motivated and driven by false-self compulsions. When one neglects giving attention to his interior life, he is not master of his house. His "programs for happiness" control him, and he goes through life unaware that his "service" is more truly frenetic activity. He is not only blind to the real needs of those he serves but to his own needs as well. True acts of service do not build up our egos but bring us into deeper solidarity with the poor, marginalized and victims of injustice, who compel us to prayer.[11]

Parker Palmer drives this point home:

> Too much of our action is really RE-action. Such "doing" does not flow from free and independent hearts, but depends on external provocation. It does not come from our sense of who we are and what we want to do, but from our anxious reading of how others define us and of what the world demands. When we react this way we do not act humanly.[12]

Our community had the wisdom to recognize the imperative value of rest in what had become a very intense bent toward service. Chris and I had leaned heavily into the question, "What can I do for God?" and neglected to regularly recognize our need to ask, "What can God do for me?" We were victims of the Puritan work ethic. We struggled to find people in similar fields of service who modeled sabbatical (rest) well. Chris and I entered pilgrimage and the season at Duke tenuously. The prospect of five months of detachment from work loomed over me and seemed more daunting than visiting former child-combatants in Sierra Leone. What in the world would I do with all the time?

And time was all I had. No obligations. No major responsibilities. The time given me amounted to a lot of waiting time. Waiting turned into longing. Longing mingled with darkness and death. The spiritual journey as a passage for growth and transformation was upon me. I didn't realize then during the long days of relative stillness in the Rose Cottage, as I sat in the darkness of my soul and felt abandoned by God, that everything I was experiencing was a part of the process of transformation. Like the caterpillar in her cocoon, I felt the distress and torment of my confinement. Everything seemed dark and I didn't understand what was happening to me. All I could do was succumb to the pain in my soul, try to grasp it somehow and try to understand it. In my desperation all I could do was cry out for mercy.

As the weeks turned into months I found myself fragmented. Through prayer, purgation had the effect of separating my false self from my true self, and I was left in pieces. I remembered the Gospel stories about sick and disabled people wanting Jesus to make them whole, and this had never made more sense to me. I too wanted to be whole. And I was powerless to make that happen. This is a work of the Divine Physician[13]—the one I doubted then and still doubt at times. And yet when the uncertainty creeps in, all I have to do is look at the changes in me and I am brought to my knees at the wonder of my Creator, Savior and Friend. My priest once said, "The opposite of faith is not doubt, it's certainty." The essence of faith anchors me even in the midst of misgivings.

Transformation, which essentially involves healing, is a slow process. It is rarely full and complete in an instant. It takes time. And during that time, it demands cycles of awakening, longing, darkness and, yes, even death. All are crucial to this most sacred work in us. Being healed of that which shackled me and prevented me from being fully me took time and space for solitude, silence and stillness. You might enter a sabbatical expecting a kind of convalescence, but it wound up being more like rehab for me— lots of stumbling and frustration and even anguish. This is how it feels when you emerge from your cocoon as you begin to live into your true self—the person loved for who you are alone and not what you can do or be for others. During seasons of transformation we have to find our footing and let our wings harden so we can make the flight of our life. An intentional sabbath season made it possible for me to enter my chrysalis and submit to a metamorphosis of my soul.

I love how Tilden Edwards explains sabbath: "Sabbath rest . . . emphasizes trustfully relaxing into what already has happened and is happening for us in God's easeful grace."[14] Sabbath time is characterized by catching our breath, ceasing and freedom from compulsion. It is a deeper communion with God, our self and our community. Contribution through acts of service or work can more easily and purely flow from this communion. Apart from communion with God, our action is more likely a compulsive, anxious attempt at imposing our will on the world.

The gifts of sabbath are available to everyone, even if you are not able to receive a sabbatical. When kept mindfully and thoughtfully, any regimen of sabbath can create optimal conditions for soul-tending, growth and transformation. If we posture our lives through the lens of pilgrimage or the spiritual journey, all we have to do is open our eyes and find that we are in the grace-filled passage of transformation. At any given point in life we can find ourselves at various places: awakening, longing, darkness, death, transformation. All are prime moments to rest in the arms of God.

GROWING ACQUAINTED WITH GOD'S SILENCE AND LEARNING TO LISTEN

While I was at Duke, the difference between compulsion and communion became more apparent. God's easeful grace led me into a long, lingering experience of *being* as I've never experienced before. I read novels—lots of them. I read a history book on the sordid past of Durham's race and class division in an effort to root myself in the city in which I found myself living.[15] I prayed and meditated—more often than I ever had before. I gardened for hours and took long walks with no destination. I took advantage of being near the Atlantic Coast, spending a total of fifteen days by the sea in a matter of three and a half months. I enjoyed some creative cooking, going to shows with Chris, and sitting and having long talks in the outdoor hot tub with him. And I even enjoyed accompanying him to a couple of football games (he took full advantage of sabbatical and his love for college football, attending sixteen games over the course of four months). I lingered in the backyard hammock—reading and dozing. I walked through Duke Forest and marveled at the changing colors of the falling (dying) leaves. From day to day, I tried to reach deep down in my soul to discover what I wanted and needed, freeing myself of former compulsions to do and be that which I thought others wanted or needed of me.

At about the halfway point during my time in Durham, a much-needed rain began to fall after a long drought. The climate had been uncharacteristically hot for the autumn and with the rain came welcomed cooler temperatures. On the first day of the downpour, since I had no real agenda for the day (like most days on sabbatical), I abandoned all convention and went for a walk in the rainstorm. With all the determination of pilgrimage, my walk turned into a run until I could run no longer. The pink Rosie Thomas T-shirt I was wearing clung to my body, reminding me of the nakedness beneath that reflected my vulnerable soul. My soul longed to be exposed and embraced in grace and freedom. I was desperate for this baptism—more so than the relatively innocent nine-year-old who was baptized many years before. How my entire being needed the Water of Life that Jesus claims to be. The rain kept pouring down and I couldn't bring myself to go inside. It was as if all of creation were crying out for me to pay attention and be present.

So I walked to the neighborhood park and swung alone on the swing until my hips were sore from the child-sized seat. The previous few days, I had experienced the trials of soul-searching and I desperately wanted to hear from the Lord. I was weary of the darkness and longed for better days of full release and freedom. I cried out to God to speak to me. I told God how much I needed to know the comforting Presence. I felt so alone.

Though I wasn't able to hear God's voice in the way I was asking for it, at that moment I *heard* God's silence, and for the first time in a long time God's silence was okay with me. I no longer felt abandoned. I longed to worship. I was shedding compulsions for the liberating gift of communion. Love was growing in my soul—slow and feeble but it was there nonetheless—a love that longed to love regardless of what it received in return; a sign of transformation.

Later that afternoon, after reading a bit from my novel of the week and drinking my favorite pumpkin ale, I took a nap. When I awoke, I turned to the Gospel of St. John in prayer. As I entered *lectio divina*,[16] Jesus broke through the silence between us and spoke to me through the words of Scripture. The reading was from the story when Jesus healed the man at the pool of Bethesda.

> Here a great number of disabled people used to lie—the blind, the lame, the paralyzed. One who was there had been [disabled] for thirty-eight years. When Jesus saw him lying there and learned that he had been in this condition for a long time, he asked him, "Do you want to get well?" "Sir," [the disabled person] replied, "I have no one to help me into the pool when the water is stirred. While I am trying to get in, someone else goes down ahead of me." Then Jesus said to him, "Get up! Pick up your mat and walk." At once the man was cured; he picked up his mat and walked. The day on which this took place was a Sabbath. (John 5:3-9 TNIV)

Clearly I was that disabled person longing to be made whole on the sabbath. Jesus took compassion on me, noting that I had been in this condition for a long time. The past months of darkness had brought me to a greater realization of that very condition. For security's sake, I had clung all these years to my pitiful human condition filled with attachments and compulsions that weren't good for me—like being defined in relationship to others and succumbing to self-abnegation. As the darkness progressed over time, I was being invited to let go of this false security of self, not knowing what would be given in return. In those moments with the Scripture before me, as Jesus asked me if I wanted to get well, I was overwhelmed and wanted to shout, "Yes!" God had heard my cry for mercy. Having come to greater understanding of my personal human condition, I wanted nothing more than to be well, to be made whole, to be transformed.

One of the things I love about Jesus is that he never imposes himself on us. He always offers but never coerces. Time and again in the Scriptures we find Jesus confronting people with all kinds of ailments, but he doesn't force them into healing. As the noblest of all gentlemen, he asks what he can do for them and asks if they want to be well. Jesus never pushes us into something we're not ready for. Jesus is so patient with us. He leads us tenderly and jealously at times, but he doesn't force us into the next season of abundant life or healing. He asks us what we want of him. In those moments with Christ, I poured out my grief and sorrow over my condition and, by faith, received the transformation that I couldn't offer myself.

As my self-perception and understanding of what it means to be woman was being healed and transformed, so also was my perception of God. Early in sabbatical I had the sense that God wanted to reintroduce God's self to me. Since so much of my understanding of God was shaped by masculine influence, my understanding was limited. And the distance I felt from God was caused in part by this misunderstanding. If God is perceived as male and men are often overpowering and all-pervasive, then there's no room for me as a woman in relationship to God or men. But here was this revelation of God in Jesus who, as a man, doesn't overpower, overshadow or impose himself. Though Jesus could fill the space of the world and is certainly self-sufficient, he restrains himself with remarkable discipline and control to make room for the other—all others, all of his creation. And he doesn't stop there. Making room for the other, he invites us into a relationship of mutuality—giving and also receiving.

Incredible. If the God of the universe can make room for me and receive what I have to offer, then certainly humanity can too—most notably, men. In Jesus we see the portrait of what it means to be the best of masculine humanity—powerful but free of ego, dominant but tempered, strong but yielding to others. He has nothing to prove and everything to give. He is a respecter of persons—he affirms that masculine and feminine are both divine reflections. In relationship to him there is enough space for all of us to live in mutuality, offering our gifts and influence to one another. Some feminists have a really hard time accepting that in the life of Christ God chose to be revealed as a man and not a woman. But when seen in this light, God's incarnation as man becomes an incredible grace to men and women alike.[17]

After months of transformative silence, I was able to finally listen. God was reintroducing God's self to me and holding up a mirror to my true self. Jesus had never been more appealing. Love was taking root in my heart as I embraced my femininity and the gifts I could freely give to the world.

QUESTIONS FOR REFLECTION

1. The process of dying makes space for transformation. Look over your life. Consider a season in which you went through a process of transformation. Perhaps it was the process of growing from childhood into adolescence or adolescence into adulthood. What was that season of life like? What were the difficulties and the joys?

2. Transformation takes time; it doesn't occur overnight. Consider the timeline of transformation. If 1 is the beginning of transformation and 10 is fully transformed, where are you in your current process of transformation?

   What is this stage like for you?

3. Change demands rest. What does rest look like in your life?

   How easy or difficult is it for you to make time for rest?

   How have you seen space and time for rest support your growth and relationship with God?

4. Practices of solitude are crucial elements to receiving rest and receptivity to the work of transformation. In what ways do you welcome or resist solitude?

   Describe a time when solitude was a catalyst for your growth or nurtured your relationship with God.

5. "As my self-perception and understanding of what it means to be woman was being healed and transformed, so also was my perception of God" (p. 143). The process of transformation necessarily involves aspects of dying and being reborn. Another helpful way to understand the process of becoming relates to the stages of construction, deconstruction and reconstruction. Which stage in the journey of transformation best defines where you're at?

   How is this stage affecting your self-perception and your perception of God?

PRACTICE

Meditate on the process of metamorphosis. Watch a time-lapse video of a caterpillar turning into a butterfly (for example, "Monarch Butterfly Metamorphosis Time-lapse FYV 1080 HD" from Front Yard Video on YouTube. Or visit your local butterfly sanctuary.

Pay attention to sensations, feelings or thoughts that are provoked in you as you observe the process of metamorphosis. In what ways do you identify with the caterpillar's process of turning into a butterfly?

What stage of metamorphosis do you most identify with at this time?

What do you most need from God during this process of transformation?

Pray quietly with what comes to the surface in you or through journaling or drawing.

6

Intimacy

Someone is standing near
Who will wash away her tears
Someday when she's been found
Her scars will become a crown

KATE HURLEY, "HEY LITTLE GIRL"

INTIMACY IS THE STARTING PLACE, the posture and the goal of the spiritual journey.

From a place of intimacy, for our tenth wedding anniversary Chris gifted me the promise of walking the Camino. Intimacy guided us through all the preparations we made to embark on the journey together. Intimacy rooted us to the experience of suffering and enduring together thirty-three days of physical feats and emotional exploits. And by the end of our journey, we had achieved greater intimacy with one another. The Camino became for me an outward, tangible experience of an invitation to journey deeper with others, God and surprisingly with myself. As I grow to understand and embrace myself more fully, intimacy with others grows too. Embracing myself requires me to come out from hiding (self-abnegation, self-effacing). Intimacy is about knowing and being known. How can I be known if I remain in hiding?

On the Camino, my apparent physical "weakness" caused me to feel terribly inferior to Chris. Biologically he is stronger. He can walk longer and faster and carry more weight. I, on the other hand, couldn't walk as far or as fast, and I certainly couldn't carry as much weight. I thought this made me less, but as I emerged from hiding I came to recognize my differences as a gift rather than an inferiority or inequality.

In light of this, on the third day when we walked from Zubri to Pamplona—the infamous day known as the "Phileena Shuffle"—I experienced a deeper intimacy with Chris. In my vulnerability and humiliation, I came out of hiding and acknowledged my difference from Chris in what felt like weakness. I owned my limitations and my needs and presented them to Chris. "Chris, I can't walk that fast. I'm in a lot of pain. I'm slowing us down. I'm sorry." And Chris responded, "Bebe, that's why you should lead the way today." "What?! You mean you accept me in this condition? You embrace me as I am in my felt weakness? And in being me, in my femininity and in my difference I can lead us?" Tears flooded my eyes as I proceeded before him.

Struggling to accept myself in this one area was an opening to a sinkhole of self-perception that had drained my influence and contribution to the marriage and to other relationships and endeavors. Being honest with who I was in that moment and revealing that to Chris—instead of hiding, trying to "buck up," "take it" and pretend like I could keep up—and being embraced in such a loving way by Chris helped me find the courage to be more truthful and honest with myself *and* with Chris (and others) about who I am.

This was the beginning of greater intimacy with Chris and a new step in confidently offering more contribution and influence to the marriage. In what seemed like inferiority, weakness and something less valued, my femininity and my unique personhood was actually a gift. It was time I embraced myself more fully. Neglecting to do so was not only detrimental to myself but could be so to others as well. Though Chris does have a different orientation and pace for life than I do, he admittedly is subject to overdoing it and getting ahead of himself and those around him. When I offer myself, my perspective, my needs and limitations to him, it can often be surprisingly liberating for him too. Often, the very part of ourselves that we are most embarrassed by or feel most vulnerable about is the exact gift others need from us. Regardless, embracing these parts of ourselves is crucial to intimacy.

The spiritual journey allows for space within us to be carved for intimacy. Intimacy is about knowing and being known. But sadly there are a lot of obstacles that keep us from achieving this most necessary of human needs. "Programs for happiness" that our false selves cling to threaten to prevent us from reaching our hearts' desires for intimacy. We seek power and control, affection and esteem or security and survival, and none of these pursuits leave us fulfilled. At the end of life's journey, it doesn't matter what we have, what we do or what others say about us. What will matter is whether or not we are known and loved for who we are, and whether or not we have known and loved our family and friends well. This is why family and old friends are the dearest. They know us—the good, the bad and the ugly—and they still love us. We want to be known, and we want to know and love others well—this is the truest success in life. Countless novels and films center on this very theme: the estranged family member on his or her dying bed seeking relationship, intimacy—they want to be known, forgiven, loved, or they want to have one last attempt at knowing and loving their family better.

The spiritual journey is an invitation to know God and to be known by God, which necessitates that one finds and knows oneself. Intimacy is something that either saturates our life or leaves us craving more. Awakening to deeper intimacy with God fuels the growth of intimacy with others, and vice-versa.[1] When we pursue intimacy and our awareness is heightened to our limitations in intimacy, we are en route toward growth and transformation.

In order to grow in the intimacy we long for, we must cultivate self-knowledge. Self-knowledge cradles intimacy. And to the extent that we grow in understanding our deepest self, we grow in relationship to others. Often, when we don't experience the intimacy we want in relationships, we point the finger at the other person or at God and focus on their shortcomings and why they aren't able to allow for intimate relationship. Though this can be true—some of the people in our lives are limited in their ability to be intimate in the way we may desire—often the key to being known and knowing others is knowing our self. When we dare to know our deepest self, with its sorrows and hopes, we encounter God who, in turn, invites us to greater enlightenment about our self and the world that we live in. In knowing and embracing our self, we find courage to offer our self to the world—most intimately to the people with whom we are in relationship. We are more inclined to put our self out there to be known when we are comfortable in our own skin. If we are hiding behind our "programs for happiness," our desire for intimacy will never be satiated. We have to come out from hiding—naked and vulnerable—look at ourselves in the mirror, embrace and celebrate the person we are. Then we are free to be known and to more truly know others. An intimate exchange can occur.

During this season of my soul, I realized that I was attached to the "program for happiness" of affection and esteem. As long as I generally did and said what I thought others wanted or needed from me, I would feel "loved," "accepted," "desirable." But living in this manner perpetuated a slow internal decay. I wasn't a human being fully alive, but in a sense was living only half of my life. The other half was in hiding and scared to come out for fear of being rejected.

Aren't there parts like that in all of us? We offer the world what we think are our "presentable" parts, and we tuck away what we think are less desirable to others. In this manner our egos are stroked and we subsist on the sustenance of our "program for happiness." But it is a survival technique nonetheless, not an abundant, thriving life. It's more like a parasitic relationship between our ego and false self. The ego feeds on our "program for happiness." The longer this goes on the more emaciated the true self becomes. Learning to know and embrace myself was not easy for a woman who was religiously and culturally inclined toward a posture of subservience.

The journey that my soul embarked on was made possible by a divine invitation to intimacy. The pilgrimage that I choose to continue on is one that grows in ever-deepening exchanges of intimacy with God, my family and friends and all of creation. Growing in self-knowledge and self-embrace is a surprising experience of being known and embraced by God.

AN AUDACIOUS PRESUMPTION

Longing is about growing acquainted with the presence of God. Intimacy is about friendship and growing toward union with God.

Several years ago, I started to wonder: *If I lived in a society of religious persecution and was imprisoned and could no longer read the Scriptures or attend church, or if I had been born into a family and culture that did not know Christ and could not tell me about him, could I still know God? Can we only know God through the influence of others, or is it possible for God to reveal God's self to us in a more direct way? Is God confined and contained in the Holy Scripture, in our church services or in others' interpretation and explanation of God? Is God only to be found in these places or does God also really dwell within me? Is it possible to be acquainted with God without the usual "filters"?*

These questions beckoned me into deeper intimacy with God. I am reminded of the disciple Thomas and how he has gotten a bad rap. You know the one—the disciple who said, "Until I put my hand in his wounds, I will not believe!" (John 20:25-31). Well, why is that so bad? I relate to Thomas in some ways. I am a skeptic and a realist. Like Thomas, I wanted to see, touch and embrace God. I wanted a more intimate exchange. Perhaps like Thomas I was calling God's bluff. "If you really are the Christ and have risen from the dead, prove it. Show me yourself. And don't stop there. Show me your wounds—the most intimate, pain-filled places in you."

Even in the most insecure and vulnerable moments of my soul's journey, I occasionally had the sense that I was not alone. In fact, I now understand those darker moments as some of the most intimate encounters with the wounds of Christ. The invitation to intimacy beckoned me toward growth and transformation, which meant also a redemptive suffering. The desire for intimacy guides us through all of the movements of the soul.

What does it mean to know God? Primarily, I have come to know God through the life of Christ. When I think about my desires to know Jesus I don't want to take someone else's word for the reality and divinity of Christ. I want to know him myself. I want to be so near him that I too can put my hands in his wounds. I've begged to know him and he has been faithful to make himself known in my life. In the words of the anonymous fourteenth-century author of *The Cloud of Unknowing,* there is a yearning for God within me, "a longing to see and taste [God] as much as is possible in this life."[2]

One of the most evident ways God has been made known to me is through my friends around the world living in poverty and suffering all kinds of horrors. One of the most compelling reflections I gained from time with our young friends in West Africa centers on the wounds of Christ. The civil war in Sierra Leone was just ending. Soldiers were being disarmed. Boys as young as five were gathered in from the combat zone and forced to turn in their weapons. Unable to return to their villages because of the atrocities they were forced to commit under compulsion from their commanders, the children resigned to whatever social welfare the government or NGO community could provide them. They were desperate to find a way to live in peace in a war-torn country.

During one of our times together, Chris shared with them the story of Thomas. He asked, "If the Scriptures are true and Jesus is the same yesterday, today and forever, and if after his resurrection he still had the wounds (they weren't healed over even though his entire body had been raised from the dead)—then wouldn't he still bear wounds today? And if so, then where are the wounds of Christ in the world?" Without hesitation one of our friends, a former child soldier, replied with eagerness as he pounded his chest, "We are the wounds of Christ."[3]

This understanding is one of the ways in which our community can celebrate suffering. We don't vindicate or sacramentalize suffering; we grieve it, but we can also embrace it as a lifestyle celebration. Let me explain. The perpetrator and perpetration of suffering are not excusable. But through Christ, companionship and hope are found in the midst of our suffering. And this is why we can celebrate it. Through suffering, the wounds of Christ are revealed, providing an invitation to intimacy with God. To the degree that we respond to the wounds, we experience intimacy with the One who suffered for us and bore *our* wounds. Drawing near to the wounds in our brothers and sisters around the world, while simultaneously acknowledging our own, allows for healing and transformation to take place. In this way we can understand the words of the Hebrew prophet Isaiah, "By his wounds we are healed" (Isaiah 53:5).

Knowing God can be a challenging endeavor for people who are inclined to limit reality to their senses, but people of all times and cultures strive to know God nonetheless. We experience life and relationships by our ability to see, hear, smell, touch and taste. Certainly we can know something of God through reflections of God. It's like knowing a fine painter whom we might never meet: we can know something of her or him as our senses encounter their piece of art. Poets and artists of all kinds help us achieve this kind of encounter with God.

But rather than knowing something *of* God, how can we know God personally and intimately? Classic Christian spirituality helps us with this. God is beyond our faculties: reason, imagination, memory, feelings and will. Prayer that makes use of our faculties is known as *cataphatic* (or *kataphatic*) prayer. Cataphatic prayer corresponds with ordinary awareness and reinforces our unique egoic selfhood. It is wonderfully self-reflective. "I" is the center of orientation for this kind of prayer. It arises from the predominant way in which we relate to the world and to others.

By contrast, *apophatic* prayer does not make use of our normal faculties. It transcends our capacities for reason, imagination, memory, feelings and will. The center of orientation for this kind of prayer—by its very nature—is abandonment of self and attentiveness to God. But this prayer does make use of *different kinds of faculties,* faculties that we are less in touch with, faculties known as "spiritual senses." Engaging our spiritual senses is enhanced through apophatic prayer, which is usually characterized by intentional silence or meditation. By way of apophatic prayer, we grow in receptivity to and awareness of God who is indeed very personal and intimate with us. In this kind of prayer, we grow in openness to God introducing God's self to us, very directly. True aspects of God that have been told to us become infused in us through the posture of surrender and attentiveness: God is gracious, compassionate, merciful and forgiving. And the most predominant impression we are left with as we grow acquainted with God in apophatic prayer is that God is love.[4]

Songwriter Kate Hurley echoes the revelation of the God of love that the ancient writer of Song of Songs understood. God is love. And the love of God is all-consuming. The essence of intimacy is experiencing this all-encompassing love.

I am my Beloved's and He is mine
When I found the one my soul loves
I held on to Him
When I found the one my soul loves
I would not let Him go
Love burns like a blazing fire,
Like a mighty flame
Many rivers cannot quench love,
Many waters cannot wash it away
Love burns like a blazing fire,
Like a mighty flame
For love is stronger than death,
Its jealousy unyielding as the grave
Place me like a seal on Your arm
Like a seal over Your heart
Love is stronger than death.[5]

Because of Christ's passion, death and resurrection a way is made for us to pass from death to life, from death to love. Christ has identified with us and with intimacy has invited us into his passion, death and resurrection. For ultimately, no death we face is stronger than love. Though the suffering and death we experience throughout life can at times seem unyielding, love always prevails. It is love's jealousy that invites us into the pain of our suffering and invites us to die so that love might be born. The invitation is to fullness of life and love. That fullness comes at a cost. We must die to obtain it. The dying may feel like it will have the last word, but the truth is that love always has the last word. The poet Kahlil Gibran explains this well:

When love beckons to you, follow him, Though his ways are hard and steep. And when his wings enfold you yield to him, Though the sword hidden among his pinions may wound you. . . . And think not you can direct the course of love. For love, if it finds you worthy, shall guide your course.[6]

Love leads us and at times it may penetrate us so deeply that we feel as if we are being wounded. But that "wounding" is actually for our healing and transformation.

Cultivating intimacy with God is not so different from cultivating it with our spouse or our friends and family. Depth of intimacy requires knowing our self and being honest with our self and with the other. I realized this in new ways during sabbatical. There were parts of my relationship with God that I didn't really want to be honest about, as my journal reveals:

> As I'm learning to give voice to things personally and in my marriage, today I realized how I must do that in my relationship with God. During the past week I've wanted to come to God out of adoration and worship and praise and yet I haven't found much of that in my soul. That has scared me a little.[7]

The truth in my relationship with God in those moments was that I didn't feel anything toward God, except a sense of being abandoned. But I was afraid to be honest. Would God accept me in that condition? Can we be honest about our doubts that God exists? Can we go to God and be honest about not really feeling like worshiping or praising? Can we show up to an encounter with God just as we are? Or do we opt for keeping a distance from God because we would rather be distant than honest? Cultivating intimacy with God in this season of my soul required honesty. I would show up in faith or reach out to God in faith, but in all honesty too, I acknowledged that I didn't know if God really existed, and if God did, I doubted God cared.

Henri Nouwen explains the role that doubt plays in intimacy:

> The [person] who never had any religious doubts during his college years probably walked around blindfolded; he who never experimented with his traditional values and ideas was probably more afraid than free. . . . But he who did, took a

risk . . . the risk of being alienated from his past and of becoming irritated by everything religious, even the word
"God." The risk even of the searing loneliness which Jesus
Christ suffered when He cried, "God, my God, why have you
forsaken me?" . . .

We can discover, with pain and frustration, that a mature
religious [person] is very close to the agnostic, and often we
have difficulty in deciding which name expresses better our
state of mind: agnostic or searching believer. Perhaps they are
closer than we tend to think.[8]

Though I feared being honest about my doubts in God, I was
learning that doubt does not stand in opposition to faith. Like my
priest said, "The opposite of faith is not doubt but certainty." In fact,
doubt is at times a necessary element to growing in faith. Being honest about my doubts and fears strangely brought me nearer to God.

EMBODIMENT LEADS TO INTIMACY

It was on a day of that kind of honesty that my walk—in the steamy
North Carolina rain—turned into a run. In my drenched, vulnerable, embodied truthfulness I encountered God. God's silence broke
through to me and I experienced an intimate exchange. This was an
intimacy of embodiment. In relationship with a God whom we
struggle to grasp with our senses, actions of embodiment—being
present in our body as well as our mind—are extremely important.
Sadly, Western culture has so prized the mind over the body that
the two have been divorced in much of our Christian experience.

Western culture has historically segregated the life of the body
from the life of the mind, creating a dichotomy in which the mind's
work is given value and the body's work is disregarded or actively
devalued. This bias is an imposition on Christian history, which
gave as much attention to the body as to the mind, developing spiritual practices such as pilgrimage, labyrinth prayers, genuflection,

the sign of the cross and other embodied prayers. These kinds of practices, in addition to reading and intellectual reflection, are helpful for embodying our faith and growing in intimacy with God. We all have practices of embodiment; some of us just need to connect those to the One who made them possible.

I like to pray in the same chair; it's become a sacred place for me to embody my prayer. I experience embodiment every time I listen to Sergei Rachmaninoff's "All Night Vigil." I remember being at the Rose Cottage, with a fire in the fireplace and the orchestra sounding through the speakers, fully present in the moment and in the wonder of the music. In those moments, intimacy with God was tangible.

I also like to sit on a quiet, empty beach and watch the tide roll in. Yet sometimes it's incredibly difficult to be fully present—can you imagine? In the grandeur of the expanse of the sea, earth and sky, how can it be hard to be attentive and fully there? This is the problem: we are fragmented—our mind, body and soul have trouble coming into harmony. We have so overemphasized the mind in our Western experience that we are always in our heads.

Because we in the overdeveloped West have become so accustomed to privileging the mind over the body, disciplines of embodiment can be intimidating and even perplexing. My friend David went to yoga for the first time with another friend. Realizing David's uneasiness and anxiety going into class, his friend said, "Dude, you've got to get out of your head and into your body." Exactly—though perhaps more accurately it would be, "Dude, bring your mind in harmony with your body."

Going to confession can also be an act of embodiment. The action of taking our body to another to confess sin is a demonstration of our desire for intimacy with God. Realizing our sin, we recognize the ways in which we are separated and take steps toward intimacy.

As I prepared for my first confession in the Catholic Church, I was encouraged to think about themes in my life that separate me from God, myself, others and creation—contrary to the misperception that I would have to bring thirty-five years worth of a laundry list of sins to confess. It didn't take very many moments of meditation to know what my confession would be. As I met with my priest, I waded through tears and deep-felt emotion and confessed the sin of self-abnegation. It was one of the most intense experiences in my spiritual journey. I kept looking at the crucifix on the wall before me in the office. (That's right, I met face to face with my priest in his office—not in the mysterious, dreaded cubicle most often depicted in movies, though that could have been arranged as well.) As I gazed on the image of the Christ hanging on the wall, I was overcome by the impact of sin; even now as I think about it, the emotion fills my heart. Succumbing to self-abnegation—hiding, neglecting responsibility for my truest self, living out of response to what I thought others needed or wanted from me—had the direst consequences on my relationship with God, myself, others and the world. In the presence of my confessor I realized how this sin caused massive separation in my life and in the world around me.

What made this confession even more painful was that in my sin I thought I was doing the right thing. I thought my posture and attitude was a godly one. I thought I had been living as a good Christian woman. It was a confusing moment of enlightenment, as you can imagine. But now that I was confessing my sin, the feeling of being known was more tangible and the depth of intimacy in my relationship with God more possible. Christ's words on the cross touched me to my soul's core: "Abba forgive them. They don't know what they are doing" (Luke 23:24). At the moment of this confession I realized the devastating effect of my sin, while at the same time I realized that when I committed the sin, I didn't know what I was doing. What compassion of Christ! As he received the direst effects of the sin of humanity—through crucifixion—he could see that the people truly didn't know what they were doing. In fact, they thought they were doing the right thing.

A God who sets rules to follow and punishes those who break them no longer seemed real in light of the grace and revelation I experienced through confession. Suddenly, sin became something that is not good for me or others, and God was revealed as a God of great compassion who is simply trying to help me live the most fulfilling life possible; sin gets in the way of that. Instead of leaving confession feeling like a terrible sinner and hoping to do better next time and to keep "the rules," I left deeper in love with the God of love—the God who *is* love.

Confession is a meditative act that requires embodiment. We take our bodies to confession in order to fulfill the impulse behind confession; by going to confess we show that we have left what we're confessing behind. With our bodies we repent and literally turn from our old way of life. Jesus' parable in the Gospel of Luke verses 18:9-14 illustrates this well for us. There are two confessors: the Pharisee and the tax collector are seen at the temple praying. Both go to pray but only one makes confession—embodying his prayer by his posture and by beating his breast, which symbolized his internal humility. The other prays "about himself" (or as some texts have it, "to himself"). Only the tax collector leaves the temple justified.

Walking the Camino reminded me daily that I cannot live apart from being connected to my Creator and Redeemer—like the plump grapes on the vine that cannot survive apart from connection to the vine. That kind of connection is of the deepest intimacy—knowing God and being known by God. I wanted to settle for nothing less.

CONFUSED WESTERN SPIRITUALITY

Intimacy with God is possible when we believe in the reality of the divine indwelling as expressed through Scripture:

- I will ask the One who sent me to give you another Paraclete, another Helper to be with you always. (John 14:16)

- Aren't you aware that you are the temple of God, and that the Spirit of God dwells in you? (1 Corinthians 3:16)

- God is the One who firmly establishes us along with you in Christ; it is God who anointed us and sealed us, putting the Spirit in our hearts as our bond and guarantee. (2 Corinthians 1:21-22)

- God made us for this very purpose and gave us the pledge of the Spirit to safeguard our future. (2 Corinthians 5:5)

According to these and other references, God dwells within us. At Christian baptism, we receive a special grace and faith to grow in response to the presence of God. Contemplative prayer provides a way to grow in awareness of the Presence. Growing in awareness allows us to respond more readily to God. As we progress in the Christian journey, we find ourselves experiencing a divine dance of moving with the rhythm of the Spirit. As the dance develops in intimacy, union is possible. In union, we are most free from our self-consciousness and are in tune with the consciousness of God. In God we live, move and have our being. God's thoughts become our thoughts. God's ways become our ways. God initiates and we respond. God leads the dance; we follow in step. Like the most eloquent waltz or most enchanting salsa, we are mystified in the embrace of our Lover. The doctrine of the divine indwelling affirms God's immanence (the pervading presence of God within the created world), yet many of us live as if God is only transcendent (above, beyond and independent of the created world). The two attributes of God are important for us to understand so that we can grow in relationship with God.

Richard Hauser, S.J., in his book *Moving in the Spirit: Becoming a Contemplative in Action,* drives this point home in his reflection on Pelagius and the Western model of spirituality. Today there is great debate over Pelagius's teaching, but the point Hauser tries to make remains valid: many misunderstand grace and the immanent presence of God because we embrace a position that makes grace unnecessary and live out of touch with the immanent Presence.

Pelagius was recognized as a respected monk before his ideas surfaced. A teacher in Rome, he was thought to have originally been from Britain. Hauser simplifies the complicated history surrounding Pelagius's ideas by pointing to a debate that occurred between Pelagius and Augustine of Hippo—one of the most influential early church fathers. The controversy centered chiefly on original sin and the role of grace. Pelagius failed to understand humanity's nature and weakness as portrayed by various passages of Scripture.

A common reading of the Pelagian theory suggests that humanity is able to perform some good deeds apart from the grace of Christ. Jesus was important to the Pelagians not because of the indwelling grace released through his life, death and resurrection, but because he provided the example for humanity to follow. The early church countered this idea by affirming that Christ saves humanity through the indwelling Spirit and apart from human actions, work or the degree to which we can imitate Christ's example. The Pelagian theory is that we can do the will of God and attain goodness, virtue and holiness apart from the grace of God, entirely by our will. This theology amounted to the Western model of spirituality that suggests that the self exists outside of God—self initiates and God rewards. The measure of grace received is dependent on good behavior.[9]

Augustine led the movement to denounce this teaching[10] and correct it with a scriptural model of spirituality. The scriptural model is self-in-God—God initiates and we respond. Grace (or love) is experienced within this union of self-in-God. In response to the Pelagians, the church insisted that the movement in our hearts toward good action flows from our response to the grace of God, not on our own initiative. For fifteen hundred years Christians have affirmed that the desire for good and the power to carry it out flow from the grace of Christ.[11]

Orthodox Christian teaching reiterates that we, in our brokenness, are unable to fully do God's will. We *are* affected by original sin, contrary to Pelagianism. And Augustine and others were determined to preserve this truth.

Hauser describes these principles in figure 1.

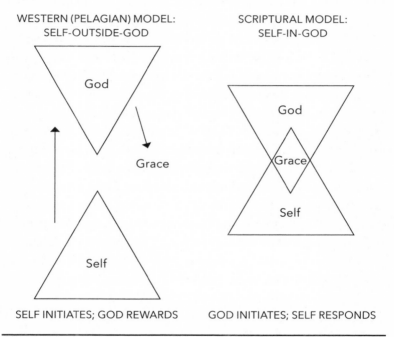

Figure 1. Western Christian spirituality and biblical Christian spirituality

Illustrated on the left side of the diagram is the "Western Model of Spirituality." God and self are depicted apart from one another. Grace is understood as something outside of ourselves and therefore separated from the origin of our good action. Grace is something that God rewards us with for the good we do on our own initiative. Our good actions are understood to originate from self. The good in our lives flows apart from and independent of grace, while grace increases or decreases based on our behavior. Relationship with God centers on punishment and reward.

In the "Scriptural Model of Spirituality" diagram, we see the indwelling of God depicted. The intersecting triangles symbolize the presence of the Spirit as the origin for inner movements toward good. As we grow in union, we can imagine the intersection of triangles increasing—this signifies our growing posture of surrender and the increase of Christ's life freely flowing through us.[12]

Intimacy is possible when I trust myself to the One within whom I live and move and have my being (Acts 17:28). God revealed the extent of this union through the annunciation, by incarnating God's self in the world through Mary. Can the imagery be any clearer? The God of the universe is not somewhere out there, distant and separate from humanity. God entered into the very womb of Mary, which illustrates God's presence within all humanity. God initiates: God told Mary that though she was a virgin, she would conceive a son (Luke 1:31). God inhabited Mary's womb. Mary responded to the grace given her and was receptive to the will of God: "Let it be done to me according to Your word" (Luke 1:38). God initiates; self responds. God has not ceased to initiate with humanity. God has made God's home within me and you, but it is up to us to awaken to the Presence.

Reflecting on the season of Advent, Carla Mae Streeter in her book *Seasons of the Soul: An Intimate God in Liturgical Time* makes this point eloquently:

> Mary is me. She is you, and you, and you. Mary is that humanness that is asked to bring forth God. . . . The message of God united with humanness in a woman's womb is the message that for me, too, locked in the darkness of faith's womb in this life, this Holy One is still taking on humanness: *mine*. Mary is a mirror. In her we find our own original face as God-bearer.[13]

Intimacy is possible when we recognize the immanent as well as the transcendent presence of God and join with the Presence in the creative process of life. Through an intimate exchange, abundant life unfolds. This is what Jesus tried to communicate in his promises of fullness of life, life eternal and the abundant life. Intimacy evokes abandonment to the object of love. Bathed in trust, we can abandon our self to the One who made us. And the Christian understanding of Christ living in us, the hope of glory, is made possible. Through this intimate exchange we are conformed to God's likeness.

QUESTIONS FOR REFLECTION

1. What does intimacy mean to you?

2. If intimacy requires coming out from hiding, what parts of yourself do you tend to hide?

   What would it be like to reveal those parts of yourself?

3. The spiritual journey is an invitation to greater intimacy with self, God and others. Intimacy is about knowing and being known. Describe the interconnection of self, God and others. How does intimacy with one relate to the other relationships?

   Recall an experience when coming to know and embrace yourself more fully meant greater intimacy with God and others.

4. Describe an aspect of yourself that you once shunned only to later realize what a gift it is.

5. Intimacy implies vulnerability, and to be vulnerable is to be woundable. No wonder it's so difficult for us to be vulnerable. So what is the point in risking such vulnerability?

   What is the tradeoff?

6. Longing is about growing acquainted with the presence of God. Intimacy is about friendship with God. In what ways have you seen your friendship with God develop?

7. Embodiment is an important emphasis in the spiritual journey. We must learn to bring the mind down into the heart, which is situated in the body. Bringing integration and harmony to the body helps us to be more fully present to the immanence of God (God's presence within us). What practices help you to practice embodiment?

In what ways have these practices been helpful to your relationship with God and your personal healing and growth?

Note: In the spiritual journey, intimacy can lead us to wounded places in our soul. When we dare to look at and embrace our wounds, healing is possible and we emerge from those depths more whole. But sometimes it's too daunting to go there alone; we need external support to be with our wounds and find healing. There's absolutely no shame in reaching out for help and support; it's actually a sign of maturity. If you are struggling to be with your woundedness, ask God to lead you to pastoral or professional help. Nothing is more beneficial than a good counselor, therapist or spiritual director.

PRACTICE

Practice embodiment. Consider these options:

- Go for a walk in nature, and whenever your mind wanders into the past or future, return to your breath and to the moment.

- Consider taking a yoga class. Reflect on how your yoga practice leads you to greater connection to yourself and the immanent presence of God.

- Walk the labyrinth. For more information, visit gravitycenter .com/practice/labyrinth.

7

Union

We shall not cease from exploration
and the end of all our exploring
shall be to arrive where we started
and know the place for the first time.

T. S. ELIOT, "LITTLE GIDDING"

DAY THIRTY-THREE ON THE CAMINO, when Chris and I walked hand in hand into the early morning city of Santiago, we could scarcely believe we had really arrived. As we turned the corner, El Catedral de Santiago jutted up before our eyes. Its weathered, westward gates gave us a tired, overextended welcome. As we drew nearer, the massive structure looked down on us as it had countless pilgrims through the centuries. We were the only pilgrims in the plaza at that hour—just Chris, me and the ancient church welcoming us. We marked the moment with a warm embrace and took our personal thoughts to silence. We had arrived. We had made a sacred passage. Our presence would be announced in the afternoon pilgrims' mass—"Two pilgrims from Nebraska made it to Santiago by foot!"

My journal entry that day captures the arrival:

It's hard to get my mind and emotions around the moment. We really did it! We made it to Santiago on foot as we hoped and prayed and cried we would. . . . In addition to the very concrete destination of the cathedral, El Camino de Santiago leads to an internal place. The way is transforming for the body, mind and soul. And the internal destination is a place of peace—a peace that is found by the way in which we journeyed—open, abandoned, dependent, broken, stripped, humbled, receptive, loved.[1]

Lee Hoinacki is so right. "The Camino is not a path leading to Santiago, but a way to reach Christ—if one can learn how to walk on it."[2] We made it to Santiago, but in a way our sojourn had just begun.

During pilgrimage, Chris and I had reflected on various aspects of our lives—our marriage, vocation, community and friends who feel like family scattered all over the world (some of them still living in poverty). All the pieces of our lives were laid out before us, and upon reaching Santiago it seemed they had been brought back together in a more proper way through our conversations, reflections and prayer. The parts had become a whole and there was a sense of union to what had been fragmented. Parts of me that had been in hiding were coming into focus and I was offering those parts of myself to Chris with courage and honesty, evaluating how those parts would be offered anew to my normal, actively engaged life. False ways in which I had previously responded and reacted to my husband, my community and the world were being revealed. The interpersonal self was giving way to the institutional self, bringing the fragmented parts of my life into a whole. The interindividual self seemed within reach.

The spiritual journey offers a similar experience of union— fragmented parts of our self becoming whole. Classic Christian spirituality describes the Christian sojourn in terms of three stages: the purgative way, the illuminative way and the unitive way. The purgative way is where we begin. As we grow closer to God we move into the illuminative way. And at a point of responding to God in love and living primarily out of that love, one is said to be in the unitive way. The Fathers and Mothers of the church teach that at each stage there are different prayer practices that aid our spiritual growth. Richard Hauser describes this in an outline called "The Christian Spiritual Path" (see table 1).[3]

As you look at the table you'll notice three columns: "Stages of the Journey," "Focus of Daily Living" and "Quality of Prayer." Each stage in the spiritual journey corresponds with a particular focus that characterizes it ("Focus of Daily Living") and a particular type of prayer ("Quality of Prayer") that usually marks that stage in the journey.

The spiritual journey is a multilayered process where we often vacillate between stages (especially before we reach the unitive

Table 1. The Christian Spiritual Path

Stages of the Journey	Focus of Daily Living		Quality of Prayer
Unawakened Self	Law & Commandments		Vocal
	(Relationship to Christ by fidelity to obligations)		
	AWAKENING OF THE SELF TO THE SPIRIT (Relationship to Christ by fidelity to the Spirit)		
Purgative Way	Imitation of Christ: Patterns of action		Talking to the Lord
	Continuing Conversion:	Temptations	Mind active
		Fluctuations of heart	Meditation
		Fluctuations of action	
Illuminative Way	Imitation of Christ: Quality of heart		Being with the Lord
	Continuing Conversion:	Temptations	Mind attentive: I-Thou
		Fluctuations of heart	Beginning contemplations
		No fluctuation of action	
Unitive Way	Imitation of Christ: Zeal for service		Being one in the Lord
	Continuing Conversion:	Temptations	Mind absorbed in the Lord
		No fluctuation of heart	Advanced contemplation
		No fluctuation of action	

way). All of the prayer practices are valuable at each stage, but the emphasis for growth lies in the "Quality of Prayer" column. In other words, the prayer practices ("Talking to the Lord," "Being with the Lord," "Being one in the Lord") indicated at each stage are best, or are naturally supported, by the quality of prayer ("Mind active," "Mind attentive," "Mind absorbed in the Lord") indicated. But each stage is not limited to this type of prayer. As one progresses in the journey, one moves through awakening to purgation, illumination and union. Each stage aids the continual conversion process we experience as we grow in relationship with God. Some compare these classic Christian-spirituality descriptive stages with the more contemporary terms "woundedness," "recovery" and "wellness."[4] However you understand the stages, the end result is growing in increasing wholeness, or union.

Contemplative prayer usually marks the unitive way. But there is no foolproof prescription for reaching the unitive way and no cookie-cutter practice that indicates one has reached it. The all-pervasive quality of love in one's life is the only probable indication that one is living in a state of union with God.

Contemplation as mentioned in this chart is understood as the state of prayer or awareness. Contemplation in this sense is a gift, and as such it is not necessarily imparted to everyone. We must not confuse contemplation with contemplative prayer. We can practice contemplative prayer or acts of contemplation by our will; but we cannot will the contemplative state of union with God—it is a grace and a gift. The marks of the unitive way are most notably peace, freedom from compulsions and freedom from major agitation. In addition, the individual's mind and heart are almost continuously fixed on God. Reaching the unitive way involves a dreadful experience of purgation and abandonment (described by John of the Cross as a "dark night" of darkness and death) which has the effect of freeing one from the false self. This freedom results in personal strength, power, energy and selfless giving of the purest, freest kind.[5]

The point of axis for the state of union is love. When living in the unitive way, we are free to receive and give love. Our motivations are rooted in love rather than in ego-centered compulsions or "programs for happiness." The true self is alive and active.

GETTING READY TO RETURN: FROM ME TO EVERYONE

In the memoir *Eat, Pray, Love,* Elizabeth Gilbert realizes at the end of her year-long journey in search of her self that "when you set out in the world to help yourself, you inevitably end up helping everyone."[6] When Gilbert reached her final destination in her journey through India, Italy and Indonesia she met a little Balinese girl whose name, Tutti, means "everybody" in Italian. Having uncovered her hidden self, Gilbert was more authentically attentive and responsive to a little girl and her family in need. From a place of freedom and love, Gilbert responded to the needs of this family with courage and generosity. She even compelled others to get involved in the liberation of the family. Gilbert realized that embracing her deepest self allows for an encounter with God, and that encounter connects us with everyone. When we are connected to God we cannot remain isolated and indifferent to the needs of others. The needs of the world call to the truest part of us that was created to respond in our unique way with courage and creativity.

The difference at the point of union is how we respond to those needs. Rather than responding from a place of false attachments and compulsions—the need for power and control, affection and esteem, or security and survival—we respond from a place of freedom from those attachments; a place of pure, undefiled love. We love with no expectation of return.

I struggled a lot at the beginning of sabbatical, thinking that taking all of that time for me was selfish. But I came to understand, like Gilbert, that sacred time of solitude and rest, whether it be a weekly sabbath or once a year or every seventh year or so, is really for everybody. In fact we owe it to the world to create time and space for dismantling our illusions. Otherwise we may be guilty of committing acts of violence. As Thomas Merton wrote,

> To allow oneself to be carried away by a multitude of conflicting concerns, to surrender oneself to too many demands, to commit oneself to too many projects, to want to help everyone in everything is to succumb to violence. More than that, it is cooperation in violence. It destroys one's own capacity for peace. It destroys the fruitfulness of one's own work, because it kills the root of inner wisdom which makes the work fruitful.[7]

Living into our true self, being free of our ego and rooted in love allows for true acts of peace and justice. Without attention to our internal motivations and attachments, we are at risk of imposing our will on the world—deceived into thinking we are doing a virtuous thing—only to find out we need forgiveness for our action (the sin of omission more often than that of commission). The ways we interact with the world can be connected so deeply to our false self that we cause more harm than good. In our misapprehension we do not realize that what we are doing may actually be reaping destruction cloaked in virtue. The greater our leadership and influence, the greater the potential domination and devastation. How else can we explain nations at war with one another, global exploitation of the poor, destruction to our planet?

During sabbatical, I was learning how necessary contemplative spirituality is to dismantling my illusions and uncovering my true self. All the months of distress and agony were transforming me. And at moments the anguish, disorientation and darkness subsided, to hint at peaceful union ahead.

In the fall of our sabbatical, Chris and I spent Thanksgiving with our friend Amey Victoria and her family in rural Rocky Mount, Virginia. What a delight to be strangers welcomed in and warmly embraced around the family feasting table. The drive out was breathtaking, winding through autumn wooded roads filled with deer, the green, red, yellow and orange leaves falling and blowing in the wind. The season was changing. The season of my soul was changing too; love was taking root.

Sabbatical was a sacred time for me. A season of time and space opened before me, inviting me to deeper solitude, silence and stillness. Weekly sabbath and regular private retreats offer the same invitation. All throughout sabbatical my thoughts returned to a familiar poem. I found myself identifying with the psalmist's expression of a similar experience:

The LORD is my shepherd, I shall not be in want.
  He makes lie down in green pastures,
he leads me beside quiet waters,
  he restores my soul. . . .
Though I walk
  through the valley of the shadow of death,
I will fear no evil,
  for you are with me;
your rod and your staff,
  they comfort me.

You prepare a table before me
  in the presence of my enemies. . . .
  My cup overflows.
Surely goodness and love will follow me
  all the days of my life,
and I will dwell in the house of the LORD
  forever. (Psalm 23 NIV)

Certainly the Lord was and is my Shepherd. Like a good shepherd with her not-so-intelligent sheep, God knew my need before I did. The essence of the spiritual journey is so evident in this psalm. The "Shepherd" makes me lie down, but also leads me; restores my soul even as I walk through the valley of death; prepares a table for me and sets me on a good and merciful path; makes a home for me while never neglecting to care for me.

God made me lie down in green pastures. Through God's generous and gracious provision, I was able to experience a pilgrimage of a lifetime. For a month in time I was transported from the trenches of an active life of pursuing and building communities of justice, compassion and peace, to the rolling, green hills of the Spanish countryside where wildflowers grew along the roadside and vineyards were laid out before me in all their splendor. The expanse of the blue sky was my canopy and the rich soil my carpet. I would wake with the sunrise and be greeted by the natural wonders of the earth every moment of the day.

I remember one day in particular when Chris and I made a difficult climb over an arid hillside with massive boulders and rocks underfoot. With every step my feet and ankles burned with pain; the Scripture about how God makes our path straight made so much sense to me. My body needed a straight path. Finally, after a couple of hours of ascending this hill we reached the top. And as we descended, a massive expanse of green, plush grass greeted us. The way was made straight, and the green pastures were literally provided for us. I broke down in tears as I received this most precious gift to my body and soul.

God led me beside still waters. For five months I was able to bring my active life to a halt and enter the stillness of the second part of my sabbatical at Duke. Five months of utter stillness, the waters of the ocean and that much-needed rainstorm.

God restored my soul. During those months of rest, God tended and restored my soul and sense of self.

God led me through darkness. I had never experienced such intense feelings of abandonment by God. The darkness I endured was like nothing I had ever known. As my life and sense of self seemed to be crumbling, God was with me. Jesus kept me. God led the way through that most disturbing season.

God prepared a table for me. And all the while as I submitted to the transformative work of God—like the caterpillar in her cocoon—God was preparing a place for me to return to, a table spread out for me to engage in a more life-giving way.

Truly my cup overflows. As I write this, my "cup" overflows—this "feeler" is spilling out tears in wonder at what God has done for her. I could not have made this journey alone. How can I not love the One who has done all of this for me?

During the last week or so of sabbatical, I grieved to say goodbye to that sweet season. I knew I would miss the long mornings—waking only when my body and mind decided to awake, lingering in prayer, reading and reflecting—free from nearly all responsibilities and obligations. I knew I would miss the quantity of relaxed, unscheduled, unhurried time by myself and with Chris and new friends. I would miss the sacred long walks and long soaks in the hot tub. I would miss the gift of Durham and Duke Divinity School and the short distance from the seaside. But I realized that there is a time for everything—a time to rest and a time to engage. A time for solitude and a time for embrace. And I realized that there was something I missed that could not be found in the same way in North Carolina. I missed the community of Word Made Flesh.

COMMUNITY AND CREATIVE ABSENCE

Jara, a friend and coworker at Word Made Flesh, gave us a hand-made bowl as we were preparing to leave for sabbatical. "It isn't until we are empty—like this bowl," she wrote, "that we can fully embrace solitude and welcome each other more intimately in our lives." The months of sabbath rest truly had been a time of self-emptying—emptying the false parts of self that hindered my true self from emerging. Greater intimacy was now possible. For several months that year I was separated from my people—making room for solitude between us. I was challenged in new ways to trust that this grand solitude of sabbatical could truly be for my people as well as for me.

Nouwen explains this paradox of solitude and relationship:

> In solitude we come to know our fellow human beings not as partners who satisfy our deepest needs, but as brothers and sisters with whom we are called to give visibility to God's all-embracing love. In solitude we discover that family or community is not some common ideology but a response to a common call. In solitude we indeed experience that community is not made but given. . . .
>
> Whenever we enter into solitude, we witness to a love that transcends our interpersonal communications and proclaims that we love each other because we have been loved first (1 Jn 4:19). Solitude keeps us in touch with the sustaining love from which we draw strength. It sets us free from the compulsions of fear and anger and allows us to be in the midst of an anxious and violent world as a sign of hope and a source of courage.[8]

Emerging from a creative absence from my community, I realized how much I wanted to be with them. I wanted to reconnect with my brothers and sisters. I wanted to return to them. My love for them had grown. I had never been more grateful for my community. I knew that I would be able to best express my deepest self in their company, rather than in perpetual isolation. Instead of being defined by my relationships, I wanted to *be in* relationship (interpersonal vs. inter-individual). It's an incredible gift to be part of a community that is a sign of hope and courage in a despairing, violent world. Chris and I are members of a community of incredible children, women and men who bring us life, and within their company God's all-embracing love is brought into focus. I looked forward to being connected with them again—this time in a freer, truer sense, and hopefully from a place rooted deeper in love. I looked forward also to being reconnected with Chris in our active life together. The transformation I had experienced was transforming our marriage also. Letting our transformed sense of self and marriage take flight was a longing to be realized.

Sabbatical was a necessary time of detaching, self-emptying, and becoming naked and vulnerable in deeper ways; and returning became time to reattach and engage community in new ways. By reengaging I would know whether or not solitude had made an empty, sacred space within me in which I could welcome all people. As Nouwen suggests, "There is a powerful connection between our emptiness and our ability to welcome."[9]

That December, after closing the chapter on a season at Duke, Chris and I drove our little, black Toyota Yaris all the way from Durham, North Carolina, to Omaha, Nebraska. As we entered Omaha and turned onto North Thirty-Third Street we started to approach our home. To our surprise, at the corner we spotted a yellow arrow! They were posted all the way down the road, leading to the front door of our apartment. Our friends in community had heard the stories of the arrows on the Camino and after a long separation welcomed us with these markers to reassure us that we had found our way.

A VOICE CALLING

When we are rooted in love—in union with God—simple, congruent communities made up of healthy relationships are formed, and service rather than domination is possible. True service is the expression of our vocation, our response to love.

The English word "vocation" is derived from the Latin *vocare,* "to call" and *vox,* "voice." The meaning centers on a "voice calling." John Neafsey, a clinical psychologist and senior lecturer in the department of theology at Loyola University Chicago, says that "vocation is not only about 'me' and my personal fulfillment, but about 'us' and the common good." He goes on to explain that "authentic vocational discernment, therefore, seeks a proper balance between inward listening *to* our heart and outward, socially engaged listening *with* our heart to the realities of the world in which we live. These come together in our heart's response to the needs and sufferings of the world."[10]

Living in a place of union opens us to our true voice, our vocation. Service is refined and redefined. We live from the truth of who we are, rather than our false-self "programs for happiness." When we live in this way, we respond to the plea of Christ in his crucifixion. For many years, I understood the crucifixion mostly as an indictment against my ugliness, unworthiness and sinfulness. This perception stands in stark contrast to the message of Christ's life. John Main explains it this way:

> The crucifixion is the divine plea to each of us to understand the meaning and wonder of our creation, the dignity which love bestows. . . . [I]n knowing this we open our hearts to the reality of our personal destiny, far beyond the narrow confines of the ego. The astonishing core of the Christian revelation is that the destiny of each person is full union with God, "to share in the very being of God," as St. Peter puts it. . . .
>
> Perhaps the greatest problem afflicting our society is that so many people feel that they are not fully alive. They suffer the sense that they are not fully authentic as human beings. A major reason for this is that there are so many living their life second-hand without a real openness to the uniqueness of the gift given to them: their own life.
>
> So many lives are lived by responding to other people's goals for us. . . . Christian revelation says that each of us is summoned to respond directly to the fullness of our own life in the mystery of God.[11]

On the cross, Christ experienced the totality of solitude, silence and stillness—the feeling of having no followers, no sympathizers, no companions, no God. But his return from solitude on the third day changed everything, ushering in the new creation and the new vocation of his people. Withdrawing at times from our virtuous, active life offers us the opportunity to identify with Christ in his absolute abandonment. And from that kind of encounter with the Divine, our action is purified, our destiny is unleashed, we grow in intimacy and we are more likely to experience union.

It is difficult to hear the voice of God calling us to fullness of life amidst the dissonance of other voices that filter through our "programs for happiness." But regular periods of solitude, silence and stillness provide a way to dismantle the dissonance. Contemplative practices provide a way to cut through the static and noise that lead us away from the voice of God. Slowly, slowly in the company of a patient God and supportive community we can find the ability to respond to "the fullness of our own life in the mystery of God." Throughout our lifetimes our vocations will develop and evolve as we grow and mature. Our response to the fullness of our lives in the mystery of God will look a particular way at each stage in our lives. All along the journey we do the best we can at the time to live and respond with integrity and truth. As time goes on, with ever-deepening awareness and freedom, our truest selves are set free.

When our sabbatical came to a close and Chris and I reentered an active life of service, some subtle and some not-so-subtle changes unfolded. I had emerged from my cocoon and it was time to test my wings. Awakened to the divine feminine, I had uncovered courage to assert myself in new ways. With greater self-awareness, I was compelled to engage the world in a way that would be true to these realized parts of myself. I was determined to assert myself appropriately in all of my relationships and creative work—in a way that would allow me to be fully present and not tempted to hide. Being free from the "program of happiness" for affection and esteem, I asserted myself at the risk of being misunderstood or rejected.

A part of the change my true self demanded of me was expressed in becoming Catholic. Also, in Word Made Flesh I gained confidence to imagine a new organizational position that would best serve the community while allowing me to live into my potential; honoring my deepest self *and* serving others was possible. The two are not mutually exclusive. Contrary to the distorted message I received as a woman, the two are inherently connected. Whereas I had formerly hidden myself (in a manner of "self-sacrifice") and allowed my potential and influence to be dictated by relationships or circumstances (in a manner of feminine subordination) through the flow from my encounters of union these fragmented parts were becoming whole. Rooted in love, my true self was free to be expressed in all areas of life. My vocation continued to evolve into ever-widening layers of truth from which my deep gladness could connect with the world's deep hunger.[12]

Reflecting on the changes in me, Chris, my marriage and my community, I have thought often about the homily at our wedding. Dr. Samuel Kamaleson, our dear friend, mentor and officiate, reflected on 1 Corinthians 6:19-20: "You are not your own. You have been bought with a price." He simply but soberly charged us to remember that we belong to God, one another and the world. These commitments keep us anchored and allow for periodic refinement of how we relate to God, each other and the world—depending on where we're at in our personal pilgrimage.

Each of our lives does not look like anyone else's. The uniqueness of our life created in the image of God is meant to shine. Our very own life is a gift to be given. We each have a unique vocation, and it is brought into community with others. Isn't this the diversity we see in the Gospels? Some left prestigious work to follow Jesus. Others, after being touched by Christ, returned to a rather "normal" life in society. There are many stories of Jesus telling some to leave everything and follow him, and others he told to return to their village. The call or vocation looked different for each one. And it looks different for each of us. The invitation is to know God and be known by God—authentic life and relationship. In that place of intimacy we are more inclined toward union and therefore freer to be who God created us to be.

The beauty of our lives is our participation in the paschal mystery of Christ again and again. With each new passage of death we receive new revelations of love. We continue in this cyclical pilgrimage until that final day when we will make our last passage from death to life and find ourselves in eternal, constant union with the One whom we have longed for since we took our first breath.

QUESTIONS FOR REFLECTION

1. As mentioned before, the spiritual journey is a process of construction, deconstruction and reconstruction. In the journey of becoming, fragmented parts of self are exposed, and with time, intention and grace those fragments are redeemed and brought together in a sense of wholeness or union. What are the fragmented parts of your identity?

   What would wholeness look like for you?

2. Look at table 1 on page 169. Which part of the classic Christian spiritual path do you identify with the most right now: unawakened, awakening, purgation, illumination or union?

   How is God at work in you at this stage in the journey?

3. Union or the unitive state is a state of love. In this stage of the journey we are liberated to love more freely with no expectation of return. In what ways have you demonstrated this kind of no-strings-attached love?

   Or in what ways have you been the recipient of this kind of love? Describe what it is like.

4. Elizabeth Gilbert wrote, "When you set out in the world to help yourself, you inevitably end up helping everyone." What does this mean to you?

5. Review the section on pages 178-81 about solitude, silence and stillness. These are critical components in the process of transformation. In solitude, our false-self attachments or disordered attachments are exposed and dismantled. We can then enter back into our relationships and responsibilities in a more true-self or ordered way, with greater love and freedom. How have you seen solitude, silence and stillness be of help to you?

6. In the state of union, what is good for ourselves is good for others. The two are not in opposition. In what ways have you experienced this?

PRACTICE

Spend time with Psalm 23. Journal the ways in which you see or do not see God doing for you what the psalmist experienced. Be honest. Invite God in. Through your honesty be open and available to the ways in which God is bringing the fragmented parts of your life into wholeness and union. Remember this mysterious work of healing and wholeness is God's. All you have to do is learn how to cooperate with God's work in you.

God makes me lie down in green pastures.
God leads me beside still waters.
God restores my soul.
God leads me through darkness.
God prepares a table for me.
My cup overflows.

Conclusion

FROM COMPULSION TO FREEDOM

FOR MUCH OF OUR LIVES we are bound by the "emotional junk of a lifetime." I have had to come to terms with my own false-self "programs for happiness." I had previously lived in a mode of reaction like Parker Palmer describes so well (see chapter five).[1] Bound by the interpersonal stage of development, I was driven by a need to be needed and I reacted accordingly. I was not always serving from a "free and independent heart." I did not have a good sense of my deepest self but rather was driven by who I thought I was expected to be by family, friends and the religious community. Patriarchal paradigms reinforced this posture of captivity. In some ways, I was letting others define me instead of the One who created me.

Our emotional wounds of a lifetime need healing. During a visit to St. Benedict's Monastery in Snowmass, Colorado, I was told by Father Micah that prayer is healing. It doesn't always feel good. In the healing of a physical wound, as the body rejuvenates there is itching and pain. Likewise, as we grow and heal we journey through seven movements: awakening, longing, darkness, death, transformation, intimacy and union. Our healing and growth often come through pain and suffering.

But in the unitive way, there is only one descriptor—love. Love defines. Love motivates. Love responds instead of reacts. Contemplative practices provide the space to move from compulsion to freedom. Contemplative prayer is a way in which we connect to love and absorb the truth of our belovedness and our unique destiny. Being grounded in the truth of who we are sets us free to live authentically, responding with generosity and creativity to the needs before us and, in turn, receiving gifts offered. As we live in the limitlessness of God's Spirit, we experience freedom like the apostle Paul wrote about: "Now the Lord is the Spirit; and where the Spirit of the Lord is, there is freedom" (2 Corinthians 3:17). Contemplative prayer is a way to grow in union because through this prayer the love and freedom of God become more corporeal to us.

Centering prayer (sometimes called "pure prayer" or "prayer of heartfulness") is a simple prayer that supports the spiritual journey. It is adapted from a prayer practice that was historically confined to monasteries and convents, dating back to the Desert Mothers and Fathers of the third century. In the 1960s and 70s, a surge conspired to make this prayer available to laypeople. Monks like Thomas Merton, Basil Pennington, Thomas Keating and John Main were monumental contributors to this movement. Because of the overwhelming response of individuals, Keating established a worldwide community of contemplatives called Contemplative Outreach. Different leaders teach the prayer slightly differently, but the principles are the same.

Silence is God's first language, according to mystics. And in centering prayer, silence is the language of communication. For twenty to thirty minutes, two times a day (though this time can be shortened in the beginning when one is getting used to it), we sit in silence with God and consent to God's presence and action within us. The use of a sacred word symbolizes our intention to consent to the presence and action. When first beginning the practice, we wait in silence to receive our sacred word. This can be any word or short phrase that symbolizes our relationship with God. It could be our favorite word for referencing God or a characteristic of God, like love, peace, joy and so on. Over time, the sacred word can change, but it is best to keep the word consistent so as not to be distracted by the changing of the word. Certainly it is discouraged to change the word *during* a prayer period. And if one wants to change their word over the course of time, it is recommended to discuss the change with one's spiritual director.

Centering prayer is a practice that is quite difficult for people of Western culture who overemphasize connecting to God through the faculties (reason, imagination, memory, feelings and will). This prayer is not unreasonable for Christians; it is beyond reason. This is a different way of connecting our whole self to God. It teaches us awareness, presence, embodiment, trust, surrender, faith and hope. This prayer is not intended to usurp other prayers or sacred practices but to be used in addition to them. Throughout the entire prayer period, thoughts that flood our minds give way to our sacred word, which represents our intention to give God our undivided attention. In some ways it might be helpful to think of this "prayer" as a discipline more than prayer as we commonly understand it—conversation in words, feelings of consolation and the like. Centering prayer disciplines our souls to be aware of and attentive to God in our active life. The fruit of this prayer is seen in our active life, and so we should not concern ourselves with an experience during prayer or with seeking after consolations during the prayer. We abandon everything—all desires, anxieties, expectations and energies—as a way of being present to the Presence.

Our office community makes time in the middle of our work day at 3:00 p.m. to come to God together in this silent prayer. During frenetic activity, many of us stop to find rest in God. In this way we remember that we are finite and only God is infinite, and we affirm our dependence on God. We cultivate an awareness and attentiveness to the presence of God to become more naturally aware of God's presence in all of our activity. This prayer time connects and roots us to the Spirit who dwells within us, who in turn connects us with our entire community spread out across the globe. It is a way of "remaining in Jesus" (vine and branches, John 15) that we might bear lasting fruit. By honoring this rhythm of action and contemplation we nurture intimacy with God and bear lasting fruit in our active lives. As Thomas Merton explained, our active lives are "leavened by peace, order and clarity."[2] As we spend time with God in contemplative prayer we experience greater freedom from our false-self motivations and compulsions and receive fullness of life. Contemplative prayer brings into focus our gifts and therefore we know more clearly and more freely where to focus our energies. This is the dance of contemplation and action.

The union of action and contemplation brings freedom and joy—even in the midst of some of the greatest poverty and suffering of our time. By abandoning ourselves regularly to God through prayer in the form of solitude, silence and stillness, we experience more freedom *from* compulsions and heavy-laden expectations and more liberty *in* our true self with all of our unique gifts to offer the world. Bringing balance to action and contemplation in our lives allows for the greatest impact in our world. And the love of God compels us to not lose heart in the journey.

Awakening, longing, darkness, death, transformation, intimacy and union. The spiritual journey is an intense sojourn. Where are you in the pilgrimage? Who do you long to be? Is your life fragmented or are you experiencing the peace of union?

Picture yourself at the end of your long journey:

Warming yourself at the fireplace, you watch the flames dance softly across the wall. Your pilgrimage has come to an end. You have traveled to the outer limits of your being and returned home full of a sense of worth, and a profound understanding of who you are.

You turn and in the doorway stands a young pilgrim. She is so young, her eyes so bright. There is a beauty about her, an eagerness to be on her way. You wonder if this was what you were like so long ago when, staff in hand, you first stepped out on the road.

"What can you tell me about the journey?" she asks. What dare you tell her?

"You will be met by demons and angels. You will have nights of crystal clarity and dark days of doubt. You will lose your way so many times you can't keep count. But over and over, you will stumble upon yourself, and in the end grow to love who you are."[3]

As we grow to love who we are, we grow in capacity to love God and one another. The spiritual journey is as much about loving our self as it is about loving our neighbor. "Love your neighbor as yourself" (Matthew 22:39). If we are not giving proper care and attention to our deepest self, we are at the least encumbered in our love of others and at the most committing acts of violence in the name of love. We owe it to the world to submit to a spiritual journey that makes us receptive to the dismantling of our illusions and self-deceit. We can be either our worst enemy or our dearest friend. For the love of God, let us choose the latter. For in befriending our self, we find the One who calls us and even our enemy "Beloved." From this centered place of union we can hope to bear witness to redemptive love and to live as cocreators with God.

Buen camino,
Phileena

Acknowledgments

THE EVENING I RECEIVED the final edits for this book, I was on my way out the door to attend one of my favorite yoga classes. As I breezed through the finished pages of what had become my first book, I felt a surge of emotion within me. I hurriedly embraced the feeling of accomplishment and finishing well, and made my way to class. The ninety-minute practice of the evening focused on back bends—a series of postures I wasn't very familiar with. At the end of the session, when it was time for *savasana* (corpse pose, in which we lay flat on our backs for several minutes to complete our practice), I was surprised to find tears quietly streaming out of my eyes, into my ears and falling softly on the mat. After we came to a seated position to acknowledge the effort of one another and to bring closure, my yoga instructor, Jed, kindly asked, "Are you okay?" That evening it was only Jed, his wife, Sarah, and me in class, so it felt intimate and safe. I asked, "Is it common to experience these kinds of emotions during yoga?" And they both proceeded to explain that it *is* common, especially after a session of back bends.

What I learned in those moments was the beauty of embodiment and how the varied layers of our lives come together. In class as I practiced the postures of back bends, I was opening my heart center—the place of love, compassion and vulnerability. And the exposure of the bodily heart center has the potential to open up some of the most vulnerable expressions of who we are. Normally the average person tends toward hiding and protecting his or her most vulnerable space—symbolized in the front body and heart center. But in class that night, I was opening that body space and also the intangible space of my vulnerable soul.

Just before class, as I reviewed the page proofs, I was experiencing the culmination of a journey I had been on for years. Through my book, my "heart center"—the seat of some of my most vulnerable places—was being exposed, soon for literally the world to see. My body and soul harmonized through the embodiment of courageous and vulnerable yoga postures. The result was emotional release of peace, love, joy and gratitude.

My teachers explained that in the tradition of yoga they practice, the front side of the body is the "individual body." The backside of the body is the "universal body." One supports the other. And so in the moments of *savasana*, as I experienced the liberation of exposing my heart center, I also became overwhelmed with gratitude for the support that has enabled me to put myself out there in the world through the expression of *Pilgrimage of a Soul*.

Immediately my thoughts turned to specific mentors who have nurtured, supported and believed in me at unique stages of my life: to my parents, Phil and Sandy Bacon; to Patrick and Victoria Samuel; and to Michael and Laura Alley. There are so many others who have accompanied me in my journey along the way—who were provided at just the right time, in just the perfect way. For each of you I am deeply grateful. A few I am compelled to mention: Eva Joyce Cunningham (my late "Mammaw"), Dr. Samuel and Adela Kamaleson, Fr. Bert Thelan, Dr. Cathy Leslie, and Bob and Anne Ginn.

Beyond these guides, there are some friends who were particular companions in the actual writing of the book. There is a common proverb: "It takes a village to raise a child." Well, it took a small village to write *Pilgrimage of a Soul*. My heartfelt gratitude is warmly extended to you who accompanied me and supported me with your readings and constructive feedback: Adriana Dakimowicz Forcatto, Amey Victoria Atkins, Bethel Lee, David Bayne, Sonya Gray, Stuart Erny and Twyla O'Callaghan. For your technical assistance I am so grateful: Hilary Wilken, Mandy Mowers and Rob O'Callaghan.

To every single person at InterVarsity Press who had a hand in bringing this book to its beautiful completion, my sincerest thanks. A special appreciation to Jeff Crosby, associate publisher of sales and marketing, for your particular enthusiasm for the book at its proposal; Cindy Kiple, art director, for going above and beyond in creativity for cover design; Rebecca Carhart, copyeditor; Ruth Curphey, Adrianna Wright and every member of the sales and marketing team who is supporting the work and making it accessible to the reader. And for being the first to read my feeble writing, for believing in me and my voice, and for teaching me how to be a better writer: thank you David Zimmerman, associate editor for IVP Books. It's been a delight to work with you.

Beauty inspires creative work, and so there are two artists I'd like to extend a special thanks to. India.Arie: you sing many of my heart songs, and in the early days of drafting this manuscript, your music gave me the inspiration I needed. Thank you. And Sarah Lance: your life is beauty and your art has the potential to lead the reader further than my words. Thank you for being a part of this.

Thank you also to my community at Word Made Flesh—to the board for believing in and supporting my voice; to my coworkers for graciously extending to me the time and space needed to devote to writing; and to those I like to affectionately refer to as the "Third Order" of Word Made Flesh—the many friends and family who support our mission with your prayer and financial support. And to all of the women, men and children who I've come to know on impoverished urban streets, in degrading brothels and other desperate dwellings—my indebted gratitude to you for sharing your vulnerable lives with me. In you I find courage to be human. Thank you for your forgiveness, grace, love and confidence. May this book and my life, in some way, honor you.

And to the one whom I love more than life itself—Chris Heuertz—my best friend and cherished husband. Your life inspires and teaches me. Thank you for always believing in me and for seeing more in me than I can usually see in myself. Thank you for affirming the importance of this book, and for your support and assistance all along the way. Thank you for making this journey with me—and not just the book. Your companionship, love and support all these years is unmatched.

Notes

Introduction

[1]Thomas Keating is a modern Christian mystic. For more than fifty years he has given himself to the ancient Christian contemplative tradition. Through contemplative prayer he has excelled in the fruits and gifts of the Spirit. He is wise and holy, discerning and kind. His life bears witness to the presence of Christ living within him. He is rooted in the Presence. And from the heart and mind of Christ, Fr. Thomas responds to the world around him. Being anchored in the real, immanent and transcendent presence of God frees him to respond as Jesus would. Through his efforts and those of others like him, he has renewed the Christian contemplative tradition and made it accessible to monks, nuns and laypeople alike. His teaching illuminates the gospel and provides a road map for the spiritual journey.

[2]The true self is our most liberated, deepest self in contrast to the false self who lives from a place of bondage, woundedness and fear. I will expand on this concept throughout the book. For further reading on the true and false self consider the following books: David Benner, *The Gift of Being Yourself;* Albert Haase, *Coming Home to Your True Self;* M. Basil Pennington, *True Self/False Self;* Thomas Merton, *The New Man.*

[3]I owe this imagery in part to Henri Nouwen (with Philip Roderick, *Beloved: Henri Nouwen in Conversation* [Grand Rapids: Eerdmans, 2007], p. 23).

[4]Exodus 20:8-11: "Remember the Sabbath day and keep it holy! For six days you will labor and do all your work, but the seventh day is a Sabbath for YHWH. Do no work on that day, neither you nor your daughter nor your son, nor your workers—women or men—nor your animals, nor the foreigner who lives among you. For in the six days YHWH made the heavens and the earth and the sea and all that they hold, but rested on the seventh day; this is why YHWH has blessed the Sabbath day and made it sacred."

[5]There are many kinds of contemplative prayer practices, like *lectio divina,*

labyrinth prayer, breath prayer, the Welcome Prayer and prayer of recollection. For a good overview of these or other contemplative prayer practices see *Spiritual Disciplines Handbook: Practices That Transform Us,* by Adele Ahlberg Calhoun (Downers Grove, Ill.: InterVarsity Press, 2005). I explain centering prayer in more detail in chapter seven.

[6]The paschal mystery refers to the suffering or passion, death, resurrection, and glorification or ascension of Jesus Christ. The center of the work that the Father God sent Jesus the Son to do on earth is the paschal mystery. The term *paschal* comes from a Hebrew word meaning "the passing over." The paschal mystery is Jesus' passing over from earthly life through his passion, death, resurrection and ascension to a new and glorified life with the Father.

[7]Thomas Keating, *The Human Condition: Contemplation and Transformation* (New York: Paulist, 1999), pp. 18-19.

[8]In the Torah, the seventh year is known as the sabbatical year. Exodus 23:10-11: "You may sow your crops and reap them for six years, but in the seventh year let it rest and lie untilled. In that year the land will provide food for the poor, and what they don't take will go to the wild animals. Do the same with your vineyards and olive groves."

Chapter 1: Awakening

[1]Austin Reparth, "Starting Out," in *Pilgrim Cards* (accessed June 10, 2009) www.pilgrimcards.com/.

[2]Esknath Easwaran, *To Love Is to Know Me* (Tomales, Calif.: Nilgiri Press, 1993), p. 87.

[3]This translation is gender-neutral though the pronoun used is "he."

[4]Thomas Keating, *The Paschal Mystery: A Journey into Redemption and Grace* (Butler, N.J.: Contemplative Outreach, 2007), p. 100.

[5]In this tradition pastors are generally referred to as ministers or preachers instead of pastors.

[6]Debi Pearl, *Created to Be His Help Meet* (Pleasantville, Tenn.: No Greater Joy, 2004), p. 23.

[7]Ibid., p. 25.

[8]Ibid., p. 29.

[9]Ibid., pp. 31-32.

[10]Ibid., p. 23.

[11]I owe this insight to my gifted spiritual director, Sr. Anne Pellegrino, O.S.M.

[12]Marianne Williamson, *A Return to Love: Reflections on the Principles of a Course in Miracles* (New York: HarperCollins, 1992), pp. 190-91.

[13]Reinhold Niebuhr was a leading American Protestant theologian of the twentieth century. He is credited with writing the Serenity Prayer. Carol Lakey Hess is a practical theologian and author of *Caretakers of Our Common House: Women's Development in Communities of Faith*. In her book, Hess says that few theologians have influenced North American theology as significantly as Niebuhr. She says that his theological anthropology both looked to historical key thinkers and themes in the Protestant tradition and projected forward a highly influential thought for Christian theology. And she remarks that his thought has raised critical questions for women. Carol Lakey Hess, *Caretakers of Our Common House: Women's Development in Communities of Faith* (Nashville: Abingdon, 1997), p. 33.

[14]Reinhold Niebuhr, *The Nature and Destiny of Man, Vol. 1: Human Nature* (New York: Scribner's Sons, 1941), pp. 137-38.

[15]Hess, *Caretakers of Our Common House*, pp. 34-35.

[16]Kate Hurley, "Hey Little Girl," from her album *Sleeping When You Woke Me* (Worship Circle Records, 2006).

[17]Niebuhr, *Nature and Destiny of Man*, pp. 137-38.

[18]Thomas Keating, *The Human Condition: Contemplation and Transformation* (New York: Paulist, 1999), p. 30.

[19]Ibid.

[20]Thomas Merton, *The New Man* (New York: Noonday Press, 1961), pp. 67, 63.

[21]For more information visit www.dnmsinstitute.com/.

[22]Personal journal, April 1, 2007.

[23]Parker J. Palmer, *The Active Life: A Spirituality of Work, Creativity, and Caring* (San Francisco: Jossey-Bass, 1990), p. 17.

[24]There are many books written about the Desert Fathers and Mothers. A couple I recommend are *The Wisdom of the Desert* by Thomas Merton and *The Forgotten Desert Mothers* by Laura Swan.

[25]John Main, *Word Made Flesh* (New York: Continuum, 1998), pp. 7-9.

[26]Thomas Keating, *Open Mind, Open Heart: The Contemplative Dimension of the Gospel* (New York: Continuum, 1986), p. 68.

[27]Keating, *Paschal Mystery*, p. 65.

[28]Thomas Keating, *Intimacy with God* (New York: Crossroad, 1994), p. 45.

[29]Thomas Keating, *The Spiritual Journey* video series, produced by Contemplative Outreach (n.d.).

[30]Keating, *Human Condition*, p. 36.

[31]Ibid., p. 35.

[32]Thomas Keating, *The Better Part* (New York: Continuum, 2000), p. 26.

[33]Merton, *New Man*, p. 56.

Chapter 2: Longing

[1]Spanish phrase meaning "have a good pilgrimage."

[2]Mayberry is a fictional community in North Carolina that was the setting for the American television sitcom *The Andy Griffith Show*.

[3]I am not suggesting that being in relationship with children from around the world is the same as motherhood. For me, having no children of my own simply makes room for me to be available to children in poverty in different ways than if I had children of my own. More on this in the "Death" chapter.

[4]Christopher Webb taught me about longing at a Renovaré Conference in 2008 in Atlanta, Georgia—the last regional Renovaré conference with Dallas Willard and Richard Foster together.

[5]Hazel wood is chosen for its strong and flexible qualities.

[6]Chris and I are not tall by average standards. Instead of being referred to as short we prefer the term "fun size."

[7]Spanish for "companions."

[8]Macrina Wiederkehr, *Seven Sacred Pauses: Living Mindfully Through the Hours of the Day* (Notre Dame, Ind.: Sorin Books, 2008), p. 32.

[9]"Flight of the Bumblebee" is a well-known orchestral interlude written by Nikolai Rimsky-Korsakov for his opera *The Tale of Tsar Saltan*, composed in 1899-1900.

[10]"The Secret Life of Butterflies," *Studio 360*, NPR, KIOS 91.5, Omaha, Nebr. (December 8, 2007).

[11]Sue Monk Kidd, *When the Heart Waits: Spiritual Direction for Life's Sacred Questions* (New York: HarperCollins, 1990), p. 14.

[12]Augustine did a lot to preserve the gospel of Christ, even though he was imperfect and vulnerable to the worldview and limitations of his culture and society.

[13]Hebrews 11:1: "Now faith is being sure of what we hope for and certain of what we do not see" (NIV).

Chapter 3: Darkness

[1]We found out later that on this very day a pilgrim was hospitalized because of the intense climb and dangerous weather conditions, and a week earlier someone had actually died on this mountain pass.

[2]In St. John of the Cross, *Dark Night of the Soul: A Masterpiece in the Literature of Mysticism,* ed. E. Allison Peers (New York: Doubleday, 1959), p. 27.

[3]I highly recommend Fr. Richard Rohr's teaching on male spirituality.

[4]Kolkata is the present-day spelling of Calcutta, capital of West Bengal, India.

[5]For a summary of the Catholic (or Counter-) Reformation see Phyllis Tickle, *The Great Emergence* (Grand Rapids: Baker, 2008), pp. 57-59.

[6]Lee Hoinacki, *El Camino: Walking to Santiago de Compostela* (University Park: Pennsylvania State University, 1996), p. 135.

[7]Kimberlee Conway Ireton, "The Gift of Darkness," *Relevant Magazine* on-line. The article has since been taken offline.

[8]Rob Bell notes these Scripture references in his Nooma film *She,* in which he explores the feminine attributes of God. Rob Bell, *She,* Nooma 021 (Grand Rapids: Flannel and Zondervan, 2008).

[9]St. John of the Cross, *Dark Night of the Soul,* p. 61.

[10]For further examination of the night of sense and night of spirit, see *Dark Night of the Soul* by St. John of the Cross or *Invitation to Love: The Way of Christian Contemplation* by Thomas Keating.

[11]St. John of the Cross, *Dark Night of the Soul*, p. 37.

[12]Ibid., p. 127.

[13]*The Cloud of Unknowing* is thought to have been written by an anonymous fourteenth-century English monk. The writing is strikingly similar to St. John of the Cross, who would likely not have been privy to *The Cloud* at the time of his writing *The Dark Night.*

[14]Cynthia Bourgeault, "From Woundedness to Union," *Gnosis*, Winter 1995, pp. 41-45.

[15]George MacDonald, *Unspoken Sermons* (Charleston, S.C.: BiblioBazaar, 2007), pp. 178-79.

Chapter 4: Death

[1]Kolkata is presumed to be named for Kali, the Hindu goddess of death and destruction.

[2]Joseph Langford, *Mother Teresa's Secret Fire* (Huntington, Ind.: Our Sunday Visitor, 2008), p. 92.

[3]Jon Sobrino, *The Principle of Mercy: Taking the Crucified People from the Cross* (Maryknoll, N.Y.: Orbis, 1994).

[4]W. Bader, ed., *Like a Drop in the Ocean: 99 Sayings by Mother Teresa* (Hyde Park, N.Y.: New City Press, 2006), n.p.

[5]Though Mother Teresa was Albanian by birth, she was granted Indian citizenship and was often mistaken for being Indian.

[6]Robert Kegan, *The Evolving Self* (Cambridge, Mass.: Harvard University Press, 1982). Kegan is a developmental psychologist and the William and Miriam Meehan Professor in Adult Learning and Professional Development at Harvard University.

[7]Henri Nouwen with Philip Roderick, *Beloved: Henri Nouwen in Conversation*

(Grand Rapids: Eerdmans, 2007), p. 12.

[8]They did in fact go through with the marriage and have been a source of beautiful grace to one another.

[9]Carol Lakey Hess, *Caretakers of Our Common House: Women's Development in Communities of Faith* (Nashville: Abingdon, 1997), p. 66.

[10]Reginald F. Christian, ed., *Tolstoy's Letters,* vol. 2 (New York: Scribners, 1978), n.p.

[11]Ronald Rolheiser, *Forgotten Among the Lilies: Learning to Love Beyond Our Fears* (New York: Doubleday, 2004), p. 188. For a broader reflection on this content see Brian McLaren's *A New Kind of Christian* (San Francisco: Jossey-Bass, 2001). On pages x and xi he elaborates on this context of change. He includes a helpful diagram and explanation for the process, using different terminology but the same core idea.

[12]Cynthia Bourgeault, *Centering Prayer and Inner Awakening* (Cambridge, Mass.: Cowley, 2004), p. 49.

Chapter 5: Transformation

[1]Personal journal, October 5, 2007.

[2]A rule of life is generally associated with the monastic tradition for outlining a way of life to incorporate work, prayer and rest. In our contemporary times, rules of life help bring balance to these areas of the layperson's life.

[3]Tilden Edwards, *Sabbath Time* (Nashville: Upper Room Books, 2003), p. 63.

[4]Ibid., p. 79.

[5]Ibid., p. 73.

[6]Personal journal, November 23, 2007.

[7]The labyrinth prayer dates back to at least the twelfth century. Historically it was used by Christians in place of making pilgrimage to a holy site. The floor of Chartes Cathedral in France has a labyrinth that has been used by pilgrims for centuries. The labyrinth is a symbol for our spiritual journey. As we walk we journey toward the center, toward God. Throughout our movement we are interchangeably close to and far from the center. But even still, as we walk we are progressing closer to the center, no matter how far away we might seem. The labyrinth is a way to be fully present in the moment of our prayer. It is a prayer of embodiment: entering the labyrinth is embodying our inner desire to grow closer to God. Walk the labyrinth prayerfully. Let your walk be your prayer. As you walk, let your thoughts come and go with each step. The labyrinth can be a slow, quiet, meditative practice, though children often enjoy running or skipping in it. Walk as you so desire, but remain mindful of others in the labyrinth with you. You can search for a labyrinth near you on the Internet. Many churches and retreat

centers make their labyrinth available to the public.

[8]Jackson's fundamental effort is Natural Systems Agriculture (NSA). NSA is rooted in the ideology that nature is comprised of perennial, symbiotic plants growing in a mixture. Being symbiotic means that two dissimilar organisms live together to the benefit of both. With the help of genetic biology Jackson has been breeding the grains we need to exist into perennials from the annuals humanity has created over a period of 10,000 years of agriculture. All plants started as perennials, and over many years, in order to create a larger seed head or yield per acre, we selected for the annual and gradually bred out the perennial qualities. For more information visit <www.landinstitute.org>.

[9]Mother Teresa, *Total Surrender* (Ann Arbor, Mich.: Servant, 1985), p. 107.

[10]Henri Nouwen, *Compassion* (New York: Doubleday, 1982), pp. 116-17. "Prayer and action, therefore, can never be seen as contradictory or mutually exclusive. Prayer without action grows in a powerless pietism, and action without prayer degenerates into questionable manipulation. If prayer leads us into a deeper unity with the compassionate Christ, it will always give rise to concrete acts of service. And if concrete acts of service do indeed lead us to a deeper solidarity with the poor, the hungry, the sick, the dying, and the oppressed, they will always give rise to prayer. In prayer we meet Christ, and in him all human suffering. In service we meet people, and in them the suffering Christ."

[11]Ibid.

[12]Parker Palmer, *The Active Life: A Spirituality of Work, Creativity and Caring* (San Francisco: Jossey-Bass, 1990), p. 39.

[13]Thomas Keating refers to God as the Divine Physician.

[14]Edwards, *Sabbath Time*, p. 76.

[15]Osha Gray Davidson, *The Best of Enemies: Race and Redemption in the New South* (Chapel Hill: University of North Carolina Press, 2001).

[16]*Lectio divina* is Latin for "sacred reading," though a more accurate definition might be "sacred listening." *Lectio divina* is a slow, contemplative praying of the Scriptures. Traditionally one progresses through the movements of *lectio* (reading/listening), *meditatio* (meditation), *oratio* (prayer) and finally *contemplatio* (contemplation). These traditional Latin movements are also associated in this manner: *lectio* (acquaintanceship), *meditatio* (friendly companionship), *oratio* (friendship), *contemplatio* (union). For more information I recommend M. Basil Pennington's book *Lectio Divina: Renewing the Ancient Practice of Praying the Scriptures*.

[17]Richard Rohr has an interesting perspective of God incarnating God's self as a man:

The "sacred feminine" is in many ways a rediscovery of Jesus' spirit, a reemergence of a well-suppressed truth, an eventual political upheaval, a certain reform of our hearing of the Gospel and someday perhaps the very structures of the churches—and all proceeding from a deep knowing in the feminine womb, the exact place from which we received Christ for the first time.

The feminist insight explains a vast majority of Jesus' teaching and style, a male acting very differently in an almost totally patriarchal Jewish society. Like Mary, the Church also has somehow "treasured these things in her heart" (Luke 2:19), but only in time will they be ready to come forth, like Jesus from her womb.

Jesus would never have broken through as a genuinely new revelation if he had acted nonviolently inside of a feminine body. It would not have been revolutionary or a challenge—because we expect and demand that women be patient, nurturing, forgiving, healing, self-effacing, and self-sacrificing. Women are expected to be nonviolent in a violent male society. But we are still not prepared for males or institutions or nations to act nonviolently, even in the church. That is why God had to become incarnate for us in the body of a man. Jesus had a male body but a very feminine soul, which was genuinely new. Unfortunately, we basically rejected most of Jesus' teachings and style as impractical and unreasonable in the pyramidal "real world" of church and state.

Adapted from Richard Rohr, *Simplicity: The Freedom of Letting Go* (New York: Crossroad, 2004), pp. 130-31.

Chapter 6: Intimacy

[1] Themes of abiding in God and loving one another are developed in John 15.

[2] William Johnston, ed., *The Cloud of Unknowing and The Book of Privy Counseling* (New York: Image Doubleday, 1973), p. 88.

[3] For a more detailed rendition of this story see Chris Heuertz, *Simple Spirituality: Learning to See God in a Broken World* (Downers Grove, Ill.: IVP Books, 2008), p. 141.

[4] For more exploration of cataphatic and apophatic prayer see Cynthia Bourgeault's book *Centering Prayer and Inner Awakening* (Cambridge, Mass.: Cowley, 2004), chap. 4.

[5] Kate Hurley, "Stronger Than Death," from her album *Sleeping When You Woke Me* (Worship Circle Records, 2006).

[6] Kahlil Gibran, *The Prophet* (New York: Alfred A. Knopf, 1923), pp. 11-15.

[7] Personal journal, September 23, 2007.

[8]Henri Nouwen, *Intimacy* (New York: HarperCollins), pp. 17-18.

[9]Richard J. Hauser, S.J., *Moving in the Spirit: Becoming a Contemplative in Action* (Mahwah, N.J.: Paulist, 1986), p. 25.

[10]Pelagius's teaching was condemned as heresy at numerous councils. Councils of Carthage (412, 416 and 418); Council of Ephesus (431); Council of Orange (529); Augsburg Confession (1530) Art. 9, 18 (Lutheran); Council of Trent (1546) (Roman Catholic); Gallican Confession (1559) Art. 10 (French Reformed); Belgic Confession (1561) Art. 15 (Lowlands, French/Dutch/German Reformed); Second Helvetic Confession (1561/1566) chaps. 8-9 (Swiss-German Reformed); Anglican Articles (1571) 9 (English); Canons of Dort (1618-1619) 3/4.2 (Dutch/German/French Reformed).

[11]Hauser, *Moving in the Spirit*, pp. 25-27.

[12]For a more in-depth discussion of the Western and Christian models of spirituality see chapter two of Hauser's *Moving in the Spirit*.

[13]Carla Mae Streeter, O.P., *Seasons of the Soul: An Intimate God in Liturgical Time* (St. Louis, Mo.: Chalice, 2004), p. 14.

Chapter 7: Union

[1]Personal journal, June 5, 2007.

[2]Lee Hoinacki, *El Camino: Walking to Santiago de Compostela* (University Park: Pennsylvania State University Press, 1996), p. 135.

[3]Richard J. Hauser, S.J., *Moving in the Spirit: Becoming a Contemplative in Action* (Mahwah, N.J.: Paulist, 1986), p. 13.

[4]Cynthia Bourgeault, *Centering Prayer and Inner Awakening* (Cambridge, Mass.: Cowley Publications, 2004), p. 93.

[5]"State or Way: Purgative, Illuminative, Unitive," *Catholic Encyclopedia* (accessed July 8, 2009) <www.newadvent.org/cathen/14254a.htm>.

[6]Elizabeth Gilbert, *Eat, Pray, Love* (New York: Viking, 2006), p. 274.

[7]Thomas Merton quoting Douglas Steere, Quaker theologian, in *Conjectures of a Guilty Bystander* (New York: Doubleday, 1968).

[8]Henri Nouwen, *Clowning in Rome* (New York: Random House, 2000), pp. 13-14.

[9]Ibid., p. 30.

[10]John Neafsey, *A Sacred Voice Is Calling: Personal Vocation and Social Conscience* (Maryknoll, N.Y.: Orbis, 2006), p. 1.

[11]John Main, *Word Made Flesh* (New York: Continuum, 1998), pp. 37-38.

[12]Frederick Buechner, *Wishful Thinking: A Seeker's ABC* (San Francisco: HarperSanFrancisco, 1993), p. 119. "The place God calls you to is the place where your deep gladness and the world's deep hunger meet."

Conclusion

[1]Parker Palmer, *The Active Life: A Spirituality of Work, Creativity and Caring* (San Francisco: Jossey-Bass, 1999), p. 39.

[2]Thomas Merton, "The Contemplative Life: Its Meaning and Necessity," *The Dublin Review* 223 (Winter 1949): 27.

[3]Austin Reparth, "At Home Again," in Pilgrim Cards (accessed June 10, 2009) www.pilgrimcards.com/.

formatio

TRADITION. EXPERIENCE.
TRANSFORMATION.

Formatio books from InterVarsity Press follow the rich tradition of the church in the journey of spiritual formation. These books are not merely about being informed, but about being transformed by Christ and conformed to his image. Formatio stands in InterVarsity Press's evangelical publishing tradition by integrating God's Word with spiritual practice and by prompting readers to move from inward change to outward witness. InterVarsity Press uses the chambered nautilus for Formatio, a symbol of spiritual formation because of its continual spiral journey outward as it moves from its center. We believe that each of us is made with a deep desire to be in God's presence. Formatio books help us to fulfill our deepest desires and to become our true selves in light of God's grace.

gravity

a center for contemplative activism

The spiritual journey makes life worth living, yet at times it can be really difficult to navigate on our own. Phileena meets monthly with her spiritual director as a way of staying rooted in the journey and connected to the Divine. Phileena also provides spiritual direction for others. Certified by the Jesuits in the contemplative-evocative method of spiritual direction, Phileena is an internationally recognized spiritual director meeting with people from all walks of life in person or over the phone or Skype. To learn more about spiritual direction or to inquire about meeting with Phileena visit gravitycenter.com/join/spiritual-direction/.